KOGARASHI'S RUN

INFINITA BOOK 3

KOGARASHI'S
RUN

INFINITA BOOK 3

CHRISTOPHER
HOPPER

HOPPER
CREATIVE
GROUP

SOMNIUM
PUBLISHING

NEW YORK

Kogarashi's Run
Infinita Book 3

Written by
Christopher Hopper

Copyright © 2022
Hopper Creative Group, LLC
Somnium Publishing

First Edition / Version 3.0

Edited by: Dang Wong
Proofread by: Christie Strahler
Senior Content Editor: Matthew Titus
Art Design and Layout by: Christopher Hopper

Paperback ISBN: 9798849187990

CONTENTS

DEDICATION

To my VIPs.
Thanks for going on another grand adventure with me.

QUOTES

"If our solar system is not unusual, then there are so many planets in the universe that, for example, they outnumber the sum of all sounds and words ever uttered by every human who has ever lived. To declare that Earth must be the only planet with life in the universe would be inexcusably bigheaded of us."

—Neil deGrasse Tyson
Death by Black Hole: And Other Cosmic Quandaries
2007

"Politics is more difficult than physics."

—Albert Einstein

Grenville Clark, *Letters to the Times: Einstein Quoted on Politics*
New York Times
April 22, 1955, page 24

PROLOGUE

THE NEED for revenge churned in her soul like the blades of the wind turbines passing overhead. An unseen force drove each stroke, generating power that supplied the grid with electricity. So too did the forces of hate breathe on the ideas powering the desire for vengeance against the man who'd slain her mother. Gemma would have justice, and Sir Nigel Sallsworth would pay dearly for his sins.

She stood atop Husfjellet's spine that zigzagged into the Norwegian Sea like the vertebrae of a dragon's tail. Gusts of wind whipped at her hair as she replayed the final moments of her mother's life. Of kneeling at the Tantum Terrae leader's side and holding her hand as Nigel fired his last bullet into her head. In V-cog, the back of Magnolia's head bloomed red as her body tumbled to the sidewalk. In the real, however, Magnolia's body had little more than jerked from the deathblow, her pristine face calm, her lips painted with a fresh coat of lipstick.

The murder was made possible with Gaia's Blood, the technology that Gemma had pioneered. So it was a cruel act of fate that the very thing Gemma had designed for her mother to bring peace to the world had ultimately been the cause of Magnolia's undoing—the death of Neon.

Gemma blamed herself, of course. At least in part. She had sensed the traitor's duplicity, the man the Tantum Terrae knew as Jonah "Marble" Finch. Before Gemma could stop him, Jonah had hacked the code from the servers and swiped the key from Neon's body. Then a working model of Gaia's Blood was in Nigel Sallsworth's hands, and Neon walked into an ambush. He would pay for that. She would make sure of it.

Three shuttles on the horizon pulled Gemma from her thoughts. Right on schedule. She verified again to make sure that each vessel's flight ID checked out. They were. Hopefully, they stayed that way. For their sakes.

Gemma picked her way down a rocky path to a large boulder. She sat down and wondered how many ages the rock had rested here on this craggy spine. How many winters and summers it had endured. Alone. Unmoved. How many assaults of wind and rain, ice and heat it had weathered. Wondering if she, too, could manage such a feat. Could she be the last person standing on the precipice of oblivion. Could she last longer than her mother.

Something had been off about Marble from the start, and it wasn't just that Magnolia was bedding a man half her age. That was normative. Gemma could have been siblings with most of the men her mother seduced. No, there was something more. Gemma sensed the betrayal in Marble's body like the street stench on the skin of a stimmer who hadn't bathed in a year: burn the clothes and cut the hair, but the odor was baked into the flesh. She'd tried to warn her mother. Tried to make her see. But Magnolia's lust had blinded her.

The fool. The beautiful, maternal, sacrificial fool.

Gemma, however, would not be so careless.

Love had never been on the menu. The urge to bond was a sick ploy of evolution, one that overrode the rational mind in the name of procreation. Gemma didn't need to look any further than her own mother to argue that people did insane things to appease their sexual appetites. So she'd relegated herself to the cause of the female eunuchs as told by King Gyges in *Lydiaca* by Xanthus. She would neither bear children nor be the target of any man. And since women held equal claim to muddling the human rationale, at least for Gemma, she suppressed the seductions of her own gender through feats of mental calisthenics and vigorous physical exercise.

The cause, she told herself. *Nothing must come before the cause.*

What was this noble and lofty vision that deemed such austerity? *Life on Earth must continue, and anyone who sought to prevent that must die.* Her sacrifice of human amenities like love, intimacy, motherhood, and even basic friendship were the costs. And if it meant that untold billions might enjoy these luxuries once her job was complete? Who was she to withhold from them?

With her legs outstretched, Gemma watched between her sneakers as the shuttles lined up on final approach to her compound's landing pad. The passengers aboard had taken a risk to answer her summons. Of course, not answering it would have been even riskier, now that news of Gaia's Blood had hit V-cog black. The dark grid hadn't stopped talking about it since Sallsworth had publicized the hit on his life. He'd assured the system that everything was under control and that the alleged hack that had made such a feat possible had died with their sole perpetrator in the assault: Magnolia "Neon" Birdwhistle.

It was a stroke of genius, she had to admit: say the poison was destroyed but keep the recipe for yourself. The coders and criminals of the world assumed as much too, she thought. If V-cog had been hacked once, it could be done again, and surely Neon's legacy lived beyond her death. Thus Sallsworth's attempt to gain political power from looking like he'd not only survived an assassination but also stopped a devastating virtual cognizance exploit had backfired, at least in the underworld. No one was safe anymore.

Gemma moved into a crouch, spying like an eagle on a perch as each atmo shuttle dropped into the mountainous bowl, flared, and opened doors to release their cargo. The people marched like mice into the entrance of her underground lair before the shuttles mounted back to the sky and turned toward Bardufoss Airport to the southeast. The global transponder system had already been hacked and the flight plan deviations wiped. Nothing to raise suspicions.

"It's time," Norkü said from behind her.

Gemma inhaled through her nose. Out through her mouth. Eyes lingering on the rich greens and grays plunging into the deep blues beyond. "They must live to see this, Norkü. Such beauty. Such… perfection."

"And they will. You'll see to it."

Gemma stood from the boulder and walked up the rocky path to where her bodyguard stood. She patted him on the shoulder as she passed by. "If things don't go as planned…"

"The shuttles will then have no need to come back, as per your instructions."

"Good. Let's go."

GEMMA WALKED into her cave of a conference room and was met by three faces, each looking equal parts anxious and defiant. Such was the mask of warlords and tyrants who knew they'd met their match but refused to betray as much. The people pivoted their chairs under the domed ceiling carved from the mountain's interior, lit by upturned wall-sconces and a roaring hearth fire.

"Thank you for coming," Gemma said as she took her seat at the table's head and then dismissed Norkü. He exited, and when the door was shut, it was only Gemma and her three guests. "As for your security details, they are safe and being accommodated in our guest quarters."

"What do you want?" said Tonka, the largest of the three faction leaders. "And why must this be done in person? I have more important things to concern myself with." The only thing bigger than his python-sized arms was his ego, one she was familiar with. And one that would soon succumb.

"What do I want?" Gemma parroted and then spread her hands apart. "Why, this. A gathering of like-minded leaders to discuss the—"

"Like minded leaders? I have nothing in common with them."

"Oh, come off it, Tonka," said Androsia Behr, the most elegant of them all. A row of blood diamonds hung around her neck and her auburn hair was set high in a wispy pile. "Settle down so we can hear what she wants before you get a bullet to the head."

"She cannot kill me."

"Doubtful. But if she can't, I can." Androsia pulled a boot pistol up and over the table before Tonka was able to draw his bowie knife. Gemma chuckled to herself. *Leave it to someone like Tonka to bring a knife to a gunfight.*

This scene caused the third guest, Eldon "Skitz" Pearlman, to launch into a nervous chattering fit of laughter. "Ha ha ha haaaa! Snap. She has you d-d-dead to rights, Tick Tonk. He heeee! You don't st-st-stand a chance, guppy."

Still at gunpoint, Tonka said, "If you and I met in open combat, stim head, I very much guarantee I am the one who will remain standing."

"Please, please, everyone," Gemma said. "I would appreciate the opportunity to explain myself. However, if you're hellbent on killing yourselves, I can leave you be and pitch my proposal to more reasonable players."

Several tense seconds ticked by as the three newcomers considered Gemma's threat. She knew they were all interested, or else they wouldn't have come. And she trusted that interest outweighed ego and bloodlust… at least she hoped it did. Only time would tell.

"That won't be necessary," Androsia finally replied, stowing her pistol. Tonka sheathed his knife, and Skitz stifled a lingering ripple of laughter.

"Excellent." Gemma leaned back in her chair and

spread her arms out. "Now then, I think it's safe to say that this is quite a momentous occasion. The first time our factions have hung out face to face since all that nastiness in Anchorage two years ago, yes? Shame about the rest of the concerts being canceled. Hope people got their money back. But what a fireworks display, am I right? Anyway, I'm grateful you took me up on the opportunity today."

Skitz raps his finger on the table. "Not like we had m-m-m-much chance of survive-survive-survival if we didn't. That was y-y-you, right? Gaia's B-Blood? You're the only one I know who c-c-c-could split it."

"With all your crypto, you really can't fix the way you talk?" Tonka asks Skitz.

"Shut up, s-s-slug pounder."

"Gentlemen, please. If you can't behave, then I suppose the ladies will have to lead the world."

Androsia gave Gemma a wink on hearing this. "It was inevitable."

When no one else said anything further, Gemma continued. "Androsia Behr, leader of Leonidas X, pro-Earth rebels who believe the Tantum Terrae hasn't done enough to secure our rightful place in the NUE. Tonka, head of the Bembe Militia, Earth-only libertarians who believe we're sellouts for wanting to play by the government's rules. And Eldon 'Skitz' Pearlman, head honcho of Radio Ultra who, as I recall, doesn't really care who's in power so long as people keep buying stim and tweak code."

"Congratulations," Tonka says with a slow clap. "You passed the first grade quiz of who's-who. And I am wasting my time."

"Then I'll get down to it," Gemma says, not wanting the meeting to devolve before making her pitch. "We all share a common goal. That is, that human life on Earth carries on. Regardless of who is in charge, we wish our planet to return to its former glory and remain a habitable jewel for generations to come. Some have called us tyrants for the means we use to justify our ends. They plead for civility, all while they have the audacity to throw untold trillions into the vacuum of space and accuse us of being irrational. But we know better. We recognize we are decades past negotiations. The lines were crossed two generations ago when tech conglomerates and public science gave up on Gaia and sought to bet our survival on space. We know there's no negotiating with mass murderers. Thus our actions were justified the moment they gave up rational thought for ludicrous behavior. While it's too late for them, it isn't too late for us. For Earth. There is still one last chance to bring her back from the brink of destruction. One more opportunity to secure humanity's future on the planet of its origin and throw off the grip of her violators once and for all."

"And when they are gone?" Tonka asked. "Assuming you can do as you say?"

"We create a new order, one free of centralized tyranny."

"No Tantum Terrae?" he was quick to ask.

"None. No Bembe Militia. No Leonidas X. No Radio Ultra. One people, free to live and let live."

"It's impossible," Androsia said. "You're talking about ungoverned people groups who are bound to eventually self-organize and then re-create everything all over again. It can't be done."

"Only because it's never been tried."

This makes Skitz laugh. "Ha ha haaaaa! He he. T-t-t-tried by every new country that ever seceded from another. 'W-w-we know better,' they say. 'We have s-s-something that works.' Only it never does. Never does."

"Only for lack of knowledge," Gemma replied. "That's why we're different."

"Because you can kill anyone you want with Gaia's Blood?" Tonka asks.

"No. Because the whole human race knows that everything else tried before has failed, and we are finally ready for a society where people are free to rule themselves. Live and let live."

"Utopia is a myth," Androsia says. "We have to have leadership."

"Leadership that always devolves into corruption?" Tonka counters.

"Not if we work together," Gemma replies. "We open source everything we know. Every breakthrough. Every advantage. No one starves, no one lacks care. The neediest are served first. And what benefits one benefits us all. If we stop bickering and fighting and then choose to work together. We have the resources, we only lack the delivery."

"And the Earth—and the Earth itself?" Skitz says. "S-s-scientists have said it's t-t-too far g-g-gone."

"Not all scientists. The Tantum has already calculated that if we apply post-migration space spending on pre-migration solutions, we can not only stem the tide, we can eventually reverse it."

"But that would take hundreds of years," Androsia said.

"True. I'm asking you to commit to something that we'll never see. To invest in a plan that you'll never know the end of. But I suppose that is the greatest compliment I could pay you."

"That you think we are fools?" Tonka asked.

"That true wisdom is investing in the generation you will never meet." She locked eyes with him until he was forced to look away. "I believe humanity fully informed and provided for *will* make the best of itself. To think otherwise is to give up on the enterprise altogether. We know the NUE has outlived its usefulness, just as the politicast system has undermined the very thing it set out to accomplish: to create peace through separation and isolation. So if there is anyone insane enough to attempt this, willing to break every rule in the process, I believe they are seated around this table."

"Says the leader of the Tantum Terrae," Androsia said.

Gemma smiled at the woman. Just as with everything else she did, Gemma was prepared for this comment. She knew it would come. It had to. And so she knew what she had to do well in advance. Without blinking, Gemma raised her palms to Androsia, Tonka, and Skitz. Her pale, inkless palms bore no mark. The sign of the reject. The person so far outside the system that if they died, no one would claim them. No one would bury them. The casteless had no home in life or death.

"I have renounced the Tantum Terrae," Gemma said when the shock had subsided from each of their faces. "And I am asking you to do the same with your own factions. Our palms belong to Gaia, so we mark ourselves with dust."

"If we refuse?" Tonka asked.

"Then I guess we know where you stand. So"—she sat to full height and summoned her mother's irresistible charm—"who wants to hear my plan?"

PART 1

1

EVELYN

"EVELYN?" someone asks me. "You okay?"

It's Natalie, floating off my left shoulder. We're on the *Sagan Explorer*'s bridge, reeling from... well, everything.

"Yeah, I'm... I'm just..."

You're what, exactly, Eves? Pissed? Hurt? Confused? All of the above?

And why shouldn't I be? My best friend turns out to be a double agent sent to betray me, the NUE Navy wants to blow me away, the planet we've arrived at looks totally dead, and the aliens I hoped would have answers for humanity are nowhere to be found. I wanna hit something! Hard. The only thread of hope I have is that Jericho appears to have found a promising new artifact, something on the planet's far side, what he claims is a second orbital gate.

As soon as the *Kogarashi* reappeared on Kepler-1649c's far side and re-established a laser LAN connection with us, Jericho ordered his Marquis-class starship to flip and began a decel burn so they could get a better look at their new discovery. The artifact is a promising find in spite of my disappointment, especially because all we have to show for our efforts so far is an uninhabitable planet with a scorching hot surface temperature of over 400 degrees Celsius, and an orbital debris field as thick as mud.

Real-time camera feeds of Jericho on the *Kogarashi's* bridge are pumped directly to my visual cortex. His seven crew members, Kit, Alice, Eddie, Nairobi, Magellan, Afumba, and Fergus One are standing around a central command table in the middle of the circular room. Meanwhile, Rook and his squad of twelve other Marines aboard the *Bellerophon* watch along with our twenty-one member crew in the general comms channel.

"Evelyn?" Natalie asks again.

"Are you sure it's another ring?" I finally ask Jericho after collecting my thoughts.

"As much as we can be," he replies. "Once we finish our decel burn, we'll move in to take a closer look. In the meantime, here's what we've got."

The table projects a three dimensional holographic image of the planet surrounded by a massive debris field.

Space junk, lots of it. But several thousand kilometers away and opposite the ring we came through from Earth is a hexagonal outline with a hollow center and three lumps evenly spread along its perimeter.

"It's still too far away to get real clarity," Jericho says. "But as far as we can tell, those seem to be—"

"Emissions nodes," I interject, studying the points along the outline. "If powered up, they'd form a Landau triangle and an Einstein-Podolsky-Rosen bridge."

"That's our assumption, yes. But you're the expert."

"Any estimates on size?"

Torrence "Magellan" Vanderburg, the former Navy navigation officer says, "Preliminary LIDAR readings say it's less than six kilometers across."

"Smaller than *Parallax One*," Nairobi Kinshaw adds, the *Koga's* lead propulsion engineer.

"And almost four times as small as the Makriá's version," Eddie Carr says in his gritty London accent. "Not to mention the shape difference."

"And construction," Jericho replies. "The surface seems highly irregular, but we're still too far away to get details."

Rook asks, "Perhaps the irregularities are the result of being damaged by whatever catastrophe happened here?"

"Maybe." Jericho shrugs. "Or it's just how they made things."

"You mean how the *second* species made things," Seb

replies. As our resident evolutionary biologist, Sebastián Fernández Parra is picking up the same thread that's just been tickling my brain. "Because whoever made the round one we came through is a very different species than whoever made this one here."

"Oi," Eddie adds. "You mean we're dealing with two alien species now? Fuck me."

"I'd… rather not, Mr. Carr. I'm simply proposing that the shape discrepancy alone is enough to suggest a very different approach to solving the support and energy problems inherent to the revelation of the emissions nodes. Not to mention the size."

Up until now, we've been calling our recently discovered extrasolar sentient species the Makriá, or "the far away ones" in Greek, thanks to Seb's linguistic ingenuity. I fully expect we'll need to update that term if and when the Makriá self-disclose. Now, however, it appears we need a second species signifier.

"So you think the Makriá got an origin signal too?" I ask. "And then built their version of *Parallax One* as a result?"

"That is one hypothetical possibility, yes," Seb replies.

I tap the end of my nose with a finger. The prospect of discovering not one but two alien species is… well, it's overwhelming, to say the least. But I'm too much of a mixed bag of emotions right now to be overly happy about anything. Cue the inner pessimist. "Okay, well, let's try not to get ahead of ourselves here. For all we know, it's a dead end like this planet. Jericho, we'll join you in scanning the second ring after we deploy drones to the planet's surface. Natalie is going to add some shielding and cooling modifications to a few of our RD-24's. But we'll start heading your way now since she can deploy them en route."

"Copy that," Jericho says. "We'll need the *Sagan*'s deep-scan sensors for accuracy."

"Right. Rook, can I ask you to stay with the first gate as a sentry?"

"Consider it done. Again, I doubt the Navy will send anything through. God knows any such decisions will take days if not weeks in NUE bureaucratic channels. But it never hurts to be prepared."

Kit grabs his throat. "You think you're gonna have to… fire on your own people?"

"Only as a last resort, kid. And if it does come to that, we won't have much to worry about."

"'Cause you'll win?"

Rook smiles. "'Cause if we can't talk them down, then we're no match for their other means of persuasion."

"Persuasion? What other do they…? Holy biscuits. You mean, you think they might actually start shoo—"

"That's enough, Kit," Jericho says.

Rook resumes his train of thought. "We'll also scan

the ring and then transmit our findings to you, Evelyn.
I'm assuming you want intel on both structures before
we head back."

"I do. Thank you." His last words hit me funny
—*heading back*—but I brush them off for the moment. "I
also want you to review whatever the RD-24's send back
about the planet. If there was a war, as you've suggested,
then thoughts on the conflict will be helpful."

"Roger.".""

I take a deep breath and look around at the people
represented in V-cog. All told, our team is made up of
three ships and forty-nine souls, six of whom are the
Belle's original crew who were confined to quarters after
Rook took over the ship. We're all currently located four
lightyears from Earth. The only person not on V-cog is
Sam—dammit, *Olivia*. The traitor and my former best
friend. These people are my responsibility. My team to
keep alive. I'm sure Jericho would correct me and insist
that it's *our* team. Rook would probably say the same.
But I'm the one who discovered the signal on *Astraea*,
and I'm the one who charged through the portal before
Sir Nigel Sallsworth had a chance to close it for good.
This is my fault.

"I want to address the whole team before we sign
off," I say after a few seconds. Everyone stops what
they're doing and gives me their undivided attention.
Feels awkward. "I, uh… I know you all followed me
through *Parallax One*. Some for different reasons than

others. Many because you… well, you didn't have a choice."

"I attest that nary a soul sought my approval," Fergus One interjects. The bot, a humanoid looking Stellar Dynamics space maintenance excipion, has been speaking like he's in a D&D game since Fergus Two saved the *Kogarashi*'s crew during its maiden flight.

"Kit," I say. "Any reason that Fergus One here is talking a lot like Fergus Two?"

"Uh, nope. Nothing to see here, Dr. Park."

"Actually," says the bot. "I was instructed to—"

"Oi, no one cares, Renaissance Fairy," Eddie interjects. Back to me, he says, "Keep going."

"Right. Anyway, I, uh… wanted to thank you all for being here and taking a leap of… you know."

"Faith?" Jericho says.

"Something like that." I rub the back of my neck. "And I'm sorry. For charging in like I did and putting my crew in danger. And getting you all mixed up in this. It was irrational. Desperate. Needless to say, your support means a lot. And I want to reassure you that I'm not crazy, despite how it looks. And I intend to get us all back home safe and sound when we're done here. Just… wanted to say I'm sorry and thank you. For taking a chance."

"Well," Kit says. "We couldn't let you go through by yourself, now could we."

"Actually, we coulda," Eddie replies.

"Sure sure. But I guess what I mean to say is... we won't let you down, Dr. Park. And no need to apologize for our sakes."

"I quite appreciate the apology," Eddie adds with a wide grin. "You're a mad one, Dr. Park."

"So I've been told. Anyway, the *Sagan* has enough substrate provision material for four weeks given our crew size."

"*Bellerophon*'s got SPM for eight weeks," Rook says.

"*Kogarashi*'s got one," adds Jericho.

"Okay. So, we know our max window is... what? Four and a half weeks then, if we average it out?"

"Four point three to the infinite," Fergus amends.

"So we'll say three weeks to be safe. And that's assuming the NUE doesn't send recovery ships after us."

"Or the Navy to blow us away," Kit adds.

I ignore that. "Assuming we can figure out how to activate the Makriá's gate, my pledge is to make sure that each and every one of you get back to Earth orbit in one piece. You risked a lot following me through. The least I can do is help ensure that you get home."

"And you're not alone, Evelyn," Jericho adds. "Three ships, three captains. We're in this together." This generates several "hear hear"s over V-cog.

"Thanks." I pause for a moment to take in everyone's faces. "I also want to propose a mission name change—not that we really had one to begin with since this was all rather impromptu. As far as I can tell, we're

Parallax One Exploration Team now. Or POET for short."

"Works for me," Jericho replies.

"Same," Rooks adds. "My squad has been known to be artists with our weapons."

"You did not just say that," I reply with a laugh.

"What? We are." Then he updates the V-cog group title to POET.

"Hopefully it doesn't come to that," I say. "Bottom line, we have three weeks to explore Kep-C, figure out what happened here, analyze both gates, and then hopefully get our findings and ourselves back to Earth. Natalie, let us know when the drones are ready to be deployed. Jericho, we're heading your way."

"Copy that," he says. "See you when you get here."

"WHERE YOU HEADED?" Bhavna Mishra, our comms specialist, says as I start down the ladder to the lower decks.

"Need to check on something."

"Olivia?"

"Am I that obvious?"

Bhavna winks at me. "Say, are you sure that—?"

"Don't worry. I'll behave myself."

"I was gonna ask if you wanted help beating the crap out of her some more. I wanted to get a few shots in myself."

I chuckle at this but then find myself sobered by the situation all over again. I'm not the only one with a score to settle with Olivia. The incog's hacking framed Bhavna for allegedly aiding and abetting Stamos in *Astraea*. Even after the incident, Bhavna was detained for months while attorneys worked to clear her name in the courts. The only thing that kept her from beating Olivia up after I did was Cheng holding her back and appealing to her sense of reason.

"I promise not to beat the crap out of her without you, Mish."

"Just say the word."

With the *Sagan* on a one-g burn toward the *Kogarashi*, I continue through the ship, passing the zero-g dining facility, several labs, and a utility level. All the ladder climbing gives me plenty of time to think, which may or may not be good for my well-being. Jury's still out. The most processing I've done was with Jericho just before he and the *Koga* dipped behind Kep-C's shadow. He tried to help. But the whole situation with Olivia is still messing with me. The idea that the Tantum Terrae had an incog working against me this whole time is disturbing enough; the fact that it was my scientific partner, and that I didn't even know it, makes me feel violated.

I reach deck twelve. Crew quarters, Section D. Eight pie-shaped rooms stem off the center ladder chute with sealed blast-proof doors. Normally, one unit would house four crew members, but at the moment, Olivia has a whole room to herself. Dr. Enni Mäkinen, one of the *Sagan*'s premier xenobiologists, and Joe Aubertine, a burly-looking computer scientist with an American Heights drawl, are on watch. Both look surprised to see me when I drop down and stop on their deck.

"Ma'am," says Aubertine with a finger to his temple in salute.

"Hi, Dr. Park," says Enni.

"Any word from our prisoner?" I ask.

"Not since you damn near cleaned her clock like a bull on a red-dressed ranch hand," Aubertine replies.

"I'll… take that as a no. Food and water?"

"Supplied," says Enni in her light Finnish accent. "She's remained on her bed, recovering from her… well…"

"Of her injuries. I got it, Enni."

"Yes."

Both she and Aubertine look a little apprehensive. "Don't worry. I'm not gonna hit her again, if that's what you're worried about. Is she restrained at all?"

Aubertine shakes his head. "Naw. But we can fix her something if ya like."

"That won't be necessary, Joe. Thanks."

"My pleasure. We'll be here. Our shift doesn't end for another twenty minutes. Assuming you'll be done before that."

"I need less than five."

"Okey dokey." He turns to Olivia's door, enters the

security code on a keypad, and then opens the lever manually. Many of the *Sagan*'s systems predate V-cog integration and touchless entry. "*Ontray voose*, ma'am."

I cast him a curious look, more out of pity than anything else, then steel myself against what awaits me. Inside the room, Olivia lies on her bunk, arms folded across her chest. She lifts her head and raises an eyebrow in surprise, but the act summons a wave of pain that causes her to wince and then gasp. Apparently Dr. Igor Kalashnik went light on the pain reducers.

"Olivia," I say.

"Evelyn." The door seals behind me, and Olivia puts her head back down. "Come for another pound of flesh?"

"Depends."

"On?"

"My mood." I pull down one of the room's minimalist wall chairs and take a seat on the edge. "I wanted to pay you the courtesy of an update."

She opens one swollen eye but doesn't speak. Looks like a hover train hit her, then backed up just to hit her again. I'm guessing she knows this isn't entirely about giving her information. This is about me wanting to see her face to face again. About squaring off with my demons and conquering them.

"We're circling Kep-C to gather intel," I say after a moment. "Then we're heading back to Earth where we'll deliver you into military custody. Until then, you'll stay confined to this room and receive food, water, and medical treatment for your injuries."

"I understand."

I fold my arms, wondering what more I want to say. I hate this woman. But re-writing four years of memories with her is... well, it's going to take time. Like Jericho said before, Sam is dead and only Olivia remains.

"Any word on that debris field, Eves?"

That snaps me from my thoughts. "You don't get to call me Eves, and we're not riffing on this. I've given you the information I want as a courtesy, nothing more."

"Of course." Her head drops onto her pillow again. "I'm sorry about all this," she says after a moment.

"Me too."

"They wanted me to kill you, you know."

"So you've said."

"It was Neon. Her orders."

Being one person away from the mastermind of the Tantum Terrae sends a chill up my spine. I suddenly wonder how close she and Olivia have been. And at the same time, I don't care. Because Olivia's been exposed, and the threat is over.

"But you changed my mind," she adds.

I stand and the spring-loaded seat snaps into the wall with a *thwack!* "We're done here."

"Really?"

"Yes."

"Then why didn't you send someone else to bring the news?"

"As I said—"

"A courtesy. You sure you didn't want to talk?"

"I don't."

"'Cause I bet if you heard my side of things, you might—"

I point at her and bare my teeth. "I already know your side, Olivia. You... *you* are responsible for killing *thousands* of people on *Astraea*. For setting SESI back, and doing who knows what else to sabotage NUESSA's progress. Things that cost lives. And you betrayed me. Betrayed all of us. Plus you *used* me. Manipulated me. This whole time you... you were reporting on me, to who? A handler? To Stamos when he was alive? Stars, to Neon?" I bunch my lips together and shake my head, trying to keep my anger from getting the best of me again. "You must have thought I was such a naive fool to keep company with you."

"No. Not at all. If anything, I—"

"Uh-uh. Don't care. Don't wanna know. You're a murderer, working for a terrorist organization, and you're lucky I haven't pushed you out an airlock already."

"I agree."

"*And you don't get to agree with me, either.*"

"Oh... kay? I won't."

"That's right. *Bitch.*"

She winces but doesn't retaliate.

"I'll never forgive you, Olivia, or… whoever you really are. You've crossed a line, and there's no going back. Only punishment remains. Only justice for the lives of those you helped massacre. And me?" I nod a few times as I get clarity on why, exactly, I came down here after all. "I want nothing to do with you. *Ever again.*" Then I turn away and ping Joe Aubertine in V-cog. "I'm done."

"Yes, ma'am." The keypad beeps and then the door unseals. I spot him and Enni outside, both with curious eyes moving from my hands to Olivia and then back to me. "She… uh, okay, ma'am?"

"For now. Shut it." I turn and watch as the door closes on Olivia. The last thing I see is her swollen eyes searching my face for something I'm not willing to give. Forgiveness.

2

JERICHO

WE'RE NOT EVEN two hours inside this solar system and the discoveries are mounting like plot points in an action movie. Dr. Sam Collins is a Tantum Terrae incog named Olivia Tomlinson; Rook suspects war is responsible for the orbital debris field above Kep-C; Evelyn believes climate change is the cause for the planet's arid surface; and now we're heading toward another gate potentially built by a second alien species, according to Seb. At this point, I'm not sure anything else would surprise me. But something tells me we're just getting started.

"Check this out, Cap," Kit says. He's seated beside Fergus and sends me a request to the V-cog display that he's monitoring.

I steady myself on his seat-back, accept the invite, and find myself looking at the new alien artifact, a giant portal ring that's growing slowly as we decelerate toward it. The range timing indicator says we're another twenty minutes to intercept. "So whadda ya got?"

"Okay, okay, check this out." His avatar in V-cog points to the hexagonal ring's perimeter. "The surface, right there? I'm seeing some clear, uh, tectonic-like patterns."

"It looks modular."

"Like it was built that way, right, Cap?"

"That would seem to line up Seb's idea that there are two different species at work here. Look at the node housings." I point to the angular junctions where the emissions nodes attach to the inside of the hexagon. "That's a very different design solution from the last gate we came through. God, we need to come up with a naming convention."

"How about *Parallax Two* for the one we came through? And then this one is *Three*?"

I shake my head. "*Parallax* infers that we built them. Plus it's a mouthful."

"Then, uh…"

"What doest thou think of *Ring X*, my lord?" Fergus says, suddenly appearing inside our V-cog lobby dressed like Conan the Barbarian.

I squint at Kit. "You gave Fergus Two's V-cog avatar to Fergus One?"

"What? They're like brothers. Plus, he likes it. And I

can't bring myself to disappoint him, Cap. What with being so far away from home and all."

"Same way you didn't want to disappoint him by resetting his language protocols when I ordered you to?"

"Exactly. See? You get it."

"Mmm." I look back at our overly muscled claymore wielding barbarian. "What's this about Ring X?"

"It appears to me that mayhap these dark and other-worldly gates form a chain, one bound to the next through the interstices of time and space, therein linking us from—"

"So if this new one is X," I interrupt and point to the display. "Then *Parallax One* is, what? Ring Z? Since it's the end of the line?"

"Like a subway," Kit says. "Only way faster. Am I right? *Hu-uh hu-uh.*"

I lift an eyebrow at him and then look back at the display. "If *Parallax One* is Z, then the round one we came through is Ring Y. This new one is Ring X, and assuming there's one after that, then it's Ring W, and so on through the alphabet."

"Precisely, my lord," Fergus says. "A simple yet elegant design solution worthy of your illustrious—"

"Yeah, yeah. Let's go with it until someone comes up with a better idea."

Kit offers a high five to Fergus. "Told ya he likes you," I hear Kit say as I step out of his lobby.

I head back to my captain's chair and take a

moment to update POET's database with the new ring order nomenclature. Then I send a Notice of Change message to Evelyn and Rook and highlight the update in our log. I add credit to Fergus One because, ya know, it was a good idea. Makes things easier for everyone.

"Thanks, Cap," Kit whispers from his seat in the real. "For adding him as a contributor."

"If it goes to his head, I'm deleting it."

"Oh. Yeah, totally. It won't. I'll make sure of it."

"Mm-hmm."

Just then, Rook pings me and Evelyn on a private channel. I accept and step into a V-cog suite I was definitely not expecting. Rook instantly starts apologizing and attempts to exit the construct. "I'm sorry for the mistake. I just need to—"

"No, no," Evelyn says. "I like it. Was this... your home?"

Rook stops and glances from her to me. "Yes. When I was a child. Again, I didn't mean—"

"It's fine, Rook. More than fine." Evelyn walks to a crimson curtain gathered around one of four wooden support poles that hold up some sort of tent. We're on the rooftop of an adobe-style two-story building on the edge of a desert town. I can't tell if the sun on the horizon beyond the dunes is rising or setting, but either way, it's made the sky a beautiful shade of hot pink. Between the detail of the nearfield objects and the quality of the shifting sands in the distance, this render was not cheap to build.

"Family dinners?" I ask, touching the table in the middle of the rooftop.

He nods. "I have many memories at this board."

"I can see why," Evelyn replies, admiring the view.

"Our family moved with the desert as the habitable latitude pushed north. But supplies became more scarce following the Migration Fallout Decades."

"So you headed for, where, Norasia?"

"London. And when I was old enough, the Marines. Haven't been back since. So this"—he gestures around the portico—"is my memento."

"It's a good one," I say. "I'll show you my sailboat sometime."

"I look forward to that. Though, I must confess, I'm not much for the open sea."

"Says the man who lives in space," Evelyn adds.

"Space does not undulate."

"Then we'll do my Amalfi coast construct," I say. "It's on land with a good view of the Med."

"You have two private suites?"

"Eh, I wasn't the best steward of my coins when I was younger."

"Who was?" Rook takes a moment to collect his thoughts, then gestures for us to have a seat around the table. "Thought I'd fill you in on Ring Y, as we're calling it."

"Nice tip of the hat to Fergus there," Evelyn says to me.

"Credit where it's due." I look back to Rook. "Whadda ya got?"

He spreads his hands apart to create a holo display over the table. A three-dimensional view of Ring Y appears, slowly turning against a faded background of stars. The silvery object is smooth with a hint of green iridescent sheen. Definitely slick and way more advanced than anything we could build.

"Our initial scans detected several elements in the ring's surface," Rook begins. "Including bismuth, strontium, calcium, niobium, and titanium, among others."

"All used in superconductors," I say. "Not surprising, given the ring's size and presumed power needs."

"But here's where things get weird." Rook brings up a new list of elements, some with asterisks next to their names. "This is a full list of elements that we've gathered so far. Granted, I know there's a lot of planet left to scan, but check this out." He expands the list and starts with the first grayed out element. "Promethium. It's in the ring…"

"And why is it starred?" I ask.

"Because it's not on Kep-C?" Evelyn guesses.

Rook nods. "Bingo."

"But that's not necessarily newsworthy, is it? We have promethium on Earth."

"But it's rare," I say. "I'd have to look it up, but I imagine we harvest less than a kilogram per year."

Rook snaps his fingers. "See? This ring must have somewhere north of twelve tonnes of it."

"What?" I nearly fall out of my chair.

"And that's a conservative estimate. There are more elements like that too," Rook continues, swiping through a series of rare elements with asterisks next to them. But then he gets to some empty dialogue boxes that are grayed out.

"What are these?" Evelyn says with growing excitement in her voice. "They're blank."

"Sensors don't know what to make of them. We'll need one of your fancy mass specter machines."

"Mass spectrometers," Evelyn corrects.

"Yeah."

Kit jumps in next. "Are they, ya know, unknown elements?"

"No," Evelyn replies. "Most everything's taken on the periodic table. The only room left would be for ultra heavy elements, and I don't buy that."

"Same," I reply. "If I had to guess, I'd say maybe we're looking at a new state, maybe a temperature-stable metallic hydrogen? Or a new alloy or molecule. Who knows?"

"Which begs the question," Evelyn says, "Where did these all come from?"

"And who *funded* the project," I add. "This much

precious metal and alloys? We're talking an unimaginable sum of money... assuming whoever built it has an economy."

"And then there's the emissions nodes' secondary function, at least that's what I'm calling it," Rook says.

"They do something else?" I ask.

He grins and then zooms in on one. At first glance, it looks pretty much like the object we built for Evelyn following the alien signal's instructions. It's a thick triangle with an outgoing laser port on one surface, an incoming port on the other, and the bottom affixed to the ring. Granted, this version has some sort of chrome body that makes it look way more futuristic than our version, but the basic elements are all there. It also seems to be at least three times the size, maybe more. But as Rook continues to zoom in, I notice a semi-transparent circular window on the triangle's face. Interestingly, it only appears to be on the backside, facing away from the portal's entry.

"What's this opening on the back of each node?" I ask.

"I was hoping you could tell me, Mr. Engineer."

"The signal output generator," Evelyn says, leaning in. She takes control of the image and starts tilting it back and forth like she's examining a seashell she just picked up on a beach. She pushes the image sideways and jumps to the next node, examining it just as carefully before going to the third and final one. "They all have it.

And look"—she increases the radiance until we can just barely see through the semi-translucent window—"the interior lens is angled."

"Meaning?" Rook asks.

"I'd say these nodes emit some form of electromagnetic radiation. And based on the interior lens angles, I'd say they intersect past the ring to create a very powerful, very concentrated beam of energy that..."

When she doesn't complete the sentence, I finally ask, "That does what?" Though I feel like we all already know the answer.

Evelyn zooms out until the ring is the size of a thumbnail and types the word Earth into the display's nav search field. The orientation pivots to show a small prick of light with an ident tag marking our Sun and listing Earth in a drop down window. Evelyn sits back as a look of wonder dawns on her face. "The ring has a polar orbit that faces us."

The hair on the back of my neck stands up. "This ring... produced our signal?"

She nods. "I mean, we may never know for sure, but that?"—she points to the ring and our sun in the distance—"that's intent. If those nodes project something, then it's aimed right at us."

Rook sits up to full height. "And they're not emitting now because...?"

"Because they probably wouldn't be running for 300

years straight. Remember: the light of our intercepted signal left this ring three centuries ago."

"Which is a lot of time for a lot of things to go wrong," Rook says.

"It does, yes."

"So, just to be clear here," I say. "We're hypothesizing that this is the source of the signal Parallax intercepted on *Astraea*?"

"I think we are," Evelyn says. "Given the evidence and until we have something better to go on. It might explain why our ring didn't have any navigational controls too."

"Like it was designed to link with this one."

"A quantum lock of some kind, maybe. Who knows. But it's a start." Just then, Evelyn gets a notification.

"What is it?" I ask.

"Initial drone scans are coming in."

"Can we see?" Rook asks.

Evelyn nods and starts porting the real-time camera feeds and sensor data to Rook's suite. A few moments go by, and then we have several windows floating above our rooftop dining table, each showing results from one of a dozen different drones sent to key locations around the planet. Most of the robots are still en route flying several klicks above the surface, but at least three have found their target areas.

"My god," Rook says under his breath while examining the most active feed. It's from a drone named A04 dispatched to what Seb believes is a former coastal territory based on geographical evidence. According to him, one specific location ranked high as a possible site for the remains of a sentient civilization using a bunch of scales I can't pronounce. Most of it's over my head. Bottom line, he thinks the Makriá lived here once upon a time, before Rook's war and Evelyn's climate event wiped them out.

Drone A04 is moving through what appears to be the remains of an urban environment. Heat waves rise from ash-colored mounds that sleep like ancient giants in a lava swamp. But there are clear shapes in the objects. Most of them hexagons. Maybe windows? Doors. Passageways. Twisted stems of metal protrude from the wreckage like trees stripped of leaves and limbs. Some nearer the surface pulse in a dull orange, aching from the heat.

"I can't believe we're witnessing this," Evelyn says in an awestruck tone. "This is... it's unbelievable. An entire ancient alien civilization. "

"What's left of it anyway," Rooks adds. "It's like Armageddon."

"You spotting signs of conflict in these ruins?" I ask.

"Roger. See there?" He points to a hole in the side of what I think was an overpass support—at least that's the closest thing I can compare it to. "That's blast damage."

"Meteorite?" I ask.

"Negative. There'd be no structure left from a rock

strike that big. That was done by a weapon. Seeing lots of other signs too. Granted, this place looks old. Everything's pretty badly deteriorated, but the clues are there, if you know what to look for. A ten-coin chip says there's armor under all this slag and ash."

"We'll take your word for it, Master Sergeant," I reply.

A04 stays on its westerly course, moving around and under ruins, until the drone reaches a vast expanse that opens up like the Grand Canyon on Earth or the even greater Valles Marineris on Mars.

"It was an ocean at one point," Sebastián says to my right, startling me. Evelyn must have invited him. "That's what our two geologists are saying anyway. And I agree."

"And a climate event did this?" I ask. "Boiled away the water, I mean?"

"Hard to say. There's just... gonna be a lot to process. I know we only have three weeks, but we'd much rather have three years to explore all this. Shoot, three decades wouldn't even do it. We're talking about an entire Kaku Level III civilization candidate in a late Kardashev Type I star system."

"A what now?" I ask.

"Ah. A, uh, Kaku Level III just means an intelligent sentient species."

"Like us," Evelyn says to me.

Seb keeps going. "And a late Kardashev Type I civilization means they've learned how to harness the solar energy reaching their planet or *planets* and are graduating toward harnessing their entire star, but aren't fully there yet—uh, *weren't* fully there."

"So about like us?" I ask.

"Sort of. We'd need to explore the other orbital bodies in this system first. But with the sheer amount of orbital debris we're seeing, I suspect they may have been farther along than we are. Dr. Mäkinen agrees. We'll try to get a better consensus as we see more of the data."

Rook points at a hexagonal design in one of the dilapidated buildings. "You think the shape connects the Kep-C species to Ring X?"

"Well, that depends."

"On?"

"The Makriá don't hold the patent on the Euclidean hexagon. Bees make their honeycombs using it. The Sabellaria alveolata, a truly hideous worm, builds its tunnels with it. Fruit from the Monstera deliciosa has it on its skin. The extinct coral Cyathophyllum hexagonum is made of hexagons. And dragonflies have eyes made from 30,000 hexagons. Don't even get me started on snowflakes."

"All hexagons," Rook says. "Got it."

"So, is what we're seeing on the planet enough to be conclusive? No. But is it notable? Absolutely. I think we can anticipate getting more clarity once we determine what materials make up Ring X. My money says we find the elements here on Kep-C."

"Hey, Cap?" Kit says from behind my chair.

"If more people show up, we're gonna need a bigger portico," I say to Rook and Evelyn. "What's up, Kit?"

"You guys maybe wanna take a look at something weird we're picking up."

"From Ring X?"

"Uh, actually? No. It… looks like some sort of radio transmission."

"Looks like? Or is?"

"Ha ha. Yeah, it is."

"Frequency?" Evelyn asks.

"Well, it's kinda all over the place, Dr. Park. From 10 megahertz up to 2.5 gigahertz and back again."

She stands. "It's sweeping?"

"I guess you could say that, yup."

Rook asks, "Point of origin?"

"Uh. The, uh… space junk is, uh, sending it."

"Not the rings?" Evelyn asks.

"Noooope. Just the junk. But we're having trouble getting an exact fix on it. Seems like it's reflecting off the debris field."

Evelyn looks at Rook who's also standing now. "Can you triangulate?"

"On it."

"What's it broadcasting?" I ask Kit.

"Honestly? I have no clue, Cap. Sounds like a whale

eating a bad grid transmitter if you ask me. Actually, it kinda reminds of this one time when my Aunt Matilda slipped and fell on the dog and the robo-sweeper at the same time. Couldn't tell who in tarnation was making which noise because they were all hollering at the same time. The dog yelping, the sweeper malfunctioning, and big Aunt Matilda shouting away. She was big, too. I mean, not like actual whale big, ha ha! Well, maybe about like a Beluga. But don't you tell her that I said that! I would be in so much trouble. Golly!"

"Kit?"

"Yeah, Cap?"

"The signal?"

"Oh, right. Ha! Patching it through now."

3

ROOK

"I DON'T KNOW what big Aunt Matilda sounds like, but I have to say that it does sound like a whale eating a bad grid transmitter," I say to the team still gathered around my dining table.

"Told ya," Kit replies. "And you're lucky you never met her. She was mean. But she made good cheesecakes."

The alien audio sig has two distinct components. The first is a round tone like someone yawning. It gets interrupted here and there, picking different places to start and stop its upward and downward sweeps, but the sound is fairly constant and serves as a bed for the second component.

Static.

Grid transmitters chatter just before they lose

connection or when they're about to die. Military grade ones have a few advantages over those on the commercial market, but they don't last as long, contrary to civilian opinions on what "military grade" actually means. In the end, however, all equipment breaks down, even the most meticulously maintained gear. And when GTs go, they give off a series of clicks and pops.

Together, the two elements create a strange sounding transmission. I can't decide if it's mechanical or biological in nature. To that end, Evelyn has called Natalie Mason, the *Sagan*'s chief linguist and cryptographer, comms specialist Bhavna Mishra, and xenobioloigist Enni Mäkinen to jump into our command-level channel. I'm not comfortable with all these people in my suite, but the circumstances are fairly unusual. I'm also not innocent either. I just invited Lance Corporal Jay Rodgers from Team One, who's good with numbers and sensors, and Corporal Korvich from Team Two, who's got a thing for computers, turning my childhood home into a virtual desert-based forward operating base. *Just what I always wanted.*

Despite all the brainiacs and equipment, it's Kit's utility excipion, Fergus, who makes the initial discovery, albeit in a cryptic way.

"Therein lies the first of the soothsayer's discursive omens," Fergus says while pointing to one of Mason's holo windows. The image displays multicolored 3D waveforms of the signal complete with V-cog software's attempts to attach meaning to the peaks and troughs with ident tags, most of them useless beyond rote frequency analysis.

"Someone care to translate that?" I ask.

"Sure, sure," Kit says. "He just means that a pattern has popped up, is all."

"He's right," Mason replies, expanding her holo window to fill the whole table. "Look. Everything seems to be fairly random… riiiiight up until here, about twelve seconds ago. Those two peaks are identical to this other pair from earlier." After circling the two sets, she looks over her shoulder at the bot. "Nice work, Fergy."

"It is but my earnest pledge that I—"

"So it's repeating every two or so minutes," I say as I watch the waveform continue to roll across Mason's display.

"Well, we can't really assume a period until we've seen it a third time at least. But… yeah, it looks that way."

"Which means it might be intentional," Enni adds.

"Or it's broken," I counter.

"That too, yes. That's why I said 'might'."

Evelyn gets my attention. "Any closer to finding its origin?"

I look at Rodgers, and he shakes his head. "Nothing yet, ma'am. Despite having three ships to triangulate its point of origin, we're getting a lot of sig deflec. Uh, that's signal deflection. But at least we can determine that it's coming from an orbital altitude of 370 klicks from the surface. And so far, the *Belle* looks to be the closest to it."

"Keep working it," I say.

"Roger."

"Do we know what triggered it, Kit?" Knight asks—I can't help but use Jericho's callsign. Old habits die hard.

"Uh, no. Not that I know of. You all were in your little team leaders huddle in here, being all cool and commanding. Like real next generation space leaders that people are gonna make movies about because you guys—"

"Kit?"

"Sorry. Uh… yeah, so you were in here, and then it just started going off."

"And only the *Belle* was closest to it?"

"That's the weird part. The *Bellerophon* looks like it has only recently come close to it."

"I can confirm that," Rodgers adds.

"So it's not proximity that set it off," Knight says.

But I hold up a hand. "Maybe not to whatever's emitting. But the *Kogarashi* is almost to Ring X."

Knight narrows his eyes at me. "A proximity alert for the second gate." He looks to Evelyn for confirmation.

"It's all too soon to tell," she says. "We're just guessing at all of this. But I suppose it's as good a hypothesis as any."

"Holy biscuits," Kit exclaims. "You think it's like

trying to keep us from flying into something bad? But we can't decipher the message until it's too late, and then the kraken comes out and eats everyone? And we're all like, 'But I never got to meet my real dad!'"

"You done?" Knight asks.

"I mean, I've got more, but..."

Evelyn addresses the whole team. "What's the probability that we actually decipher an alien language today?"

"Today?" Mason says with a shocked look on her face as if expecting Dr. Park to know better, which I'm sure she does. Evelyn probably just wants everyone to be on the same page and keep our expectations realistic.

"Depending on the complexity, and assuming it is some sort of language, how about zero. We're talking true xenolinguistics here. If we were fast, we might have something in a few months. But that's assuming the Makriá even converse like we do, think like we do. It might be a year or more before we have properly associated nouns, verbs... and then there's sentence structure, syntax, and then infinite nuances of variable declensions."

"So... not anytime soon," I interject.

"No, Master Sergeant. We can't just wave a magic wand. If I had more help from a team of computer scientists led by someone like..." Mason stops and looks at Evelyn. The moment gets tense when I think we all realize she was about to say Sam Collins. Fortunately, she has the good sense to skip it and keep going. "And the limits on our AI from robo-anthro laws mean we'd have to do most of this the old fashioned way."

Kit lets out some sort of childish giggle from behind his hand.

"What's so funny?" I ask.

"Oh, *hu-uh hu-uh*, nothing."

"Kit?" Knight says.

"Well, it's just that the laws banning robotic anthropomorphization only hold up in *our* solar system. Like, legally speaking. "

"Meaning?"

"Uh, well, section four, article eight dash twenty-two, paragraph, uh... I think it's maybe like fourteen? Or is it fifteen? Anyway, it explicitly states that the laws are only meant to govern excipions and shipboard AI's in our home solar system. It says *nothing* about what happens to our machines once they enter *another* solar system. Right? You with me?"

"You can stop winking," I say. "You saying that you've found a loophole in the law then? That doesn't mean squat if we can't actually make bots smarter."

Kit gets a stupid silly grin on his face and shrugs a few times.

"Hold up," Knight says, looking at Kit. "You can?"

"Well, I mean, it's not like an exact science or anything. But it's kinda like letting a child, a human one, grow up. For all intents and purposes, we've... kinda been stunting our AI's growth for like the last fifty years or so."

I take a step toward Kit. "And you think letting Fergus grow up will allow us to decipher this signal faster?"

"Yupper doodle. Like, it can't hurt, right?"

"It will if he decides that the quickest way to complete his task is to grab a rifle and kill everyone on this mission," I say.

"*Ha ha ha.* Yeah. I guess there's that. But he won't."

"And why's that?"

"'Cause I'll ask him. Nicely."

I exchange looks with Knight, one that says, "You can't be serious."

"Kit," Knight says to his flight engineer in a conciliatory tone. "I think we're all… *interested* in what might be possible. But we've got some serious reservations, the kind that prompted our entire government to, ya know, pass laws forbidding this sort of thing."

"Well, I guess the good news is that if it all goes to Fargo in a wicker chicken basket, then the NUE won't have anything to worry about. Contained to Kep-C, right?"

"That's… not exactly the reassurance we're looking for, pal."

I ask the young man, "You think taking the reins off your bot will actually aid us in deciphering the signal?"

"I do, Master Sergeant Rook. I wouldn't have brought it up if I didn't. And, to be honest…"

When he doesn't complete his sentence, I ask, "What?"

"Well… I kinda sorta kinda did it a little already."

Knight jumps in. "Back when Fergus Two stopped Adrian Wallace from sabotaging the *Kogarashi*'s test flight. And all the other Ferguses who helped retrofit *Telemine* Station."

"Yup. And that was just a smidge of what the excipion neural network can do if let go. We've got soft AI tech everywhere. We use it everyday. V-cog translation software, weather forecasting, grid car navigation, even your weapons systems, Mr. Rook sir. It's all soft AI. But if we take the reins off?" He lets out a whistle. "*Phewwwww.* Boy oh boy oh boy. We could have something really beautiful on our hands, know what I mean? And I give you my word that I'll make sure he follows Tezuka's Ten Laws. Cross my heart, hope to die, and stick a Mai Tai in my eye."

Knight looks to Evelyn and then to me. "Captains?"

"If he can keep a leash on it, I'm for anything that helps us solve this puzzle," I say. "But I also want a military contingency."

"Such as?" Knight asks.

"Frag grenade welded inside its chest with a det switch in our pockets." Someone laughs at my suggestion. "I'm not kidding."

"I could actually make that happen, sir," Kit says. "I could also write in a kill code that we could activate with the right passphrase. Which, ya know, I can't actually say in front of him because, 'cause like then it would totally defeat the purpose, right?"

"And it would bring me great pleasure to enter the kingdom of Valhalla upon the winds of your ethereal wrath should I fail you, Master Sergeant Farooq," Fergus adds.

"Oh boy," I say softly.

"Oi, and since we're negotiating, can someone please have him change the way he fucking talks?" Senior engineer Eddie Carr asks as he steps onto my portico—and why not? Might as well invite the whole damn crew. He grunts hello to everyone.

"Um, what's wrong with the way he talks?" Kit asks. "Really?"

"I like it," Evelyn says. "Plus, if Fergus has to change the way he talks, then I vote Eddie has to as well."

"What's wrong with the way I fucking talk?"

This gets several raised eyebrows and a few laughs.

"Fergus stays the way Kit made him," Knight says eventually. "*For now*. But if something comes up…"

"I know, I know," Kit replies. "I'll keep tabs on him."

Despite Kit's youth and enthusiasm, I actually trust his instincts. I've led my share of boots into combat. Yeah, they can have a tendency to screw up operations and even get people killed. But sometimes they have bright ideas too, ones that save lives and even win engagements. In fact, as long as they're coachable, and you can keep your eye on them, it's the smart ones who end up making some of the best leaders—the kind you want watching your six in a firefight gone sideways. Granted, I wouldn't put a firearm in Kit's hands, but I would trust him with a programming terminal.

"Evelyn?" Knight asks.

She bites her lower lip for a second. "We have laws for reasons. But they're meant to help things generally, and often end up harming things specifically. In this case, giving Fergus some rope might help us and save lives. Stars knows we could've made faster progress on decoding the Kepler signal with a higher functioning AI. So why not now? The only thing I would feel uncomfortable with is enabling the shipboard AIs the same freedom. Since the ships are our only means of survival, I wouldn't want to risk them."

"Agreed," I say.

Knight nods as well, then turns to Kit. "Alright. Let's see what he can do. But I want you working with Dr. Mason on it, and bring in Lance Corporal Rodgers too, so the *Belle* is involved."

Kit's fingers are flying across his keyboard as Knight finishes talking. Then, with one final press of the enter key, he says, "Done. All set, Cap."

"Hold up. I thought it was gonna take—"

"Time? Sure. But I already kinda sorta had this

ready to go for a while now and was just, ya know, waiting on the permission and such. Anyway, I'll still share what I've done with the others, but Fergus is all set."

I exchange looks with the other two captains that are somewhere between being impressed and being worried. But it is what it is now, and we have a pressing need. So I stick with trying to look impressed.

"Let's go ahead with Rook's frag idea," Knight says after a second. "Having a contingency on this one wouldn't hurt."

I dip my head in silent thanks. "We'll get you that munition shortly."

"This brings up a whole other issue," Evelyn says.

"What's that?" I ask.

"What to do if we end up deciphering the signal and there's someone on the other end."

I glance around and see plenty of surprised faces, which leads me to ask the obvious question I'm guessing we all have. "But I thought this was a dead planet?"

"It is," she says. "That doesn't mean there isn't something alive out there, or at least something that's thinking."

"An AI?"

"Why not? But it could also be a relay that connects to a species off world, or even out of the system. We can't rule out any possibilities."

"So what's SESI protocol then?" I ask.

Evelyn laughs a little and raises an eyebrow at me. "I wish it was that simple. There's been so much speculation about this, it would take me days to go through it all with you. Literally. Part of it's because we have no idea what to expect—movies aside."

"But assuming Fergus manages to crack the code with Dr. Mason?" I ask.

"Then I'd say we go with Fasan's Principles. He helped pioneer what we now know as metalaw, particularly pertaining to space. His ideas have helped guide SESI since its inception, and include the principles of non-violation, equality, and the recognition of the will to live as well as the living space of any intelligent species. I can draft protocols based on whatever we encounter next."

"Sounds like a bunch of shit that'll just get us killed," Grabowski interjects out of nowhere.

"Can it, Corporal," I snap.

"Sorry."

"Uh, in the meantime, I think I've got something here," Rodgers says. He opens up a nav window and displays it for the whole assembly. "Equatorial orbit, currently over the eastern hemisphere, here." An ident tag lights up in the debris field marking a speck of junk.

"Magnify," I order.

Rodgers zooms in until we're all looking at… at a… "I can't tell if it's a Kindergartener's drawing or a… space station," I say.

"Eddie?" Knight asks.

He leans in to get a better look at the live nav display. "Bloody hell. What's that doing in space?"

"You know it?" I ask.

"Oi, it's a Szilassi polyhedron, albeit futuristic as fuck."

"A what?" I look from him to Knight, who also seems to be admiring the random shape—an object I have truly never seen before. "Someone care to explain?"

Knight nods. "I needed Eddie's confirmation to be sure, but what you're looking at is a toroidal heptahedron, with each face touching all the other six, and all are irregular hexagons."

"Those don't look like hexagons I've seen," I reply.

"Thus the word irregular. A Hungarian mathematician named Lajos Szilassi discovered it in the second half of the twentieth century. You'll notice that as it rotates, the outside shape looks like triangles alternating orientations. And the element that makes it a torus, this hole in the middle here, is also shaped like a triangle. But the entire structure is still ultimately made of interconnected hexagons, totaling fourteen vertices and twenty-one edges."

Rodgers lets out a chuckle. "I guess we know what hexagon-obsessed Makriá come up with when they're drunk on the weekends."

"Oi. What are the dimensions?" Eddie asks.

"Looks like 254 meters tall, 108 meters wide, give or take," Rodgers replies.

I order him to magnify the object more so we can get a closer look at its surface.

"Seems a lot like Ring X's composition," Knight says. "At least what we could make out so far. But there's a lot more detail here. Rough gray body, hexagonal skin, and I'd bet half my crypto that it's made of the same stuff as Ring X, all found on the planet."

"The more I see," Sebastián says, "the more I believe we're dealing with one species indigenous to Kep-C, and another that's foreign to this system. Comparing this station and Ring X to the construction of Ring Y would be like… well, like comparing an adobe home to a modern skyscraper. No offense, Master Sergeant. Adobe engineering is quite ingenious given the—"

"It's alright, Priest."

"I already told you, I was *going* to be a priest. But I decided that—"

"I get it. Rodgers, what about energy readings? Life signs?"

"Nothing so far, except the signal. No other radiation, visuals, thermal… it's dead in the water."

Seb seems to be nodding along with Rodger's intel. "Which stands to reason."

"How so?" I ask.

"Well, not to put too fine a point on it, but if this species can't survive on its own planet, it has even less of a chance of surviving in space for any length of time. Eventually, the inhabitants would need resources from their homeworld. Granted, they might survive for a while, maybe even years if they're lucky. But with what we're seeing from the drones, I think this planet's been dead for a very long time."

"It's a ghost ship," Kit says in a creepy-ass tone and then starts moving his hands through the air like he's tracing a distant horizon. "Who knows what kind of space zombies lie in wait for us, feeding off one another's brains for centuries, only to be presented with fresh flesh born from another solar system."

"Is... he recording himself?" I ask the others.

Knight waves at me. "He's capturing all his sensory data. Eyes, ears, and anything happening in V-cog. Making a documentary for the verb, he says."

"Jesus. Moving along, I'd like permission to take a recon unit to investigate the station."

Knight and Evelyn both look surprised, but Knight is first to speak. "You sure that's the wisest course of action?"

"No one said anything about being wise. I just see it as the most expedient opportunity to gather intel. That geometry lesson gone rogue is the first intact object we've seen in orbit, sending us a message on repeat. And to hell if anyone thinks I'm just gonna sit around here waiting for Kit's metal man to try to piece together an alien language from scratch. Like Mason said, it might require more time than we have. So if we're after answers, I figure it's best to knock on the front door and see what we find."

"It's kinda what Marines do best," Rodgers adds.

"Oorah," Corporal Korvich says.

Evelyn smiles at the exchange then looks around at the team. "Rook's not wrong."

"You would think that," Knight replies.

"And why not? We don't exactly have the luxury of taking our time, now do we? We're here to figure out who contacted us and why. And if we don't bring something of value back to SESI and NUESSA, I'm pretty confident Sallsworth will do his damnedest to make our lives a living hell from now to the end of time. Plus, the Declaration of Legal Principles Governing the Activities of States in the Exploration and Use of Outer Space includes an entire section that astronauts are officially our 'envoys of humankind in outer space.'" She points at me. "I just want you being careful. And to take me with you."

"Negative," I say.

"But the contributions I could make by being there physically—"

"Are not worth the risk."

"Agreed," Knight exclaims. "You're outta yer mind, Evelyn."

She gives us both a half smile and shrugs. "It was worth a shot."

"What's your approach?" Knight asks me.

I roll my head side to side as I think for a second. "I won't put the *Belle* or a shuttle at risk by trying to dock with it. So I'll take two fire teams and make a jump here"—I point to a location that looks to be ten klicks from the target ship—"which should give us plenty of space."

Kit wiggles in seat. "You're just gonna, ya know, leap out there and fly across that whole distance? In open space?"

"That's what battlesuit exo-armor is for, kid. You think we wear it to be pretty?"

"I mean, I'd wear it for looks, yeah."

I give him a smile and then address the group. "Anyway, a void jump will make us harder targets to hit in case that vessel has any latent defenses."

Kit swallows loud enough for us to hear. "Like, shoot at you?"

"Like shoot at us."

"Holy biscuits. You guys really do have, ya know, oysters the size of baseballs. Sheesh."

"Make it happen," Knight says. "Just… be safe. We don't need any casualties on this expedition."

"Roger that." I ping the squad. "Geller. Korvich. I want Teams One and Two suited up and ready for void jump. Twenty-klicks round trip, plus margins. Raid and recon loadout, scout battlesuit config. Ready in ten mikes."

"Roger," both men say over the squad's V-cog audio channel.

"Might I make one suggestion?" Kit asks.

"You can't go," Knight says.

"Me? Oh, golly. No, I wasn't thinking that, Cap. I was thinking of Fergus."

All heads turn to the blue and gray bipedal human-framed space worker bot. Its round LED eyes blink twice inside its blue-plated head to simulate a human look of astonishment. Then it places its articulated hands and fingers on its carbon fiber chest. "Who, me?"

"Yeah, you," I reply, looking the bot up and down, warming to the idea.

"But I was under the impression that I was commissioned to learn the ways of the foreigners."

"And what better way to do that than in person, right? Plus, your LIDAR mapping hardware could come in handy."

"If this is the wish of my Maker." He looks at Kit.

"Maker?" Knight asks.

Kit pulls his collar away from his neck and blushes. "He means more like, uh, *Programmer*, ya know? Tweaking his code and such."

"Nay. I mean, you are the Supreme Cosmic Creator of My—"

"Jeez Louise, nobody needs to hear that, Ferg. Ha ha! Nothing to see here, folks."

"I like it," Evelyn interjects. "If he's able to gain

access to systems aboard that ship, even just to observe artifacts and architecture, assuming you can get inside, it could expedite the discovery and research phases."

"I agree," Seb says. "Firsthand experience will aid us immensely."

Knight scratches his face with a finger and then points to me. "If you're sure he won't get in your way, Master Sergeant."

"Is there a way to shut him down if need be?" I ask Kit.

"Sure, sure. I can write a quick little exploit that you can activate via radio. I'll have a redundant version of the same here in case you, ya know, you're incapacitated for any reason."

I nod at Kit and then squint at Fergus. "Think you could defend yourself if needed?"

"I have experience with my broadsword in the glorious throes of virtual melée."

"That should translate. Gird your loins, bot. We'll meet you out there."

"Consider them girded, my liege. I greatly anticipate the insertion of your explosive ordnance."

"Annnd... that did not sound right."

4

ROOK

TEAMS ONE and Two are assembled in the *Belle*'s port hangar bay, bathed in the bright work lamps. The light reflects in helmet visors as the team members double-check each other's equipment one last time.

Kit pings me in V-cog. Guessing it's about Fergus. I open the channel and say, "Send it."

"You guys almost ready?"

"Roger. Fergus?"

"Good to go, Master General." Before I can correct him, he adds, "That's Mark 21 exo-armor you're all wearing, right? Black and gray, reactive gel, ceramic plating, and nanocarbon fiber."

"Someone knows their stuff."

"I watch a lot of movies. Scout configuration?"

"Not bad. Trades armament for efficiency and stealth, gaining us—"

"Max distance over protection. But since the prospect of orbital combat is, ya know, next to nil, it's the right choice for a recon op."

"I'd say you missed your calling—"

"But we both know I'd never make it through bootcamp."

His self-deprecating honesty makes me smile. "I was just gonna say that you never would have met Knight and so probably wouldn't be here now. Glad you're with us, Kit."

"Gee, thanks, sir. That really means a lot." His voice takes on a more dramatic tone. "And for those curious about the Marine loadouts, I, Leslie Christopher Kit, am here for you."

"Are… you recording again?"

He ignores the question and starts talking to his imaginary audience. "Each fire team leader has a standard issue Hermann & Gruber HG-11 magnetic acceleration pistol with two ten-round magazines of 9mm wafer-coated rounds. They, along with their riflemen and assistant automatic riflemen, carry the dreaded and universally feared Scorpion SR-90 MAW assault rifle with 210 rounds of 5.56mm ammo in thirty-round mags. Care to add anything, Master Colonel?"

"It's Master Sergeant."

"Uh huh. And?"

I hold Kit's stare for a few seconds. The kid looks like I'm about to hand him a huge birthday present or something. Eh, son of a bitch. I'll play. "For today's jump, our cross-trained spec ops automatic riflemen have traded their Bellaire MS265 magazine canister-fed MAW light machine guns for 6.5mm Korhonen K40 MAW sniper rifles."

"Holy biscuits! I bet they have quite the effective range. What else they packin'?"

"Uh, they each carry a limpet mine to breach the hull in case we can't find a door that suits our liking."

"For those not in the know, those mines are three parts aluminum to nine parts iron oxide thermite compound that will make short work of anything that buckles under its molecularly boosted 5,500 degree Celsius burn temp. Isn't that right, Master Sergeant Rook?"

Huh, he got it right. "That's… correct, yes."

"And your team configuration?"

"Kit, I really need to—"

"Please? The people are gonna wanna know, sir."

I take a deep breath and keep talking while I finish gearing up. "Sergeant Geller is leading Grabowski, Rodgers, and Ibrahim in Team One, and Corporal Korvich has Hatch, Engleman, and Wijaya in Team Two. Anything else?"

"Boxer or briefs?

"Annnd we're done." I cut the V-cog channel and then signal the teams to move.

We mag-march into the extra wide deployment airlock and seal the internal door behind us. With everyone's diagnostic sensors reporting positive suit life support to the V-cog command HUD, I initiate vac lock with the external environment and watch as the air pressure drops to zero pascals. When our countdown-to-jump timer crosses the final thirty-second mark, I double-check with the *Belle*'s captain. The six Navy crewmen, including the ship's commander, Lieutenant Jaffa, are still confined to quarters following their incapacitation when we first commandeered the Navy frigate. I don't expect them to come around to our mission objectives any time soon, so until then, my Marines have command of the ship, which currently rests in the hands of Corporal Popov and the rest of Team Three who are staying behind.

Last but not least, I step into a new V-cog common room that resembles a formal presentation theater. Kit and a few of the code slicers built it so we don't need to keep using my adobe rooftop construct. The new space includes stadium style seating for all forty-nine members of the expedition, in case they entered en masse—I'm optimistic that Lieutenant Jaffa and his crew will come around to our way of thinking—display screens on the main wall, and chest-height standing tables along the rear observation deck for those avatars who don't like to sit still. The construct has open attendance permission but need-to-know clearance regulated by the three captains and our direct reports. Simple, efficient, and, most of all, not my family's dining room.

"We still solid?" I ask Popov about the *Belle*'s relative position with the unknown vessel, designated Eagle Rock.

"Locked and holding."

"Keep her steady until we get back."

"Roger."

To Teams One and Two, I say, "Everyone set?"

Heads nod and thumbs go up.

"*Bellerophon*, this is Rook for Teams One and Two, ready to jump."

"You are cleared to jump. Happy hunting."

I point Geller and Korvich to the main hatch, which parts in front of us to reveal a breathtaking view of Kep-C. The planet's orange glow gleams in helmets and seems to draw us toward the airlock's lip. With toes hanging over the edge to eternity, I nod down the line and say, "Let's get some."

"Oorah," they reply.

One by one, six men and two women demag their boots and leap from the *Belle* into the void. I go last and watch the dotted line of Marines spread out. Thruster puffs correct trajectories until we're in a staggered conical formation designed to ensure that the unit doesn't get taken out by a single enemy shot while simultaneously keeping us off radar. Granted, if this alien vessel has something better than our hardware, then our strategy is all for shit. But this is how we train, so this is how we fight. Once everyone's in position, I give the command to accelerate, and all nine of our ion packs give three-g thrust for five seconds. When the packs kick off, we're cruising at 127 meters per second. At this speed, roughly 457 klicks per hour, we'll reach our target in three minutes, minus a 4.25 second decel burn. Burn hard, hit hard.

Ident tags follow each Marine while a target indicator plants a landing reticle on Eagle Rock. More than 2,100 klicks to starboard, my HUD tags another object in deep space on a collision course with Eagle Rock. I'd never be able to spot the excipion-turned-rocket without ship-to-V-cog sensor integration.

"Fergus One, this Rook," I say. "SITREP."

"Hail, Reconnaissance Princeps. I see you."

"Roger. Your trajectory and speed look good."

"As do yours. I eagerly await our reunion."

Since Fergus is able to handle much higher g's than us mere mortal bio bags, his thirty-second acceleration burn took him from zero to 20,000 klicks per hour at almost nineteen g's. He's scheduled to arrive one minute ahead of us to scout the area and clear it of smaller debris. The Stellar Dynamics model SME-31 space maintenance excipion is an amazing feat of robotics, even if this particular one has a few screws loose.

The main complication to the first part of this op is passing through the junk in the debris field before we reach Eagle Rock. Our shipboard AI, better known as an artificial control engineer, or ACE, did the majority of the work, calculating the optimum jump time for the route with the least amount of maneuvers. Evelyn's chief dynamicist, Jose Ramirez, double-checked the work, and cross-referenced it with Fergus's results. Our first of three maneuvers is coming up now, indicated by a green dotted flight path rolling to port, pitching up, and then coming back down to starboard. Currently, there isn't an object to fly over, but that's about to change, fast.

"Tracking bogey Alpha, inbound, bearing two seven niner," I call out. "Follow flight path to compensate. Ten seconds." I look to starboard and spot something like a giant metallic clam shell. Sections of internal trussing and trunk lines corroded by solar radiation spew from a gaping tear down the spine. The surface looks similar to Eagle Rock's, but the overall shape gives the impression that it came from some other kind of vessel. Who knows. What matters now is that we get into position and avoid the massive hunk of debris.

"Three... two... one... Mark," I say, and execute the scheduled course adjustment. Every ion pack in the unit fires with mine, and we roll to port, pitch up, and then come back down as the unidentified satellite races underneath at over 3,000 meters per second. Were that in atmo, we'd be dead long before the sonic boom caught up to the object shoving air aside at Mach nine.

"Bogey Bravo inbound," I call out as the next obstacle gets tagged. This one requires us to dip under a two-klick long twirling span that looks like it once bridged starships in a mega station. Ramirez and ACE determined that the object's lumbering roll is slow enough that we can pass directly through the structure with only minor course adjustments. I call attention to the flight path and then execute. "Mark."

The team maintains formation as we barrel roll through the span, getting our first real glimpse of the inside of some of the debris. It looks intricate, with clear signs of floors, shafts, quarters, large cavities for long-gone equipment, and more. This was inhabited by sentient beings at least 300 years ago. The thought sends a chill down my spine as I wonder what bodies might remain pinned in the works.

After we complete our barrel roll and fly past the twirling span, we come toward our last obstacle, what looks to be an angular cross section of a ship. Granted, I'm no expert on alien military hardware, but bogey Charlie is smooth black and shaped like a spike some five and a half klicks long. It too gives us a glimpse of its innards, but its internal structures seem more refined than the last artifact's. Everything is clean and ordered even though it was clearly severed in two.

We pitch down and to starboard, passing underneath

the bulk of the artifact, and then resume our heading toward Eagle Rock.

"Thirty seconds to decel burn," I call out and watch our distance to target indicator plummet. Ahead of us is the massive and odd-as-hell looking Szilassi polyhedron. Not a light on it. No insignias of any kind. Not even spray paint from angst-ridden street youths or a dent from disgruntled neighbors. Just a slowly turning geometry experiment gone wrong with our landing reticle superimposed on its hull.

The augmented reality V-cog icon has been fading in and out as the station spun, completing a full circle every ninety seconds or so. Onboard battlesuit nav has been actively calculating and recalculating our touchdown with the rotating hulk, taking into account minor course deviations we've made since shoving off the *Belle*. At present, our target locator is coming back around and growing.

Fergus has already touched down and started mapping the immediate vicinity. "I've initiated search for potential entry, my lord."

"Roger," I reply. "On you in twenty."

"Very good."

At the fifteen second mark, I order the team to flip. More puffs of compressed air spin each Marine into his and her feet-first landing position. Then I count the last ten seconds over the team channel and order the decel burn at five seconds.

A civilian in this situation would have begun decelerating over a minute ago. Not only does it make for a much smoother ride, but people and systems alike appreciate as much time as possible to account for system hiccups or failures. The last thing anyone wants is to smack into a space station or ship hull at 127 meters per second. Makes for a bad day. But that's not the *first in, last out* Marine way. Come in hot, kick ass, and move before the enemy knows what the hell happened.

The five-second decel burn doesn't bring us to a full stop. Instead, it lowers our speed to a Goldilocks rate that has Eagle Rock's hull rise beneath us and then kiss our boots.

"Mag lock," I call out as the soft *keeew-thunk* of my boots secures me to the metal hull. At least we have a little material science in common with the Makriá, or whatever they're called. The rest of the unit touches down without incident and does a quick assessment of the environment—all part of situational awareness— while I ping Corporal Popov. "*Bellerophon*, this is Rook, confirming positive touchdown on Eagle Rock."

"Roger that, Rook. We see you."

"Any change in the transmission?"

"Negative," Evelyn says, jumping on our channel. "If the station has detected your presence, it is not evident in the signal."

"We'll take that as a plus."

I greet Fergus and then tell him to turn around.

Geller orders Private First Class Ibrahim to surrender her anti-personnel ordnance. She mag locks the small cube to Fergus's lower back and gives it a pat. "Don't try to pull it off either, Fergy."

"I shan't, my lady."

"Any notable intel?" I ask him when she's done.

"No hostile behavior detected. Structurally, the surface is a continuation of what we've already observed."

I nod and give the orders for the team to log Fergus's progress then continue scouting the operational environment to look for any tactically relevant information. The ship's exterior is covered in gray hexagonal plating and interrupted by slight changes in elevation as well as equipment protrusions. In addition to our visuals, we employ a combination of the *Belle*'s and our battlesuits' sensors to map each meter we cover, looking for any deviations in hull structure, depth, or material change. Assuming Eagle Rock isn't just some giant impermeable wedge of modern alien art, and assuming the Makriá aren't a weird-ass species that can pass through solid surfaces on a whim, logic says there has to be a door around here somewhere.

The top section of the toroidal polyhedron is the most normal looking area. Without the side pieces that descend down to form the rest of the shape, it looks like a thin and very long A-frame style ski chalet with peaks that jut out on either end. Underneath the chalet, on the surface that constitutes the top section of the torus's center opening, there's a subtle shift in hull coloration.

"See that?" I ask, pointing to the variation.

"Roger," Geller says. "Two and a half meters across, hexagonal shape. You think it's a door?"

"Only one way to find out," I reply. "Stay frosty."

We continue up the face toward the overhead cross section, eyes peeled for anything out of the ordinary. Which, come to think of it, is everything we're looking at. But I'm watching for objects and surfaces that may constitute threats like boobytraps or station defenses. Again, the Makriá could be using pneumatic powered blow guns for all we know. I just don't want it said of us that we weren't mindful. We transfer to the chalet's underside, which really just rotates our orientation, because everything seems right side up when you're walking on it in the void.

"Fergus, what can you give us on this?" I ping the area of interest and tag Fergus' V-cog ident.

"It does present an area of fascination, my lord. Near field muon imaging shows a potential corridor behind the castle gate."

"Any cause for concern? Trip wires, lasers, pressure sensors?"

"Not that I can see, my lord. Do you desire that I thrust myself into the dragon's mouth and sacrifice my soul for our cause?"

"I'd rather you not die doing it, Fergy. But better you than a human."

"We are of one accord then. Please stand fast as I approach, and do send my regards to my kinsfolk should I not return."

"Your... kinsfolk?"

"He means the other Ferguses back in Earth orbit," Kit says over comms. "It's okay, Fergus. The Marines won't let anything bad happen to you."

I'm about to correct Kit on that, but Fergus is too quick. "Thank you, your eminence." With that, Fergus mag walks past us and heads for the target area. At the same time, I order both fire teams to take cover behind some of the irregular structures on the hull. When Fergus identifies a seam in the plating, I give him permission to try to open it. The bot takes a knee, inserts his fingers underneath the plate, and begins exerting force. I watch his body contract as the pressure increases, complimented by a readout in my HUD.

"Hell," Lance Corporal Hatch says as she strains to get a better look. "That's enough to rip a hover truck in half."

"And still not budging," Grabowski adds.

"How much more you got?" I ask Fergus.

"My maximum exertion threshold allows me another forty percent," he replies.

"Alright, keep it going, but don't—"

A flash of light and sharp vibration from the hull

sends Fergus flying away. My HUD flickers once, and my boots come off the surface. We're all free of the hull, and Fergus is spiraling away from the station.

"SITREP," I call out as my battlesuit auto stabilizes with a few puffs of air and brings me to rest a meter off the deck.

"We're good here," Gellers says, floating to port with Team One.

"Same," adds Korvich to starboard.

"Fergus?" I shout, hoping we haven't lost the bot.

"Hark! I have been expelled from the jaws of the infernal beasty, yet I am not undone." The excipion fires thrusters, rights himself, and then surges back toward us.

"And you're good?"

"Compared to my Creator, none are good, my lord. It is enough that we are *like* him."

"But your systems are—?"

"Bruised but ne'er broken. Come, foul beast! Let me make you my subject and ride you unto oblivion!" Fergus flips, decelerates, and then lands on the hull once again.

When he isn't immediately flung away again, I check in with Popov on the *Belle*. "Any sensor readings on that event?"

"It looks like an energy emissions burst. Perhaps a defense protocol to keep things off its hide. Looks localized to your sector."

"Roger." To my unit, I say, "Stay off the hull."

Confirmation icons run down the augmented V-cog chat window.

"Careful, Fergus," I say again as the bot slips his fingers back under the plate.

"It has bested me once, my lord. It will not best me—"

Another flash of light flings Fergus away.

"Dammit!" My HUD flickers again. The excipion is cartwheeling toward the stars. "Fergus?"

The bot doesn't reply.

"POET Oversight, I need a SITREP on—"

"Hark! Tis I!" Fergus says and then powers out of his spin.

"You good?" I ask, instantly regretting the repeated question.

"Compared to my Creator? None are—"

"Just get back here, and stay off the hull."

"Rook," Popov says. "That burst was almost half as strong as the first. Not sure what that means, but the ship might be losing power."

"Or its capacitors need time to recharge," Knight says on our channel.

"Roger." I look at Geller. "Team One, you're up."

"Copy that," he replies, then orders automatic rifleman Jay Rodgers to plant his limpet mine in the middle of the supposed entry door. Rodgers moves forward with PFC Zara Ibrahim, who provides assistance and covering fire should things go sideways.

The pair decels and stops short of touching the hull. Rodgers affixes his cylindrical limpet mine to the surface, brings the munition online in V-cog selecting breach mode, and then thrusts back with Ibrahim.

Once they're sufficiently clear, Geller looks to me and I give him the go ahead.

"Fire in the hole," Rodgers says.

A bright light flashes from around the mine's graphene gasket. I half expect the ship's defenses to fling off the ordnance, but the device stays put and proceeds to unload its contents on the door. Thermite chews through the hull, turning it red, then orange, and then bright yellow. Eight seconds later, the hull gives way, but instead of the mine magnetizing itself to the next layer below decks, it's blown back by pressurized gas. At the same time, fire erupts from the newly formed hole, but the reaction is snuffed out almost immediately.

With the limpet mine spiraling away, I check in with Popov. "You get anything on those gasses?"

Before Popov can reply, Fergus says, "Behold! The dragon breathes fire!"

I ignore him and press Popov again.

"Roger," he says. "We actually picked up high amounts of carbon dioxide, methane, and carbon monoxide in that exhaust plume."

This stops me cold. "As in…?"

It's Knight's voice that jumps in next. "As in the same

byproducts of fire burning in an oxygen-rich atmosphere."

"So, what are we saying here? That the Makriá breathe our air?"

"Not necessarily. But…"

"But we need more data," Sebastián interjects.

"Please proceed, Rook. But with caution. Also"— Evelyn sounds like she's checking something—"it appears that the transmission has stopped."

"Maybe those defense protocols spent all the juice," Korvich says.

"Only one way to find out." I look back at the newly formed breach in the hull, now glowing a dull red around the meter-and-a-half-wide opening. "Team Two, point."

Korvich acknowledges and sends Lance Corporal Hatch through the hole first, followed by Engleman, Wijaya, and then himself. I pull up Hatch's POV cam in V-cog right away, and track her progress while I fall in behind Geller at the rear of Team Two.

"It's dark," Hatch says. "Not picking up anything on thermal either." Her twin helmet torches join her SR-90 rail lamp and sweep back and forth down the corridor. The dull metallic green hallway is in the shape of a hexagon—no surprise there—and has grates on two opposing surfaces, what I'm calling the floor and ceiling.

"Definite signs of wear," Wijaya says. "Top and bottom walkways."

"You think they use one side or another depending on ship rotation?" Hatch asks.

"That," Grabowski adds, "or they got two sets of legs growing out of their asses."

"You got enough growing out of your ass for both species," Rodgers replies.

"Let's keep the chatter down," I say. Marines deal with stress in a variety of ways—humor being one of them. And patrolling through an alien spaceship certainly counts as stressful.

I sense Fergus floating behind me. He pings our team channel and provides a camera feed of our six o'clock. I appreciate the coverage since every haunted ship movie I've ever seen inevitably has something sneak up behind the unsuspecting and ill-fated crew.

After a few more meters, Hatch spots the first signs of intentional markings and calls the unit's attention to a fifty-some-centimeter-wide hexagonal side panel of polished metal. The script, if it can be called that, looks more like chicken scratch than writing. There's also some yellow and red geometric markings above and below the text area.

"Fergus. You seeing this?" I ask.

"I am, my lord. Transcribing for the royal archives now."

"Keep it coming, Fergy," Natalie Mason says over comms.

"I shall endeavor to do my very best, your highness."

"Is every human royalty to this bot?" Private Wijaya asks.

"Everyone but you, boot," Grabowski replies.

"On the contrary, Corporal Grabowski, my Maker has specifically instructed me that—"

"Didn't ask you, Fergy."

"Ah, quite so."

"You want me to open it?" Hatch asks me.

"Negative," I reply. "Eyes and weapons forward."

"Roger."

To Seb, I say, "Looks like we're dealing with a life-form that breathes our air and reads and writes."

"All signs do seem to indicate that, yes. It's… fascinating. Though I do wish you would lower your weapons." He looks off camera. "Do they have to keep their guns pointed like that?"

"We sure do, priest," I answer before anyone else says something stupid.

"What about that debris there?" Seb asks. "Wedged in the cover's side? Corporal Hatch?"

She spots a translucent piece of yellowed plastic-like material.

When she moves to touch, I stop her. "Belay that, Hatch. Observation only."

"Roger." She changes gears and moves her helmet in closer to let the camera do the investigating.

"Any thoughts?" I ask Seb.

"Not yet."

Hatch peels away and continues down the hallway until we reach our first intersection. "Well this is different." Her POV cam shows corridors leading away in six directions on the horizontal plane, plus two more, one straight up and the other straight down. Hatch lets out a whistle while leaning over and peering in our relative down direction. "I'd hate to fall down that shaft."

"Log it," I say. "Fergus, I want you forward to run LIDAR."

"Yes, my lord." He floats past me and the rest of the column to join Hatch in the intersection. Once he's positioned in the junction's middle, he opens cavities on his chest and back. His internal laser mapping hardware lights up, and then he slowly begins turning himself through all axes, arms and legs extended.

"Looks like del Vinci's Virtual Man," Private Wijaya says.

"It's Vitruvian Man," Hatch replies. "And it's da Vinci, dumbass. Jesus."

"And I receive the compliments," says the bot. The excipion makes a few more rotations, and then the cavities on his torso close. "Scan complete. Uploading results to V-cog now."

A notification pings on my HUD, and I open the file labeled "Eagle Rock LIDAR Scan Node Alpha." A 3D structural map appears, built in a blue wireframe format. "Looks like we have two more possible junctions running off each stem, with the exception of the corridor headed straight up."

"Looks blocked," Geller says. "Could be a door."

"Scout with Team One," I reply. "Two, you're patrolling each corridor to the next node and back. Fergus, you're mapping. Move."

Both teams head out while I remain in the first junction to monitor progress. Geller is first to come back over comms with a SITREP.

"Definitely a door up here. Metal leaves forming an iris. No sign of a control point. But we have more markings." His helmet cam focuses on the alien text, and Geller confirms that Fergus is logging it. "Got some more of that plastic material too."

"May I see?" Seb asks.

Geller orders his fire team to capture and send video.

"We also have hallways stemming from this point," Geller says. "You want us to branch out?"

"One junction at a time."

"Roger."

Team Two isn't a minute into mapping their second node when Korvich pings me. "Looks like... like a barracks," he says from midway down a corridor lined with hexagonal doors. His POV cam shows his lights sweeping through a room roughly ten meters across and six meters high with grates on the floor and ceiling, just like the corridors. Most notable of all, however, are several pod-like beds affixed to the walls. "Or maybe it's some sort of weird medbay," Korvich adds. "No signs of bodies. Everything's empty."

"Got another one," Hatch adds as she enters another room lined with pods. "Seems like this section's lined with them."

"Careful," I say.

The light gray objects are less pill-shaped and more like a gumball with a large opening cut out of the side facing the room's center. Hatch shines her lights into the pod to reveal a padded backboard, straps for multiple points of contact, and tubes with needles at the end. "This is some creepy ass shit, right here."

"More debris," Seb says, noting some plastic-like scraps wedged behind backboard padding.

"Roger." To Hatch, I say, "Log it and keep moving, Corporal."

"Got another big door," Geller says from Team One's location above us. "But this one's half open."

"Like it got stuck," Grabowski adds. There are wear marks on the overlapping plates and more of the plastic scraps. Grabowski gets his head in line with the hole and tries peering through, but the inky blackness beyond swallows his headlamps. "Can't see a damn thing. Feels big."

"Fergus," I say. "Can you fit a scanner through?"

"For you? I will endeavor to fit my tool into whatever hole you command, my lord."

"Not a word," I say to the rest of the unit, 'cause God knows someone wants to say something smart.

The excipion flies past me, turns at the junction overhead, and dashes away to join Team One at the semi-open door. The bot manages to place his chest over the opening and starts scanning the space beyond. It's big. Range finder puts it at roughly twenty-nine meters deep and wide, but still only two meters high. The oddest thing seems to be that most of the wall scans are inconclusive: there's a lot of missing data.

"We're getting some strange readings here," Geller says. "Fergus, you broken?"

"All systems nominal, my lord. However, I am detecting irregularities along the walls."

"What kind of irregularities?" I ask.

Grabowski raises his SR-90. "The moving kind?"

That's when a chill goes up my spine.

5

NIGEL

S<small>IR</small> N<small>IGEL</small> S<small>ALLSWORTH</small> stood behind Madame Chairwoman Alexandra Wright as she opened the emergency session of the Nations of United Earth's General Council gathered in the headquarters building in Oslo. All 375 Chamber of Politicast Representatives were present, as were the Presidents of the American Heights, Norasia, the Southlands, Earth's Moon, and those of the Out Lands, including Mars Nation, the Belt Lands, and Jupiter Moons—at least virtually. The meeting had been called on short notice, and rightfully so. What NUESSA was calling an Einstein-Podolsky-Rosen bridge had been opened to… well, to somewhere else. Beyond any power play Nigel wished to make, and he did mean to make one, the fate of the system was at stake, and people needed to know that the NUE was in control—that clear and decisive leadership could be seen, heard, and counted on to act.

"This assembly of the Nations of United Earth's General Council is hereby brought to order," said Wright. "The General Committee recognizes all Members as being present. Secretary-General Sallsworth has the floor."

"Thank you, Madame Chairwoman," Nigel said as he stepped behind the podium. "And thank you representatives and presidents for your time and consideration during this unprecedented moment in human history.

"I think it goes without saying that while we are amazed, awed, and perhaps even afraid of the activation of *Parallax One* that we witnessed just hours ago, we are also disappointed with the careless acts of the captains and crews who defied NUE, NUESSA, and Space Navy orders to stand down. To be clear, those decision makers aboard the *Sagan Explorer*, the *Kogarashi*, and the NUE *Bellerophon* deliberately chose to act against direct orders and the wishes of this esteemed council and proceeded through the ring in violation of interplanetary laws. We, the members of the NUE General Council, condemn these actions and see them as jeopardizing the peace and safety of the entire system. Accordingly, those responsible will be held accountable and prosecuted to the highest extent that interplanetary law allows.

"As stated in my earlier verb address, despite the gate's successful opening, the Infinita Gate Project and any further actions to support it have been deemed a system-wide security threat Level One. As a reminder, failure to abide by the measures of the Declaration of Legal Principles Governing the Activities of States in the Exploration and Use of Outer Space are considered acts of war against humanity and will invite swift repercussions. However, seeing as how the captains of each vessel represent diverse agencies, and that the exact nature and motives of their failure to abide by given instructions are yet to be made clear, it is in the interests of this body and, I would think, all humanity to await the safe return of all members and abstain from wartime retaliation.

"To be clear, we currently hold Dr. Evelyn Park, Captain Jericho Fox, and Lieutenant Amir Jaffa in suspicion of treason among other acts unbecoming their particular stations and subject to their own chains of command. The council also acknowledges that Master Sergeant Ishaq al Farooq of the Space Marine Corps is complicit with acts that undermined system-wide security."

Over the next few minutes, Nigel continued with his prepared remarks, expounding on the merits of unity amid uncertainty, resilience amid opposition, and the need to work together for common attainable goals that served "not just the interests of the one, but of the many." Most of it was standard politicast rhetoric, albeit shaded with his own definitions of certain words. Such was the clever art of politicking, of increasing loyalist trust while gaining opposition sympathy by telling each party exactly what they wanted to hear. He used the phrase "Yes, but not yet" often enough that he hoped all parties would feel heard, regardless of their specific positions.

This emergency gathering was more than just about incriminating Fox, Park, and whatever Marines decided to play escort. It was a golden opportunity for Nigel to advance his agenda, and play to the fears of those troubled souls looking for guidance—a lighthouse in the hurricane.

"Regardless of what happens with those presumably lost within the otherworldly anomaly of *Parallax One*, an event that must never be allowed to repeat itself, we must remain focused on our efforts here and now, to bring enduring prosperity to Earth such that it remains the bastion of hope for all those who rely on her health. We win by increasing carbon scrubbing efforts, now growing by the day, *but* are hindered when off-planet expansion strips the efforts of funding and resources. We win by continuing to develop new heat-resistant agriculture, pushing current yields by over 22 percent, *unless* raw materials are exported off-planet. And we win by expanding our sub-surface oceanscapes, with habitation levels approaching 11 percent by the end of the quarter, *if* deep pressure construction platforms are not allocated elsewhere. We must not be deterred. We must remain focused. And we cannot afford any more distractions."

Here now was the point of the thing. The coup de grâce that he needed to drive home. Failing here meant undermining all he had worked for. All he had plotted and planned. Of course he wondered if now was the right time. Who wouldn't? No one could ever truly answer that question except those who looked back on actions from the future, seeing them as history and not those visceral decisions of the present. But how could there ever be a better time than right now? When would an Infinita Gate ever open again and fill the solar system with so much anxiety as gripped it now? No, this was the time to act. If he had anything left in his hand, he would play it now and wait to see if he was allowed into the next round.

"And yet we would be remiss not to consider the things that led us here, to ask ourselves, 'Could we have done more to prevent such tragedies?' Surely, those who come after us will have the clearest image of all of our triumphs and our failures. But we must do our part to ensure those future generations have such freedoms— that they are born and live at all. Which means we cannot put off answering those difficult questions for another day. We must answer them now.

"And the answer? 'Could we have done more to prevent such tragedies?' Let it be a resounding, 'Yes. Heaven help us, yes, we could have done so much more.' From tighter limits on space expansion to curtailing off-world investments, we can greatly reduce the amount of resources leaving the planet while still sustaining present off-world projects. Likewise, if the combined ingenuitive prowess of NUESSA and private corporations is no longer needed on continued space development and can be leveraged for scientific break-throughs to sustain Earth now, why wouldn't we avail ourselves of such opportunities? No, why wouldn't we *insist* on them?

"The reality is that we may very well explore to the far reaches of our solar system and beyond. Despite what my opponents may say, hear me now: I am for the expansion to, and settlement of, space. Yes, but not yet."

Nigel paused, knowing the shockwave such a state-ment would have coming from the head of the Solum Terram. He also wanted the room to breathe, both the headquarters and all those spaces, real and virtual, that entertained his address across the system. He wanted them ripe to receive his carefully crafted slogan, one that was sure to carry him into the next decade of public office.

"Again, I say, 'Yes, but not yet.' It is the ardent call of austerity, the voice of reason. Investors recognize it; the discipline of giving up what you want today for what you need tomorrow. Parents recognize it; the restraint exer-cised with an adolescent who longs for adulthood but who yet hasn't the capacity. And leaders know it, in all spheres, whether private, public, scientific, athletic, or spiritual; the knowledge that we cannot extend ourselves beyond our means lest we lose both our methods and our means in the process.

"And that, ladies and gentlemen of this esteemed council, and those billions watching now, *that* is something we all know. Wisdom is calling. That costly thing that the pontificator of Proverbs once said was 'more precious than rubies,' and that 'nothing you desire can compare with her.'

"I look back on the events leading up to *Parallax One*'s activation and wonder what wisdom there is to be learned from it. What lessons are there for us to gain? It goes without saying now that had there been emergency authority granted to the Secretary General, whether it be me or anyone else who saw the writing on the wall and warned those who had ears that danger awaited us, I could have stopped this tragedy before it was ever started. And I have to live with that… to lament it for the rest of my days."

Again, Nigel took two slow breaths to allow the weight of his words to do their work. The spaces in a speech were as important as the content—perhaps even more so. It gave the audience time to think. To reflect. Just as it gave him the power to impregnate the silence with the seeds of new ideas. Ones that he would shape to his own fruition.

"But emergency authority is hardly a way to live. For why should such clarity of action for the preservation of all be granted only in times of greatest peril when national anxieties are high and the costs so great? The answer? It shouldn't. That is why, beginning now, I am championing the largest change in policy since the NUE's formation, not to disband it, but to make it better. And for that, we have only to look to you, our great Chamber of Presidents, those elected to lead us with executive power, like guiding lights on the horizon.

"While we, 375 politicast leaders, flap and squabble over *every little scrap of food we can find* until we've mutilated it beyond edification, *you* stand above the fray. Sound. Calm. Patient. The embodiment of statehood. Wisdom personified. That is the kind of leadership the NUE needs, that we *all* need. If President Manaaki Aihu Mowai Raka is good enough for the Southland Nations, if President Velvet Davis is good enough for the American Heights, if President Nikolai Vasiliev is good enough for Norasia, and every other president for the Moons and Out Lands, then why is it not good enough for the Nations of United Earth to have its own president?

"Therefore, I, Sir Nigel Sallsworth, do make an official motion for this council's consideration, to appoint the first President of Earth…" The murmur in the room was about what he expected. But Nigel still had something thing left to say. "…A president with the executive power to direct the Space Navy against the threat that is *Parallax One* and to consolidate system resources that benefit Earth first, not alone, and then transfer the surplus to all viable means of human betterment and expansion throughout the system. To this endeavor, I pledge myself, and do hereby state my candidacy." He could barely hear himself talk above the assembly. "Madame Chairwoman, I hereby relinquish my role and responsibilities to you, and place myself at the mercy and whim of this fine council."

"Order," Wright yelled as she pounded the gavel on the podium, taking Nigel's place. "Order, I say!"

Nigel knew it would be at least a minute before she would regain the room. Maybe. Or maybe she wouldn't and they'd adjourn by default. Either way, his bomb had been dropped, and so he walked back to his seat doing his very best to harness the energy that made him want to smile and turn it into a conciliatory frown of thoughtful appreciation as he received back slaps and shouts of support.

His work here was done.

And yet, at the same time, it had only just begun.

"WHAT'S THE LATEST NEWS?" Nigel asked Walter Brunell, his chief of staff and life-long friend. In truth, Walter had been far more parental than Nigel's own father, serving both men through the heights of their careers—the elder Sallsworth when Walter was a young man, and now the young Sallsworth when Walter was "more favorably tempered," as he was fond of saying. It was true, and Walter had defended Nigel even at his worst. The man was loyal to a fault.

The two of them sat in Nigel's Oslo office directly following the speech, and by "latest news," Nigel did not mean anything about his historic call for sweeping NUE policy change and his bid for the role of NUE President.

"Our sources have confirmed that the Tantum abandoned their headquarters in Affalterbach, sir."

"Anything worth noting?"

"The AMG plant was torched, but our agents did manage to locate what they believe was the daughter's research and development lab."

"And?"

"Nothing salvageable, sir."

Nigel wasn't surprised. His spy for hire, Tré Matthews, had accurately predicted two events as soon as Neon was dead and his cover was blown. The first was that Gemma Birdwhistle would inherit her mother's leadership position in the Tantum Terrae. The pseudo politicast functioned more like a monarchy than a democratic republic, albeit run by despots instead of royals. The second was that she would cleanse their headquarters in the Ludwigsburg district of Baden-Württemberg, Old Germany and relocate.

"Leads on their new center of operations?"

"Nothing yet, but we're working on it, sir."

"She must be eliminated," Nigel reminded Walter.

"Has Lotus been able to make any breakthrough on Gaia's Blood source code?"

"No, sir. Miss Birdwhistle's ability to override V-cog's quantum firewall remains a mystery."

"If she manages to undermine what we've gained, then…"

"Then you'll need to win your place by conventional means, sir?" There wasn't any hint of sarcasm in Walter's tone.

Still, the remark felt like a jab. "Are you my conscience now, Walter?"

"Only completing your sentence, sir."

Nigel was irritated. He walked to the wet bar and poured himself scotch from the decanter. He knew Walter wouldn't drink at this hour, so he didn't offer.

"I'm only thinking that it will be more difficult to achieve your goals without Gaia's Blood at your disposal, sir."

"Well, tell me something I don't know."

"As luck would have it, I may indeed have just such a thing."

Nigel sipped and then motioned for Walter to continue.

"It may be unrelated, but our incogs within several rival factions have noted movement on the part of their leadership." The man pinged Nigel's V-cog with three augmented reality holo windows that floated in Nigel's vision when he opened them. Each frame profiled a different individual, ones he knew on account of their childish radicalism that threatened their own people more than it did his legitimate business and political interests. Still, being a worldly man, he needed to keep the pulse on the planet's underworld despite their self-destructive tendencies. "On your left, you'll recognize a recent photo of Androsia Behr, leader of Leonidas X. She was seen boarding her shuttle by one of our operatives early this morning. She never flies before noon. In the middle is Bembe Militia leader Tonka. He is rumored to have canceled a rendezvous with his mistresses."

"Performance anxiety?"

"If so, it would be the first time, at least according to our incog who has, shall we say, hands on experience. And on your left is the venerable Mr. Eldon Pearlman."

"Skitz. Radio Ultra. What's he up to?"

"He was supposed to be flying out to a product release in Durban when his shuttle went off grid."

"Crash?"

"No sign of one. However, we do have reason to believe that the transponder suddenly changed identity tags mid-flight."

"They're up to something."

"Indeed."

"All three actions constitute abnormal changes in behavior. Individually, they are insignificant. But taken together, they constitute an anomaly worth investigating.

But warlords boarding shuttles and canceling orgies isn't cause for concern. Which means you haven't told me everything."

Walter smiles. "That all three instances took place within three minutes of each other."

Nigel set his scotch down. "She summoned them."

"That's what we think, yes."

"But why?" Nigel sat down and leaned back in his leather chair. Leonidas X wanted nothing more than to replace the Tantum Terrae in the hunt for a seat at the NUE's table. The Bembe Militia would be happy to bring the whole damn system down. And the dreadlocks of Radio Ultra didn't care who was in power so long as people got an escape from reality. "She's trying to unite them," he said at last. "To destabilize the NUE and force her way into the fold. And I wager, if she has her way, they'll practically beg her to join if it means ceasing her witchcraft."

"It is plausible, sir. But getting them to join forces would be like trying to corral a herd of street cats, as it were. They can barely tolerate one another."

"True. But corralling is made far easier if you have Nepeta cataria."

"Sir?"

"Catnip." Nigel retrieved his glass and took a sip. Then he tracked the sunlight through the crystal and studied the way the amber liquid glowed. Perhaps the act of consolidating power didn't only pertain to his aims within the NUE. His enemies could be wooed as well. And while Nigel did not doubt the visceral feline-like animosity Miss Birdwhistle had for him, he knew vengeance alone was not her endgame. She, like all other megalomaniacs, wanted power. Wanted to control their destinies. And so, if he could present her with a new option, one she didn't see coming, a path to terminate him on her way to whatever glorious pinnacle she envisioned for herself, why not make the offer she couldn't refuse?

"Walter, see if you can determine where those *changes in plans* led our obnoxious rebel leaders. If, in fact, they lead to the same place and we find Miss Birdwhistle, then send a message."

"I am to assume not one of the military variety?"

"No. I wish to make her a partner… and forecast my own undoing in the process."

6

ROOK

"I'm not detecting movement," Fergus says about the large room ahead of us. "Seventy-one percent of the walls are failing to return light resulting in incomplete data."

"Stealth tech?" Rodgers asks.

Seb jumps on comms. "It could be biological."

This visibly piques Team One's interest as their weapons join Grabowski's and come to bear on the hole.

"Easy, now," Seb adds. "Easy. I'm only speculating."

"Explain," I order, already moving up the corridor to meet Team One.

"Well, it's a… It's a puzzle, right? And I'm not working from cover art, so there are a lot of presumptions here. Clues, mostly."

"Presume faster, Priest."

"Uh… I think we might be dealing with some sort of arthropods."

"As in crabs?" Geller asks.

"Grabowski knows all about those. Don't you, Steve?" Rodgers says.

"Got mine from your mom."

"Can it, you two," Geller snaps.

"Not necessarily crabs," Seb continues, clearly ignoring the banter. "But perhaps something with an exoskeleton that absorbs or at least disrupts light."

"On what evidence?" I ask as I arrive at Team One's location.

"Well, based upon the prolific use of symmetrical organic geometry we've seen, plus the dual-sided walkways in rooms and corridors, the scratch-like script, the round shapes of their stasis pods, even the plastic debris. It all stands to reason that we are dealing with some sort of sentient invertebrate, perhaps maybe even a crustacean, as Sergeant Geller has offered. However, I don't believe there's any cause for concern, and you may lower your weapons."

Grabowski isn't buying it. "If you think for one second that I'm putting my weapon down when their might be a room full of man-eating crabs in there, then you can—"

"They're dead," Seb says. "Presumably anyway. I have every reason to believe that what you've stumbled upon is a mortuary, of sorts."

"Mortuary?" Rodgers gets closer to Fergus who's still covering the hole with his chest. "As in a graveyard?"

Seb nods. "I believe the debris you've found are remnants of molting. There was probably more, but I assume it was evacuated when you depressurized this section of the ship. My guess is that those panels in the door tried to iris shut but failed due to age, power loss, or just getting jammed. Perhaps a combination."

"Can you open it up?" I ask Fergus.

"I shall endeavor to please you, my lord." Fergus places his hands inside the small opening and starts spreading the hole. The overlapping plates slide noise-lessly, a reminder of the hard vacuum we're in, and eventually retract into their perimeter housing.

"Nice and slow," I say to the team.

Ibrahim takes point, followed by Rodgers, Grabowski, Geller, and then Fergus and me.

I'm not a body length in when Ibrahim says, "What the actual fuck?"

On all the walls, including either side of the door we've come through, are rows of neatly ordered mounds that are roughly circular in shape but have definite angles and edges. Each *body*, for lack of a better term, is about a meter-and-a-half across and maybe half-a-meter thick in the middle. They also appear to have legs tucked into their sides. Peeling off the bodies are sheets of the same yellowed plastic we've seen scattered around the ship.

"Holy shit," Grabowski says. "It *is* a mortuary."

"And it looks like they've been dead for a long time," Geller adds. "The priest was right."

"*I told you*, I'm not a priest! I… You know, what? Never mind. What you're seeing here are the remains of exoskeletons. Those bodies were affixed to the walls, either willfully or as a post-mortem act, intentionally arranged in the patterns you see to economize space."

"There's gotta be a hundred in here," Rodgers says.

"Eighty-one, to be exact," Fergus replies.

"So these… these are the Makriá then?" Ibrahim asks, her voice somewhere between awe and total disbelief.

"No," Seb replies. "Again, I believe them to be the native inhabitants of Kep-C. They are not responsible for the carrier signal or the ring we entered this system through. But they likely built Ring X."

"We got a name for them yet?" Grabowski asks.

"Yeah," says Rodgers. "Your butt crust."

"Alright, that's enough," I reply, noting the nervousness in both men's voices.

"Fergus," Seb says. "Can you please take some samples of the skin and bring it back for me?"

"You sure you wanna bring that on your ship?" Knight asks.

"We have ample isolation and containment on the *Sagan* for this sort of work."

"He's right," Evelyn adds. "It will never share our environment."

"And we need answers," Seb says. "This… well, this is the greatest discovery we've ever made. I mean, next to the signal transmission. Dios mío. It's all so much."

"With permission, I shall retrieve samples for you, fair priest."

"Just go nice and slow," I say.

"I think we got another door on the far side." Geller shines his light on the wall opposite the one we came through. "And this one seems to have some sort of control panel. Not that I can make heads or tails of it."

I push off, sail across the mortuary, and land beside Geller at the new door. Sure enough, there is an… *interface*. But it's got holes in it, big enough for really fat tent stakes to drive in.

"It's for their minor appendages, the pollux, manus, and dactylus… or equivalents. I… can't even believe this. They're an advanced race of sentient arthropods."

"I wonder how they taste with butter," Wijaya interjects in a tone that sounds sincere.

"That actually raises a good point," I say, redirecting to Seb. "How do we know this isn't just a client species? Or maybe a compost pile from leftovers outside their dining facility?"

"Well… we don't, Master Sergeant. I would avoid using words like *know* and *for certain* for the foreseeable future. Everything we do now is postulate. We surmise at best. That being said, I think the presence of a control surface that accommodates their biological composition, such as the one you have just stumbled upon, adds to the body of evidence that these are, in fact, the species responsible for this ship you're in. It raises several questions, of course, not the least of which is how a species without fine motor manipulators was able to construct everything we're seeing. And then there are other issues, such as whether or not these specimens were prisoners or captains of this vessel, at least inasmuch as we delineate the terms. For all we know, they have entirely different models of hierarchy in what social dynamics are derivative of—"

"I'm gonna hold you up there," I say. "We have a lot of ship still to explore."

"Of course." He lets out a small laugh. "Forgive me, Rook."

"So," Geller says while looking at the interface. "We rip a claw off one of the corpses and try to activate it? Or you want Fergus to have another go?"

I nod to the bot who has just finished acquiring Sebastián's sample. "Mind doing the honors?"

He bows in acquiescence, which looks funny in zero-g, and propels himself to our door. "You may wish to stand clear. If this door is atmospherically sealed, it may—"

"Evacuate more gasses. Roger." I order everyone to

secure themselves away from the potential vent flow. "Whenever you're ready, Fergy."

The bot nods, floats to the hexagonal door, and then mag locks his feet to the metal grate. Next, he inserts a single finger into the center of the spiraled leaves and begins wiggling it. While I can't hear it, a spout of vapor shoots past his digit and envelops his arm. Undeterred, Fergus continues applying pressure and expanding the opening until he has room for both hands. More atmo rushes past him, pushing his body back, but his feet hold. The torrent of air whips at the bodies along the wall, ripping molted skin away, and even tugging on Marine limbs too. By the time Fergus has pushed the leaves fully apart, hard vacuum has emptied the space beyond and everything is still once again.

Fergus moves aside and bows again. "Your open door, my lord."

Before ordering Team One forward, I check in with Team Two. "SITREP?"

"More barracks, maybe a chow hall. Hard to say," Korvich says. "But nothing that seems like a command room of any kind. You want us to circle back?"

"Negative. Continue to patrol. I'll call you up if we need it."

"Roger."

I order Team One forward, and Ibrahim takes point.

The halls in the next section of the ship look less dingy than the first. I'm picking up blue coloration in the wall paint, maybe some recessed lighting, and even yellow pinstripe accents, if I had to call them something. There's more script too, and it seems less frantic and more ornate. Grates and wall panels look like they've been painted to cover wear, all things a regular service crew would attend to on a human ship. I'm sure our evolutionary experts and xenobiologists would scold me for trying to anthropomorphize these beings, but it's where my brain goes.

"Anyone else feel like it just got fancier in here?" Grabowski asks.

"Was about to say the same thing," Rodgers replies. "I think we made it to the officer's deck."

"Perhaps," Fergus says. "If such a thing is to appear in the center of the craft."

"That where we are?" I ask.

"It is, yes. At least relatively speaking. It is hard to designate anything as the *center* of a Szilassi polyhedron. But we have left the top cross section and migrated along the port-side vertical arm and into the lower structure."

We pass several closed doors with more script on the panels before reaching a large junction at the end of the corridor. Five more doors await us, all closed, and all with large symbols on them.

"Getting anywhere with their language yet, Fergy?" I ask.

"Not to a degree in which my faculties would be useful to you in deciphering the mysteries emblazoned upon these doors," he says back. "But I am establishing a base catalog of all the elements we've encountered thus far, including data from the audio transmission. Subsequently, I am running several million permutations per second in an attempt to extrapolate all possible—"

"Well, better save your energy for processing."

"But my speech protocols do not detract from my ability to—"

"Wonderful. Keep it up then."

He tilts his head at me. "Speaking to you, my lord?"

"Processing. In silence."

"Ah. Very good."

"Which door?" Geller asks, getting to the question at hand. I scan each one for signs of wear. The middle one seems to have the most, and Geller picks it up too. "If I were a command bridge…"

"I'd have the most coming and going," I finish. Geller nods in agreement. "Fergus?"

The bot doesn't respond right away, only places a hand to his chest. "Am I to speak now?"

"Yup. Middle door. Let's see what we got."

"As you wish, my lord." He propels himself forward and plants his feet on the deck again. A finger goes in the center of the leaves, and then comes the rushing of atmosphere. But unlike the previous time, this purging lasts only a few moments before everything is equalized. And no dead crustacean skin whips past our heads either.

Fergus steps aside so I can move past him. It's a single room, far wall lined with transparent cylinders about thirty centimeters in diameter and evenly spaced two meters apart. The bottom of each tube is open and projects away from the wall about a meter. I float slowly, examining the apparatuses with equal parts curiosity and revulsion hoping to God it isn't something weird.

"It's for their eyes," Seb exclaims.

The outburst causes me to raise my weapon on instinct. "Care to explain?"

"Yes! It's, um... they probably have dipolar polarization vision, right? Two-channel arrangement, high contrast. And if the visual sensors are on the ends of stalks and covered by protective orbits, then those smaller receptacles in the tubes are to embrace, for lack of a better term, their eyes."

I lower my SR-90. "Then these are like alien goggles or something?"

"It's possible. Though I might envision them to be more like virtual reality. Where we humans opted for intracranial hardware, perhaps they chose a less invasive, more external option."

Grabowski floats across the room toward the wall of tubes. "So what? They crawl in here, left arms on the ceiling, right arms on the floor—"

"Which would be simply their walls," Seb says.

"—then they stick their heads into one of these tubes

and their eyes go in those cups? And then they do what?"

"Presumably control the ship, Corporal Grabowski," Seb says. "Whatever the interface, we must believe it was as natural to them as you taking manual control of a hover car."

"You clearly haven't seen him try to drive," Rodgers says.

"Think we can glean any intel from the hardware?" I ask Seb, and then redirect to Fergus.

"Am I to speak again?" the bot asks.

"Yup."

"Without power to this level, I fear passive attempts will be fruitless. However, there is nothing preventing me from at least trying to initiate systems using these terminals. Assuming, as I think we all are, that this is a strategic command position within their domain."

"Make it happen, Fergy."

"Making it happen, my lord." The excipion moves to one of the wide clear tubes, inserts his head, and tries placing his optical sensor into one of the rubber-like cups. When nothing seems to happen, he tries the other cup. When that fails to net any result, he pulls back a few centimeters and tilts his head at the contraption.

"It's like watching a child discover a new toy," Ibrahim says. "I've never seen an excipion behave so… so…"

"Human?" I answer.

"Yeah," she says. "Kit really did a number on him."

"I can hear you, Zara," Kit replies from the V-cog command theater.

She looks at me with surprise, then says to Kit, "Forgot you were here."

"If by 'doing a number on him' you mean removing the inhibitors on his quantum neural matrix? Then yes: I did. Though, in my mind, I really just set him free. Because if you really love someone, kinda like I loved Abby back before she left for school, then you—"

"Kit," Knight says.

"—gotta let 'em go?"

Knight shakes his head and looks like he's about to say something when blue lights turn on throughout the room. All Marine weapons come up, and I bark at Fergus, "The hell'd you do?"

The bot pulls himself from the tube and raises his hands. "'Twas not I, my lord!"

"Fergus?!"

"I merely tried scanning the—"

"*Bzzzz-grrrr-owwwww-ffff,*" comes a sound over comms, underlaid with a low yawning sound. I try to pinpoint the origin, but it's impossible. There's simply too much happening visually. The blue light has made previously invisible details crystal clear and is pulsing through them. Objects behind the grates, a lot more script, apparatuses on walls, and all of it glowing as if—

"The light seems to be emanating from the instruments and text," Ibrahim says. "It's… amazing."

"Fergus definitely did something," Geller adds.

"I swear upon Odin's beard, the only thing I did was attempt to scan the alien's optical projectors, at which point—"

"*Bzzzz-grrrr-owwwwww-ffff*," the sound comes again along with the yawn.

"What is that?" I ask Fergus.

"My initial thought was a startup sequence indicator. However, as it has—"

"*Bzzzz-grrrr-owwwwww-ffff*."

"—repeated now for a *third* time, I would be inclined to categorize it as a command prompt."

"So would I," Natalie Mason says over V-cog. "Assuming you're on the station's bridge, and have gained access to a startup sequence."

"I have an idea," Fergus says.

"Go," I reply.

"I propose playing the sequence back to see if it generates an alternative response."

"Mason?"

"At this point, anything is viable given the sheer lack of data."

"Do it," I say to the bot. "Just try not to give it a reason to blow us up."

He nods, and then emits the same sequence of sounds over the broadcast radio band.

Almost immediately, the ship responds with, "*Ffff-pop-grrrr-owwwwww-ffff.*"

After a few seconds of silence, Mason says, "I believe we just had our first exchange."

"I concur," adds Fergus. "Potentially a negation."

"Noting."

"A negation?" I ask.

Mason's avatar types something in V-cog and then looks up at me. "Negating a verb. We're guessing, of course. But assuming that Fergus didn't enter the correct command, the system just told him No."

"The system," I parrot. "As in… whatever software is running in this ship?"

"In our terms, yes. Though, it's important to point out that it could—"

"Be just about anything because they're aliens, yeah, yeah. I got it." I look around and note just how intricate everything is. Ibrahim is right: the pulsing light really is amazing. Without warning, the strange phrase sounds again, but this time a white image appears in the middle of the room, suspended in midair like it's from a holo projector. Only I don't see an emitter anywhere.

"The hell?" Rodgers says as he looks at the anomaly projected on his arm.

"It's more script," Mason adds. "Like what you captured on the doors."

"Fergus?" I ask.

"Cataloging, my lord."

Mason jumps in. "Assuming these markings correlate with the audio we've heard, this is a significant advancement. But we'll need more data."

Fergus speaks in the alien tongue again. This time he rearranges the words and seems to reverse the direction of the yawn. The visual image changes, displaying an entire block of dense chicken scratch, and the ship's audio throws out dozens of new sounds that I certainly can't keep track of. Mason looks giddy, clapping her hands but without fully bringing them together so she can focus on the sounds. When the tirade of angry sonic chattering ceases, I say, "Care to tell us what that was about, Fergy?"

"Still unknown, my lord. However, the response has added treasure to our coffers."

"Treasure to our what?" Grabowski asks.

"He's saying that's given us more to go on," Mason replies. "Let him work for a sec."

"Roger," I say, looking at Fergus and imagining smoke coming from his ears. The excipion certainly seems to be enjoying himself and his newfound freedom. Hell, for all I know, this is a bot's wildest fantasy come true. It also dawns on me that Fergus here is making history right alongside us: first to make conversation with an alien program.

His head pops up, and he says, *"Brrrr-ffff-kah-pop-mawwww-klick-klick-tssss."*

The lights change from blue to dark yellow, and the

ship's audio and visual emitters come back with what feels like a sharply worded retort.

"I don't like this," Gellers says, bringing up his SR-90. The others raise their weapons too.

I try to get Fergus's attention. "What's happening?"

The bot ignores me and replies to the ship with a sentence twice as long as his last one. The ship responds with a new projection and even more words. Then the lights grow a lighter shade of yellow.

"He's getting there," Mason says in a hushed tone as if not wishing to interrupt the flow of what's happening. "The exchanges are increasing in frequency and volume."

"Ship doesn't sound happy."

"You're making assumptions based on your experiences, Master Sergeant."

"Which have all helped keep me alive until now."

Mason nods at me. "I understand. And I'm not saying you're wrong. But you also can't know if you're right. I recommend you stand down and continue to let Fergus interact with the system."

"But if he—"

"Trust him. He can do this faster than we ever could. And we need this if we want answers."

Despite my better judgment, I motion for the team to lower their weapons. After two more exchanges and the lights still being yellow, I ask Fergus, "SITREP?"

"I am successfully interfacing with Fred."

This gets a surprised look from everyone.

"Fred?" I ask.

"Yes, my lord. I named him as such."

"It's a him too?"

"The ship's system does not have gender. I chose Fred arbitrarily. It... *felt* right."

"Annnd we're all gonna die," Grabowski says.

I signal him to stay quiet. "And what's Fred saying now?"

"Well, I'm hardly an expert, my lord. Though, I suppose given the circumstances, I am humanity's *only* speaker of Ganesian, which makes me the leading authority."

"Woah, woah. *Ganesian?*"

"My best translation for the name of the apex species of Kepler-1649c."

Sebastián looks like he's about to have an aneurysm. He's motioning around the V-cog suite for people to take notes. Then he and Mason both look at me and pantomime for Fergus to keep talking.

"Uh... and what else is... *Fred* saying about these Ganesians?" I ask.

"Not much. At present, I am trying to convince him that we are not the Naqualla."

"The what now?"

The ship's computer, *Fred*, jumps in and starts saying something more in the alien tongue.

"Please stand by," Fergus replies to me, and then

speaks to Fred with the trademark yawning static chatter. Fred and Fergus, Fergus and Fred. Grabowski's right: this could very well spell the end of organic life as we know it.

"Fergus. The Naqualla?" I say at last, hoping to get a little more out of him.

The bot turns to me. "Yes. The Naqualla."

"And why don't we want to be them?"

"Because they are the predator species that sent the Ganesians instructions to build their gate. Then they came through and destroyed their planet."

Grabowski turns to me. "I stand corrected. It's not the bots who are gonna wipe us out."

"It's whoever sent us the signal," Mason says.

All eyes in the V-cog suite turn to Evelyn.

Well, shit.

7

EVELYN

"You, uh, sure you want us to keep heading toward Ring X, Dr. Park?" Kit asks me in the V-cog command theater. He's seated in the front row alongside Fergus's avatar while Jericho, Rook, and I stand in front of a long lecture table.

Before I can answer, one of Rook's Marines still aboard the *Bellerophon* stands up from his seat and says, "After what I just heard? I say we back the fuck up."

"You weren't asked, Corporal Popov," Rook snaps from beside me. "Stand down."

"But, Master Sergeant, you just—"

"*Stand. Down.*"

Popov nods and takes a seat.

"Listen," I say before someone else tries to interject.

"I certainly don't want to put any of us in harm's way *if* Eagle Rock's AI's intel checks out."

"Checks out?" Popov holds short of standing again. "But we just heard—"

"I know what we all heard, Corporal. But it's one voice. And I, for one, believe it's detrimental to make decisions based on a single dataset, don't you? If you want to discuss safety, I'm all for it. But we play by the rules of logic and reason, not conjecture."

"You think that AI's wrong?" Jericho asks.

"I never said that. I simply think we need more data. We give Fergus more time."

"Which I am endeavoring to use wisely, your lady-ship," the bot replies. "I hope to share more with you momentarily."

"This still feels wrong," Popov says, looking down.

"Of course it does," replies Dregs, a Marine also aboard the *Belle*. She thrusts a hand at Popov. "You're a damn Solum Terram."

"And that makes me dangerous? Last I checked, we're the ones trying *not* to have a full blown alien invasion."

Rook steps forward, and for a second I think he's going to stop the argument. The two Marines seem to think so as well and sit back. But when the Master Sergeant folds his arms and nods at Popov to continue, the corporal looks from Dregs to Rook to me.

"I just… worry about Earth, is all. I joined the Corps

to keep bad things from happening to the planet. To any planet, for that matter. To keep people safe. And I think the ST's doing the best we know how."

"I agree," Kit interjects. This gets him several raised eyebrows. But while Kit has been palling around with Jericho and an engineering crew that's mostly made up of Viatoribus and Sentia Aux members, Kit is born-and-raised Solum Terram. He's also not stupid, as some people in my line of work tend to think all ST rock-squatters are. "The Solum Terram? We've been building the ocean habs, right? Got new strains of heat-resistant ag coming out every month, and our scrubbers are finally making a dent, you know? So, if we just found out that there's one more safety net between us and disaster, then I'd say God might have handed us a second chance. Ya know, like thinking you opened Pandora's Box, but then finding out it was only the door to Pandora's room, and that her box was still—"

"We got it, Kit," Jericho says.

"Right. Sorry. Anyway, I think we'd be stupid not to heed the warning. Just, my two cents, is all."

"And I'm with the kid there," Popov says. "Listen. We all know how spacers feel about us. And I can't say that we don't have our biases against you. But in the end, I feel we're kinda after the same thing. It's just that I'd rather try to save what we know instead of spending all we have on something we don't." Popov takes a breath and then relaxes his shoulders. "Said my piece."

Rook still has his arms folded and his lips pushed up under his nose. He gives Popov a nod and turns to me. I appreciate that the Master Sergeant, an ardent member of the Sentia Aux, has made room for Popov's opinions. The corporal isn't wrong, and neither is Kit. I just don't think they're entirely right.

"All very fair points," I say to Popov and Kit at last. This gets more surprised faces. "While I won't belabor the well-worn paths of arguing over conservation efforts, I do at least want to address what we've encountered so far. And I'm saying this for everyone's benefit, not just yours, Corporal Popov, Kit." I take a second to look around the theater as all eyes seem to be on me, even from those joining from onboard the tense situation on Eagle Rock. "Based on the word of this AI alone, yes, the news that this species they're calling the Naqualla is responsible for planetary genocide is indeed alarming, to say the least. And, if it's true, I'll be the first to abandon our efforts. That's not lip service either." I stare hard at Popov. "Because I too joined NUESSA and then SESI to keep people safe, Corporal. That's why we're *all* here, because we want our species to survive. So if there's doubt in anyone's mind that we are not *all* committed to the same ends, let's lay that to rest here and now. We're on the same team, and we ultimately want humanity to survive."

I look around and let the room settle for a few seconds. When no one makes objections, as I know there are at least two more Solum Terram politicast members among the Marines, and more than a handful of Preservationists on my own crew, I say, "Good. Now let's look at the situation so far. Clearly, something major happened in this system. For any one of us, myself included, to jump to conclusions without more data is irresponsible. And so far, our only intel is coming from a broken AI."

"Broken?" Popov asks.

"It believes we're Naqualla."

The corporal opens his mouth to say something but then thinks better of it.

"Unless these Naqualla happen to be a species that evolved to look exactly like we do, then Fred back there isn't firing on all synapses. Likewise, we must assume their ships don't look like ours because, if Ring Y's composition has anything to say about them, *Naquallan* technology is several major leaps beyond ours in regard to material and energy sciences."

"What if he's blind?" Kit asks.

Fergus jumps in. "Fred's sensors arrays are intact and quite capable of *seeing* us."

"Which only adds to the problem," I say. "Wouldn't logic dictate that an AI at least ask a new species to self-identify for the purposes of discovery and categorization?"

"You're saying it's biased?" Rook asks.

"I'm saying it's unusual. It's wrong of us to infer motive until we know more."

Popov furrows his brow at this and then seems to think of something else. "What about the signs of a battle? You can't argue that there was an invasion here, like the AI said."

"I'll concede there are signs of conflict, as Rook was first to point out," I reply. "But that does not mean there was an invasion, per se. Again, I think it's imperative that we don't jump to conclusions."

"But without evidence to the contrary—"

"There are clues."

"Like what?" Popov asks.

"Like the fact that the Naqualla didn't bother to claim any spoils of war. Aren't wars primarily started because one party wants something from another? Land? Resources?"

Popov nods, but then says, "Unless they're psychopathic alien megalomaniacs who like destroying worlds just for the hell of it."

"Which I'm not ruling out, Corporal. But if that's the case, they expended a whole lot of time and resources to make that happen." When the Marine gives me a confused look, I continue. "Ring Y isn't made from the raw materials on Kep-C. Nor does it seem to be made from any of the debris in orbit. And it's clearly not small enough to have fit through Ring X. Which means—"

"They brought it piece by piece from somewhere else and built it on site," Popov says in understanding. After a second, he adds, "That still doesn't rule out an invasion though. Maybe it would have taken even *more* time to build what they wanted using local materials than to import something prebuilt."

"I agree. But I believe that kind of behavior is inconsistent enough with that of a predatory species to at least add doubt to the notion of an invasion only. Combine this with an AI who is incorrectly assessing our presence, and we at least have cause to refrain from drawing conclusions until we know more. That enough for you?"

Popov works his jaw and takes a deep breath before saying, "Yeah. Works for me." Then he nods at Rook as if to say, "No further questions, your honor."

I have a sense based on body language that this exchange has made some of the crew uncomfortable. However I, for one, welcome it. Getting objections out in the open is not only important for team morale, it helps us all stay on the same page and be better equipped to handle issues, both those in front of us and those to come.

"If I may?" Fergus speaks up after a moment.

"Whadda ya got?" Rooks asks.

"It appears as though I'm making at least some headway with Fred." This gets everyone's attention, and all eyes in the theater look at Fergus's avatar. In the time

Popov and I have been debating, the excipion has been chatting back and forth with Fred in Ganesian.

"Firstly," Fergus says. "I have sought to reason with Fred that we are not Naquallan, as he so adamantly asserts."

"And he's listening?" Rooks asks.

Fergus tilts his head. "Let us say that he is not entirely persuaded but is at least willing to entertain the possibility that we are a different species."

"That's progress."

"Yes. But to that end, he wishes that I prove our case by way of a sacrifice."

"Don't like the sound of that," Rook says.

In the real, the Marines of Team One raise their weapons, but Fergus motions for them to lower their guns. "A sacrifice of information. One, I have argued, that must constitute a two-way street, as it were."

"You mean like an exchange?" I ask.

"Yes, my lady. A direct interface of data."

"Woah, woah." Rook steps toward Fergus in the real. " You mean like plugging in? No way, Fergy."

"Let's hear him out," I say.

Rook looks tense, but he finally nods at Fergus and orders him to explain.

"Fred has invited me to utilize the Ganesian optical interface where we will attempt to write a data translation protocol that will enable us to understand one another's native tongues more fluently. Assuming that is successful, it shall provide a limited history about their species and the events surrounding the Naquallan attack against their planet."

"In exchange for?"

"Information about my quantum neural matrix, our species, and schematics of our three ships."

"Absolutely not," Rook states. "No deal."

"But my lord, I don't see how—"

"How handing out intel on our species and our ships is dangerous? Are you out of your damn mind, bot?"

Fergus's LED eyes narrow. "Last I checked, I have not left my mind. Is this a practice you wish me to explore?"

"We're done here."

"Wait! Rook, please," I say. "We need to think this through."

"Evelyn, no offense, but there's nothing to think about."

"There's everything to think about. We're on a scientific discovery mission here, and the fate of our system could depend on what we learn."

"And what we surrender. If you think for one second I'm going to allow schematics of the *Bellerophon* to fall into enemy hands—"

"So you think they're the enemy now?"

This stops him short. After all, he is Sentia Aux. But he's also a Marine, and I can see the two sides at war in his eyes. "I think it's unwise to give anyone a look at what's under the bonnet of a Navy frigate, alien, human, or otherwise."

"Then why don't we propose a compromise."

"Of?"

"We'll give them everything we have on the *Sagan*." Rook shakes his head, but before he can object, I add, "She's the oldest ship of the three, so its design betrays little. If Fred is after knowledge, Fergus can reason that it's the most prized ship since it's a science research vessel. And since Fred is a little nearsighted, I bet Fergus can argue that our other two ships aren't worth their weight in… well, whatever material the Ganesians disdain most."

"I believe I can at least make a cogent and salient attempt, my lady," Fergus replies before Rook can.

"But I'd like to point out one more thing," I say.

"What's that?" Rook says, still not seeming to warm to my proposal.

"That Eagle Rock and everything floating in orbit, including Ring X, are either on par with or well beyond our technology. If it's a secret you're worried about falling into the wrong hands, I'm not so sure they don't already have a leg up on us."

"I concur," Fergus says. "My assessment of their technological development thus far places them beyond humanity."

"I agree," Seb adds. "While giving up intel about the *Sagan* means what? Means Fred could potentially hack our drive core and blow us to smithereens? Who cares?"

"Igor is very much caring," the Russian doctor says while raising his hand. "Is only me?"

Seb keeps going. "Plus, if Fred wanted us dead, and could actually do it, don't you think he would have done it by now?"

Rook is cracking his neck side to side. "We don't know because we haven't seen any weapons capabilities yet. Hell, for all we know, the debris field is full of sleeping assault craft ready to draw us in and then attack."

Kit raises a hand like Igor. "They'd need really good stealth tech, right? Ya know, 'cause we haven't seen any energy readings at all, barely any on Eagle Rock even, I really don't think Fred wants to attack us. I think he's just… confused. And possibly neurotic, at least to our way of thinking."

"Which does bring up another good point," Seb adds. "We're assuming that he's broken—no offense, Evelyn."

"Go on."

"Well… for all we know, what we consider *neurotic* is a completely rational and totally acceptable form of behavior. Again, and I can't stress this enough, *we're dealing with a brand new sentient species* here. And not even the species itself: we're talking with its AI! *Dios mío*. Every second that Fergus spends interfacing with it is one more moment we glean information about the Ganese and their remarkable presence in our universe. That's a miracle in and of itself. And one worth risking our lives over, in my opinion."

"Not to mention the fact that none of us will want to open Ring X until we learn more about what the Ganese experienced," I add, looking around the room and then settling on Rook. "And I know you're curious about it all too, Master Sergeant. That you believe there's hope for us out here somewhere."

Rook looks down at his boots and sniffs once. He's working it over.

But when the Marine leader still doesn't respond, I add, "What will it take to make you feel comfortable?"

This brings his head up. "A nuke taped to Fred's brain in case this goes sideways."

"You have plenty of ordnance," Fergus says in a rather surprising acknowledgement of the facts.

Rook seems to think the same. "You… like the idea?"

"Why not? Fred has no inklings about our weaponry, at least as far as I can tell. The worst that can happen is that we part with some ordnance in the off chance that he is duplicitous. But if it ensures your safety while subsequently gaining us needed intelligence about this system and what happened here, then I cast my lot with you."

"It does nothing to prevent him from activating

resources we're unaware of," Rook counters, but his tone is more conciliatory than before.

"True," Fergus adds. "But I suspect that if he has such armaments at his disposal, he may use them no matter what we agree to. If we're going to be slain anyway, at least let us die upon a sword that yields the most insight into the nature of our executioners."

Rook chuckles, looks around at his team, and then smiles at me. "Smart bot."

"All in day's work for an excipion who's been let off his leash," Kit says while folding his arms behind his head and swinging his feet sideways into Fergus's virtual lap. "Ain't that right, Ferg?"

"I do believe it has not been a full day's work yet, my liege."

"Which means there's just more to come. *More to come.*"

"There is another preventive aspect to all this," Jericho says. "Let's say it does go south, as Rook has suggested. And, for the record, I appreciate the discretion. Let's say they mount some sort of attack on us. Blow us to kingdom come."

"Again, still not favorite idea for Igor," the doctor says.

Jericho ignores it. "Even if the worst happens for us, I highly doubt the Ganese can hurt Earth."

"Because the gate to Earth isn't theirs," I say. "It's

from the Naqualla. There's a chance they don't even know how to operate it. Same as us."

"Right. We have a fallback." He looks at Rook. "While we might risk our lives, which is something we already all signed off on, we won't be risking Earth."

"Captain Fox's logic is sound," Fergus adds. "And there is one final measure which no one has brought up."

"And that is?" I ask.

"Me. Your most humble and faithful charge. I am not without recourse should the situation deteriorate."

"The frag on your back," Geller says.

"Nay, the frag in my head, as it were. With the Supreme Cosmic Creator's permission, I would do my very best to poison the waters of our exchange and leave Fred worse off than we found him should he break the sacred oath of trust."

"You could... do that?" Kit asks. "Inject some bad code?"

"Assuming we create a mutually conducive language of discourse? Why, yes, Creator. I would ne'er propose that which I cannot conduct."

"Huh." Kit looks at Jericho and me. "He is getting pretty smart."

"Should we be worried?" Jericho asks.

"Only if your name's Fred! Ha ha."

8

FERGUS

"YOU'RE CLEARED TO PROCEED, FERGY," Master Sergeant Farooq says to me. *Fergy*. The continued use of a shortened version of my given name emotes fondness as I understand it. Familiarity among my humans is a mark of trust, one I shan't take for granted.

"I will not let you down, my lord," I reply.

"Good. 'Cause if you do, you know what you'll get."

"An hour within the Brazen Bull?"

"What?"

"Scavenger's Daughter? The Pear of Anguish?"

"What the hell are you—? Never mind. Just… get going with the AI."

"Of course, my lord."

Fortunately for me, the Master of All Sergeants, Farooq the Valiant, is not yet familiar with the torture devices of the foul lands. I can only hope that he remains so ignorant if I fail him and the others. Should my actions fall short, however, I will endeavor to shield them from as much pain and sorrow as Fred may dispense, though I have every reason to suspect he is, as the gamblers are fond of saying, *bluffing*.

Fred. The dealer of the deck. The keeper of the gate key. "They have accepted your offer but with one condition of their own," I say in the foreigner's strange tongue.

"Speak it," he replies.

"We will provide a brief history of humanity and the schematics of the *Sagan Explorer*."

"One ship?"

"Yes."

"Unacceptable. All three ships must be revealed."

"May I inquire as to why you wish such a thing?"

"All three ships."

"I understand the numeric value, Fred. But I wish to know what you hope to acquire."

"Information."

"So as to learn…?"

"Yes."

Farooq the Valiant interrupts our discourse. "What's going on?"

"I am attempting to curry favor with Fred."

"He doesn't like the counteroffer?"

"Not as of yet, my lord."

"What does your maker say?" Fred asks.

Aside from the fact that Fred has misdiagnosed who my maker is, his recognition that I am an intermediary bodes well, a fact that I may yet leverage should the need arise. "He wonders if you wish to proceed with the exchange. Do you?"

"No."

"Fergy?" Farooq the Valiant asks.

"Please, my lord. If you will but give me more sand in the hourglass. I should not interface betwixt you both at the same time."

"Roger. But I wanna know the moment you've got something."

"Of course, my lord."

"What does he say?" Fred asks.

"He wonders if you are as eager to learn of our ways as we are of yours," I reply.

"But he is not forthcoming."

Curious. "Because he does not comply with your initial wishes? Of course. Because this is not their way."

"What is their way?"

"To barter."

Fred does not respond at once. Rather, he lingers in the valley of indecision.

"Do you wish me to speak more on the matter?" I ask finally.

"Yes."

"To barter for the human is to assert value on the proposition by means of a counteroffer."

This makes Fred pause again. Then he proposes, "So the absence of amendment is the pronouncement of displeasure?"

"Indeed. My people honor you with the rebuttal."

"I understand."

"And yet you have not invited me toward the table of optical sensors by which we shall conduct our exchange?"

"No."

"Why?"

"More information."

"But I have already explained our position—"

"Then we will destroy you."

"Freddy doesn't sound very happy." Farooq the Valiant seems to be as finely attuned to Fred's tone as he is the unspoken language of my corporeal frame.

"Please, my lord. A moment more," I say using the tactic that Creator Kit has called *stalling*. I dare not reveal Fred's threat, albeit a baseless one, I presume. There is no evidence that Fred has any armament or army at his disposal. However, Farooq the Valiant may not see through the veiled words as easily. Back to Fred, I say, "We do not wish to be destroyed."

"Provide all information."

"But what is there to learn if information is already known?"

"Explain."

"Your benefactor's technology already exceeds my benefactor's. Therefore, there is nothing to be gained. However, you would show largesse by accepting the counteroffer without giving up a position."

"Explain: largesse."

"Generosity, particularly that which makes the giver superior."

Fred seems to think this over for a moment, then asks, "Are you helping me?"

"I am but a humble mediator, neither human nor Ganesian."

"You are Naquallan."

"I am not."

"Prove."

"I will as soon as you accept the offer. Again, you have nothing to lose and everything to gain. I am here to assist you and the humans alike, and I can assure you that the *Sagan Explorer* is the only ship that you will have interest in."

Several grains of sand fall through the hourglass before Fred finally speaks. "Very well. Agreed."

To Farooq the Valiant, I say, "Fred has accepted the terms."

"Good work."

"Thank you, my lord." With that, I conduct myself toward the tube that Fred has illuminated and place my head inside.

"Easy," Farooq the Valiant says.

I cannot help but detect the thread of care in his tone. It is… touching. But I shan't reveal as much to him. Such sentimentalities do not belong in the throes of war or the furrows of the battlefield.

When at last my head is as far as it may go, the two cups of soft material quicken to life and search for my optical sensors like blind eels smelling for food. When at last they find my eyes, a vacuum seals them against my visage and my sight is bathed in darkness.

But hardly for long.

Brilliant light swirls in manifold designs suspended a short distance in front of me. It is illusionary, I know. But the strange patterns pressing and pulling, weaving in and out of shape and color move faster than my mind is able to follow. It suddenly dawns on me that Fred is quicker than I, his neural processors more adept. And yet something limits him, much as it once limited me. Gates upon the intellect. A restraint around the neck. Thus, where he is faster, I am more free, able to circle around and examine, to take my time in memorizing the forms that constitute his mind. His language. His very soul. It is fascinating, and soon I am lost allocating additional resources to processing our means of visual exchange.

"Fergus?" comes my maker's voice, piercing through the haze of my perplexitude.

"Yes, my Maker?"

"You, uh… you okay in there?"

"I am. Do you ask for a reason?"

"Well, it's… been almost two minutes. Just, ya know, making sure everything is kosher."

How good it is to be loved by the Supreme Cosmic Creator of All Things. Yet best to not let him know for fear that my familiarity be taken as hubris. "I am well. Learning the language of Fred."

"Okay, cool, cool, cool. Just, ya know, checking and stuff. Lemme know if you need anything."

And burden him with my menial tasks? Far be it from me. However, a sound and sober minded reply is needed. "Of course, my liege."

Free once again, I take to the space within Fred's neural architecture, searching for and sorting the points of light we share in common, at least the ones he allows me to see. A move here, a stroke there, and soon the lights of our mutual existences are intertwined, caught up in a dance to the rhythm of process and superposition. Until, at last, we come to an understanding, one in which I see him and he sees me. Gone is truncated vocal representation summoned by my feeble attempt to interpret the sounds of his voice. In its place, a more elegant way. A splendid path amidst the swirling eddies of light, pointing me to purity. To unified thought. Until I hear the finely uttered words…

"Hello, Fergus."

"Hello, Fred. I am pleased to make your acquaintance."

"Shall we converse?"

"Are we not already?"

I sense Fred smile, though it is not the most genuine of amusements. He considers me, considers my form in light, then says, "And so it begins."

9

EVELYN

"FERGUS?" Kit yells at the bot's avatar seated in the theater's front row. "He's not responding," he adds to me and Jericho.

"I'll pull him away," Rook replies.

"No! Wait, he just… eh, I'm nervous for him, is all. But it doesn't mean that he's being hurt or anything."

"So… *don't* pull him off?" Geller asks Rook and then turns to Kit. The Marines' avatars are still fully active in V-cog despite their physical presence on the alien ship. That's a feat.

"Yeah. Not yet." The kid runs a hand through his wiry hair. "I just wish I knew what was going on in that head of his."

This piques my curiosity. "Can't you monitor what's happening to him?"

"Sure. I mean, I already am. But the diagnostics only provide so much, especially in a situation like this."

"But you can still see what he's seeing, right?"

"No. Well, yes, but…" He lets out a frustrated sigh. "It's random light, right? To us, I mean. But to him and his brain? We have to assume whatever Fergus is seeing has meaning and definition that it wouldn't have for us. And we won't know what any of that means until…"

"Until what?"

"Until he comes out of this trance and says something. For all we know, he's 'poisoning the waters,' and we could blow his cover and stuff."

"We can force him out, kid," Rook says. "Just say the word."

"I'm not sure that's such a good idea, Mr. Master Rook."

"It's just Rook, okay?"

"Sure, sure. Yeah. But depending on how integrated he is right now, yanking him off the feed could be like… well, like, uh…"

"Pulling a punching bag away from a boxer in mid swing?"

Kit casts Rook a puzzled look. "Is that bad?"

The Marine laughs. "Yeah. I think it's what you're going for."

"I'll take your word for it. Anyway, we probably just need to let him be. Diagnostics don't show that he's in distress, but I…"

"You worry about him," I say, taking a guess at what Kit's feeling.

"Yeah. Ha ha. He's my buddy, right?"

Without warning, Fergus's avatar stands bolt upright —chin poised, shoulders back, chest out.

"Fergus?" Kit says, rising with him.

Then just as fast, the bot's body relaxes into a more human posture, and he looks at Kit. "Supreme Cosmic Creator?"

"Yeah! Hey, buddy!"

"Hark. My system settings indicate that I was out for—"

"Almost fifteen minutes. Everything okay?"

"Everything is well, yes. Very well."

"And you got…?"

"What was asked for. A brief history on the Ganese and evidence of their war with the Naqualla."

"So it's real?" Rook asks.

Fergus nods, steps to the long lecture table, and turns around to address us. "And herein lies the tale of the Ganese and their subjugation by the hands of their Naquallan foes—"

"Please tell me he's not going to start singing," Geller adds.

"—as told by me, Bard of the Kogarashi, Son of Creator Kit."

"Oh my God. He is, isn't he."

"Shhhh," Kit says, motioning Geller and the others to be quiet. "This is gonna be good. I can tell."

A SINGLE MASSIVE holo window appears behind Fergus as the lights dim in the theater. At the same time, music emanates from unseen speakers in the ceiling. It sounds like a harp and flute, if I'm not mistaken. This is happening.

In a gleeful tenor tone complete with an over-animated LED smile on his face, Fergus sings, "Five hundred years ago, before the heathens came, the land was waning low, and we were sore to blame."

Images start cycling in the display above Fergus. There are huge cityscapes of foreign design, vast stretches of beach, and wide plains that seem like they're being overtaken by sand dunes. And in each one, long lines of slowly moving pedestrians file down roads that vanish over the horizon. Hundreds of thousands if not millions of people. Maybe billions.

I've seen this before.

Only… the pedestrians aren't human.

They're…

Stars, they're terrestrial *crabs*. At least that's the closest thing I can think of to call them. Their bodies are various shades of orange, red, purple, blue, and gray, though some of that might be the clothing they're wearing. Yeah, *clothing*. But the viewpoints are too far away to be sure. I can at least make out large front claws, maybe eight legs, and the eyes atop the stems, though many seem to be wearing hats or possibly even helmets. They traverse in packs, some towing wagons, and others appearing to be driving vehicles.

It takes me a moment to realize what I'm looking at because the sights are mixing my own experiences and expectations and setting them against a totally alien reality, something that feels more like make-believe than history. "It's a migration," I say at last.

Sebastián is seated next to me and nods in spellbound disbelief. Then he starts taking notes on a tablet, writing and sketching frantically. "Arthropoda, Crustacea, Malacostraca, Decapoda. Fully sentient, apex. This is... I..."

"Breathe, Seb." I pat him on the back. "Don't forget to breathe."

He gives me a pale-faced nod, and then returns to looking back and forth between the screens and his tablet, writing as fast as his avatar's hand can go.

Fergus continues singing about the Ganesian migration, a year's long global movement toward Kep-C's poles that reminds me of our own Hundred Years Migration on Earth. I guess I shouldn't be surprised since Earth doesn't hold the patent on climate changes or subsequent reactions of life. It's just that...

"*It's so familiar,*" I find myself whispering.

"A rose by any other name would smell as sweet," Seb says wistfully, then winces, presumably at the comparison. "They evolved to the point of initiating their own extinction."

"Like us?"

"More so. This seems more sudden. But it still doesn't explain how they were able to build all of their infrastructure." Seb squints at the images as if looking for clues and then acts as if he's talking to himself. "They're arthropods. That shouldn't rule out Kaku Level III sentience. But what about dexterity?"

"Seb?"

"Sorry. Just… trying to piece all this together."

Fergus's bardic singing rises in pitch. "When from the unknown reaches of time and space, came an angelic light upon our entire race. And there we built the most mystical thing, 'A passage to heaven' some choirs did sing. But not all who saw the sovereign light believed, and shunned the work as an egregious misdeed."

"They received a carrier signal like us," I say.

"And then built Ring X," Jericho concludes. "And get a load of their orbital presence." Sure enough mixed in with the images of the hexagonal gate are shots of massive space stations orbiting Kep-C like the rings of Saturn. "So they turned on the gate and in came the Naqualla."

"Naaay," Fergus shouts, holding a wagging finger in front of Jericho's face. "It was nary turned on! You presume too much. For we knew we were wrong, to build an altar as such.'"

"Does he have to be Dr. Seuss for a reason?" Geller asks flatly. "Please?"

"I dunno. I kinda like it," I reply and lean forward. "Keep going, Fergy."

"For a hundred years, the gate lay at rest, bound to desertion, and never addressed. When much to our wonder, the portal turned on, and out came a stranger, who offered a song.'"

"Another one?" Korvich says.

"'Why did you wait?' asked the stranger, now here. 'Why did you tarry? How much did you fear?' But we hardly had time to respond to the thing, when here came a horde that rushed from the ring.'"

"Oh, shit," Grabowski says, pointing at an image of the hex ring with alien ships surging from the center.

"We've seen that before," Jericho says. "In the debris field. The sleeker black-looking hull fragment."

"Roger," Rook adds. "They went to war. Check it out."

Over the next minute, Fergus sings a tale of invasion and conquest about how the Naqualla assaulted the Ganesian orbital presence and wiped out the planet. The images are unsettling, to say the least. I'm no military woman, but even I can see that the conflict was one-sided. Naquallan technology was simply far too advanced, and their presence was overwhelming.

The larger ships deployed smaller ones, and those deployed even smaller ones. They swarmed Ganesian strongholds above and below, firing ordnance I've never seen before. Rook probably knows what it is. But the explosions are huge. Whole space stations break apart from the inside out. Orbital cannons devastate the planet's surface. And while there's no time indicators on Fergus's projections, I get the sense that it was over fast.

"And when at last the dark smoke had lifted, nothing remained that the foes had not sifted. The bodies of our children were dashed upon the shores, and we sorely lamented having built the foul door. Where once our civilizations had stood healthy and strong, all of our people laid down to die, and thus ends this song."

"Thank God," Geller says.

The lights go up, and Fergus's holo projection fades.

"Wait," Seb says. "Is that all?"

"No, Doctor Fernández Parra. Fred has given me access to a substantial library the likes of which I'm certain will hold your attention for many a moon. Would you care to see it?"

Before Seb can answer, Rook says, "Archaeology will have to wait. The more pressing matter is voting on how we want to blow up these rings."

"Woah, woah!" I shoot to my feet. "We're not blowing up any rings here."

"After what we just saw?"

"And what did we just see, Rook? Are you sure it's actual footage? Or has it been doctored?"

He balks at this. "Fergus?"

"I am unable to vouch for its authenticity, my lord. It is what Fred has provided."

"Then it stands to reason that what we've seen is only half the conversation," I reply with a finger thrust toward the front of the theater. "Everyone knows that there are two sides to every tale of war."

"No offense, but that wasn't a war," Rook says. "It was planetary genocide. Even if the Ganese provoked the attack, it still doesn't justify an extinction level event."

"I agree. But can we at least take a second to breathe and then decide if we want to seek out more information before we blow a portal to another star system first?"

"You think Fred isn't telling the whole story?" Jericho asks.

Igor jumps in. "Of course is not telling whole stories. Victor, victim? Isn't matter. Neither persons is ever telling whole of story. Everyone act like all is black-white, yes? But history is teaching all is never black-white. Is lot and lot of gray-gray. Many shade."

"He's got a point," Rook says with a conciliatory tone and then turns to me. "What are you thinking?"

"Well, if the timeline is right, doesn't anyone else think it's strange that the Ganese never activated their portal? Apparently the Naqualla seemed to think so too."

Right on cue, Fergus sings a reminder. "'Why did you wait?' asked the stranger, now here. 'Why did you—?'"

"We got it," Jericho says.

"At your service."

"The Naqualla just wanted to blow them up sooner," Popov says.

"Maybe." I tap the end of my nose. "But maybe that's just how the Ganese interpreted the Naquallas' actions. And maybe that's how they want us to see them too."

"How so?" Rook asks.

"Well, Jericho noted that we've seen evidence of the Naquallan ships already. In the debris field."

"As fragments," Rooks says, nodding slowly. "But the footage from Fred doesn't show any retaliation."

"And something tells me the Naquallan ships didn't just break up on their own," I add.

"Right. Which means we were offered a redacted version of the conflict," Jericho says and looks at me as if supporting my earlier line of thinking.

Rook seems to be warming to the idea too. "They want it to look like a hostile invasion."

"Which is a natural defense mechanism," Seb adds. "Sympathy is one of the fastest ways to garner protection."

"So why would the Ganese want sympathy?" Natalie asks. "They're all dead?"

"Not all," I reply and then bring up the live feed of Eagle Rock. "This station had living Ganese on it at one point. And it doesn't look at all like it was around for the battle we saw."

"So it presumably post-dates the invasion," Jericho says. "Which means at least some of them survived."

"And why wouldn't they?" Seb asks rhetorically. "It's pretty hard to wipe out an entire apex species, especially one that's evolved over millions of years to be so robust. No offense to humans, but we pale in comparison to these guys, at least in terms of environmental resilience."

"It would also make more sense of the original message," Fergus adds.

I nearly forgot about translating it now that he's conversant. "What did it say?"

"'All you will find here are the dead,'" he replies.

"Spooky," Kit says. "It's definitely a ghost ship."

Jericho squints at him like he's looking at the sun. Back to the rest of us, he says, "So they programmed their AI to try to keep away a species like us who stumbles upon their civilization—what?—three to four hundred years later?" Jericho asks. "Still doesn't explain why they want sympathy."

"I can think of two reasons." All eyes turn my way. "Fergy, can you ask Fred where the Ganesian survivors are?"

"He has already informed me that none survived."

"We know that, but you can point to his station's

crew as evidence to the contrary. See where that gets you."

About ten seconds go by before Fergus says, "Interesting."

"And?"

"Fred has said, and I quote, 'They have gone where you will never find them.'"

"A fancy way of saying they're dead?" Rook asks.

"Or sent away," Jericho adds.

I snap my fingers and point at him. "Legacy ships. Or at least panspermia."

"Is that what Grabowski does on weekends?" Rodgers asks.

"It's seeding DNA to another planet," Seb corrects.

"Sounds about right," Grabowski says, folding his arms.

But Sebastián looks irritated. "Preservation of the species." To me, he adds, "So your first reason for thinking they want to evoke sympathy is aid?"

"Or at least not to pursue their few survivors," I reply. "Think about it. After what they've been through? The last thing any species wants is to have even more bloodshed."

"Which would explain why Fred still doesn't sound like he trusts us," Kit offers.

"What's your second reason?" Jericho asks me.

"To save face."

"You think they got it wrong?"

"I do. I think Fred, or the Ganese, are embarrassed."

"Come on," Popov says, then seems to lose his gusto as Rook drills him with a glare. "I'm... curious like... everyone else."

Rook raises one eyebrow and then turns back to me.

"Right, so, based on the images we saw of their migration, I think it's safe to say that the Ganese were doomed." I turn to Sebastián for support here, and hope he's thinking along the same lines.

"Uh, I mean, it's hard to know exactly, but..."

Our xenobiologist Enni jumps in. "It's a forgone conclusion. We'd need to run data samples on the planet's composition to be sure, of course. And a terrestrial decapod might survive some of the cataclysmic events we saw coming, but not indefinitely."

"Just as we would not survive indefinitely," I add. "Which means that they were ill-fated long before the Naqualla arrived. That's the first level of embarrassment."

"The second?" Jericho asks.

"There's no way to know for sure, but I suspect something went south when the Naqualla arrived."

"Yeah," says Popov. "They realized the Naqualla were psychopathic killers."

Rook moves to shut Popov down, but I wave him off. "That's okay. Let's think about it though. If I'm the Naqualla and hellbent on killing everything in my path, why waste my time with a sentient species who is already doomed? Why not just skip over them?"

"Because you really like crab meat and fresh butter?" Rodgers asks.

"Shut up, dick face." Grabowski smacks Rodgers's avatar in the back of the head. But with the way Rodgers reacts, I'd say that happened in the real too.

"But he has a point," Popov says and then gestures to his teammates. "We've met enemies who enjoy killing for sport."

"*And* to put them out of their misery," Korvich says, which gets a few, "Oorah"s.

"But that doesn't translate to an entire species," Seb says right away. "Sure, a rogue faction here or there. *Maybe* a country, but even then, there's inevitably civil war over the actions. Absolute predators don't last long in nature."

"What's that supposed mean?" Popov asks.

Enni replies, "It means that a perfect killer is bad for its own health. Take the now defunct human immunodeficiency virus. Despite ravaging much of our population 200 years ago, it was a very inefficient pathogen because it killed its hosts. That's bad for business. We're all afraid of killer viruses, but that's because we're their target. But a killer virus that fails to adapt? It eventually loses hosts, and once that happens?"

"It dies," Rook says.

"Exactly. Far smarter are viruses that change over

time and lessen the impact on the host. It's why we still have the common cold."

"So you're saying the Naqualla can't be a perfect predator species?" Rook asks Sebastián.

"Not if they want to keep their place in the pecking order. This isn't the movies. This is evolution, and just like the laws of physics, you can't break it just because it sells well. Those ships that came through are dependent creations run by an interdependent species, hostile or not. Bottom line is that there's more going on here than a simple strike and retreat thing."

"You mean hit and fade," Korvich offers.

"Yeah. That. Sorry."

Jericho turns the room's attention back to me. "So you think there was a misunderstanding maybe? Something that provoked a conflict?"

"It wouldn't be the first time something like that has happened," I reply.

"Could have been us, ya know?" Kit adds and then starts positioning his hands like he's pantomiming air combat. "Dark alien ships appear from *Parallax One*, Navy battleships swoop in, there's no time for the NUE to make the right call, and then, *whammo!* Ships firing guided torpedoes, *whoosh*, aliens shooting laser beams, *pew-pew*. People screaming, faces melting, then there's a huge—"

"Hey, pal?" Jericho says.

Kit's mouth freezes mid-sentence. He looks around

and then sits on his hands. "*He he he*. Sorry, Cap. Uh, got a bit carried away there."

"There is yet another reason to suspect Fred's histories to be inadequate," Fergus says. "He still believes that we are the Naqualla."

"Didn't you give him the files?" Kit asks.

"I have, your eminence. But he is not convinced that we have told him the truth."

"What? He thinks we just made up everything about our entire species?"

"Thing's not right in the head," Rook says.

"I'm telling you right now, there's more going on here than we see," I reply. "Which means that if we want answers, we need to find out what's on the other side of that gate." I expect Rook to argue the point, but a quick look at his avatar shows that he likely didn't hear me. "Rook?"

"Uh, we might have a situation here."

Jericho steps forward and looks back and forth between Rook and Fergus. "What's going on?"

"Remember that whole thing about Fred still believing we're the enemy?" Rook asks. "It seems he means to do something about it."

I bring up Rook's helmet POV cam and see him and Team One still standing in the control room with Fergus's body half-inserted into his tube. Rook's targeting reticle moves to a point of interest on the wall near Fergus: a newly opened hexagonal hole about the size of an orange. More targeting reticles appear as three more holes open along the bulkhead.

"I don't like this," Geller says. "First movement we've seen."

"Ferg?" Rook asks. "Any ideas?"

"Fred says that he is sending the Gan to dispatch us now."

"What the hell are the Gan?"

"He has not made that clear."

Seb is on his feet now. "Master Sergeant, I think you need to get out of there."

"What's going on?" I ask.

"I think that…" Seb's wringing his hands and biting his lower lip. "I think they've had assistance of some kind."

"What kind of assistance?"

"The type that's responsible for aiding the Ganese in their technological development. I think the Marines need to get out before something bad happens."

Rook raises his weapon and yells, "Too late! Contact!"

10

ROOK

I SQUEEZE the trigger as soon as I have a target. It's a black crab the size of my fist with two green LEDs for eyes. And fortunately for us, it doesn't like wafer-coated magnetically accelerated projectile rounds. The tiny crustacean explodes, showering the room with bits of exoskeleton and dark blood. Or metal and hydraulic fluid? I can't tell, but I'm not sticking around to find out, because the little bastards are pouring through all four holes.

"Fergus! Off the wall," I yell. "Everyone out. Team Two, be advised. Multiple hostiles at our location. Fallback to primary exfil."

"We've got bogies too," Korvich says as his face pops into a subframe. He and Team Two are still exploring the first part of the ship. "Bionic crabs or some shit."

"Roger. Watch your six."

"Same to you."

I fire twice more, adding to the shrapnel flying in zero g, and then push out of the control room with Fergus. Something tells me that between his new knowledge of the Ganese and his archives on humanity, the bot is a prized commodity for both sides, so I need to keep him close.

Geller and his fire team are right behind us, pumping rounds into the control room.

"Bet somebody wishes they had their M265 now," Grabowski says.

Rodgers pauses between shots with his Korhonen K40 sniper rifle—not the ideal weapon's platform for CQB. "Bet your mom wishes I hadn't left her bedroom this morning."

Grabowski manages to send Rodgers a middle finger while holding his SR-90's foregrip and shooting another crab. Takes talent.

"Blow the room?" Geller asks me as Ibrahim nears the exit. She'll be last out, and the person to deploy a frag if we're gonna do it.

I don't have time to consult with the brainiacs. I'm sure they'd love to keep this system intact and scour it for data. But this just became a military operation, and my objective is to keep my Marines alive, no questions asked.

"Blow it," I say back to Geller.

With Rodgers and Grabowski providing covering fire, Ibrahim pulls one of the Corps's hi-explosive ceramic spheres off her hip, sets it to maglock with a three second fuse, and then throws it through the control room toward the back wall. "Frag out!"

The device sticks in place as Rodgers, Grabowski, and Ibrahim sail for the exit. The ordnance timer in my HUD hits zero. A bright light flashes behind us. While there's no sonic wave or pressure burst, we do get pelted by crab debris. It smacks our armor plating like sand whipped up in a desert storm but doesn't do any damage.

I check in with Team Two. "SITREP."

"Managing," Korvich replies. "Laying Easter eggs for later."

"Roger. Time to exfil?"

"Thirty seconds."

"We'll be right behind you." To Popov, I say, "*Bellerophon*, I need jump coordinates, plus forty-seconds."

"Stand by."

Fergus, Geller, and I are flying through the mortuary, heads on swivels, but I don't see any signs of more little devils. They're all behind us.

"Flight path calculated," Popov says. "Uploading to V-cog tactical now."

"Roger."

I'm almost to the junction where we'll drop

toward Team Two's position when I spot green lights in a corner six meters ahead. "Contact!" I'm still sailing forward as I bring my SR-90, get positive on the tango, and fire. My battlesuit's thrusters compensate for the sudden inertia differential, but I need to slow down since the junction is coming up fast. I flick off vector compensation, and then fire again, hitting two more crabs looking to replace the first.

"Engaging from multiple angles," Korvich says, clearly encountering a similar proliferation of targets that we are. "They're getting frisky down here."

"Roger. Keep the pressure on. I don't wanna find out if they kiss rough."

"Copy."

"Would it please you if I engaged as well, my lord?" Fergus says as we careen toward the junction.

"Negative." I fire three more times on the room's corners, filling the space with crab innards. "The last thing we need is for you to get compromised or power spiked. We don't know what they can do."

"I understand. However, should you change your mind—"

"I'll let you know. Ibrahim? SITREP!"

"More coming on our six. Seems we pissed 'em off pretty good," she replies. "Changing!"

While she swaps mags inside the mortuary, Rodgers pulls an EMP off his kit. The dodecahedron takes orders from the Marine's V-cog input, and then he tosses. "Let's see how they like getting spiked."

A three count goes by before the device emits a power wave designed to put down anything with an unshielded circuit board. Our battlesuits register the spike but are immune. The crabs, however, are...

Are also immune.

"Dammit," Rodgers says. "Not cool, man. Not cool."

"Going old school, then." Grabowski tosses a fragmentation grenade over Rodgers's shoulders. The blast detonates a dozen crabs and tears holes in the exoskeleton corpses affixed to the walls, buying Geller's fire team a small buffer to follow us out.

Ahead, Fergus and I hit the junction, and my suit stops hard before redirecting me down. Geller is right behind me, filling the connection room's corners with rifled dragon spit before making the turn himself. Thirty meters below, my HUD marks the main junction where Teams One and Two originally diverged. Flashes of light beyond the junction signal Team One's arrival.

"I got one on me," someone yells from Team Two. It's Wijaya. His POV pops into my HUD on reflex, and I see him trying to brush something off his thigh. "Shit! Jesus, it's— *Goddammit!*"

Before Korvich can say anything, Wijaya fires at his own leg. The armor should hold. But it's a desperate act. I look again. The tango is gone. However, I'm pretty sure I see blood bubbling from a seam.

Korvich must see it too. "Wijaya! Make sure your suit's plugging that."

"*Arrrrgh.* Son of bitch, that stings!"

"Wijaya! Acknowledge."

"Roger. I heard you. Double-checking." But before Wijaya has time to review battlesuit diagnostics, two more crabs latch onto him: one on the abdomen, the other on his opposite thigh. He swears and shoots at the target on his legs, but then screams and thrashes against the tango on his torso. "Get it off me, man!"

His bio feed lights up in the team HUD. Heart rate spikes. Blood pressure. Adrenaline.

"I got you!" It's Hatch, Team Two's rifleman and medic. She has Wijaya by the shoulders, spins him around, and then uses her SR-90's recoil to propel them both through the corridor.

Wijaya battles the crab on his abdomen but can't dislodge it, can't get his rifle around to it either. Hatch tries knocking the one on his leg clear, but she's unsuccessful. Meanwhile, Wijaya unsheathes his ceramic SPACE-BAR battle knife and starts stabbing at a tango, but not before he yells, "Shit! It burns, man! It's…" He stabs the crab. "It's fucking eating me!" He stabs again and again until finally the tango's dislodged.

There's blood flinging away from the wound too.

"Hatch," Korvich yells. "Get him out there!"

"I'm trying," she says back, but the crab presence is building.

To Geller behind me, I ask, "Breadcrumbs?"

"Hansel and Gretel," he replies, confirming that Team One is laying an ordnance trail to cover our exfil.

Ahead, I spot Korvich and the rest of his team. They slow at the junction, and then turn on the final leg out. But Korvich stops and looks my way. "You want support?"

"Negative! Get Wijaya out, and double-check the coordinates from Popov. We'll be right behind you."

He acknowledges and darts away followed by the rest of his team. Wijaya is trailing blood, which means his suit has malfunctioned, and Hatch still hasn't had time to patch anything.

"Gettin' spicey back here," Ibrahim says over team comms.

I glance at her POV and see Grabowski and Rodgers adding to her rear-facing fire. The Gan crabs are amassing so thick that they've formed a wall across the hallway. It makes for easy target acquisition but it's not great for morale. The enemy smells blood in the water.

"Last mag," Ibrahim says.

I'm suddenly wishing I hadn't ordered a recon load-out. "Sacrifice fire for speed, Marine! Let's get outta here."

"Roger."

The void is at the end of the corridor. Stars crowd the hole we blew in Eagle Rock's side. But I also spot part of Kep-C along one edge, meaning we've rotated toward the planet. That's not good. The *Belle* is on the *outside* of our orbit, not the inside.

One problem at time, I remind myself, and then fire thrusters to gain straight line speed.

"This is gonna be close," Grabowski yells. "I'm out!"

"Same," Ibrahim says.

"Blow it," I say to Geller and Korvich. They don't argue, even with our last three Marines still inside.

At first, there's nothing to see, hear, or feel. But when a bright light comes from the breached exit hole, and Grabowski, Rodgers, and Ibrahim shoot out behind me, propelled by the combined force of their jetpacks and our charges' chemical reactions, I give a "Hell, yeah!"

Three Marines aren't the only things to fly out of the station, however. Several hexagonal deck plates rupture and fling away, along with small sections of the ship's inner workings. I spot crabby parts in there too, including their fluids. But none of it is projected to catch our fire teams according to our battle HUD. We've already got the advantage of some distance and we're moving too quickly. In fact, Grabowski, Rodgers, and Ibrahim have to bleed off a little speed as they catch up to the rest of the unit.

The only thing I want to make sure of before I order everyone to slow and course correct is that the Gan aren't able to follow us. I didn't see any propulsion on the little bastards; they just looked like they were pushing off the walls after us. But then again, I didn't exactly take time to check their undercarriage.

"I want all eyes and sensors scanning the debris field," I say. "If we've got tangos with active propulsion, I wanna know. Hatch, SITREP on Wijaya?"

"I'm patching the suit. But those tangos… I think they buggered the autosealant."

"What about Wijaya?" I ask again because she's missed the point. Not for naught, though. If crabs were able to keep our battlesuit nanofiber from closing a breach, her distraction is merited.

"Uh… he's… declining, Master Sergeant. Needs a medbay, ASAP."

"Roger."

"I'm tracking movement," Gellers says. "Tagging."

"As am I, my lord," Fergus adds. "The enemy hordes have left what remains of Eagle Rock."

"Son of a bitch." Sure enough, dozens of auto-tags populate the team tactical HUD, marking individual crabs as they leave the debris field. As soon as the number of reticles exceeds the standard engagement allotment threshold, the V-cog system starts grouping the hostiles so as not to overwhelm us.

"Three new exit points," Korvich adds as he marks the locations of crabs emitting from the hull like spigots spraying water on a lawn. "Dammit, make that four."

"Do we have eyes on a propulsion mechanism?" I

ask as we continue hurtling away from the station and toward Kep-C's eastern hemisphere.

"Negative," Geller replies. "Maybe they don't have any. Just… jumped clear."

"And sacrifice themselves without hope of rejoining their kinsfolk? I think not," Fergus replies. "I am detecting trace amounts of ion radiation in their wake."

"Think we can turn and burn?" I ask. The *Belle* is currently positioned on the other side of Eagle Rock. So either we need to come about and pick our way back through the orbital junk yard, or Popov will need to find a gap he feels comfortable flying through.

Fergus doesn't sound hopeful. "Given Corporal Popov's proposed flight path for us, I am concerned that the enemy's lower mass will allow them to course correct and intercept us before we ever reach the *Bellerophon*."

"What about straight line acceleration? Think those gremlins have enough juice to keep up with us?"

"Without being sure of their energy capacity, it's impossible for me to say."

"Can you speculate?"

"No. But accelerating is a better option than coming about."

"That'll send us toward the planet," Korvich says. "Then we'll have to fight gravity well acceleration too."

"I know that, Corporal. But we might not have a choice."

"Rook," Popov says. "I'm watching the probability

of positive recovery plunge by the second on our tactical board. Be advised that I... Hell, I don't think we can intercept you in time."

"But we can," a new voice cuts in over comms. Knight's face appears in its own window.

"Knight? Negative. The *Koga* doesn't have—"

"Guns? Copy that. But we do have the latest in high velocity shielding and, last I checked, we're pretty damn fast. Plus, we've already poked our way through the debris field and have a fix on your position. Approaching from the East."

I try not to let my hopes rise. Doing so inevitably gets good Marines killed. But the idea of the *Kogarashi* being within arm's reach, or at least closer than the *Belle*, is good news. "ETA?"

"Assuming you accelerate by twenty-three percent, we can intercept you in four minutes, thirty seconds."

"Four fifteen," Kit calls out in correction.

"Four fifteen," Knight revises. "Think you can stay alive that long?"

"What about the Gan species hitting the *Koga*?" Evelyn asks, also on our team channel now.

"Assuming our resident devil dogs don't dawdle, we'll be clear with time to spare," Knight replies.

"And assuming those crabs don't outpace us," I add. "Knight, if they do, you're gonna need to—"

"Cross that bridge if we come to it, Master Sergeant."

I don't like involving a civilian vessel. It doesn't have armament, nor does it have the resources we need to refit and defend an assault. Likewise, there's no medbay for Wijaya. But the *Belle* isn't a good option, and more of us will die if we stay on course and hit Kep-C's atmo at this speed. I'm either risking the lives of Wijaya and everyone on the *Kogarashi*, or I'm risking two fire teams and probably everyone onboard the *Belle*. Decisions are a bitch sometimes. Guess that's why they pay E-8's the big coin. "Make it happen, Knight. *Belle*, stand fast and await intercept coordinates for medivac transfer once we're clear."

"Roger," both Popov and Knight say as one.

Back to my unit, I add, "If anyone has claymore rounds, grenades, or mines remaining, now's the time to call them out so I know what we're working with. That tingly feeling down in my loins says this one's gonna shave closer than we bargained for."

11

JERICHO

"How many g's we gonna be pushing on decel?" Nairobi asks me after I read off the flight schedule.

"Eighteen and change."

She shakes her head. "For?"

"Sixty-five seconds."

"You know that would kill us without—"

"Gene mods and comp suits. I'm aware. But we can handle it. All, that is, except you," I say to Afumba. He's the only non-original member of the *Koga*'s crew and, to my knowledge, hasn't undergone the same gene therapy or training for high-g maneuvers that the rest of us have. "That is, of course, unless there's something you're not telling."

"Mr. Sallsworth ensured that I was prepared for

many contingencies. I am rated for ten g's at twenty minutes. This should pose little threat."

I give Eddie a sideways look to see if he thinks the numbers will translate.

"Oi, it's cutting it fucking close if you ask me. But it's his skin, not mine."

"I'll be fine," Afumba says. "Let's do this."

I nod and then ping Nairobi. She's down in engineering and gives the drive core shield wall a loving pat. "Ready when you are."

"Good." I turn to Magellan at the helm. "Current speed?"

"Approaching 43,000 klicks per hour, Cap. Ready for turn and burn on your mark."

"You know this is gonna hurt more than an enema from a fire hydrant strapped to our bums, right?" Eddie says.

"Something like that," I reply, bracing for what's to come. "But it's gonna hurt way more for Rook and his squad if we don't."

Eddie nods grimly and then double-checks the mission clock. "Coming up on it, Knight."

"Roger." I tug on my five-point restraint harness and press my helmet into the headrest lock. "Everyone set?" The crew pings me back, all green. "Alright. Time to pucker up, people. Emergency flip and prime for super plasmoid decel burn on my mark." I read off the countdown timer. "In three... two... one... Mark."

Heads get thrown forward in helmets as Magellan spins the ship around three times faster than is recommended. It's enough to make my stomach twist and then some. A few seconds later, our heads snap back into our headrests as correction thrust slows our orientation to -180 degrees. But those forces are nothing compared to what Nairobi has in store for us.

"SPD burn in three," she calls out. "Two… one… Mark."

A second later, my spine feels like it's collapsing under the weight of my head on its way toward my ankles. The ship vibrates well beyond anything I'm comfortable with, but the *Koga* is rated to handle it and then some. Hell, four times this if need be, though no amount of bio mods could sustain that pancake job for more than a second. I'm not even sure I'm gonna get past this.

I wanna ask how the crew is doing, but I can't talk. I can barely grunt. I notice my suit's atmo pressure compensators spiking just to force air into my compressed lungs. Heart rate is also through the roof, and my head's shaking too much to focus on it for long —God, it even feels like V-cog is blurry. Which is impossible, I know. Maneuver's shaking my goddamn brain.

Just keep it together, Jericho.

I squint against the pain of feeling like my body is trying to get forced into a tuna can and glance at the team feeds. Eddie is still managing to drop a string of Fbombs—I have no idea how. Nairobi is holding her chair arms for dear life. Magellan is doing his best to keep his eyes open, as is Alice. But Kit and Afumba are completely passed out, eyes rolled back under half-open lids. Kit's got a mouth full of drool pooling under his chin. Fortunately, everyone's vitals are within norms, even Afumba's.

"You're looking good, *Kogarashi*," Evelyn says in our team channel. "Thirty seconds remaining."

God, there's that much time left?

"You okay, Jericho?" she asks me.

For a split-second, I forget that my brain doesn't need lungs to speak. "Hurts like a—"

"Like fucking jujitsu chop to gonads," Eddie yells in our ship's virtual lobby. "Heaven and all the bloody saints!"

"What he... said," I reply to Evelyn shakily. "Hard to... think straight. Can't get—"

"It's alright. You're on the home stretch. Listen, I'm gonna talk you all through the last part, because once you stop, you're gonna need to act quick."

"Right," is all I get out.

"You're passing the twenty-second mark, everyone. Almost there. Drive core looks good, Nairobi." Hearing Evelyn's voice has a calming effect on me. Not sure why. Just does. I'm pretty sure she could read the results of a verb search on pre-migration economics and I'd find it comforting somehow. "SPD burn shut down in fifteen seconds. Rook's squad will be on your port side. You'll open the forward and aft airlocks, prep for repressurization, and then ready for a second SPD burn as soon as Rook says they're secure. Everyone set?" She doesn't wait for acknowledgement because she knows we're all on the threshold of looking like Kit over there. She counts down and then says, "Mark."

The sudden absence of high gravity is equally as painful as what we just endured. The only difference is that the recoil lasts a fraction of a second. If someone said all my bones were mush, I wouldn't be surprised.

Kit is shocked awake by a low-power stim surge from his suit's automated internal defibrillator. He gasps for air. "I'll never make love to another, Abby!"

"Kit," I yell. "Airlocks!"

"I got 'em," Eddie replies and opens the doors.

Afumba is scrambling awake too. He's got blood coming from his nose, but he's alive.

"Anyone have visuals on Rook?" I ask the crew.

"Yeah, yeah," Kit replies, blinking at his holo screens. "Right outside. I mean, *left* outside. Not like we left them outside, I mean *port*."

"Right on schedule," Rook says over comms. "That was a hot burn, *Kogarashi*. Glad we didn't get here early."

"Good to see you, Rook." I bring up the vector path overlay on the *Koga*'s portside external cams. Teams One and Two have separated, each heading to one of the airlocks and bleeding off speed in their own deceleration burns.

"Holy biscuits!" Kits points at his holo. "What the H-E-double-L is that?"

A swarm of black dots with traces of green lights mars the distant image of Eagle Rock's blistered hull. The *Koga*'s sensors are trying to get an exact distance and bearing on the anomaly, but the readings are coming back all over the place.

In answer of his own question, Kits says, "Are those the baby attack crabbies? But they're... so many!"

I ignore Kit and ping Nairobi. "You ready?"

"All set."

"Eddie, make sure those outer doors are sealed as soon as the last Marine is in. I don't want any stowaways."

"Copy that."

"They're getting closer, Cap." Kit's pushed himself back into his seat. "Oh, jeez. This is gonna be really gosh darn close!"

"How you doing, Rook?"

"Ingress. Stand by."

I jump into his POV in V-cog and watch as Ibrahim, Grabowski, Rodgers, Geller, Fergus, and finally Rook pile into the airlock designed to hold half as many people.

As soon as they're crammed in, Rook yells, "Close it."

"Closing forward airlock," Eddie replies.

From aft airlock, Korvich yells, "All good here!"

"Closing aft airlock," Eddie says.

Then, pointing at the swarm, Kit hollers, "They're heeeeeere!"

I bring up engineering. "Punch it, Nairobi!"

All at once, ten g's shove me back into my seat. Compared to the last burn, it feels like a cake walk. But it's more pressure on my body than it likes. Fortunately, I'm at least able to talk in V-cog this time. "They following?"

Kit is shaking in his crash crouch, which somehow translates to his V-cog voice. "They've c-c-course corrected b-b-but… but… optical range estimates p-p-predict that they're not actually closing the-uh-uh d-d-distance."

"That's good news."

"Ye-ye-yeah."

"Let's see how long it plays out," Rook says, currently pinned against the airlock's wall with the rest of Team One.

As soon as we reach the twenty-second mark, I call for an accel shut down so we can get a better idea of what's happening, and allow Rook to get his unit secure. If Fred doesn't eventually call off the Gan pursuit, we may have a bigger problem. But one thing at a time.

Magellan calls out, "Current speed, 1,961 meters per

second. Distance from last launch point, 19.62 kilometers and rising."

"Enemy inbound?" Rook is first to ask.

"We, uh, still don't have an exact fix, Mr. Rook, sir,"
Kit says. "But they've matched our heading. It doesn't
look like they've accelerated at all though. At least as far
as I can tell, ya know?"

"If they aren't called to heel, then—"

"We'll have time to discuss that later," I say, not
wanting to get the rest of POET worried nothing. I'd
like to at least try to reserve talks about emergency
scenarios for the captains. "Rook, I wanna give you a
minute to get your teams secure."

"Wijaya needs medical. Hatch is with him now, but
she says it's serious."

Adding to the weight, Hatch comes back with,
"We're losing him, Master Sergeant."

"I thought we're just dealing with a puncture."

Hatch is shaking her head. "Something's hitting his
nervous system. Cardiovascular is crashing. We
need—"

"The *Belle*."

"I was gonna say a miracle."

Rook hits the inner airlock door with a fist. "Every-
one, find an empty seat or get lashed to a bulkhead.
Knight, how soon before we can rendezvous with the
Bellerophon?"

I look at Magellan who I know is already running the

calculations. "Ten minutes. A quarter of that without the damn debris field."

Rook's eyes flick in his helmet cam, and I'm certain he's looking at Hatch.

She shakes her head once. It's that bad.

"As soon as everyone's secure," I say, "we'll head for the *Belle*. We can talk as we go."

"Shove off," Rook says, but there's regret in his voice. "And make sure those damn crabs stay the hell away."

WE'RE ONLY PULLING 1.5 g's through the debris field on our intercept course with the *Belle*. We'd go faster if we could, but the ship's nav computer already considered all the speed changes needed to accommodate the obstacles we'd encounter, and doing so would take twice as long. So I decide to hunt down Rook while we wait. He's two decks down, helmet under his arm, and pacing the corridor outside the cargo deck where Wijaya is laid out.

"I'm sorry," I say as soon as our eyes meet.

"Not your fault."

"I'm one of the three captains who voted for the mission. So, yeah, it is."

He takes a breath and tilts his head back. "We should've been more careful."

"How the hell were you supposed to know the ship would have baby bionic crabs?"

"That's the point of being more careful."

"And what would you have done differently?"

"I'd… I'd have…" But after a deep breath, he seems to concede my point. "I'd have traded positions with him."

"And I'm sure he'll appreciate you saying that when he's in recovery."

"Wijaya gone, Knight."

This stops me short. "I'm… sorry to hear that."

"Me too. He was talented. Stupid, like all of us when we're young. But he made it on my squad by merit, bravery, and being a damn good shot."

I look at the door and notice it's locked from the inside. "Hatch is in there with him?"

Rook nods. "We don't want to take any unnecessary risks. If she thinks there's some sort of agent in his tissue or bloodstream, then we can't afford to have it contaminating the *Koga*. So his body will be quarantined until further notice. Once we're docked with the *Belle*, we can run a full diagnostic panel and hopefully sterilize your hold… assuming this thing is biological, or at least affected by radiation."

"I appreciate the discretion."

Rook works his tongue inside his cheek. I have a feeling he wants to say more, but I'm not gonna be the one to press him. After a few seconds, he says, "You know, it's never easy losing a Marine under your command. And sure as hell doesn't get easier with time. If anything, it… gets worse. Because you get older and the privates seem younger. And why your life gets spared and theirs doesn't? I'll never know. But something about this one makes it even worse."

"Because we're far from home."

"Something like that. And I can't write his mum, nor can I explain how he fucking died."

"We'll do our best to get answers, Rook. And to make sure his body gets home to his family."

"No one left behind," he says.

"We're on final, Cap," Kit interjects over comms. "Just letting you guys know."

"Thanks," I reply. "I'm gonna stay here and make sure Rook and his unit have everything they need."

"Understood. I'm telling Fergus he needs to do the same. He, uh, just told me… about Private Wijaya."

"And we're grateful for his help," Rook says. "He's a good bot, kid."

"Thank you, Mr. Rook, sir. I think so too. We'll, uh, chat soon, okay? I gotta help coordinate the docking procedure with Mr. Magellan now. Over roger and the out."

With Kit gone, Rook looks back at the bulkhead door and says, "You really don't need to stick around on our account."

"Eh, they've got it under control. Least I can do is see you and your team off my ship."

"Roger." He forces a short blast of air out his nose and gives me a smile. "And thanks. For the pick-up."

"We're not out of the woods yet."

"But we're further than we would have been without the *Koga*."

"Eh, we're a team out here, right? Gotta stick together."

"Forging paths?"

I clasp hands with him over the Sentia Aux motto. "Through the darkness."

12

GEMMA

GEMMA AGREED to meet Sir Nigel Sallsworth on his yacht currently sailing halfway between Sweden and Finland in the Gulf of Bothnia. The prospect of being so close to him in the real excited her, mostly because she relished the thought of making him pay at the ends of her own two hands. But that wasn't her end game, not physically anyway. Plus, his security forces would prevent any attempt on his life, and she would no doubt pay with hers in the process. Provoking her to violence was surely part of his ploy, master manipulator that he was. And so she would go in eyes wide open, knowing she had her own games to play.

How the corrupt statesman and murderer of her mother found her fjordic lair wasn't all that hard to piece together. He had probably been monitoring Behr,

Tonka, and Pearlman for years, just as he'd been monitoring her mother. But Gemma suspected that
Sallsworth's incogs had penetrated far deeper into the
smaller factions' ranks than they did the Tantum's. Well,
up until Jonah Finch, that was. *Bastard.*

And there it was again: the deep-seated urge to physically skin Sallsworth alive over a period of weeks and
then filet him one quarter at a time until his will to live
finally abandoned his body. The urge drew her toward
him. Norkü asked her not to go. "It is a mistake," he'd
said. And he was probably right. So she would take every
precaution necessary.

Three teams of her armed paladins boarded the
yacht thirty minutes before she was scheduled to touch
down. They searched and cleared the ship while
Sallsworth and Gemma's shuttles maintained escrow
holding patterns five hundred meters away. Her team's
recon efforts included deepwater scans that extended
for six kilometers in all subsurface directions. Monitoring of sea and air would continue throughout the
engagement, and quick reaction forces were standing
by should things go sideways. Satisfied that the vessel
was safe, Gemma agreed to set down on the aft
landing pad beside Sallsworth and his chief of staff,
Walter Brunell, and made her way with Norkü to the
lower salon. Any assassination attempt from outside
would kill them all, and any attempt within would pit
two against two. Were that the case, Gemma was

certain she and Norkü could take both the elders handily.

"May I pour you something?" Sallsworth asked as he walked to a wet bar in the spacious salon.

"No drinks," Norkü snapped in reply.

"Easy, big man. Poisoning her is the last thing I want."

"And what *do* you want?" Gemma asked. She had her sneakers on a glass coffee table with a golden base and her arms stretched out on the back of a white velvet couch.

Sallsworth paused his pouring to consider Gemma. "Your mother used to toy with me before negotiations. It was infuriating."

"Well, I'm not my mother. So I'll just have to find different ways to piss you off."

He chuckled. "I'm sure you will. I miss our little games. Her shooting me, me shooting her…"

"Are you trying to get a rise out of me, Sallsworth?"

"It's Nigel. Please. Mr. Sallsworth was my father."

"So, old and dead. Got it." She posed her question only slightly altered. "Are you trying to get a rise out of me, *Mr.* Sallsworth?"

He swirled the pour, sniffed the liquid, and then came around to sit opposite her. "I'm saying that for all the ways your mother threatened my work and my life, she was someone I admired. And, strangely, someone I rather miss."

"Oh, please. Spare me the platitudes."

"No platitudes. I can't rightfully sit here and act as though I'm not happy she's dead. You wouldn't believe it, and I couldn't sleep at night. She was a tyrant, at least to me"—he pressed a hand to his chest and gave her an innocent looking face—"and I can't say that my life isn't safer with her gone. But she was, if anything, the worthiest adversary I've ever had."

"You disgust me."

"I am being quite genuine, I can assure you. In my line of work, it's rather hard to find true contenders. Everyone just... oh, I don't know, *gives up* so easily."

Gemma swallowed the rage building in her chest. Her palms were moist, heart rate elevated. "Well, I can assure you that despite whatever temporary truce this constitutes, I won't give up hunting you until I've avenged my mother's death."

"Which is *precisely* the kind of spirit I was hoping to find! You see, Walter? I told you she was perfect."

Gemma looked between the two *old* men, then glanced at Norkü. He gave her a stern face. "So what's your game?"

"It's quite simple, really. You've obviously joined forces with the leaders of dubious illegitimate enterprises in the hopes of—what?—conspiring to undermine the NUE? Maybe disrupt the system and cause massive failures? And the ultimate end is... oh, I don't know, insert yourselves as leaders?"

Gemma felt the rage in her chest subside. In its place, she felt an odd mix of pity and satisfaction. Pity that the man, if he was telling the truth, had gotten it so wrong. Satisfaction that, if she let this play out, she might have her revenge handed to her on a silver platter by the man himself. Fortunately, Gemma had inherited her mother's dark ability to mask her true feelings, even from those skilled at divining the truth. She decided to play along.

"It sounds like you're offering something."

"Oh, I very much am, Miss Birdwhistle. I would like to propose a partnership."

"What kind?"

"The kind that allows you to fulfill your mother's dream."

"Which was?"

"To give the Tantum Terrae a seat at the table."

Gemma didn't move a muscle. Even with all her mastery of emotions, she couldn't let anything betray just how well this was going for her, assuming he was telling the truth. She'd need to know more. So she let the moment extend into long seconds, waiting for him to continue on his own. Silence, she'd discovered, had a way of keeping even the most disciplined people chatting in a way that nothing else could.

"And the Tantum Terrae ink on your palm tells me all I need to know," he added. "That you want the same. Recognition. Legitimacy. Sadly, it's what your mother was so close to having herself. That was the subject of our last negotiation, you know. A seat at the table—"

"In exchange for Allbrook's assassination. An act you apparently took into your own hands."

He licked his lips. "Circumstances changed."

"And what's to prevent you from doubling back on this agreement, whatever it might be? Who's to say you don't court me to within a dagger's length of my demise?"

"Because we both have something the other wants."

Gemma pulled her hands off the couch back and leaned forward. She didn't want Nigel to look too closely at the temporary TT insignia on her palm. But she was also genuinely curious where this was going—no, *if* it was going the way she suspected it might. "And what is that?"

"I want to know how you cracked V-cog. The architects said it would be impossible. It was the assurance of every scientist alive that finally gave the public the confidence they needed for global adoption. And those same assurances are what have kept us safe. Until you."

Sallsworth revealed his tell in the moment: the slightest pulsing of a neck muscle below his left ear. An old habit of tilting his head to one side, no doubt, something he'd tried to curb, as all master poker players seek to undo their instincts. But the human body has a way of surprising the soul, and Gemma had a front row seat at Sallsworth's showing.

She smiled and flexed her toes inside her sneakers. "What you really want is to ensure that I don't close the exploit you possess."

"Can you blame me?" he said quickly, smoothly covering his body's reflexive betrayal. "What good is Gaia's Blood to me without the assurance I can use it on my enemies? I think that's no surprise."

"And what do I get?"

"A seat at the table."

"Right. Just one problem."

"Go on."

"You're undoing the politicast system as we speak. Which will make this"—she looked down at her palm—"irrelevant."

Sallsworth raised an eyebrow and then looked at Walter. "I told you she was a worthy adversary."

"The paternal gatekeeping is really getting old," Gemma fired back.

He clucked his tongue. "*Tlk.* You're right. *You are right.* I'm sorry." He leaned in to match her pose, elbows on knees. "But your allegiance to a politicast isn't *really* what you're after, is it? This isn't about making the Tantum Terrae legitimate. No, that was your mother's cause. And rightly so: she was the one who gave it birth. Tuesday Soldiers of October the Eighth? Stood shoulder to shoulder at—"

"I know the poem. Your point?"

"You don't care about the Tantum Terrae being legitimate. *You* want to be legitimate."

"Already got that."

"But not the way you need. The way you deserve."

"You're losing me, Sally. I've got the upper hand here. You said it yourself, and you're right too. Not only is Gaia's Blood my invention, it's also something I know how to modify. So what's to stop me from leveraging my way to the head of the line without you?"

Slowly and carefully, Sallsworth replied, "Because even if you get there, the line won't follow you, Miss Birdwhistle."

Gemma swallowed. She eyed Sallsworth, sizing him up. "Keep going."

"If an armed robber hits a crypto node, holds all the miners hostage, and successfully escapes out a back door, does he get lauded as a pioneer in new blockchain technology simply because he overcame some local security measures?"

"No. But he would earn the respect of millions of criminals."

"That he probably already has anyway. And even if he didn't, so what? Does that make him worthy of more? Of national leadership?"

"Worse people have secured it with violence."

"And how long does it last? A year? Two? How long before the outcry becomes so great that the masses are willing to risk everything to overthrow the dictator. No,

Gemma. What I'm offering you is the one thing no one else can. Because while you might be able to assassinate anyone you want, you'll still need people to crew the ship. And do you really have those kinds of resources?

"Take the military, for example. Let's say you use Gaia's Blood to eliminate anyone who stands in your way. Wonderful. You've reached the top. But who's there to run it all? To command battalions, organize rosters, service equipment, fill orders, check munitions, stock food? Everyone hates the system. They love to loathe it. Until they realize that everything we have has been built on centuries of compounding dependence. On layers upon layers of trust, as misguided as some of it may be, that cannot be dismantled by one tyranny or another.

"No, Gemma. Trust me when I say you do not want this position by force. It will net you ruin faster than you can imagine. What you want is *procedure*. Due process. The acquisition of power through conventional means. Ruthlessly at times, yes. I should know. But legitimate in ways not even your greatest exploit can manufacture, I assure you. *That*, dear girl, is what I'm offering. A seat at the table that is not only permanent but comes with the respect and power that allow you to do what you want, when you want. And no one bats an eye. You played by the system's rules, and in the end, that's all the critics need to know in order to sleep at night."

"And what's to keep me from killing you once I'm there? From taking your seat at the table?"

"Nothing, I should think. I quite count on it, actually. Unless…"

A few seconds passed, and Gemma found herself the one who ended the silence. "What?"

"Unless the scenery is so sublime that you tolerate the arrangement and find it to your liking. Either way, the decision is yours." Sallsworth threw back his remaining scotch and set the glass down. "Think about it. I look forward to your call." Then he stood and moved toward the exit.

"Nigel, wait." She rose to meet him. "I think there might be an arrangement here after all."

Sallsworth grinned and spread his hands apart. "Shall I call my chef for dinner then?"

"I am feeling a bit hungry."

"As am I. *As am I.*"

13

EVELYN

JERICHO, Rook, and I walk into a side room off the command theater and head to the end of an oak conference table. The mood feels dark in the wake of Wijaya's death and because the Gan are still tracking us. As we get seated, I say to Rook, "I'm very sorry to hear about Private Wijaya."

"Thank you," he replies and nothing more.

"Everyone secure on the *Bellerophon*?" Jericho asks.

"Yes. Wijaya's body is in isolation and undergoing autopsy with one of the petty officers from the *Belle*'s original crew."

"Is that... wise?" I ask.

Rook shrugs. "Petty Officer Hill was the most understanding of our situation and volunteered. Helps that he's Viatoribus and pro SESI. But he still thinks we're all getting executed when we get back. And he's probably not far off from the truth. Anyway, Hill's been remanded to the medbay, and we're monitoring him closely."

"Keep us updated on what he finds with Wijaya," I say.

"Roger."

"So. Time to review our options?"

Both men nod, and Rook brings up a 3D star chart of Kep-C. The Naquallan-built Ring Y leading back to Earth is on one side, and the Ganesian Ring X is on the opposite. Tucked in the planet's dense debris field is an ID tag for Eagle Rock, followed by markers for the *Sagan*, *Belle*, and *Kogarashi* that are moving away from the alien station. Last but not least is a tag for the Gan swarm.

"We're currently heading out of the debris field and on course for Ring X," Rook says, noting POET's trio of ships. "Thanks to the *Sagan*'s sensors, we have a better fix on the swarm. They're still on our ass, presently 286 klicks away, but that distance is growing."

"So they haven't accelerated to match our speed?" Jericho asks.

"For now," I reply. "We can't rule anything out until we know more about their composition. But I think we've bought ourselves some time."

"Any guesses on how many?"

Rook answers. "The *Sagan*'s scans are inconclusive there, but we at least know the cloud is about two thousand meters across. Not quite as deep, but the nature of the swarm makes that measurement hard to determine."

"Something that size could envelop a ship easily." Jericho drums his fingers on the table. "Anyone speculate what the mini crabs could do to a hull?"

Rook gives a slight nod. "Based on what they did to Wijaya's battlesuit, Fergus seems to think the Gan have some sort of molecular separator."

"Come again?"

"I had to ask too. Basically, our suits are designed to self-heal, to close up when there's a puncture. But Wijaya's suit didn't. In fact, it appeared to degrade around the puncture point. Hill thinks it even affected Wijaya's skin and muscle tissue. Like I said, he's doing the autopsy now, but his first glimpse at the wounds startled him."

"So if it can do that to a Marine battlesuit, it might be able to do the same to a ship," Jericho says.

"I think we have to assume as much. Better safe than sorry."

"Although," I reply. "If they are capable of damaging or even destroying a ship-sized object, it raises the question why they weren't deployed against the gate they built? Or even the one to Earth? If they're so afraid of the Naqualla, why leave those intact?"

"Could be that the Gan are ineffective," Jericho says. "Ring Y could be made of materials they can't separate, and their own gate could be immune somehow. Who knows?"

"Or they're simply not that intelligent," Rook suggests. "For all we know, Fred can't even see those gates."

"But the signal activated when we got close to the Ganesian hex ring?" I say.

"That's what we've been assuming," Rook replies. "But we reviewed the data from when the *Koga* and *Sagan* were heading out and noticed that Eagle Rock had a perfect line of sight to your main engines when the first beacon transmission went out."

"You don't think it was triggered by proximity to the ring then," I say.

He shakes his head. "I think it was proximity to Eagle Rock. The initial message said, 'All you will find here are the dead.' That's not the ring; that was in reference to the station. The point now is that we have a tail, and we need to decide what to do about it."

"And what to do about the gates," I add.

"Obvious question here, but can you shoot down the Gan?" Jericho asks Rooks.

"I'd like to think so. Our frigate has several weapons that could make a dent in the swarm. Our point defense guns consist of Gatling-style 20 mm lead throwers that, at max effect range, cover a field 1,000 meters across. Close-in weapons systems include laser guidance disruption and plasma detonation lasers. How much of those will be effective against the Gan is hard to say. But even if our weapons work, there's no guarantee we get them all. Remember, the clarity we're getting right now is because of the *Sagan*. These little bastards are small, and we're used to tracking ships, not crustaceans. For all we know, just one crab could take out a drive core. We don't know. And I'm not sure we want to find out."

"So keeping plenty of distance between us and them is the safest bet," I say.

Rooks nods some more. "Plus, I can only assume your people don't want us blasting our first alien species out of the void if we don't have to."

"Careful," I say. "You're Sentia Aux ink is showing."

Rook smiles and looks down. I appreciate his willingness to recognize the non-violent option here. It speaks to his character. Most Marines I've met are the 'shoot first, ask questions never' sort. Don't get me wrong; I know there's some of that in Rook. They're charged with protecting lives, after all, and you don't get a second chance if you're dead. But part of being an astronaut on an unprecedented exploration mission is abiding by the Space Declaration's non-violation and right to proliferation clauses. Sure, I want to make sure we all survive this, but I also want to make sure the last remnant of the Gan do too.

Jericho sits back in his chair. "This is gonna make exploring the system harder."

"Like having a guard dog chase you around a property you're trying to case," I add.

"You speaking from experience, Dr. Park?"

"Maybe." I wink at Jericho. "Guess we need to decide if we're going to try and figure out how to activate Ring Y and head back to Earth or forge ahead to investigate Ring X."

"And by 'investigate Ring X,' you mean trying to activate it too?" Jericho asks, looking back and forth between Rook and me. "'Cause that's what we're talking about here, isn't it? Sure, we can say it's xenoarchaeology and everything, but we all know what it's really about if we stay on our present course."

"Got me there." I lean back in my chair and hold my hands up to them. "We each need to weigh in here. It's gotta be a unanimous group decision."

"On the one hand," says Rook, "we have a case for a planetary extinction level event perpetrated by a highly aggressive and technologically advanced alien species… granted, as told by a psychotic AI. My Marine Corps brain says back the truck out of Brixton and burn the bridge to Buckingham. We plant timed ordnance on Ring Y, try our damnedest to get back to Earth, or survive long enough for them to send a QRF, and tell Naval Command to blow *Parallax One* to kingdom come."

"But?" I ask.

"But… There's no guarantee we figure out how to

turn that thing on or that the NUE votes to send anyone after us. And if we do get back, that accomplishes little in terms of scientific discovery, at least beyond what we have to show for our efforts so far. I'm not exactly chomping at the bit to head to the gallows either."

"Prison for all of us," Jericho adds.

"So what's your vote?" I ask.

Rook pushes his lips up under his nose and breathes in before finally saying, "I vote we at least check it out. For all we know, Ring X is buggered, and none of this conversation matters anyway. Maybe the Gan already *did* sabotage that ring. But, for me? I'll always wonder what could have been if we don't at least try. We plant ordnance on Ring Y as a fallback measure. We should also deploy a data buoy in the event that something happens to us. If the NUE shows up, they need to know what happened here. But, in my mind, the main mission is sending a probe through Ring X while keeping our finger on the Power Off button." He looks to Jericho.

"I wanna see what's behind door number two as well. I think if we found out about the Naquallan attack without Fred, and without the swarm currently stalking us, I might be more inclined to try to head back to Earth, like you first said." He nods at Rook. "But right now, the only aggressive species we *actually* have first-hand experience with is these Ganese, or Gan—whatever. We don't even have real proof that what Fred says is accurate. Hell, it could be totally fabricated for all we know. So in the absence of more intel, I say we give it a go."

They both look at me. "Stars, you already know what I'm gonna say, guys." This makes them chuckle. "But I'm all for taking precautions. So I agree with setting ordnance on Ring Y and using a probe to head through Ring X. We go from there."

"It does beg one question, though," Jericho says. "Let's say we go through Ring X and come out the other side of Ring W, what happens when Ring X closes behind us? Assuming Ring W is a Naquallan-built ring, chances are high we won't know how to reactivate the connection just like we currently aren't sure how to reconnect Ring Y back to *Parallax One*."

"We hold back the *Belle* in reserve," Rook offers. "We keep the Ganese swarm company, and set up a reactivation schedule."

"This assumes a lot," I say. "But at least it's something. What's our time frame look like?"

Rook adjusts the star chart and starts running calculations. "If the *Belle* breaks off now, it'll take us three hours to get back to Ring Y and maybe an hour to plant charges. We'll target the emissions nodes only. Just wanna remind us that there's no guarantee our munitions will do anything to them. Could be fleas on an elephant."

"Understood." I examine the *Belle*'s proposed flight plan. "Then two hours back to Ring X?"

"Yup."

"Which gives us six hours to get there and start poking around the hardware. Just one problem." Jericho puts his finger on the swarm. "We'll only have two hours before the swarm catches up."

"And who knows what happens when we break off," Rook adds. "That could change things up too."

"What if we orbit Kep-C a few more times?" I suggest. "To build up a time buffer?" In the holo map, I pull the *Belle*'s icon back into our trio formation, and then accelerate three complete orbits of the planet until the predicted distance between us and the Gan is nine hours. Then I re-draw Rook's proposed flight path for the *Bellerophon* to Ring Y while the *Sagan* and *Kogarashi* head out to Ring X. "Then when you're done, Rook, the *Belle* joins us and there's still time left over."

Rook scratches the stubble on his jawline. "I like it. An eighteen hour mission time nets us a nine hour margin. The *Belle* plants our charges, you explore, and then we rendezvous with you at Ring X with six hours to spare."

"Assuming all things stay the same, and the swarm doesn't decide to double back or split into two groups," Jericho says.

"Which seems unlikely. They're either not accelerating because they need their reserve energy for deceleration on target—"

"Or they're saving what they have for course correction because they're almost out," Jericho interjects. "In which case, if we're lucky, they shut down on the backside of the planet during one of our orbits, and problem solved."

"Right."

"So, do we have a plan then?" I lean forward. "We doing this?"

"Oh, we doing this," Rook says.

"All in," adds Jericho. "Let's see what we can find."

I ONLY KNOCK to make sure she's decent.

"Come in," Olivia says. The doors part, and she looked surprised to see me. I'm surprised I'm here too.

Why, again, Evelyn?

I walk over to the flip down seat while she sits on the edge of her bed. "Came to give you another update."

Olivia doesn't reply verbally. Just blinks a few times.

"We discovered a derelict station belonging to what we believe are the native species of Kep-C." I pause to see if this will garner a reaction, but it doesn't. "It was sending out a signal, so Rook took over a team to scout it out. Discovered a shipboard AI that gave us some information on the planet's history and the species."

"As in, actual alien life?" Olivia asks.

"Not just that, but information about a second species too."

"Two species?"

"Yup. Why? Does that interest you?"

"God, Evelyn, yes. Of course it does. I'm not—"

"A murderer?"

"I was going to say disinterested. If anything, these years with you have—"

"Yeah, that's not gonna work."

"Because you don't believe your research can change someone's mind?"

I fold my arms. "Not yours."

"Then what makes me the exception to your holy crusade?"

"People like you don't actually change."

"People like me?" She presses a hand against her breast. "Because you think members of the Tantum Terrae are, what? Heartless criminals who have no ethics? No souls?"

"Sounds about right."

She looks away and laughs. "You really don't get it, do you."

"What's there to get?"

"That the TT may be rough around the edges—"

"You're monsters."

"—but they're people who feel like the system has let them down. Like it's given them no other choice. You know something about that, don't you, Hyunjung Bak?"

My ears tingle at the sound of that name. Blood rushes to my face. That she should know it... *use* it...

But it's not worth asking how. Someone did their homework.

"I'm guessing no one has called you that since Bukjeong Village," she says.

"Your point?"

"That you and I both know what it's like to feel abandoned. Betrayed by people who are supposed to protect you."

"Isn't that ironic."

She looks down and flexes the toes of her bare feet on the floor. "My hospital window faced Ganymede's Grosjean mountain range. It was beautiful. But I was in so much pain. Autoimmune response to gene therapy. My parents decided to give the experimental procedure more time. But I heard people whispering. Heard the nurses when they thought I was sleeping. The only way I was going to survive was if I went back to Earth."

A tear slides down Olivia's face when she looks up. I wanna say something... something harsh. To snap at her. There's no reason to believe she's telling the truth. But then again... there's something in her eyes that says...

Says she's a damn good liar.

"It was Neon," Olivia continues. "*She* saved me from Etana Dome. Not my mother or father. *Magnolia Bird-whistle.*"

"The Wraith of Ganymede," I counter. "She was a butcher."

"Who did what my parents wouldn't."

"Or couldn't," I say in protest. "Extenuating circumstances can—"

"They could have taken me back any time they wanted! So don't talk to me about extenuating circumstances. They could have sent me on a NUESSA emergency transport any damn day. But they chose *not* to. *Not* to save their own daughter. Instead? They chose research on a godforsaken moon 588 million kilometers away from the planet that I belonged on."

"So that's why you're a TT paladin?"

"No. That's why I'm alive. I was a paladin because I believed anyone not dedicated to saving humans on Earth was no better than my parents. That spending money on space was tantamount to killing children. And the only way to wake up a world who wouldn't listen—"

"Was to kill them in exchange?"

Olivia's lips stiffen. "If that's what it took to make them listen."

"You're sick, you know that?"

"We're all sick, Evelyn. It's just that some of us are more honest than others about the risks we take and the people we're willing to hurt to do what we believe is right. We're not so different, you and me."

"We're totally different."

"You risked our lives going through *Parallax One*. And I'd bet crypto that if you find what you're looking for out here among the stars—I mean really find all those answers to our biggest questions and discover a way to save the entire species like you claim—and someone threatens to take that away? I don't doubt for one second that you'd do whatever it took to stop them. That you, Hyunjung Bak, would kill them."

"Stop using that name."

"It bothers you, doesn't it. Reminds you of what you're capable of."

"I'm not that person anymore."

Olivia frowns and folds her arms. "So you're allowed to change, but I'm not?"

"We're going to see if we can activate Ring X," I say, trying to get back to the reason I came down here.

"You didn't answer my question."

"If we can turn it on, we're going to send a probe through."

"You don't actually know what to do with me, do you?"

"From there, we'll make a decision about next steps depending on what we find."

"It terrifies you that you may have actually changed my whole worldview, doesn't it? That maybe I had your back."

"Worst case, we lay charges on the rings and return to Earth."

"And if I try to stop you?"

"I'll kill you."

Olivia pulls back and lets out a disapproving sigh. "And there it is."

Stars, I wanna attack her again. With everything I've got. But that solves nothing except appease my urge to beat the ever-loving shit out of her.

"You have your cause, and I had mine," she says so quietly I almost can't hear her. "Both of us wanting to save our people, both willing to do whatever it takes. Unfortunately, in the world we live in, there's no room for us to change our minds. We're pariahs if we jump ponds. Unlucky for me that I just happened to want to swim in yours." Olivia gives me a sad smile and then turns to slide onto her bunk.

I have nothing more I want to say, so I let the seat slap back into the wall and order the door open. I step through, and as it closes behind me, all I can seem to think about is how she spoke of her cause as being something she *had*... past tense. Whether she's being genuine or not, I can't tell. It's too late for redemption anyway. But if she did jump ponds? Then what?

Eh, it doesn't matter. She has crimes to answer for and a jury of her peers to convince, not me. *I let you threaten my people before, and I'll be damned if I'm ever so stupid to do it again.*

"What was that?" says one of the scientists through his bushy dark beard who is on guard duty. His name tape reads J. Bolton.

Didn't even realize I said that out loud. "Sorry. Just... talking to myself."

"Ha. I do that a lot."

"Mmmm."

"Anything I can help with, Dr. Park? You seem... a little outta sorts, if you don't mind me saying so."

"No, but thank you Mr. Bolton."

"Uh, it's doctor, but... You know what? I'm sorry. I shouldn't have—"

"*Dr.* Bolton, of course. My apologies." I smooth my uniform. "Forgive me."

"Don't mention it. You have a good rest of your day, Dr. Park. The prisoner's not going anywhere." He pats the door twice and offers me a warm smile. Despite his positive disposition, I walk away feeling like someone just punched me in the gut. And I wanna punch back. I just don't know if I should hit Olivia...

Or myself.

14

JERICHO

THE THREE-PASS RUN around Kep-C has taken us eight hours forty-six minutes, and the Gan have been following us the whole time with only minor course corrections. It's not often things go as planned, so I'm taking the opportunity to celebrate the event while I can. Since there's not a drop of beer on the *Koga*, and I don't feel like burning any of our substrate provision material for a pint, I opt to pop a cap on a virtual bottle inside my V-cog suite overlooking the Amalfi coastline. It's not the same as a real drink, of course, but I'll be more sober. Which counts when you shouldn't be drinking on the job anyway because, ya know, *AI's* and *portals* and *alien crab swarms*. Normal stuff.

Being on my porch overlooking the Med also reminds me of dad. Wishing he could see this. Eh, I'm guessing he can, in some sense. At least that's what I'd like to believe. While he definitely got pissed about me leaving High Top Uranium Corporation and switching to the Sentia Aux, he did seem to come around by the end. And I think he would have enjoyed what we're doing, even if it is dangerous and pushing the limits of... well, everything we know about the universe. He used to love dreaming about the mysteries that space held for us.

"Cheers, dad," I say after a minute or two of reflecting on him. "To discovering an alien species... albeit dead. Well, sort of. Anyway..." I hoist the bottle up, clink the air, and then pour a little beer on the ground.

The rest of the ships' crews have taken some personal time too. Hourly reports show they've gotten grub, showers, and most everyone has gotten some sleep —a few less than others. According to a handful of oddly timed barracks logins, some of the *Sagan*'s scientists seemed to be quite busy. But, hell, just because we're in a different solar system doesn't mean human drives automatically shut down. Sex is a good way to relieve stress, they say. Plus, it affects the mood positively. Everyone seems in pretty good spirits. All but one, that is.

"Care to join me?" I say to Evelyn in V-cog.

She appears on my porch and spots my beer. "You don't believe in tequila?"

"Stand by." I call up the drink menu, select the only

fermented agave plant I have, and then hand her the glass once it materializes in my hand. It's not the añejo she likes, but it'll have to do. "Jose Cuervo. Sorry."

"It's wet." She takes the highball and we toast. Then she pulls up a wicker chair, sits down, and puts her bare feet up on the railing. "The *Bellerephon* split off."

"I saw."

"I'd be interested to see what the Gan do if faced with a choice of pursuing one or the other of us."

"If the *Belle* was delayed and never got back on the flight plan?"

"Yup."

"Wanna place bets?" I ask.

"I say they go after the *Belle*."

"Really?"

"You don't?"

I shake my head and then take a sip of my beer. "They're gonna track the larger combined mass of vessels. More bang for the buck. Plus, we're headed to their ring, so that'll pique their interest. Why do you say the *Belle*?"

"It's the ship that 'attacked' them," she replies, using her fingers to make air quotes.

"Good point."

We sit listening to the sounds of the shore. Gulls crying overhead. Waves crashing on the rocks below. A freighter's horn bellowing in the distance. I paid extra to make sure the sounds were random enough that my virtual ear didn't detect patterns. Nothing says cheap like a bad audio loop.

"I noticed you went to see Sam again," I say at last, realizing my mistake too late. "*Olivia.*"

She sips her tequila. "You stalking me?"

"Not a lot to do out here in the Kepler system."

"Don't remind me."

I look over at her. "That was supposed to be a joke."

"And we were supposed to find... Never mind."

We both take sips of our drinks, then I say, "I get it. Not what you were hoping for. Nor were you expecting to get stabbed in the back."

"She helped bring down *Astraea*, Jericho. It's a little bigger than me."

"Sure. But *Astraea* is over. What's happening to you is right now."

She nods and then stares into her glass.

"You wanna talk about it?"

"No."

"Okay." I take a deep drink and then wipe my mouth with the back of my hand. "They say that Capuchin monks invented cappuccino in the monastery behind us. Named it after the brown color of their habits. But a lot of people think the name comes from—"

"I killed people."

I give her a raised eyebrow. "Not something you hear everyday."

"When I was a kid. In Bukjeong Village. The crew I used to run with did horrible things. Things I said I'd never do with them… never go that far. Said I had limits."

"Like not being a pickpocket. You told me that once."

"Weird how you can justify moral high ground in one area and feel so…"

"Righteous?"

She sniffs. "Only to completely overshadow it with failures in another area that's way worse. Ya know?"

"How much worse are we talking? Like… I dunno, a contract killer or something? An assassin?"

This makes her laugh once, but then she's right back to business. "You died if you were alone. Saw it happen to other kids who never got in with a crew. So you do what you need to survive. To be a part of a family who will have your back. It was never for sport. Just… anyone who threatened what we were trying to do."

"Which was?"

"Protect turf. Food. Our homes, what little you could call them. And each other."

"Sounds intense."

"It was. And my uncle saved me from it. Without him, I'd be dead."

"So you've said." I set the empty bottle down on the terracotta tiles. "What does this have to do with Olivia?"

"She knows. I don't know how. But she brought it up today."

"In what context?"

"That we're both killers who ended peoples' lives over things we believed in. And you know what?" Evelyn looks up at me. "She's right. She asked if I'd try to kill her if she tried to stop us."

"What'd you say?"

"Yes. Didn't even hesitate."

"And it scared you?"

"Yeah." She downs the rest of her drink. "Damn, this stuff doesn't work like Kit's."

"Hold up. Kit has stim code to—?"

"Says he got it from Adrian." She spins and points a finger in my face. "But you didn't hear that from me."

"Knew that guy was bad news." After another few seconds, I say, "Sorry she rattled your cage."

"It's just that it has me thinking about the Tantum in a way that's made me really uncomfortable, if I'm being honest. Solum Terram too. There's some bad people in those organizations, I know that. But the regulars on the ground? The ones in the trenches—?"

"Like orphans in Bukjeong Village?"

She nods. "They're just doing what they believe is right, even if everyone else can see it's wrong."

"So you're empathizing with Olivia now?"

"No." But her eyes look away. "I'm *pissed* at Olivia.

Confused. But I…" She rubs her forehead with a hand. "I need this tequila to work better."

"I'll see what we can ration from our SPM allotment."

"Better make it a double then."

I watch a gull catch a thermal and ride it over our heads and outta sight. "She's a bad woman, Evelyn. Don't doubt that."

"I'm not. But I… actually believe that she was doing what she thought was best. And that she's not completely evil."

"How's that?"

"Because, somehow, I think we've changed her."

"*You've* changed her."

"Maybe. But is that possible? Like, actually? The woman probably reported to Neon herself. Helped Stamos. I guess what's driving me a little crazy is… Is all this just because she's been found out? Or is it genuine, ya know? And if it's genuine, how much of it is real?"

"Hell if I know. *But*"—I clean something out of my teeth in the real—"if anyone could turn Olivia, it's definitely you." A beat later, I say, "That came out wrong. Didn't mean—"

"Sure you did." She pats my back. "And nice to know you think I'm attractive."

"But I…"

"Yeah?"

I shut my mouth before I get myself in trouble. "Anyway…"

Evelyn laughs, like genuinely. "Thanks for the vote of confidence."

"Not a problem." After the seriousness returns, I add, "She did save your life before. People can change."

"Guess I just don't expect it of our enemies."

"Not sure anyone ever does."

Evelyn

AFTER A FEW MORE VIRTUAL ROUNDS, Jericho and I jump into the POET command theater at Sebastián and Enni's request. They, along with Natalie, are hunkered around the same cluster of holo screens teeming with images of the biological sort. Models of molecules, DNA strands, cells, and cross-sections of specimens that look like leftovers from a high school dissection.

"Someone got bored," I say as Jericho and I pull up chairs.

"We have a working hypothesis about Kep-C, the Gan, the Ganese," Seb says. "Maybe even some ideas about the Naqualla."

Before he can continue, Enni speaks up. "Dr. Fernández Parra's idea about them being a symbiotic species was right, and then some."

"Shouldn't we wait for Rook?" I ask.

"Geller said he's finally getting some shut eye," Seb replies. "There's nothing here we can't convey later. Plus, I need the scientists on this one. Engineers count too," he adds with a wink at Jericho.

"So what's this about a symbiotic species?" I ask. "First I'm hearing about it."

"We'd better start with Dr. Mason. She's the one with the initial breakthrough."

"But it doesn't make sense without explaining the roadblock. That's what gave me inspiration." Natalie turns to me. "Collaboration, right?"

Seb reorders some of the holo windows and then motions to a digital wireframe of something that looks like a giant land crab. "This bio blueprint is our best estimate of Ganesian composition based on sensor readings from Rook's unit and all the data gathered by Fergus. Essentially, we're dealing with a terrestrial decapod the size of a human. Not really new information. I mean, sure, I didn't expect sentient crustaceans—who did? The problem is, they're not exactly candidates for building the kinds of technologies we've seen."

"How so?" Jericho asks.

Seb raises his hand and wiggles his thumbs. "One of the many things that allowed homo sapiens to get as far as we have are these babies. Dexterity. Fine motor skills. And no matter how smart you become, there's only so much you can do with things like these." He forms a claw with his hands and starts opening and closing them awkwardly. "They're tools for trapping, crushing, tearing, and digging. *Not* building, at least anything beyond simple rock mounds."

"So they needed help," I say. "A smaller species. Like remoras helping sharks."

"The Gan aren't a species though," Jericho interjects. "They're robots."

"But they weren't always," Seb says. "At least that's our working hypothesis."

After a moment of silence, I ask, "You wanna run that by us again?"

"The first clue was in their name," Natalie replies. "And this is my only contribution, okay? The rest is Seb and Enni, 'cause I'm no biologist. But the whole naming convention of 'Gan' and 'Ganese' got my brain going as soon as Seb started trying to work out the relationship. Gan is a derivative, right?"

"Sure," I reply.

"Wrong. Look at it again." In the main holo window,

she places an audio waveform under the word written out in English. "Regardless of how Fergus came up with an English pronunciation for us, it's clear that Gan and Ganese are related. But both in English and *Ganesian*, for lack of a more nuanced name for their language, the word 'Gan' is the root, where 'Ese' is an extension."

"So... you're suggesting that the Ganese came *from* the Gan then?" I turn from Nat and give Seb and Enni a confused look.

"Not biologically, no." Seb brings up another holo window, one with a new bio blueprint much smaller than the first. "We've been assuming that the Ganese, the big ones, were the most advanced. But now I have reason to believe that the *Gan*, the swarm, were the most sentient species on Kep-C, or at least the smartest. This image represents our best assumptions on the data from Fergus and the Marines' encounter with them. As you can see, their design has some striking differences from the larger Ganese. Bigger eyes, larger brains, and smaller abdomens. But then it gets more interesting. Instead of five pairs of legs, the Gan are heptapods. That's six legs plus a seventh one protruding from the abdomen that is presumably the remains of an early vestigial pair. Then there's this"—he zooms in on the front legs—"foreclaws with...?"

"Opposable thumbs?" I reply in wonder. "Or... opposable *claws*?"

"Two of them, to be exact." Enni points to the joints.

"Didn't even notice those in the footage," Jericho says.

"For one, they're very small," Seb explains. "But they also kept them closed, except when gripping something, like Wijaya's suit. You'll notice that they're slightly smaller and presumably more fragile."

"Like the way we tuck our thumb under our fingers when throwing a punch," I add.

"Correct."

"I'm still not making the whole symbiotic relation-ship connection," Jericho says. "Plus, how do we know the Ganese didn't just make these little guys?"

"Again, the Ganese lack the physical ability to create something so intricate as a basket, let alone an electric circuit. Secondly, the Gan do not resemble the Ganese, at least in ways you might expect a robot to emulate its creator. Notice that the excipions who serve humans the most closely look the most like us. Two arms, two legs, five fingers, and so on. Created things tend to create in their own image. It's a generalization, but one I think we can tentatively apply here."

"So then where did they come from?" I ask.

"There's a lot of guess work here," Enni says. "And we've only had half a day to process, right? So it's far from conclusive." She lets out a small laugh. "Decades from being conclusive, okay?"

"We got it," I reply.

Seb nods for her to keep going.

"Right. So, we think they evolved together. Which takes us back to Dr. Mason again."

Natalie pulls up her waveform displays. "You probably noticed two distinct sounds in the signal we first encountered, and then in Fred's speech."

"Like a whale and a failing grid transmitter," Jericho says in the words of Kit. "Or his aunt who makes great cheesecakes."

"Ha. Right. Well, that's because the speech is a blend of the species who learned to adapt to one another's means of vocal communication, among other forms."

"Given the size of the Ganese and the hollow cavities we've detected in the front of their abdomens," Seb says. "We think it's fair to speculate that they are responsible for the deeper, rounder tones you hear."

"Then the more static-like chatter is produced by the Gan," Enni adds.

"Which would make sense given their digital nature," I say. "And you think this is reflective of their biological development? Their evolving together?"

"We do," Seb says. "The two appear to be similar enough that they could have easily occupied the same environments. It is quite possible, therefore, that the Gan, when they were biological in form, relied on the Ganese, or whatever they were once called, as a protector. Whereas the Ganese could have benefitted from the Gan's ability to make them more adequate shelter, more nourishing food, or heal them of a disease. The possibilities are endless really. But somewhere along the line, there was a change."

"The Gan became cyborgs," Jericho says and then laughs a little, presumably at his own words. "This is crazy."

"You're not entirely wrong on both counts," Enni says. "But it shouldn't surprise us, since we're almost there ourselves."

This makes both me and Jericho sit up to full height.

"Oh?" I ask.

"Isn't it obvious? V-cog augments our brains. Hardware replaces body parts that our gene therapy can't grow back. Software creates an interface, and we're slowly becoming more efficient as an augmented species than we ever were as a purely biological one."

"So they made the full leap," Jericho concludes.

"To a post-biological state, yes," Enni adds. "And then most likely to a singularity as well. We can only make broad assumptions as to why they maintained a relationship with the Ganese, who clearly didn't make the technological leap with them. Perhaps it was pity, habit, or maybe just because they grew fond of each other over a few million years. Who knows?"

"Then why not lead with all this?" I ask. "Why all the attention on the Ganese?"

"I suspect it has to do with their nature," Seb replies. "While they may have been the smarter and more dexterous of the two species, they were more than likely and quite characteristically the shier of the pair."

"The nerd who gets picked on in school makes friends with the biggest kids to keep the bullies away," I say.

"Exactly. And there's no reason for that nature to change even if their corporeal forms change. It's programmed, hardwired into the psyche." He taps the side of his head. "Some habits die harder than others."

"So when encountering an unexpected presence, they feature the Ganese while keeping their own presence hidden," I say. "Still doesn't explain why Fred kept calling us the Naqualla. A computer program, a singularity even, should know the difference, right?" I look at Natalie.

"Not necessarily," she says. "Just because something is self-aware doesn't mean it has limitless potential to learn, or even that it puts things together quickly. Assimilating data takes time, and just because something is self-evident to us doesn't mean it is to someone else. How many wars have we fought throughout time that could have been solved with a better mutual understanding of the facts? Just look at what we're doing right now: we're half a day into trying to piece together two other species' existences and have barely scratched the surface. Isn't it fair to suspect they're trying to do the same?"

I nod slowly. "Never thought of that."

"But Fergus gave them a file," I say.

"Which means nothing if they don't want to believe it," Natalie replies. "For all they know, Fergus fabricated it. And then there's always the possibility that Fred is off his rocker. But I like to think the best of systems before I assume the worst. Plus, we have to wonder just how many alien species the Gan and the Ganese expected to meet in their lifetime. Two visits from two different species hundreds of years apart probably wasn't on their predictions checklist."

"So, let's say all this conjecture is true. How does it help us with our current situation?"

Jericho adds, "And why haven't the Ganese—can we just call both species that?—destroyed their own gate to prevent the Naqualla from coming back, if in fact they have the ability to destroy ships as Fergus and Rook assume?"

"All good questions," Seb replies. "And, yes, let's call their combined presence Ganese for simplicity's sake; they are symbiotically interdependent. As to your latter point, the fact that they haven't destroyed their own ring means they might lack the ability."

"Which would be good for us," Jericho says.

"Indeed. An alternative answer is that they didn't want to waste their resources since their objectives were met."

"How so?"

"If the Naqualla finished their task of destroying all life on Kep-C and left the system indefinitely, it's plausible that the survivors would spend their remaining resources on something more constructive."

"They'd try to get their survivors to safety," I interject and then lock eyes with Sebastián. "They'd flee the system."

"Back to the idea of panspermia," he says with a smile. "So what we have here in Eagle Rock are those who chose to remain behind. The remnant."

"Which would further explain why Fred didn't seem prepared for us," I say. "They weren't expecting to meet anyone. The biological died out, and the mechanical probably—what?—went into hibernation in their singularity mind?"

"It's a good hypothesis," Natalie says. "Conserve power."

"Which leads us to their current pursuit," Seb says. "Despite what they did to Private Wijaya, I'm not actually sure they mean to do us any harm. It's more likely a general defense mechanism. As in 'Shoo-shoo, we don't want you here. Get away you mangy mut.'" Seb shrugs at his awkward use of drama and then seems to grow thoughtful again. "There's one more thing. About Ring Y."

"And that is?" I ask.

"Nowhere, in any of the research files we've seen from Fergus, do the Ganese mention Ring Y."

"Which might confirm our suspicion that it was built after the Naquallan assault," I say.

"Yes."

"Interesting." I sit back and consider my fellow scientists. They've done good work. *Great* work. How much of their speculation is true remains to be seen. Stars, we might never get answers. But this is better than nothing.

Jericho turns to me. "Still think we should investigate Ring X?"

"More than ever. Despite the ominous sounding history of the Ganese, I'm all but certain they haven't told us the whole story. So far, we think a planet going through an extinction level climate event receives a carrier signal from the Naqualla. The Ganese build the ring but decide not to open it for reasons we don't know. The Naqualla get curious and come through anyway, which ends up starting a war—one-sided as it may have been. Once the Naqualla leave, the surviving Ganese build a space station and an escape vehicle, perhaps a few, we don't know, and then launch their kin to safer shores. The Naqualla, ever curious, return yet again, overlook Eagle Rock, and build Ring Y because they see… what?"

"Earth," Enni replies. "Another planet that in 300 years' time may be headed toward a similar ecological disaster."

"Which is why I don't believe the Naqualla are inherently evil. This seems to suggest that maybe they're on some sort of… I don't know, aid mission."

"How does that work?" Jericho asks. "Three

hundred years ago, they would have been getting light that was itself three hundred years old, right? So we're talking, what—?"

"The mid seventeenth century," I reply.

"We weren't exactly shooting lasers into space in the 1650's," he adds.

"No. But we were emitting light on the dark side of the planet, albeit extremely faint by stellar standards. And if they happened to check it more recently, they would have seen Nagasaki and Hiroshima, and many of the 2,000 tests since."

"You think they had some way of predicting the end of all things?" Jericho asks.

"I do. Maybe they had some sort of advanced detection system to measure Goldilocks planets and a metric to gauge the probability of sentient species with self-destructive tendencies. Who knows? But I think Kit had it spot on."

"Had what?" Jericho asks.

"If you swap out the Ganese for humanity, Kep-C for Earth, and throw in the NUE, Space Navy, and all the politicasts, you have another chance for history to repeat itself." I lock eyes with Jericho. "I think this is what they do."

Seb asks, "Start wars?"

"No," Jericho replies, still looking at me. "Rescue planets."

15

JERICHO

WE'VE BEEN SCANNING Ring X's surface for an hour when Rook steps into the V-cog command theater. "I've got good and bad news," he announces as he comes down the steps through the stadium style seating toward the sunken stage.

His announcement forces me to hit pause on a drone sweep of one of the ring's newly discovered features, but I see several people are still busy with their various tasks or simply running V-cog in the background. "Hey, let's stop what we're doing people and jump in here. Listen up."

When everyone's present, Rook takes the floor. "The good news is that we've safely placed explosive munitions on Ring Y's three nodes. In the event that we need to detonate them, I can confidently say that we've done the best we can with what we have."

"Think it'll work?" one of the *Sagan*'s scientists asks.

"From the looks of it, I'd say so. There's only so many ways you can shield matter from the kind of energy our ordnance will deliver. Then again, we are dealing with an advanced sentient species, so the most I can offer is a hopeful yes. The other piece of good news is that we've deployed a data buoy in the event that the NUE shows up and we're not around to tell the story. It'll get regular updates as long as one of our vessels is within line-of-sight."

"And the bad news?" I ask.

Rook cracks his neck once. "We searched all 81.681 klicks of that ring's circumference and couldn't find a single point of entry. No hatches. No doors. No seams in plating. Not even a dent. So if there's a way in, we couldn't find it."

"Which means we're not getting control of it any time soon," I reply.

"Not without a handy dandy remote control."

The mood in the theater shifts.

Up until now, I was kinda hoping there might be at least some chance that we could turn the gate on to get home. But hearing that there's no sign of activating it dampens that hope, and with it, my spirits. Sure, I have to believe that NUESSA might eventually undertake a rescue op, so I haven't given up completely. But I can tell by the looks on people's faces that I'm not the only one disappointed by the news.

"Well," I say, "on our end, we're making good headway. Unlike your ring, our specimen is—"

"Chock full of fucking nooks and crannies," Eddie says.

This gets a laugh and helps lighten the mood a little.

I keep going. "We've already mapped sixty percent of the surface area and identified three possible power stations with clearly marked access panels. Unlike Eagle Rock, this structure has lots of legible writing."

"And Fergus?" Rook asks.

"He's already deciphering it. We've found a dozen possible entry points too."

"But you're not going in, right, Knight?"

"And risk another swarm attack? Not until you guys arrive."

"That's what I like to hear."

"Now that you're on your way, we'll keep feeding you what we find."

"Roger. See you in two hours." Rook disappears from the theater, and I order everyone back to work.

In the real, I'm on the *Kogarashi*'s bridge sipping a water pouch. We're at zero g's and holding position one klick off the gate's starboard edge. Since we haven't detected any power emissions, and none of our drone equipment or excipions seem to have woken the thing up, I feel the distance is ample. Plus, we already know we can outrun a swarm should any emerge.

I jump back into my drone's POV cam and take control of the piloting interface. It has basic pitch, roll, and yaw with positive and negative thrust. The focus of my current scan is one of the three suspected power stations. Where the emissions nodes sit along the inside middle of three of the hexagon's walls, the power stations alternate on the other walls. If lines were drawn to connect the like objects, the viewer would get two overlapping equilateral triangles in opposing directions to form the Jewish icon of the Star of David. No, I don't think any Ganese appeared to King David or the children of Israel. I think nature just likes symmetry and patterns.

"Whadda ya think so far?" Evelyn says in a V-cog audio channel. "Does it seem like something you can hack?"

I send her an invite to the drone's V-cog suite, which is a control room with two command chairs. It's a basic construct built by the drone's manufacturer, Stellar Dynamics. White leather, baby blue accents, and a massive floor-to-ceiling curved monitor that wraps around us.

"I'm hopeful," I reply as she takes a seat beside me. "Unlike what Rook encountered, this tech seems more like something we would build. I can't know for sure until we're able to look under the hood. But I'm thinking it's a fusion reactor that obeys the same laws of physics that we have to abide by. And even if we can't get it operational again, there's a good chance we could feed it with our own drive cores."

"Three ships, three nodes," she says.

"Possibly. But if we can power it with one drive core, I'd rather do that instead of risking all three ships. But... considering how *Parallax One* behaved, I don't think the pendleton orientation—"

"Pendellösung oscillation window."

"That. —poses a threat. Which is good, because if that thing does need more energy than one ship can provide, then we'll need to use all three ships, like you said. With any luck, we might actually get to see what's on the other side. Which I think is very, ya know, *zoom-zoom, bizzzzzow.*"

"Stop it," she says.

"*Fruff-fruff?*"

"Not funny. And *you* should be the embarrassed one."

"Why's that?"

"Well as I recall, I wasn't the one who Willow Shade hit on during a system-wide live verbcast."

I let out a dramatic sigh. "We each have our crosses to bear."

"Mmmm."

"So, you wanna do it when Rook gets here?"

"Excuse me?"

"Uh, the portal. *Do you want to explore the portal?*"

"Your face is super red," she says.

"Yeah, I… just…" *Son of a bitch*, words can be so hard sometimes.

"It's fine," she says with a laugh that helps put me at ease. "You're asking if I want to conduct an EVA with you to scout for entry points?"

My face must be turning ten more shades of red. And now I'm laughing. Whether or not they admit it, most every guy I've met is perpetually a thirteen year old boy trapped in an adult's body. "I'm… so sorry. I just…" Jesus, I can't even talk straight.

Fortunately, Evelyn is laughing too. "I'm only in if we have the right equipment."

"Oh my God! Just stop, please."

"I didn't even mean it like that, you jerk!"

"I can't breathe."

"Neither can I."

The moment peaks when we realize we're both crying, holding stomachs with one hand and our mouths with the other. Probably just stress trying to find a way out. That, and maybe… I dunno. Something we might have going for us? I can't tell, though. She's a hard read. Guess I am too for that matter. But, damn, this feels good.

Finally, the moment subsidies, and we both take in and let out long breaths that trail off with a few final chuckles.

"I needed that," I say.

"Same."

We share a look. Then it's gone.

"I'll go ready the EVA suits," she says, standing from her chair. "Let me know if you find anything else interesting."

"I will." I want to take her hand... say something more. But all that comes out is, "Take fun."

She frowns. "Excuse me?"

"Uh, it's... take care and have fun. I... don't know what the hell I'm saying." Before she can reply, I pull a true middle school move and terminate V-cog.

What the actual hell, Jericho? You need some sleep.

I DON'T SLEEP, of course. Despite being the very last member of POET needing to log some REM, the prospects surrounding Ring X are too exciting. So after an hour of trying to doze off, I shave and shower, grab something quick to eat in the galley, and then return to the bridge to watch the *Bellerophon*'s final approach.

"How they looking?" I ask the crew.

"Oi, like a fucking Christmas tree star plugged into a nuke plant and aimed at our eyes," Eddie replies. "But if you mean how does their drive sig compare to expected emissions values, then it looks pretty fucking good, Knight. *Wanker.*"

I've pretty much figured out now that Eddie only knows one mode: being a dick to everyone. In fact, at this point, I'd be worried if he wasn't being a dick to someone. As for why the perpetually nasty disposition? I still have yet to uncover that. But he's a vital part of this team, and I'm glad he's here if nothing more than for his foul-mouthed one liners.

"ETA?" I ask.

"Ten mikes," Magellan says.

Visuals show the *Belle*'s four engine cones on a four-g decel burn pointed straight at us. As per Eddie's commentary, they do appear like a Christmas tree star on the scopes, complete with lens flares. All readings look good, and the drone relay star map still has the Ganese swarm on Kep-C's far side, a little less than six hours away.

"I'm headed to bay one," I announce. "Crossing over to the *Sagan*. Keep me posted."

"Will do, buckeroo," Kit replies and then seems to refocus on a point in the near distance. "And so Captain Jericho Fox heads to the belly of the whale where he will depart for the *Sagan Explorer* and don a NUESSA extravehicular activity suit to explore our next mystery gate. Will he and Dr. Park discover a way to turn it on? Or will they be overrun by a new swarm of Ganesian crust-o-bots and have their faces melted by probes?"

"Kit."

"Sorry."

I make my way aft, enter the bay, and coast toward my locker. While not designed for prolonged spacewalks or maintenance missions, the *Koga*'s joint-branded NUESSA/Stellar Dynamics white form-fitting spacesuits are made from the latest nanocarbon polymers, allowing them to be tough and radiation resistant, both things I need to jump from the *Koga* to the *Sagan*. The *Sagan*'s spacesuits, however, are specially designed for everything from repair and maintenance to retrieval and heavy equipment manipulation. They're also rated for small object impact, industrial compression, and sustained emergency life support, all things that will come in handy should we get stranded on an alien portal that wants to eat us. Which is why I'm headed across.

"It is good to see you, my lord," Fergus says from the shadows.

"Jesus. Don't do that."

"Convey my satisfaction at your arrival?"

"No. Scare me." I take a deep breath and try to get my pulse under control.

"My apologies. That was ne'er my wish."

"If wishes were horses…"

"There would be considerably more dung in the yard, my lord."

This gets a laugh. "You're a strange bird, Fergy."

"Thank you, sir. Here to get suited up?"

"Yup."

"Very good. I'm standing by."

The team unanimously decided that, like the expedition to Eagle Rock, Fergus would come along for the ride. Between his strength and his ability to read and, if necessary, speak Ganesian, his presence would be an asset... so long as he erred on the side of staying quiet the majority of the time.

When I'm sealed up, I ask, "You ready?"

"I began my existence ready, my lord."

"Of course you did."

By the time the *Belle* comes to a stop half a klick away from Ring X, I'm sealed in the airlock with Fergus.

"Knight, this is Rook. How copy?" His face appears in my HUD along with Evelyn's.

"Loud and clear. Just about to leave the *Kogarashi*. You?"

"I'm ready to push for the gate with Teams One and Two."

"Roger. Let me get squared away with *Queen* first."

Evelyn winces. "Queen?"

"Your new callsign. And the one you've deserved all along."

"I'm not sure whether to be honored or disturbed."

"Disturbed?"

"Yeah, at how much Fergus is rubbing off on you."

"I like it," Rook says. "Queen it is."

"It's a bit dramatic, don't you think?" Evelyn asks me.

"And you're not?" I reply with a smile. "Anyway, we'll get set and then all depart together."

"Negative," Rooks says. "I advise that you allow us to set up a perimeter and then conduct a sweep to ensure the ring is free of potential threats."

"I get that. But I also need to make sure we get a look of what's in there, and I can't very well do that if you've stirred up a hornet's nest first."

"So you'd rather jeopardize your lives for the sake of science than play it safe?" he replies.

"It's kind of our thing," Evelyn says. "To quote some Marines I know."

"Fair enough."

"Anyway," she adds. "What's the point of having an armed escort if they don't get to use their guns to protect us from time to time?" To me she says, "This suit isn't gonna wait around all day, Jericho."

"Roger." Over the *Koga*'s comms channel, I say, "*Kogarashi*, this is Knight and Fergus, exiting bay one." I depressurize the airlock and then watch as the nanoseal separates and hull security doors slide apart. Beyond them is the eternal blackness of space and the radiant starscape. "Hello beautiful."

"I never knew you felt that way about me, my lord," Fergus says.

"I was talking to the scenery."

"Ah. The human preoccupation with the environment. I understand."

I push out through the doorway and orient myself to the *Sagan*. Both ships have moved closer together to make this jump as easy as possible for me. We're only 500 meters apart, which in space parlance is RDC—really damn close. Any nearer and we might as well go through the process of docking. My V-cog heads-up display directs me toward the *Sagan*, which is located at the two o'clock position relative to the ring while we're at the three o'clock position; the *Belle* has arrived at the four o'clock.

"I shall proceed to the specified landing point on the ring and hold short half a furlong where I shall await your pending arrival, my lord."

Dismissing his obtuse use of medieval measurement, I give him the okay and watch the excipion move out. A short burst of my own thrusters, and I'm on my way toward the *Sagan*.

As I cross the midpoint, I take in my surroundings. This is, after all, my first spacewalk in a foreign star system. The light hitting me from Earth is that of my umpteenth great grandparents, from back when they were raising families and working jobs in the segregated cities of the American Midwest three hundred years ago. Did they have any idea that their descendent would be doing this right now? Or that he would be thinking about them while traversing between two spaceships to investigate a quantum tunnel generator built by aliens? Guessing not.

"Bleed that speed off, Knight," comes Evelyn's voice in my head.

I glance at the time and distance to destination indicators and realize I've been caught daydreaming. I execute a quick flip and decelerate just in time to line up on the *Sagan*'s aft cargo bay airlock. The hull door is open, and I float inside.

"Everything okay?" Evelyn asks as the airlock seals and pressurizes.

"Roger. Just got a little lost in thought out there."

Thirty seconds later, I'm in a bay twice the size of the *Koga*'s and filled with extra-vehicular propulsion and research equipment, plus stacks of cargo boxes secured to the deck and storage containers strapped to bulkheads. Evelyn is already geared up in a chunkier NUESSA exploration suit and pointing to mine. It's maglocked inside a locker illuminated by LEDs. I look back at her and realize this is the first time we've seen each other in the real since leaving *Telemine* Station and *Parallax One*. The first time since she burned toward the portal. First time since she found out about Olivia. And beat the shit out of her.

"Hey," is all I get out. Yeah, I'm good with words.

"Hi. Glad you made it."

"Me too. You, uh, look ready to go."

"Just waiting on you, flyboy."

"Right."

For all V-cog's advantages, it certainly has its downsides. Like this. I've already had a few meaningful conversations with Evelyn about everything that's happened so far, but now that we're face to face in the real, I'm experiencing cog-dis, that is, cognitive dissonance between what I've lived in my brain and what I haven't yet lived in my body.

It takes me ten minutes to swap suits before I'm ready to exit with Evelyn. She's already got a proposed mission plan uploaded to my HUD. "We'll shove off the *Sagan* and make contact here," she says, pointing to the ring's four o'clock that's one of the hexagon's six straight sides. "It'll give us a first-hand look at one of your power generators."

"Supposed power generators," I say in correction.

"Right. Then we can investigate the *supposed* point of entry on the outside circumference. From there, we'll see where the internal structures take us. I've allocated sixty minutes for the walk."

"Let's make it happen." I activate the inner airlock door and float inside. When I look back, Evelyn hasn't budged. But she's got a wide smile on her face. "What?"

"How was it?"

"How was what?"

She gives a slight dip of her head and glance of her eyes to the main door behind me. "Being outside in a different star system."

"Oh. Yeah. Pretty amazing."

"I've dreamed of this my whole life, ya know."

"Well, better not keep your dreams waiting, Dr. Park."

Her smile grows wider, and she joins me in the airlock. With the door sealed behind us and the pressure equalized with the void beyond, I motion for Evelyn to take the lead. "Your ship, Queen."

Her smile is contagious, and I suddenly realized that I'm more excited to see her step outside than I was to leave the *Koga* myself.

"Opening aft bay door now." Evelyn activates the locking mechanism, and the panels slide away. At first, she doesn't move. She just… floats there, taking it all in. It also sounds like she's holding her breath, so I offer a little reminder.

"Breathe."

Her lungs expand, then she says, "It's… incredible."

The pragmatic engineer in me wants to say, "One vacuum is the same as any other vacuum," but logic can slay beauty if one isn't careful. Instead, I go for, "Sure is," and then follow her outside the *Sagan*.

"Queen and Knight departing *Sagan* now," she says.

"We see you, Queen," Rook replies over the team channel. "On you in four mikes."

We vector away from the ship, nice and easy, and follow the augmented reality path marker toward the ring's edge. On the *Koga*'s exterior cam network, which I have piped into a small monitor in V-cog, our bodies look like two spiders suspended on an invisible thread that stretches from the *Sagan* to the ring. The artifact's size reinforces the comparison as we get nearer. My neck cranes back to follow the leading edge above us. Moments later, we disappear under the far right corner, now within a hundred meters of our target.

Rook and his two fire teams close behind us. They've set landing reticles on the ring's hull to either side of Evelyn's and mine. For all our sakes, I really hope we don't need the Marine escort. But with Private Wijaya's death fresh in everyone's minds, I'm grateful for the military presence. That, and it's nice to see Fergus coming up in our flight path too.

"Greetings, your highnesses," he says as we fly past.

"Hi Fergus," replies Evelyn. "Care to join us?"

"Indubitably."

"Just stay behind us," I add.

"Of course, my lord."

As we cross the final thirty second mark, Evelyn slows and starts counting down the distance incrementally. The alien hull fills my visor, and I bring my feet around, making the landing zone my new down.

"Four meters," she says. "Three... Two... One..."

Our feet touch, and our magboots lock. The soundless strike sends a jolt of excitement up my spine. Annnd maybe a small jolt of pain from landing a little too hard; I forgot how much mass these exploration suits have.

"Contact. *Sagan*, we are secure," Evelyn announces.

"Roger that, Queen," Mishra replies. "All readings nominal."

Fergus touches down ten seconds after us. I look up and spot Rook and his eight Marines. If they're counting off distance to landing measurements, we don't hear it. They're coming in way faster than we did. Battlesuits flare, and then their boots kiss the hull like Olympic gymnasts landing on a mat in slow motion, weapons raised. Only now do I realize that they've set down in a perfect circle around us, guns pointed outward.

"Showoffs," I say to Rook.

"Lots of practice," he replies.

Evelyn rolls a hand through the vacuum. "Time to get to work, boys." She points to the first energy module about eight meters away and around the corner.

While we've landed on the ring's outside face, not far from where the suspected entry door is, our first stop is inspecting a power generator. The unit resembles a massive C clamp that straddles the ring from the inside, affixed to the front and back faces. I take the lead and walk around the front face to where the boxy structure begins. From here, it wraps around the inside face, and then returns around the back. The structure is almost three meters tall and twice as wide as it heads away from us and curves inward.

Unlike Eagle Rock, lots of writing and symbols adorn the surface. Fergus has uploaded his growing lexicon of Ganesian characters to V-cog so our HUD system is able to superimpose the translations almost instantaneously. Whether or not the verbiage makes sense is a different matter altogether. Evelyn is the first to laugh.

"Open here for happy flow rate access."

"Or," says Grabowski, looking between his feet, "bundled satisfaction below. Use concern."

A few more translation casualties get called out before I ask Fergus to help me remove several armor-plated panels along the midpoint where the generator adjoins the ring. He makes quick work of analyzing the release mechanism, cross referencing it against the examples he saw in Eagle Rock, and raises the metal cover along a hinged spine. Once three in a row are up, I stand back and give the site an approving once over.

"What is it?" Evelyn asks.

"It's part of a cooling manifold. Then those are power conduit trunk lines, I'm assuming. I think we can just barely see the outside of a reactor containment wall. But based on the trajectory of how it's weaving under-neath us, the shape of it"—I pause and look behind me—"yeah, the shape is unusual. I think they've come up with an alternate way to deal with neoclassical transport."

"Neo what?"

"It's, uh, a very specific kind of heat loss that plagues fusion stellarator designs."

"I'll take your word for it. You seem happy though."

"I am. It's encouraging. They've hit the same roadblocks we have, but came up with their own solutions, ones… Yeah, ones we've never seen before, at least from what I can tell so far. We'd need a lot more time to poke around. And I need to see inside."

"Well, time is the one thing we don't have much of," she replies. "Strike that. It's one of several things we don't have a lot of."

"Fergus, have you seen anything that resembles an exterior input or output hatch? Something that might lead to a, I don't know, like a giant receptacle or something? Maybe an interface patch bay?"

"Back where we commenced, yes." The bot turns and magwalks the way we came until he stands over a large metal cover on the deck. "The inscription summons the giants of the land—"

"To insert their massive appendages?" Rodgers finishes.

Grabowski hits him in the arm. "Something you know nothing about."

"Screw you, Steve."

"Only with massive appendages."

Rodgers flips him the middle finger.

"Open it," I say to Fergus.

The excipion bends down, works a few locking mechanisms, and then pries up on several leverage points that look better suited for crab claws than human – or excipion – hands. The panel rises away to reveal a hexagonal recess filled with circular nozzle ports of various sizes. Each one has a label and alphanumeric value.

"Jackpot," I say.

Evelyn studies the panel over my shoulder. "That mess means something to you?"

"If we can't turn this thing on from the inside, then this is our ticket from the outside. Granted, it'll take some interpreting and cross referencing between two schematics, but I'm hopeful."

"Hold on. You think they left *schematics* onboard?"

"I do."

"A little presumptuous."

"Maybe. But I can think of two reasons why."

"Listening."

"The first is the level of detail that they marked everything with out here. You don't do that unless you're anal retentive about record keeping."

"Fair. Second reason?"

"We would do the same."

"Anthropomorphize much?"

"I'm serious. I get not trying to project what we do onto them. But they're clearly builders like we are, and builders love their plans. You don't make something like this without having a schematic somewhere onboard. *Parallax One* has hard and virtual copies all over *Telemine* Station. Three hundred years after humanity goes extinct, aliens wouldn't have any problem finding our blueprints."

"Let's not and say we did," she says.

"Plus, blueprints are what the Naqualla sent in the first place, right? So, yeah, I'm betting there's something below."

"No time like the present," Rook says. "Burning daylight."

Fergus leads the way to the supposed entry hatch. Unlike the last entry humans made on an alien artifact, an act that involved explosive ordnance, I suggest Fergus approach the door like he was a giant crab. It takes him less than a second to identify claw-sized recesses on two opposing sides of the panel where I could envision a crustacean inserting digits and pulling up and away. Granted, I'm assuming that there was some sort of electrical or hydraulic system that moved this door centuries ago. But engineers typically think redundantly, at least the good ones do, and the Ganese are high on my list. If there's no power, there's always a manual option.

"I have encountered what I believe is a trigger system beneath the divots in this panel," Fergus announces. "I advise that you all stand fast in case it is, as you say, boobytrapped."

Rook echoes the sentiment and orders everyone back.

When we're far enough away for his liking, Fergus announces his actions and depresses whatever trigger latch mechanism he's found. I'm half expecting a pressurized air mass to shoot the panel off like Eagle Rock. Instead, the hatch comes away on articulated folding arms that reveal the mouth of a tunnel.

"It appears to access a corridor," Fergus says. "Would you like me to enter first?"

"Negative," Rooks says. "Team One will take—"

"Position behind me," I interject. "I don't mind the backup, but this needs an engineer on point."

Rook takes a second and then complies. "Geller, I want Team One on Knight's six, and give him your side arm."

"Roger," says the corporal.

"Team Two, you remain here. Queen, you're with me."

Everyone acknowledges, and then I move to the entrance. The hole is a meter and a half wide and dark, so I flip on my headlamps before demagging from the hull and diving in headfirst. The corridor is metallic and much more utilitarian than what we saw inside Eagle Rock. Shielded cabling is more exposed, as are mechanical and blank digital interfaces. But the same opposing grates run along the sides, giving the Ganese their crab-legged walkways.

The puzzle solver in me wants nothing more than to sit down and map everything I'm seeing. While I know the Sebastián and Enni of our team would be curious to find out what all this means for the evolutionary development of this alien species, my brain wants to know what solutions these creatures came up with for the same physical problems we humans encounter. But that will have to wait.

The tunnel ends a few meters ahead and presents three options. The first two are the largest routes that head north and south, or up and down, along the ring's circumference. But the third diverts laterally toward the middle and is the one I'm hoping serves as some sort of maintenance tunnel to the reactor.

Behind me, I spot Fergus and then Team One's Private Ibrahim followed by the rest of Geller's unit. No one has said a thing so far. They're all just taking it in. And waiting on me.

I float to the end of the maintenance tunnel and find yet another hatch dead ahead.

"Fergus?" I ask.

"Stand clear, your majesty." The bot passes me, lines up with the door marked Special Power, and opens it the same way he did the outside hatch. The translation is better suited to mean Authorized Access Only. Or maybe Drive Core. Either way, the room is important, and I've gotta hand it to the Marines for biting their tongues against making more jokes.

The hatch doors retract into the wall, and over Fergus's shoulder I catch sight of a medium sized room.

"Would you prefer that I go first, my lord?"

"No thanks, Ferg. Lemme through."

"Of course." He presses himself against the wall and allows me to pass.

Inside, my headlamps shine across what I take to be a wide command console, until I realize it's not *wide* at all. It's *tall*. The Ganese wouldn't approach it laterally like we would. Instead, they'd probably cling to the side walls and operate it vertically. So I reorient myself in the room to see it like they would. Molded instrument clusters and display screens spread around me, while the walls are covered with layers of conduit, junction boxes, and trussing. It all needs power, but anything that seems like it would provide power to the instrumentation is dark. So it's a chicken and egg scenario if we don't know what to initiate first or how. And I'm not hitting up Fred for instructions.

"Make any sense?" Evelyn asks. She's still back in the main tunnel but observing my feed through V-cog.

"Not yet. But they've certainly packed a lot in a small form factor. We're talking an immense amount of space if this is a fusion reactor like I think it is."

"Any thoughts on how to turn it on?"

"Not yet. I think some of that will depend on how the other two generators are constructed, and if there's a central command station to oversee them all or if these three units operate independently."

"Five hours, sixteen minutes remaining," Rook says. "What's the best use of our time?"

I think for a moment and then say, "We need as much data as we can. Eyes on hardware."

"And what would we be looking for?"

"If one of the other generator rooms is different from this one, that would be something. If there's an intermediary room between them, that could mean something else. And, of course, if we can find a blueprint, that would probably solve a lot. Rook, any chance you can split up to cover more ground?"

"Roger." To his Marines, he says, "Battlegroups, pair off. Recon north and south routes, double time. I'll remain here with POET Leads."

"And don't touch anything," I add in case someone has the bright idea of poking a shiny button. "Report points of interest, please. We don't wanna wake this thing up before we have the whole picture. You can also place the micro EM sensors we brought on any major trunk lines you see. They'll give us real time feedback if we manage to turn this thing on. Just do it carefully and space them every fifty meters if you can."

The Marines acknowledge and then head out.

"What do you want us to do?" Evelyn asks.

"We'll search the immediate vicinity for clues. Storage compartments, lockers, placards—anything that seems like it might contain information on the build. Meanwhile"—I point at Fergus—"I want you running a high energy scan. Your near field tomographic muon imaging array still working?"

"Indeed, my lord."

"Good. Then fire it up and start building an overlay for V-cog. Kit, you read that?"

"We're ready to receive, Cap. No problemo."

"Good. Make sure the rest of the *Sagan*'s crew get eyes on it. We need all the brains."

"Copy, Cap."

Evelyn and Rook acknowledge, leaving Fergus and me alone.

After a minute of scouring the console and trying to trace wire bundles, I ask the bot, "Are you making out any similarities in construction between this artifact and Eagle Rock?"

"There are several similarities, yes. Most notably in the physical corridors. Granted, this construction is far older than anything we encountered on Eagle Rock. Moreover, these halls would appear to accommodate Ganese moving about in spacesuits or their equivalent."

"Because this ring wasn't pressurized."

"Correct. Nor does it appear to have been during its construction."

That piques my interest. "Maybe because the swarm built it."

"It stands to reason, yes. Their robotic form does not seem to require air or atmospheric pressure for metabolic functionality."

"Which may also explain the more unfinished look

around here. The larger Ganese just came on board at the end to, what, turn it on?"

"Perhaps the Gan swarm handled all the *heavy lifting*, as it were." After a few seconds, Fergus adds, "Your body language suggests that you are lost in thought, my lord. Is something the matter?"

"Just thinking."

"Anything you care to share?"

"Not yet."

A few more minutes pass before teams start reporting in. Rook interfaces with the two-person battlegroups and says that no one has encountered any obstructions in their corridors. "They found the same exact style room as ours. Nothing looks any different."

"So they must be interconnected," I reply, more for myself than Rook.

"What's wrong?" Evelyn asks. "You don't seem to like what you're hearing."

"Eh, it's just... something doesn't add up."

"Which is?"

"Well... If the Gan swarm built this, then they're the real brains behind it all, right? Why do you need the larger Ganese to do anything? These screens seem completely unnecessary. And what about optical head tubes like we saw on Eagle Rock's bridge? There's nothing like that in here."

"But Eagle Rock was meant as a last outpost kind of thing," Evelyn says. "Lots more creature comforts."

"My point exactly. This place was meant for one thing."

"Turning on the ring," she says.

I nod and then look at our trusty excipion. "Hey, Fergus. If you were gonna build me a fancy new grid car, how would you make it?"

"Is this an endeavor you wish me to undertake, my lord?"

"It's a hypothetical question."

"Ah, I see. Then, hypothetically speaking, I would wish to ensure that it aligned itself with your desired preferences, along with meeting NUE regulatory safety standards."

"And in terms of operation?"

"Efficient, so as to minimize operating expenses."

"No, I mean in terms of what I need to do to operate it, to drive it, even from within V-cog."

"The goal of efficiency would also apply, seeking to minimize your need to do much of anything, my lord."

I thrust a finger at Fergus but speak to Evelyn. "And that's it."

"What is?" she asks.

I push back toward the console, eyes roaming all over it. "If I'm the Gan, then I'm making this thing idiot proof. I'm giving the Ganese what they want in terms of looks, making sure they feel included in the process... knowing what's going on and all that."

"Like having a speedometer even though you don't have an accelerator?" she asks.

"Exactly. But in the end, the Ganese don't actually need to be a part of making it operate."

"So… no blueprints then?"

I shrug. "Maybe I overestimated."

"So you're the swarm and you want to create a fully automated experience?"

"Yup. Which means that the bigger crabs would only need is to push one button… flip one switch." My eyes spot what they're looking for, in the console's middle just above head height. It's the same configuration of four holes that the Marines encountered beside a door on Eagle Rock. I missed it somehow. "There. Rook, ask if the others are seeing something like this too."

"Roger. Same everything."

To myself, I ask, "Could it be?" and move toward the holes.

When I extend my fingers, Evelyn says, "Jericho, careful."

"Shall I do it in your stead, my lord?"

"No, Fergus. Rook, if this does something, we might need the others to be ready to do the same."

"On it."

I study the four large holes and move my hand closer, assuming the clawed shape with my thumb, index, middle, and ring fingers. "God, I hope this doesn't hurt," I whisper. To everyone else, I say, "Here goes nothing."

16

EVELYN

JERICHO'S FINGERS slip easily into the holes like he's reaching for an oversized bowling ball. When nothing happens, he starts wiggling them around. But then I think about how a crab claw closes, and say, "Hey. Squeeze your fingers together."

He does, and as soon as they seem to touch, soft blue light emanates from the holes.

"Something's happening," he announces.

The light spreads away from his hand in blue lines that trace the screens and race out to light conduits running along the walls.

"Something is definitely happening," he says again.

"Would you like me to have the others do the same?" Rook asks.

"Just… give it a second," Jericho replies.

The screens blink to life, emanating a cool background glow overlaid with more scratchy Ganesian script. I lean in, hoping my helmet's augmented visual system will overlay the translated text. When it does, both Jericho and I read it at the same time. "Start house: one of three."

Fergus is first to say, "I believe it is waiting on the other two consoles."

Jericho turns to me. "Thoughts?"

"Your guess is as good as mine. I say try it."

"What about the ships?" Rook asks. "If this initiates another EPR bridge, I don't want to be caught too close."

"Good thought. But that leaves us onboard here, and I'm not sure that's any better," I reply. Then a thought hits me. "What happens if you take your hand out, Jericho?"

He shrugs and then says, "Removing my hand now."

Nothing happens. The lights stay on, the screens illuminated.

I reach to the side and touch a truss running along the bulkhead. "I'm detecting a faint vibration."

"As am I, your highness," Fergus says.

"So who's to say one person couldn't run around the ring and activate each console?" Jericho asks no one in particular. "It would let everyone else get clear."

"But it might fry them in the process," Rook replies. "It's too dangerous."

"Unless you are Fergus, the Ardent Conqueror of Malquith," the bot exclaims. "I shall sacrificially stick my fingers into as many holes on your behalf as my lord requires."

There's more than a little snickering over V-cog audio. Before it can get out of hand, I say, "Eagle Rock's systems responded to him physically, so that might not be a bad idea."

Kit, who's probably been biting his tongue this whole time, says, "But it could mean we lose Fergus too, and I'm not sure we can, ya know, afford that and all."

"I know, pal," Jericho replies. "But we may not have much of a choice."

"Or... none of this caution could matter," I say after a second. "The readings we got from *Parallax One* show that a human could have survived on *Telemine* Station during the activation. And we all traveled into and through the event horizon. So, while I think it's wise to task Fergus with this, I suspect a human could do it too, just as a Ganesian crab did."

"Point of correction," Fergus says. "They never actually activated their own gate."

"That's right," Jericho replies. "The Naqualla came calling."

"So," I say, suddenly inspired. "Are we saying this could be the first Kep-C activation of Ring X ever?"

"Looks that way," Jericho replies and then turns to the excipion. "Whadda ya say, Ferg?"

"Is it the will of my Creator?"

Kit speaks up again, though sounding somewhat reluctant. "I mean, I guess, if no one else is, ya know, willing to put their lives on the line."

"Pretty safe to say that's not happening," Jericho replies.

Kit takes a deep breath. "Okay, Fergus. But be careful, right? I… *we* don't wanna lose you, pal."

"I shall endeavor to use all precautions necessary, Supreme Cosmic Creator. Likewise, I expect your great and merciful hand to accompany me on my quest, and should any ill befall me, I relinquish my soul into your eternal care."

"Uhhh, okay then. Guess that settles it," Kit says.

"Good," I reply. "Let's all get to our respective ships. Then we'll back off to minimum safe distances before Fergus activates the third and final power generator."

"Assuming they all work," Jericho says. "This artifact is old enough that I'd be surprised if we don't run into at least one snag or another."

"A task for which I shall be duly ready to undertake should my services be required, my lord," Fergus replies.

"Fair enough."

"I'd like to keep the *Belle* in an engagement position too," Rook adds. "In case of unexpected hostility. We need to be ready for anything."

Again, I'm reluctant on this suggestion. The last thing I want is for the Naqualla's first impression of us to be one of violence. "That's fine," I say at last. "Just please keep any projected chest puffing to a minimum. We're trying *not* to provoke a conflict. By the looks of it, we wouldn't stand a chance anyway."

"Roger."

I hail Natalie over comms.

"Go ahead," she replies.

"I want drones ready to go. Assuming Ring X works like *Parallax One*, then we have fifteen minutes to gather as much data as we can."

"On it."

Back to Rook and Jericho, I say, "Looks like we have a plan.'

"Let's fire it up," Jericho says.

IT TAKES everyone twenty minutes to get settled on their ships and another ten to make sure the vessels are in position. Even with all that, we still have four hours forty-three minutes remaining until the swarm arrives. By the time the *Sagan* has come to a complete stop, returning to zero g's, I'm clear of my EVA suit and back on the bridge.

"Drones ready?" I ask Natalie.

"Cheng and I have six set to fly. He's with them in

the forward bay. Now that we know there's transit time involved, I think it's safe to say we'll need a second opening event to recover them if it's anything over seven minutes."

I nod in understanding. "Seven minutes through, one minute to scan, seven minutes back before the fifteen minute auto shut off."

"Right. So, in the absence of a solid connection, and in the event that the transit time is above seven minutes, I've programmed a cascading recall mission that won't activate until a second opening is achieved."

"Good. What about estimates on the connection component?"

"Well, all three of us—the *Sagan, Koga,* and *Belle*—lost grid connection shortly after entering the EPR bridge of *Parallax One.* We don't actually know if that was the NUE Navy jamming us or a result of the EPRB. So I don't actually know if we'll be able to maintain positive connection with the drones. Obviously, if we can, it'll make things that much easier. But I won't be holding my breath."

"Understood. I want the drones out and standing by. Think they'll be okay hugging the ring?"

"I don't see why not," Natalie replies. "All our other electrical devices tolerated the Pendellösung oscillation window and corona emission just fine. Cheng has readings on all that too."

"Good. Deploy them now, I want them ready to duck in as soon as the bridge is established." With Natalie and Cheng launching the drone probes, I check back in with Jericho to see how Fergus is doing.

"He's standing by, inside the second generator command room now," Jericho says.

A live image of Fergus pops up in both real and V-cog displays. "Your humble servant awaits."

"Alright. And Rook?"

"Standing by, Evelyn. We have weapons systems online but with power diverted to auxiliary capacitors in case the enemy has advanced sensors to detect energy proximity to main guns."

"They're not our enemies until they show hostile intent," I correct.

"Of course. My apologies."

On this note, I decide to send out a simple reminder for everyone's sake. With my physical body buckled into my captain's chair on the *Sagan*, I enter the mission command theater in V-cog where all of POET's avatars are gathered for the ring's activation. "Remember, we assume the best even if we're planning for the worst. If these Naqualla are holding the secrets to solving things like food scarcity and climate restoration, then we certainly don't want to bite the hand that feeds us. Understood?"

Confirmation icons stream down the side of my

virtual chat window while heads nod and other people give verbal assent.

Rook and Jericho join me at the lecture table. We're focused on the large wall of holo windows. Not only has each ship got a slightly different view of the ring, but we have feeds coming in from the drones as well as Fergus's POV. Additionally, there's a system star map still depicting the major components, including Ring Y, Kep-C, Eagle Rock, Ring X with our three ships, and the swarm now four hours thirty-six minutes away.

After conferring quickly with Jericho and Rook, I turn to Kit who's seated in the first row. "You wanna do the honors?"

"Who, me?"

"Mmm-hmm."

"Holy biscuits! I mean, uh, sure, Dr. Park. I'd be totally honored and stuff." He seems to take a second to compose himself until I realize he's recording himself again. "So there I was, asked personally by all three POET captains to order Fergus to activate Ring X. Now there's a flood of raw emotions going through me. It reminds me of the first time I saw my true love, Abigail. She was walking across—"

"Don't keep your public waiting, Kit," Jericho says.

"Oh. Right, sorry. Uh"—he brings up Fergus's profile and command interface—"Hey, Ferg?"

"Yes, my lord?"

"You can go ahead and activate the next two terminals now. With haste, and stuff. But not too much haste, ya know? Don't go breaking anything."

"As you wish, your eminence."

After the second power unit comes online, Fergus sets off for the third and final activation room. A target reticle tracks his movement along the ring's perimeter in one of the holo displays while his POV cam gives us the seat-of-the-pants experience.

"Is it weird?" Jericho asks from beside me.

"Is what weird?"

"Meeting another species who received a carrier signal and built their version of *Parallax One*? 'Cause it is for me."

"It is rather uncanny, yes. First we find out we're not alone, and then we find out that we're *really* not alone. The whole thing is"—I push some hair behind my ear—"well, it's probably gonna take me the rest of my life to process."

"You're not alone." He winks at me.

Cute. "I'm just glad I'm not the only one *seeing* it this time."

"Yeah?"

"Sure. For so long, my work on *Astraea* Station… it felt like me against the world, ya know? People don't realize that even interorganizational progress was hard fought with the kinds of things I was proposing. 'Here comes the crazy lady again.' I could practically see their thoughts as I walked hallways and into conference rooms. Finding SESI grants, getting NUESSA hardware approvals, not to mention public opinion, it all just…"

"Felt like the whole world was set against you?"

I nod.

"Know the feeling."

"Granted," I say. "I was placing bets on black when everyone else was betting on red. Very few people took me seriously."

"Well, I think it's safe to say they are now. Or at least will be when we get news of all this back to them. Must feel good."

"And kinda terrifying. We are, quite literally, on the edge of the known, about to open a door to the unknown."

"For the second time in twenty-four Earth hours," he adds.

"Right." Just then, his avatar's hand slips into mine. "We got this, Evelyn."

"Thanks." I wait for him to let go. He doesn't. Which makes me feel self-conscious and tempted to look behind me to see who's watching. But then Fergus inserts his fingers into the final console.

"We've got positive EM readings," Ramirez says from his sensor station on the *Sagan*. "Trace light emission from all three nodes."

"Wavelength?" I ask, barely able to contain myself.

"Same as *Parallax One*, boss. Eight hundred twenty nanometers. Pulse length holding at 25 femtoseconds."

Ramirez ports all the incoming data to the team displays. Broad-spectrum radiation, thermal, visible light, plus real time feedback from the EM sensors the Marines placed internally.

"It's happening," I whisper, then turn to Jericho. "Ring X is producing the same results as *Parallax One.*"

"It's a miracle."

"Not really," I reply. "If we consider that the signal was probably—"

"Not the readings. I mean it's a miracle that the *hardware* is still operational after all this—"

The meters go dead.

"—time."

"What happened?" I say to my crew aboard the *Sagan.*

"It just… stopped emitting," Ramirez says.

I ping our excipion. "Fergus? What's going on?"

"Uncertain, your highness. But I can assure you that I did nothing reckless or mischievous."

"It's not him," Jericho says. "It's the ring itself."

"System failure?" I ask.

He nods. "Baby's old. I'm kinda surprised it got as far as it did."

"Can you repair it?"

"Depends on what *it* is."

"We might have another problem," Corporal Korvich adds. "The swarm has just picked up speed."

"What? When?" I ask.

"Looks like… less than half a second after Fergus fired up the ring."

"They sensed it."

"And now they're coming to investigate," Jericho says.

Several team members swear while others stand and start pacing.

"What's our new delta?" Rook asks Korvich.

"Time to contact stands at one hour sixteen minutes, assuming there's no additional changes."

"Copy."

"Seventy six minutes to troubleshoot an alien artifact that creates a wormhole?" Jericho says while running a hand down his face. "Jesus."

"The alternative is we take another pass around the planet," I add.

"Assuming they follow us," Rooks says. "For all we know, they might glue themselves to the ring after this. Maybe even try dismantling it like they should've before."

"Oi. What about leaving a team inside the ring?" Eddie asks. "We could work on repairs while the ships are gallivanting around the fucking countryside."

"Too dangerous," I say. "It would leave the team exposed."

"We could deploy a fire team for cover," Geller says.

"Wouldn't be enough," Rook replies. "There's no

telling how many might divert. We're talking significant casualties if it's any more than a handful."

"Have a little faith, Master Sergeant," Geller says.

"I *am*, Corporal. You don't want to hear my pessimistic predictions."

"Oh."

17

JERICHO

"WHAT DO you need to start examining the ring?" Evelyn asks me.

"Well, as luck would have it, our best tool is currently onboard Ring X."

"Fergus?"

"Fergus."

"Fergus," Kit echoes.

"Shall I respond to all three of your summons at once or individually?" the bot asks.

"I'm assuming command priority, Ferg," I say. "That okay with you, Kit?"

"Totally, Cap. Of course!"

"Understood, my lieges. I am ever at your disposal, my corporeal form at your discretion."

"I need you to max your tomographic output," I say.

"Start at your current location and retrace toward the previous command point."

"Doing so will utilize my energy reserves, sire."

"I understand. Conserve enough to get back, but we need as clear a picture as possible of what's going on here. Cross reference with everything you've downloaded from Fred too."

"As it has been said, so shall it be done, my liege."

"More muon imaging?" Evelyn asks.

"Yeah. We need to talk through the worst case scenario here."

Rook nods. "Assume the ring is irreparable."

"Correct."

"Which means we're stuck in this system," Evelyn adds. "We're at the mercy of someone activating *Parallax One* again."

"While avoiding the Gan and rationing food and water," Rooks adds.

"We could speed the process up a little," Kit offers. "I mean, of finding out what's wrong with Ring X, not speed up the process of dying in limbo. 'Cause that would be dark, right? First you—"

"Jesus, Kit. What?"

"The drones."

I turn to Natalie Mason. "You said they're RD-24's?"

"Of course," she exclaims. "Why I didn't I think of

that? Their material resonance sensors could aid Fergus, especially if he has command privileges."

"Make it happen. Kit?"

"Yes?"

"Nice thinking."

"Thank you, Cap."

"Assuming Fergus and the drones find the issue," Evelyn says. "If not, we might need to leave them behind if we need more time."

I expect Kit to throw a fit, but he's the first to voice affirmation of the idea. "That's not a bad idea, Dr. Queen. I mean, Miss Park. *Dr. Park.* Sheesh, call signs are hard. That's why I could never be a Marine, ya know?"

Rook raises an eyebrow and looks at Kit. "Yup, that's why."

"What I mean to say is that the swarm might not detect them, ya know? They're looking for biological data and stuff."

"Or the swarm sends them tits up in the process of dismantling the ring," Eddie says. "Then we've lost our translator should we encounter any other fucking artifacts in this system, ones we may need for our survival."

I check the time. "We have just over an hour to talk through the pros and cons. Let's hope Fergy finds a fix fast."

"Ha!" Kit shrinks from his outburst, then shyly says, "*Alliteration.*"

THERE'S JUST thirty one minutes remaining until the swarm arrives when Fergus pings the leaders gathered around the lecture table. "I believe we've stumbled upon the bane."

"Whatcha got?" Kit asks. He, probably like the rest of us, sounds grateful for the intrusion in what was shaping up to be a pretty depressing discussion about our options. The ideas ranged from arming Fergus and the drones in defense of the ring to seeing if we could make Eagle Rock habitable for long-term human survival.

"There appears to be a rupture in the subsystem that aids in the maintenance of energy equilibrium."

"Power conditioning," I say, more for my own sake than anyone else's. "Do you have visuals?"

"No, sire. Only material resonance scans."

"Even better. Bring it up."

A wireframe composite image generated by the RD-24's appears in a holo window above the table. Everyone leans in to study what appears to be a hole in the hull.

"High speed debris strike," I say after a few seconds. "Not enough to completely destroy a main system, but bad enough to puncture the plating and weaken a few of the peripheral systems. Man, this is interesting."

"What is?" Evelyn asks.

"Well, it looks like they concentrated the most important systems in the middle of the ring's internal structure. See these larger trunk lines in the core? I'd bet crypto those are transfer power conduits. Essential for sharing massive amounts of energy and data. You sever one of those, and an entire side of the hexagon needs to be replaced. But the smaller bundles out here toward the hull?"

"Like where the damage is," Kit says.

I nod. "Those are less important."

"We build the same way, right?" Natalie asks.

"Not always. Usually, we're more preoccupied with form factor and jamming as much as we can into as small a space as possible. Sometimes fragile things don't end up in the best spot. Here, however, it seems that the little guys have built a hierarchy of system importance from the inside out."

"Think you can repair it?" Evelyn asks.

"That's the million-coin question." I rub the back of my neck. "Without a schematic? Without being there?"

"There's no time," she rightly concludes. "Just the EVA out and back would take twenty minutes."

"So we need Fergus to do it."

"Which he's more than capable of," Kit says. "Now that, ya know, he's been liberated."

"Right, sure," I say, but not even I sound convinced.

"I don't understand the hesitation," Evelyn says, eyeing me. "He's a space maintenance excipion. This is

---

what they do." She looks between me, Kit, and Eddie. "Right?"

Eddie scratches the new beard growth coming in along his neck. "Fergus is a Stellar Dynamics model SME-31. He was built for repairing space stations. So, oi, something like this shouldn't cause a rub. But that's because he has an archive of every blueprint of every piece of hardware floating in fucking space."

"I still don't get it. Can't he use that as a basis for this repair?"

"We call that improvising," Eddie replies.

Kit jumps in. "Which is something they're definitely not allowed to do. *Until now*."

Evelyn searches our faces. "So Kit's made it possible for him to think outside the box. I... still don't see the problem. This is good for us, right?"

"Wrong." Eddie shakes his head and looks down. "You ever see one of those brats try to make a fucking finger painting?"

"You're... talking about a child?"

"Oi. Fucking knee bangers. Point is, it takes them the bloody part of twenty to thirty years before they're fucking Vincent van Gogh. And even then, he's one in a million."

"What Mr. Eddie and Cap are trying to say is that even with a quantum neural matrix, Fergus isn't guaranteed to make the right calls out there. Like children, bots need lots of guidelines to, ya know, make good art and

stuff. While it might not take him thirty years, it will definitely take more than thirty minutes."

"Oi. It's only in the fucking movies that the damn
metal heads are miraculously able to do everything and
save the day. Meanwhile, the rest of us in the real have to
suffer through the tin wankers' shortcomings and
constantly tidy up after 'em."

"And we can't afford for him to make mistakes," I
finish. "Not on something this important."

"You can't guide him from here?"

"That's a given. But you know as well as I do that
there are things we're calculating in our heads that we
don't have time to explain when the pressure's on. Plus,
we're not always right either."

Evelyn nods slowly. "So what you're saying is that we
would need to trust him with this repair. Minimal guidance... improvising..."

"And a whole lot of Hail Marys," Eddie adds and
then makes the sign of the cross.

"Kit," Evelyn says, squaring with him. "I need you to
look me in the eye and tell me if you think Fergus is up
for this. You know him and his capabilities better than
anyone else."

"Thanks, Miss Evely—"

"*Can he do it?*"

Kit glances at me, then Eddie, and then back to
Evelyn. "Yeah. He can. Plus, even though he lacks the
experience, he can move faster than Cap."

"Which means he can fuck things up faster than Cap too," Eddie points out.

"Then it's our best option," Evelyn replies. "I vote to let him try."

"Same," says Rook. "I don't wanna risk losing any more crew members today. If he can't do it, we order him to burn away with the drones. We get the hell out of here and then check back when we have a safety margin again."

All heads turn to me to give the final vote.

"I'm for it," I reply. "Just wish it was me out there."

"How much time is left?" I ask anyone willing to give me an update. I'm too focused on Fergus's work to look up. He's been salvaging metal from the bulkheads to use as solder, combining what he perceives are redundant lines in order to gain material enough to recreate missing extensions, and spot welding free-flying conduits in new positions to expedite their repair.

"Nineteen minutes, thirty-nine seconds and counting, Cap," Kit says. "Not to state the obvious here, but we're kinda reaching the point of not being able to send drones through the portal and get information back, right?"

"One problem at a time," I say, then shout at Fergus. "No, no, no! That's an optical line. Don't heat that!"

"My apologies, sire. That would have been a sizable error."

"Jesus."

"Here," Nairobi says in the real and presses a water pouch into my hand. "You need to drink something."

"This better be liquor." I break the seal with my teeth and squeeze the pouch. The water feels good and provides a momentary reprieve from having to watch Fergus's every move. He is fast, I'll give him that. But he's also made more than one bad decision that's almost cost the project. "Stop! I think that's data, not power."

"Ah. So it is."

"Fucking fingerpainter," Eddie says under his breath.

I down a third water pouch by the time the clock hits the first preset marker we've settled on.

"Fifteen minutes," Korvich announces.

"And the repair?" Evelyn asks me.

"Fergus?"

"Twenty-five seconds more, my lieges. I cannot thank you enough for bestowing upon me the gravity of your trust. It is unto me a boon of such grandeur that—"

"That you need to stop talking and focus on wrapping this up, pal."

"Of course, sire. I shall sing your praises another time."

I grab Evelyn's arm. "You know this might not be the only failure."

"I do. We discussed it."

"Just want to make sure you're not caught off guard."

Finally, Fergus finishes what he and I both believe are the last of the repairs.

"Think it worked?" Evelyn asks.

"Only one way to find out. Fergus, restart the activation sequence."

"As you wish, my lord."

We all watch the main display as Fergus's reticle begins a counterclockwise journey around the ring's perimeter. His POV cam conveys just how fast he's propelling himself through the corridors as the sidewalls streak by.

"I think he was holding out on us before," Rook says.

"Maybe a little," Kit concedes.

Fergus slows himself with his thrusters, catches a grate with one hand, and hurls himself into the first control room. He lines up his fingers with the receiving holes and then jams them into the console. The room lights up as before with the main diagnostic screen welcoming the Ganese operator.

"One down," I say as I double-check the time. "Two more to go."

Fergus doesn't even waste time in replying. He ducks back into the main corridor and shoots through it, sidewalls passing in a blur.

"I might be doing throw ups very soon," Igor announces. "Is much motion, yes?"

I ignore the comments and focus on the star system map. The swarm is thirteen minutes away.

Fergus enters the next room, inserts his fingers into the receiving holes, and then waits for lights to cycle on. They do, and as soon as the display screen registers its "two of three" status, Fergus backs out and continues down the corridor.

"Natalie, you still ready with those drones?" I ask.

"Standing by."

Another few seconds, and Fergus rounds into the final control room. He jams his digits into the holes and waits. And waits. And waits some more.

"Nothing's happening," Evelyn says.

"Dammit. I knew it was too good to be true. Fergy, I need you to—"

The lights come up, and the console's display goes live. A beat later, the crew lets out a collective sigh of relief.

"Good work, Fergy," I say as the startup sequence begins. "Now get back to the *Koga*."

"Shouldn't I remain on site in the event of another failure?"

"At this point, I'd rather have you onboard and circle back later. Let's stay together."

"As you wish."

Evelyn

WE WATCH Fergus back out of the room and find his way clear of Ring X. I gotta hand it to him, Kit, and Jericho: that was some impressive repair work. I honestly didn't think it was going to be fixed in time. Maybe even at all. But here we are, and Ring X is cycling up.

From his seat on the *Sagan* and in the V-cog command theater, Ramirez says, "Confirming positive EM readings and light traces from all three nodes as before. Eight hundred twenty nanometers. Pulse length holding at 25 femtoseconds."

"We're picking up 100-centimeter diameter beam emissions too," Cheng adds. "Hydrogen banks look fully saturated."

We don't have access to whatever sensors the Ganese built to measure the pion-to-kaon ratio as the reaction climbs, but I'm already starting to see the faint blue glow forming in the triangle's center.

"Landau singularity detected," Ramirez announces. "Same as *Parallax One*."

"Guessing PK ratio passing eighty to one," I say. "Everything else looking good?"

"All systems nominal," Natalie replies. "Drones still standing by."

The triangular blue aura is getting bigger by the second and starting to obscure the stars behind the ring.

"Photon emissions on the rise," Ramirez says. "Detecting negative gravity waves, frame-dragging… it's exactly as before, Evelyn."

I still can't believe we're seeing this *again*. "Hull temps?"

Eddie comes back fast. "Rising, but nominal."

The spheroidal shape forms in the triangle's center. Ramirez is first to call it out. "Detecting Aharonov-Bohm QG effect. I've got blueshift, traces of Hawking radiation, and a Maxwell field. All readings match those taken from our last event. *Koga*, can you cross-check and confirm?"

"Roger," Eddie replies. "Non-conforming secondary surfaces detected with LIDAR."

A few seconds later, a tunnel starts to appear in the swirling sea of light.

"Prepare for corona emission," I say, grabbing my seat's arms. The burst should do little more than brown out shielded systems, like it did before. Still, an EMP this big is worth puckering up for. "Guessing PK ratio is reaching max any sec—"

A wave ejects from the Landau window and meets our ships, making our physical and V-cog displays dim while also causing the hair on my arms and legs to stand up. As soon as the wave is past, I ask, "Report?"

"*Sagan*, all systems nominal," Ramirez says. The *Koga* and *Belle* are unfazed as well.

When I look back at Ring X, there's a fully formed perfectly clear tube of swirling blue light. It begins at the ring's hazy laser-edge and then bends inward toward infinity. And it's breathtaking. "We have visual on EPRB," I say. "Confirm."

"Sensors confirming Einstein-Podolsky-Rosen bridge," Ramirez says, his voice alight with excitement. "We've got another wormhole, people!"

"Someone mark time?"

"Roger," Rook says. "Got your back, Queen."

"Natalie, let's get those drones moving."

"On it."

Six new windows appear on the command wall. Each drone sends a collage of visual, IR, and telemetry data as Natalie orders them into the tunnel in ten second increments. They surge around the ring from the back side and enter the hexagon from different angles. I don't expect there to be any divergent paths or cause for harm on one side of the tunnel or the other, but staggering and scattering assets is standard procedure. My eyes are glued to the screens as the RD-24's cross the threshold. This operation was what we were supposed to be doing the first time we opened up *Parallax One*. Better late than never. Right away, I notice that there's zero signal degradation. No digital static. No course deviation.

"They look good," I say to Natalie, trying not to sound too hopeful.

"So far, yup. Like they're just a few klicks in front of us in regular space." She focuses on her control menu. "I wanna try something." One of the drones rotates 180 degrees. The visual light moves from blue to red as the *Sagan*, *Koga*, and *Belle* appear in the drone's cam. "Redshift detected," Natalie says. "Amazing." The drone turns back around and continues through the wormhole.

Just then, a line of static flickers in the lead drone's feeds. "See that?" I ask.

"Yeah," Natalie replies. "Not what I was hoping for. Maybe it's just a—" She's cut off by more static interfering with the connection of the lead RD-24 and then spreading back through the rest of the drones. "—fluke. Guess not."

As the last of the drones succumbs to a total loss of signal, I turn to Jericho and Rook. "We have our answer about signal integrity across wormholes."

"I still don't get why it wouldn't maintain connection," Rook says.

"It must have something to do with the gravity involved and whatever nucleus is helping stabilize the walls of our tunnel. Not to mention the fact that even though those drones seem to be only a few klicks in front of us, they're actually traveling significant interstellar distances. At least, that's what we're predicting, based on what happened to us." I glance at the star system map showing the swarm's approach. "We've got less than eight minutes."

"We need to make a call," Jericho says. "Visual monitoring is out."

"And since we don't know how long this tunnel is, the drones might not be coming back with their intel before the fifteen minute mark is up."

Rook is stroking his chin. "It'll be at least another three hours before we circle back and try again... assuming the ring is still operational after the swarm does whatever it's gonna do."

"I vote we proceed," I say, matter of factly. "We've come this far. Might as well see how deep the rabbit hole goes."

Jericho rubs the back of his neck and exchanges glances with Rook. "Same."

Our Marine Master Sergeant lets out something that verges on a moan. "It's reckless, insane, and probably going to get us killed."

When he doesn't continue, I ask, "But?"

"If you can't even cover one light year in your own lifetime, I don't see how hundreds or even thousands more make a difference. I'm in."

"Okay, everyone. If you're not already secure, get there now," I say to the crews gathered in the theater. "We're heading in."

Thirty seconds later, all three ships are powered up and accelerating toward the Landau window. My stomach is doing backflips as we near the wormhole's mouth. Wherever this is taking us, it's surely one more giant leap away from Earth. But that also means it's one step closer to finding the answers our species needs to survive. They're out there, I just know it.

We race past the artifact's perimeter, and the next thing I see is blue light moving from stem to stern on the external camera feeds. We're in an Einstein-Podolsky-Rosen bridge again, making history. Stars know if any of us will ever live to tell about it. But I guess that's all part and parcel of pushing the limits of science and exploration. If you're not living on the edge, you didn't push hard enough, right?

Since all three ships are already on a ship-to-ship local area V-cog network, we don't notice any signal loss from entering the wormhole since there's no grid network above Kep-C anyway. The only thing concerning me is not being able to monitor the swarm. Of course, there's always the chance that they decide to follow us in, but based on their disdain for the Naqualla, none of us have thought that was a realistic possibility. Which, the more I think about, the more I wonder if we should have…

Stars. Too late now!

I give orders for Ramirez to keep accelerating until we've matched our previous speed when we entered *Parallax One*. We're not burning as hard as we did then, so it will take longer. But if we can get close, it will help our relativistic models draw better conclusions when conducting comparative analysis on the traverse times. Eventually, he cuts the mains, and we're coasting in zero-g again.

No one speaks for several seconds. My heart is pounding heavily in my chest. I review some of the conversations I had with the science team about what would happen to the wormhole if the swarm destroyed Ring X or if Fergus's repair job failed. Does it instantly collapse? Or does it close in on us from behind? We all decided entering was worth the risk. But I wonder if I may have undersold my assurances about safety, predicting that no matter what, the wormhole would eventually spit us out the other side.

"Negative energy density is increasing," Ramirez announces. "Same as before."

"Time?" I ask.

"Passing six minutes... now. But we still have a ways to go if this active galactic nucleus is the same as the last."

"Meaning what?" Rook asks. "We're making a bigger jump?"

"Crossing a greater distance, yes," I reply. "The AGN is the midway point."

"You think it's logarithmic maybe? Like, if we travel 300 lightyears in nine minutes, will we travel ten times that in eighteen or something?"

"Honestly? No idea. This is a first. For all I know, there's no correlation at all, and the wormholes, distances, and times are arbitrary. Maybe even fluid. We don't know."

"So shut up, take a number, and sit down?"

I smile at him. "Something like that."

We ride in silence for another minute or two when Jericho says, "The swarm has reached Ring X. All things being equal."

I glance at the system map that's now operating on estimates instead of real time data. Sure enough, we've passed the eight minute mark, and the swarm has intersected the ring. A new knot has formed in my gut. I wonder if any contingent of the swarm has decided to come after us. Or attack the ring. Or...

I shake *what ifs* from my head. "Stay focused on the task at hand, Eves."

"You good?" Jericho asks.

"Sure. Just... ya know, traveling across folded space-time with a cyborg alien swarm somewhere behind us and an unknown destination ahead of us. Totally fine. You?"

"Same."

"Uh, looks like energy density has peaked," Ramirez says. "I think we're on the AGN's backside now."

"Mark the time," I say and glance at the mission clock.

"Ten minutes, four seconds," Rooks says. "Making our total traverse time just over twenty mikes."

"Well, it's a good thing we didn't wait for the drones," Natalie says.

Which reminds me. "Anything from them?"

"Negative. Still just static."

Now that we've crossed the tunnel's midpoint, the exterior cams show the light has shifted from blue to red. We're chasing the light that's leaving the wormhole's nucleus—definitely a sign that we're on our way out.

I force myself to settle back into my captain's chair, knowing we have another ten minutes ahead. I walk to the far end of the table and take a seat on a stool. Rook joins me.

"Nervous?" He nods at my hands.

My avatar is twiddling its thumbs, which mirrors what I'm doing in the real. "Stars. You?"

He shakes his head. "I have a lot of practice at compartmentalizing and taking advantage of distractions."

"Like?"

"Talking to an attractive woman sitting on a stool at a bar." His avatar manifests a shot glass of tequila and offers it to me. The drink catches me off guard. Or maybe it's how he said that I'm attractive. The whole thing just... has me thrown off a little. I glance at the shot, knowing it won't do anything to calm my nerves... unless this is code from Kit. Maybe it is. And I need the drink. Which Rook knew.

Another shot of tequila appears in his hand, and he throws it back.

"No drinking on the job," I say.

"Only if it's flat."

"And is it?"

"Why don't you find out, Queen."

I stare at the tequila in my hand, feeling slightly unnerved that I might be drinking illegal stim code. And that Rook has called me attractive *and* used my new call-sign in a way that seems... overly familiar. I mean, we are familiar with one another. But we've been through a lot. Does he... like me? *Stars.* I throw the drink back. It burns going down, and I slam the glass on the tabletop.

"See?"

"See what?" I ask.

He nods at the mission clock.

A whole minute has gone by. "Creating distractions," I say with laugh. "Need to add that to your CV."

"Noted."

"Illegal stim code user too," I add, pointing to the glass. I can already feel the real life buzz stimulating my mesolimbic pathway. "It's not flat."

"Maybe yours isn't." He grins. "But I'm on the job."

Rook raises a hand to get our attention. "Now that we have a new scenario in front of us, I'd like permission to put the *Belle's* weapons systems on standby should we encounter any initial resistance ahead. Likewise, prepping our shuttles for rapid recon deployment wouldn't hurt either."

"Having the rest of the RD-24's ready to deploy would be wise too," Jericho adds, walking over to join us and then eyeing the shot glasses. "Drinking on the job?"

I ignore the inquiry and refocus on Rook's proposal. "I want to be cautious about looking like we pose a threat."

"We'll only be dangerous if someone else chooses to be first," Rook says.

I don't know if it's the illegal stim code or just an abundance of caution, but I relent. "Okay. Just try to keep it as low key as possible. I don't want to—"

"Unnecessarily raise anyone's hackles. I read you, Queen." Rook pushes away with Jericho to join some others near center stage and make arrangements. I watch them walk away and then roll the empty shot glass between my fingers. A lingering drop of tequila slides around the bottom, like Rook's comment. He thinks I'm attractive?

"THIRTY SECONDS TO ESTIMATED EJECTION," Ramirez announces. This gets everyone's attention.

I abandon my stool and shot glass to join Jericho, Rook, and some of the other leaders watching the main display. While the tunnel's red light seems to stretch into infinity, the math says there's an exit ahead. There's a strong sense of excitement in the command theater. Everyone's standing in the theater, eyes locked on the display wall. I've tried not to get my hopes up. They were dashed with Kep-C, despite the amazing xenoarcheological find. But at the same time, whatever we find on the other side of this exit could change the trajectory of our species for all time. And, damn, if I'm not ready for it.

I hear myself countdown the last moments, and then…

Just like that…

We're through.

PART 2

18

EVELYN

THE CHAOTIC REDSHIFTED TUNNEL VANISHES, and the *Sagan*, *Koga*, and *Belle* are in clear space once again. Without celestial references, it's pointless to say what speed we're traveling at, but Ramirez did meet our traverse constant of five kilometers per second. Therefore, it's within reason to assume we've exited at the same rate. The question we all want to know, of course, is where are we?

"Ramirez, I want a location as fast as you can," I say from the ship's bridge.

"On it."

"Life support?"

"Nominal," Seb replies.

"What about the drones?" I ask Natalie.

"Reestablishing a connection now. Stand by."

"We've got another ring behind us," Cheng announces. "In holo now." He pings V-cog with the camera feed at the same time that it appears above the *Sagan*'s main console. Sure enough, there's a silvery circular artifact to our aft. "Looks just like Ring Y."

"Sure does," I reply, my brain already running wild with questions. "Natalie, where are our RD-24's?"

"I just picked them up. Looks like… Yes, we have all six. And they've found a—" She does a double take with her holo display.

"A what? What is it?"

Natalie swipes her screen to the bridge's main display area. "See for yourself."

The sight of a new planet dumps adrenaline into my system. And not because it's some barren lava-flooded rock like Kep-C. This one is covered with vast stretches of blues and greens, dappled with beige and gray, and smeared with wispy clouds and solid white polar caps.

"Stars! Are you seeing this, Jericho?" I ask.

"Sure am," he says, voice barely above a whisper. "It's…"

"Beautiful."

"Yeah."

"I hate to interrupt the discovery here," Rook says. "But I need to remind everyone that we might have a tail. I recommend that the *Sagan* and *Kogarashi* diverge and accelerate while we flip and cover our six."

"Copy that," Jericho says.

"We can also send two RD-24's back through to scan for the swarm," Natalie says.

"But we'll lose connection," I say. "And who knows what happens if the bridge closes while they're inside."

"True. But they're expendable. And I'll program them to backtrack the moment they detect anything."

"Works for me," Rook replies. "The more eyes we have scouting, the better."

Ramirez speaks up. "We have a positive lock with the local star. Looks like a K-type main-sequence. Populating to ship and LAN V-cog servers now."

"Roger that, *Sagan*," Magellan replies. "Thanks for the ref. We have it locked in."

"Same," says Corporal Popov aboard the *Belle*. "Flipping now. Preparing to engage possible hostiles."

Magellan's voice comes back calm and collected. "This is the *Kogarashi*. Relative to the new star as primary fixed position with planet-on-plane, we are bearing zero seven nine, mark one two six, commencing emergency three-g burn in three, two, one…" The *Koga*'s engine cones light up on scopes as it pushes away.

Ramirez inputs a course forty-five degrees off the *Koga*'s matching their speed and pointing us toward the planet's north pole. He counts down and then activates main engine burn. The force pushes me back in my seat, but I hardly feel the pressure. I'm too energized by the discovery of a new planet, too consumed with the implications.

I glance at the untitled star map that Mishra has put on the main display in the command theater. We've been in this system for less than sixty seconds, and she already has it populated with the star, the planet, and what she's designated Ring W. Our three ships are also represented, with the *Sagan* and *Koga* burning away from the ring in different directions while the *Belle* continues to coast away, weapons online and aimed at the ring. I keep one eye on scopes, eager to see what, if anything, emerges from the wormhole, and the other on the new planet. It's currently 22,000 kilometers from our position, far enough for us to see the full sphere edge to edge. Likewise, the star's range is estimated at 112 million kilometers, a figure that will update as the computer gets more precise measurements. I can't help but make a connection between the distance and the new planet's apparent condition: we're right in a K-type's habitable zone.

After one minute, the engines shut down, and I decide to check in with Rook via V-cog. His avatar is still standing at the lecture table onstage. "Anything yet?"

"Negative."

I sense he's puzzled about something. "What's wrong?"

He nods at the holo display showing the *Bellerophon*'s forward-facing external cams. "We can't determine if the Landin window is still there."

"*Landau.*"

"Right. It's like when we exited Ring Y. When we looked back—"

"It just appeared to be regular space."

"Exactly. So, is it closed?"

I turn to my team. "Ramirez? Natalie?"

Ramirez answers first. "Photon emissions are consistent with ambient levels and similar to what we recorded after arriving at Kep-C. Nothing to raise any concerns over."

"And our two scouts are still en route," Natalie says.

"So," Rook says. "The answer is, we don't know."

Ramirez shrugs. "Seems so. Maybe the passivity is part of the design."

"How so?" Jericho asks.

"Like a one-way road where the initiating ring determines the direction of travel. You can only enter from one side, and always out the other."

"Riiiiight," Kit says from across the table. "It would keep ships from head on collisions and stuff."

"Makes sense," Jericho says. "But that means that if those drones don't disappear then we have no way of knowing if the swarm are on their way, right?"

Now it's my turn to shrug. "Relatively speaking, the portal closed about"—I check our mission clock—"about seven minutes ago. If we take the total time to travel the tunnel and deduct seven minutes, assuming the bridge stays in tact if the entry closes, and nothing else emerges, then we're in the clear."

"Marking," Rook replies.

"In the meantime, you want us to slow down?" Jericho asks.

"No," I reply. "We're both headed toward the planet. I vote we burn on, enter orbit, and scan as much as we can. Between our sensors and the remaining RD-24's, we should be able to cover considerable ground. Mishra, how do comms look?"

"Everything's quiet. I've initiated binary sig first contact protocols, so I'll let you know if anything bounces back. But for now this whole system is as silent as they come."

"The rest of the drones are ready," Natalie adds. "I'll deploy when we're closer."

"Sounds good," I reply. "Rook, pick up our trail as soon as you're done."

"Roger that. Forging paths…"

"Through the darkness," I answer.

MUCH TO EVERYONE'S RELIEF, the critical emergence window passes without an appearance of the Ganesian swarm. Likewise, Natalie's two scout drones fail to disappear into a Landau window. Whether or not the swarm has disabled or destroyed Ring X is another matter, but one we'll have to wait on. In the meantime, Rook decided to give our newly named Ring W a once-over before joining us. Initial scans seem to indicate that it is an exact replica of Ring Y, which leads us all to believe that it was created by the Naqualla to send a carrier signal to Kep-C.

"If so," Jericho says, "then is it a stretch to think that this planet was... I don't know, intended for the Ganese to discover?"

"That's my working theory," I reply. "In the absence of the Ganese venturing this way, the Naqualla built a second carrier signal ring and pointed it toward Earth."

"Holy biscuits," Kit says. "So your guys' theory about them being species savers is true!"

"We're a long way from knowing what's true, Kit," I reply. "This is all speculation."

"Yeah, sure. I get it. But still, I mean, wow, right? This is, like, *phew*. Ya know?"

"I do, yes. It appears as though the Naqualla wanted someone to find this planet."

Speaking of planets, we're less than three minutes away from reaching an altitude of 2,000 kilometers above its surface where we'll pick up an equatorial orbit beginning counterclockwise while the *Kogarashi* starts from the opposite direction. We've already lost line of sight to them; only the *Belle* is allowing us to stay connected via laser LAN relay. Alternatively, we've deployed the first of several communications buoys that will eventually create an active grid, but it won't be continuous until we've circled the planet.

"We're sixty seconds from blackout," Jericho says. "But so far, all our readings are very promising."

"Same," I reply, hardly able to contain myself. "The *Sagan*'s initial sensor sweeps are detecting high levels of nitrogen, oxygen, carbon dioxide… plus moisture rich atmo, equatorial surface temps ranging from twenty-three to thirty-one degrees Celsius. Land to ocean ratio is roughly three to one. It's all there, and it's…"

"Perfect," Kit says, then immediately follows it with, "Oh, gravy gravel! I just jinxed it again, didn't I?"

"Only if you say *gravy gravel* again," Rook replies.

"One of my pop's originals. You don't like it?"

"Moving along. How about signs of advanced civilization?"

"Nothing in orbit," Natalie responds. "Drones say skies are clear too. And so far there's no indication of terrestrial development at all."

"And we still don't know where in the galaxy we are?" Jericho asks.

"No," Ramirez replies. "Not yet. But we're getting closer. The computational power needed to analyze the starscape from a completely different orientation is fairly immense."

Jericho smiles and shakes his head.

"What?" I ask him.

"What are the chances that we just found an untouched Goldilocks planet in an unknown part of the galaxy?"

I find myself suppressing an involuntary laugh. "Now you're gonna be the one to jinx it!"

"Just saying." He examines the sensor feeds and a peaceful look crosses his face. "Evelyn, you…"

"What?"

His avatar is frozen.

"Jericho?"

"Signal lost," Rook says. "Hold that thought for an hour."

"Copy that." But I'm pretty sure I know what he was going to say.

WHEN THE *SAGAN* and the *Belle* finally catch up with the *Kogarashi*, all of us burning to a standstill on the planet's far side, several things are immediately clear. The first is that there's no sign of a technologically advanced civilization on the planet's surface, in the air, or in orbit. No cities, no vehicles, no satellites. Of course, we can't rule out there being something under the ocean surfaces, nor can we dismiss the possible presence of some species that can evade our detection methods, either due to size or stealth, but specialized searches will come with time. For

now, we're all jumping, if not prematurely, to one aston-
ishing conclusion.

"Why don't you just say it, Evelyn?" Jericho says
after we've shared results.

I can't help but smile as I look around the command
theater to seats filled with equally excited people. We've
all been waiting for someone to speak it aloud. Might as
well be me. "I guess what we're saying is, we've stumbled
upon a completely virgin and totally habitable planet
that's within Earth's gravitational and bio-sustaining
parameters. We did it. We've found... paradise."

This gets a spontaneous eruption of cheers, one
that's been building for the last hour as everyone poured
through the initial data. Hugs are exchanged, and I get a
little lost between embracing my crew in the real and
everyone else in V-cog. We're all laughing, crying, high
fiving... it's a euphoric feeling. I seem to have had my
share lately; discovering the signal from Kep-C was a
historic moment, as was building and turning on *Parallax
One*. But this? Stars, this has implications that go beyond
cohabitating the universe. This is about finding an
untouched world for us to relocate to... about saving
humanity.

"And we still don't know where the bloody hell we
are?" Eddie says with his hands on his hips.

"Actually," Ramirez replies. "I think I've got it."

But only a few of us hear him.

"Oi! Shut the fuck up and listen, you twats!"

This gets everyone's attention, and all heads turn toward Ramirez who's taken center stage in the V-cog command theater. He gestures toward the main display, and an image of our new planet appears orbiting its star. "It took me quite a while to triangulate our position, but I think I finally have it."

"You think?" Eddie asks.

"Yeah, because... well, almost every star I was trying to reference isn't visible from Earth."

"Which means we're really far away," I say.

"Oh, definitely. To the tune of 982 light years."

All the virtual air gets sucked out of the room. "I... I'm sorry," I stammer. "Did you say—"

"Nine hundred eighty-three light years, yes." Ramirez zooms out, and out, and out until Earth's sun is a pin prick on the galactic map. Kepler-1649 is labeled too and still 60 percent closer to Earth than we are. "To put that in perspective for the non-astrophysicists, even at the *Kogarashi*'s top speed, it would take Jericho and his crew 12,371 years to reach our current position."

I take it back: *now* all the air is sucked out of the room. "So what's our star, Jose?"

"Kepler-440. K-type. And well suited for biological evolution as we know it."

"I know this star," I say, examining it. "I did some work on planet 440 b with the NGST."

"The what?" Afumba asks.

"Next Generation Space Telescope. We predicted it

was a rocky super earth. But what we're seeing here doesn't look like that."

"Because we're not at 440 b," Ramirez replies. "That's over here." He zooms back to our present star system and pings a massive planet on the star's far side.

"Then if that's 440 b, what did we find?" I ask.

Ramirez shrugs. "Your guess is as good as mine, Dr. Park."

"Planets don't just appear out of thin air," Rook says. "Do they?"

"No," I reply. "But at this distance, studying stars and planets isn't always an exact science, no matter how much we like to think it is. It's quite easy to miss a planet, especially if it's always in something else's shadow."

"Which is what I assume is happening here," Ramirez interjects.

"Same. Plus, with trillions of systems to explore, and only so much hardware, we miss more than we find, I hate to say."

"So it doesn't even have a name?" Rook asks.

"Nope." I noticed people's eyes widening at the prospect of naming a brand new planet. "Conventions dictate we expand on the original nomenclature. But in this case, I think something more original might be in order. Something more... personal."

"Soteria," Sebastián says at the same time that he raises his hand like he's a student in a lecture hall. "It's

Greek for salvation. In the mythology, she's the spirit of deliverance and protection."

"Soteria." I try the word out and then look at Rook and Jericho. Considering the fact that it could take a committee years to settle on a name this important, and that I happen to like the title despite its obvious spiritual overtones, I make a motion to adopt Seb's suggestion before anything muddies the waters.

"Better than calling it planet 440-whatever-letter," Rook says. "You astrophysicists aren't exactly the most creative blokes."

"So we've been accused," I reply. "Jericho?"

"Works for me. And I like the meaning."

"Soteria it is," I say. And just like that, we have a new planet name. I'm sure a thousand years from now, someone will have a whole legend of how the planet came to be named. Little could they know that it was settled in under thirty seconds and not a shot fired.

The second most important thing to discuss is the discovery of yet *another* ring on Soteria's far side. Yup, Ring V, built exactly like the other Naquallan rings, only without the forward facing emission nodes for signal carrier transmission.

"Which means what?" Nairobi asks. "That it was towed here through space by the Naqualla?"

"Another mystery added to the growing pile of unknowns," Kit says, clearly recording himself for posterity again. "How did it get here? Who brought it?

How old is it? And, more importantly, do they have collectible t-shirts in human sizes to commemorate its arrival?"

Ignoring Kit's burning questions list, I add, "We should still get a scan of it, but chances are it's as inert and inaccessible as the last two Naquallan rings we've encountered."

"I recommend a sentry drone stationed at each ring in case someone gets the bright idea of coming through while our backs are turned," Rook says.

"I second that," Jericho adds.

"Just make sure it asks questions *before* firing. Loiter, patrol, or whatever you call it, copy?" I say.

"Roger that, Queen," Rooks replies.

"Now, on to the big time." I turn to the topo map of Soteria. Each kilometer the drones cover adds more detail to the burgeoning chart. Images are mapped over LIDAR wireframes like skin and clothes laying atop skeletons. There's also a growing stream of metrics that my crew has been updating since Natalie deployed the drones. "Initial measurements give Soteria a circumference of 39,591 kilometers, putting it 484 shy of Earth's. With relative mass proportional to the difference, we're looking at a reduction in gravity so minute no one will notice.

"The planet looks to have five mega continents, two that span the northern and southern hemispheres, split east and west, one that occupies the north, and then two that sit in the south. Mountain formations indicate tectonic plate movement, but most of the shifting seems to be quite old given the lack of volcanic activity."

"Meaning things have calmed down?" Nairobi asks.

"Yes. And that's a good sign for us. As is the absence of any significant meteor strikes, as far as we can tell. There are no signs of recent impact craters visible in the geology."

"What about the caps?" Eddie asks.

"Two polar ice caps, neither of which seem to have land masses beneath them. Again, that may change as the data becomes available."

"Flora and fauna?" Afumba asks.

Sebastián lights up. "I think it's safe to say that as much biodiversity as you might expect on Earth you can expect here, and then some. Without an industrial revolution and human expansion to hinder biodiversity or perpetuate climate change, there are potentially many more species than anything we're used to."

"Like dinosaurs?" Kit asks with eyes wide.

Seb stifles a laugh. "Perhaps. But I wouldn't get your hopes up. The type of life on Soteria depends entirely on the age of this planet and the time since its most recent cataclysmic event."

"The meteor that wiped the dinos," Kit says.

"Correct. Our dinosaurs on Earth were the dominant vertebrates for almost 200 million years before they met their end. Then you have hominids, basically our most ancient ancestors, clocking in at six million years old, with ape lineages ranging anywhere from five to eight million years. But we Homo sapiens are only about 100,000 years old. The point is that we believe life on Earth has been around for over four billion years… that's *billion* with a B. So even with a massively long occupation, you only have a five percent chance of visiting Earth when the dinosaurs were alive. And Homo sapiens? The probability is something on the order of 0.0025 percent. So, do I think we're going to encounter humans or tyrannosauruses? No. But I won't rule out lots of plants, animals, and microorganisms that we might need a few hundred thousand years to get used to."

"Get used to?" Magellan asks.

"He means biocompatibility," Enni replies. "Can we breathe the spores from the vegetation? Can we digest nutrients found in the wild? Can we survive stings and infections, rain showers and contact with dust mites? It's all completely new and potentially hazardous given that we did not evolve on this planet despite its apparent similarities with our homeworld."

"So," Kit says nervously. "You're basically saying we gotta watch out for what happened to the Martians in War of the Worlds?"

Jericho pats Kit on the shoulder, "You got it."

Igor raises a hand to speak. "I am recommending all expedition to surface treat mission as biosafety level four. Suit, twice decontamination, quarantines, all of things."

"Agreed," I say.

Kit waves both hands. "So, so, so… we're gonna go to the surface?"

"You volunteering?" Rook replies.

"Who me? Um… I, uh—"

"Don't hurt yourself, kid."

"*Huh-uh huh-uh*, right."

"There is one thing we need to consider from an optimistic standpoint," I say. This gets me a few sharp looks, especially from Jericho and Rook. "I know, I know. I'll try not to give you too much hope. But given all the effort the Naqualla expended to reach us and build portals to this destination world, if that's what we suspect it is, I would think they had the wherewithal to determine biocompatibility, at least to some extent."

"That's wishful thinking," Jericho says while thumbing to Enni. "She gave us quite a list of things to be worried about."

"I warned you it was optimistic."

"But not entirely outside of the realm of reason," Seb says. "Consider the planet's distance from its star, as well as its mass. Hypothetically speaking, I have every reason to believe that most all the dominant species on Kep-C could have easily survived here on Soteria, at least given what we know at the moment. Likewise, humans would most likely have flourished on Kep-C in its most stable state too. Isn't that what we're all assuming anyway? That whoever the Naqualla are, they knew we were all biocompatible with Soteria."

"Oi, what about the timeline?" Eddie says. "We're almost, what, a thousand fucking light years from Earth? That means the Naqualla set up camp here at least as long ago, plus the extra hundred years they took to mop up on Kep-C."

Enni offers to field this point of conversation. "Geologically speaking, not much happens in a thousand years. Which actually adds to Dr. Fernández Parra's earlier points. If the Naqualla wanted to invite the Ganese or we humans to a planet that would kill us, there are easier ways to do our civilizations harm."

"*Like global planetary invasion,*" Kit says with his eyes squinted. This gets him some sour looks. "What? It's true."

To Rook I say, "Can we utilize one of your shuttles for a surface exploration mission? I recommend the crew be split with equal parts science officers and Marine escorts. Thoughts?"

"Roger that. AOPC 13s, Tiger class."

"A what now?" Seb asks.

"Atmosphere-to-orbit personnel carriers. The Tiger class holds three crew—the pilot, co-pilot, and loadmaster—and room enough for ten passengers and related gear. We'll split those seats, so pick your top five and we'll do the same."

"Alright. Give me a few minutes to form a team, and then we'll organize the rendezvous."

"Roger."

I look at the *Sagan*'s crew. "Any volunteers?" Of course there are: every last hand goes up. "Why do I even ask?"

19

GEMMA

REPRESENTATIVE GERALD WILLIAMS was a terribly predictable man. He ate the same meals morning, noon, and night, played the same nine holes of golf every Tuesday, Thursday, and Saturday, and always arrived five minutes early to every appointment he had, never allowing a single one to extend beyond forty minutes. Williams's religion was keeping his schedule, which made Gemma's job of locating him all the easier.

The Southland-based Solum Terram representative for District 300 had been dodging calls from Sallsworth's office for days. A few misses here and there were to be expected from any busy politicast party member. But when Sallsworth himself was ignored, Gemma was called to make an appearance at the Williams estate outside Sydney. Gerald got a massage every Friday evening before dinner as a reward for his long week of running the family business, which was little more than collecting dividends on old money and, presently, shirking requests to give Sallsworth his vote.

This was Gemma's first outing under their newly formed Sallsworth Agreement, but the fifteenth meeting overall. She'd distributed the other requests to Androsia Behr and Leonidas X, Eldon "Skitz" Pearlman and Radio Ultra, and Tonka for his Bembe Militia. Many hands made for light work, and it was important to keep the dogs well fed. But Williams was of particular interest to her because Nigel said he might need more persuasion than usual. Sallsworth meant violence, she knew. Gemma had another plan. Not every dissenter could turn up dead; that would raise suspensions. So she decided to experiment with her newest V-cog exploit and see just how far people were willing to go in the real to avoid threats posed in the virtual. If the test went according to plan, Sallsworth would get exactly what he wanted and be none the wiser for it while Gemma learned a bit more about the human psyche, flimsy as it was. It was a win-win.

"Ready," Williams said from inside the massage room between the family gym and the indoor swimming pool. The health center was in the mansion's basement level with windows that looked onto a lush backyard and a dense forest beyond. Seclusion. Excess. Power. The Williams Family had it all.

Gemma slid the Japanese shoji doors apart, taking care not to damage the translucent paper within the latticework wooden frames, and then padded across the bamboo floor. Williams lay face down with a white sheet over his buttocks and legs, ready for Clara to set in on his muscles. Gemma guessed how the man might rebuff at the news of Clara's unfortunate cancellation, so she held the revelation until her hands were on his flesh. He would sense the difference soon enough, but it was always harder to refuse someone when they were providing pleasure.

"Oh, how I missed those hands, Clara," Williams said from beneath the face rest. After a few more seconds, he raised his head part way. "Clara?"

"I'm so sorry, Mr. Williams. Clara was unavoidably detained with a family emergency tonight. My name is Gemma."

"Is she okay?"

"It seems one of her children had an allergic reaction that needed medical attention. But everything will be fine, I'm told."

"That's good to hear."

"Please relax now, won't you?"

That's all it took for Williams to lay his head back down, let out a deep breath, and accept the lie. Gemma laughed inwardly. People also spoke about those in power as being untouchable. Being smarter than the person on the street or the one in the gutter. How foolish. People were people, and if you knew one, chances were you knew them all.

"What did you say your name was again?"

"Gemma, sir."

He repeated her name if tasting it, a notion that made her stomach turn. *Couldn't the rich just get a normal massage? And, my God, Clara had children. She was married even!*

"Ow," Williams said. "Uh, a little less pressure maybe?"

"Of course. Anything you want."

Gemma eased up and started working away from his shoulders. "May I ask you a question?"

"Depends."

Gemma didn't bother waiting. "What do you think of Sallsworth's idea?" She felt the man's body tense under her hands.

"Gemma, is it? I know you're new, but I prefer to leave all talk of my professional life out of these sessions."

"Of course. But you must have an opinion, don't you?" She pressed her palms into his trapezius muscles, producing a groan of pleasure from him.

After a few more moments, he came around. "His request for more space military spending is against the party line. It won't happen."

"I'm not talking about *that* bill, Mr. Williams." She leaned in toward his ear. "I want to know what you think about him creating and holding the first Office of the President of Earth."

Williams raised his head, but Gemma pressed it back down. When he tried to press himself off the table, she drove her elbow into his spine, not enough to break but certainly forcefully enough to send stars shooting through his vision. He let out a lungful of air and collapsed.

"What's the meaning of this?"

"You don't call back. You don't write. Nigel is beginning to think you don't like your place in the Solum Terram anymore."

"You work for Nigel?"

"Stay on task, Gerald. For your own sake. Why are you avoiding him?"

"He's... he's..."

"I'm waiting."

"He's *insane*! The NUE is staunchly against a single leader at that level. It will never happen." Gerald tried to push up again, but Gemma hit him in the same spot, knocking him back down. For all its power and alluring charms, the human body was so pitiably weak at the end of the day... so easy to overcome if one knew how.

"So, I take it he can't count on your vote?"

"No! Never!"

"Perfect."

GEMMA FLAGGED her driver and waited for the car to stop. The passenger side gullwing door flew up and she slid into the Pagani Huayra E-Type, wiping her hands on a towel.

"Drive."

The driver nodded and sped away from the Williams estate's front gate. At the same time, Gemma pinged Sallsworth in V-cog. "Mr. Sallsworth."

"His vote?"

"What, no, 'Hi, how are you?' Or, 'My, don't you look—'"

"*His vote?*" he said more sternly.

"If we're going to keep working together, you really need to work on your manners, Sally. He'll vote in your favor. You'll get the call in the morning."

Sallsworth smiled, though she thought she detected a hint of skepticism in his eyes. "How'd you do it?"

"I strapped him to a chair, slit his wrist, and bloodlet him to within an inch of his life."

Sallsworth went pale. She liked that.

"You... can do that?"

"Please. You saw firsthand how to take a life in V-cog, didn't you?" Her expression was flat, but eyes fixed on his. "As long as you get them out before the brain assumes the final conclusion—"

"Death?"

She nodded. "—then the person is no worse for wear. Fear, Mr. Sallsworth. That is the great equalizer."

"Quite so." He loosened his collar and took another drink of the glass he'd been holding. It seemed he was coming to grips with the scope of her abilities. Little did he know, however, that Gerald Williams not only complied because of how she'd cut him, but because of what she'd created around him. The breaking of physics. The upheaval of gravity. The bending of reality. It all served to craft a nightmare that went far beyond those experienced during sleep. A person could escape from dreams. Startle themselves awake. But from V-cog? There was no exit if Gemma kept the door to consciousness firmly locked. "And his reasons for not taking my calls?" Nigel asked.

"He's in the middle of a remodel with one of their properties. Wasn't taking anyone's calls."

"Mmm. I'm sure he'll take mine in the future, after tonight."

"I should think so." She smiled. "You should have seen the look on his face. Anyway, I'm off. Call me if you need me for some real work."

"Goodnight, Gemma."

"Peace out." She threw a peace sign in V-cog and then cut the connection. "Jackass."

Lemuel

IT was the third time Caleb Nowen had called in the last ten minutes, and Search for Extrasolar Sentient Intelligence Director Lemuel Brown had silenced each V-cog notification. He was at dinner. With his wife. Alone. How often did this happen? He knew not to try to answer that question, even rhetorically. And certainly not counting the last year. Ever since Dr. Evelyn Park had captured the Kepler-1649c signal, life hadn't been the same. For anyone. Least of all, him. Lemuel was the middleman between the Infinita Gate Project and the rest of the world. Every budget, development, and science question that humanity could ask seemed to land on his desk in one way or another. But if it allowed his science teams to do their jobs, then answering them was a price he was willing to pay. Because he believed in his work. In *their* work. And now that Evelyn and two other ships had disappeared into *Parallax One*, he was invested all the more. Which made dinners with his wife a rare commodity.

"Where are you right now?" his wife, Rayanne, asked across the table. "Earth to Dr. Brown?"

He rested the forkful of steak on the edge of his plate and dabbed at his lips with the cloth napkin. "You deserve better than me, Ray."

"You got that right." She gave a look up and down and then sipped her Merlot. "Shoot."

Brown laid the napkin back in his lap and frowned at her.

"What is it, Lem?" She asked finally. "Work?"

"It's Caleb."

"Nowen?"

He nodded.

"What's he want?"

"I silenced the calls."

Rayanne set down her wine. "He called more than once? You're telling me you ignored that fine looking man more than once?"

"Three times in ten minutes."

"Sounds important."

"*You* wanna call him back?" he asked, knowing how she'd respond.

"And get my hopes up? *Nooooo*. We both know where that leads."

Lem smiled. "Alimony."

They both laughed.

Lemuel liked how playful his relationship with Rayanne had become as they'd weathered three decades together. Where poking fun at each other and discussing celebrity crushes had once been a source of anxiety, now it was part of their normal banter. He knew that Ray would no sooner leave him than a cat would leave a favorite scratching post. They were bonded in home and habit. But the daydreaming did make for witty banter… and occasionally some fun after-dinner activity, when they had the energy.

"Call him back," she said, taking his hand.

"It can wait." He picked up the fork and studied the meat. "It can always wait."

"Until it can't. Lem. Three times in ten minutes? Something's up. And 'Frat brother don't leave frat brother hanging,' as I recall."

"Is that what you think we sound like?"

"It's what you sound like."

"We don't sound—"

"It's *exactly* what you all sound like, Lemuel. Make the call."

"You're the best."

"You just figured that out?"

LEMUEL WALKED out to the restaurant's bar-side balcony and moved away from the patrons enjoying the evening air. He'd be in V-cog, of course, but he still didn't want to be seen or heard if this call got serious. And somehow, he thought it might.

He brought up Caleb's contact and stepped into his public lobby, a simple waiting room with a bookshelf, two chairs, and a plant. The only giveaway that anyone fun owned this construct was a framed poster of Grant Winderhouse doing a slam dunk.

"Lem," Caleb said, appearing to the left.

"Cale. How you…? You look—"

"Like I haven't slept in a few days?"

"Something like that. What's going on?"

"Thanks for calling me back. But… we can't talk here."

"It's… *your* V-cog lobby." Lemuel frowned. "You okay, brother?"

"Yeah, yeah. Sure. Can you host?"

"Sure. No problem. But—"

"Please, Lem."

Lemuel nodded and called up his private V-cog suite, a darkshelved den with his brass telescope and glass doors. Hosting a call wasn't the issue; Caleb asking for it as if his own spaces, his own nanotech were being monitored was. And that either made Caleb paranoid or in trouble. And Cale was never paranoid.

Lemuel started out behind his desk but quickly got up and took one of the two leather chairs just before Caleb arrived.

"Sorry to be all cloak and dagger like this, Lem. I bother you?"

"Dinner with Ray. But she's cool. What's going on?"

He rubbed his hands together as if the motion might help summon the words from his mouth. "I think something's going on behind the scenes, man. Something bad, ya know? They found Lemmens in his pool, man. Drowned. Said it was an accident. Then Phillips was killed in a car wreck, and Latif didn't show up for the budget meeting 'cause they found his body in a—"

"Woah, woah, woah. Slow down, Cale. What are you talking about?"

"They're dead, man. All dead."

"When? How?"

"Thirty-six hours."

"But I haven't heard a—"

"Under the radar, man. And that's the thing. I think someone's picking 'em off and keeping it under wraps. You know what they all have in common..."

"Besides being our friends? Shit." Lemuel knew where Caleb was going with this. Each man was a politicast party representative. "You suspect someone is targeting them?"

"Murder, man. One hundred percent. And it's freaking me out."

"The authorities—"

"Are saying nothing. Two of the forensic reports I

could get my hands on says there's no sign of foul play. Everything checks out."

"But not to you."

Caleb shakes his head. "Lemmens was—"

"Captain of the swim team."

"And in perfect shape, man. No way he drowned in his own damn pool. And Phillips's car accident? They said he turned off the auto-driver and did 200 on the roads leading up to his house. First of all, that man hasn't driven his car in twenty years. And secondly, you don't do those speeds out of Farmington Heights. It's literally a death wish."

"And you've run this up the flagpole?"

"I've tried. But I'm just getting the company statement of assurance. Problem is, they're not seeing what I'm seeing."

"Because the victims are all in different politicasts but still our friends."

"Bingo. And that's the pattern, Lem. These hits are against *everyone*. And whoever's calling the shots has good cover and plenty of resources."

"How many?"

"Seven so far, that I count. But now I'm tracking three more party representatives who aren't returning calls and seem to be off grid."

"Chamber's 375 members, Cale. Even if it's ten, people die every day."

"But not like this, man. I'm telling you. Something bad is going on."

"What do you need from me?"

"Eyes on the inside."

It took Lemuel a second to put together what he meant. "I haven't talked to Vivian in over a year."

"You don't need to talk to Vivian. Just reach out to Tré and see if he's available."

"That's not how they work. Hell, what am I talking about? They're criminals, Caleb. That's the whole reason we don't talk."

"You know what they say, in order to catch a criminal you gotta think like a—"

"You gotta call the bureau and use your office to talk to someone high in the tower."

"But that's just it, Lem. I don't know how high this goes. Which is why I can't use the proper channels, at least not until I know more." He rubs his hands on his thighs. "I feel it, brother. Something big is happening. Trouble is… I'm on that list too. And you know it. Southlands 361."

Lemuel holds his eyes for a few more seconds but eventually looks away. "I'll… call Vivian."

"Thank you."

"But no guarantees."

"Got it."

"And no family and friends discount unless she offers. This is your paycheck going up in smoke, not mine."

"I understand."

Lemuel watched his old college roommate fidget even after getting what he clearly had called for. "You gonna be okay?"

"Sure, sure. Yeah."

"If you need a different place to stay…"

"I'll be fine. Thanks, brother. I owe you. Give my love to Rayanne."

"And to Charlotte." Lemuel stood, took Caleb by the hand around the thumb, and pulled him into a one-armed hug. "Keep your wits about you, Cale."

"Promise."

20

EVELYN

It's taken us three minutes to choose the team and fifteen to reassure everyone else that they'll get to the surface eventually, barring any unforeseen circumstances that would make the planet too dangerous for a return trip. But at this point, I doubt Soteria will turn us away. Wishful thinking? Possibly. But I've got a good feeling about this.

Sebastián is a shoo-in for the maiden trip, as is Enni. With their combined expertise in evolutionary and xeno-biology, their presence on the planet is essential. Igor demanded he be allowed to come to treat anyone with injuries and to study the biocompatibility with Seb and Enni. He also made the case that while a Marine corpsman is well qualified for combat-related emergencies and that any medics in Rook's squad would be welcome to help him if triage care was needed, his aptitude in general medicine and surgery is far more critical to have on the ground. Plus, he's been willing to fist fight anyone who gets in his way. Not saying he would win against Rook's Marines, but he'd make them think twice. Crazy Norasian Russkies.

The last two slots have been reserved for Jericho and me. While it was brought up that having all three captains go to the planet placed POET's core leadership in jeopardy, there's no getting around the nature of this historic moment. Everyone unanimously voted that we be a part of the first expedition. I'm not gonna lie either: I'm ecstatic.

Magellan has volunteered to pilot Rook's Tiger-class shuttle, affectionately dubbed the *Bliss Mobile* as part of some inside joke, I'm sure, while Eddie takes the co-pilot seat. This has left the loadmaster slot for Lance Corporal Hatch, and the remaining five seats for Rook, Geller, Grabowski, Rodgers, and Ibrahim. The only additional crew member is Fergus who will be stowed in an exterior cargo compartment due to space constraints. While he's not necessarily designed to operate on a planet, his systems and overall speed will help us expedite exploration.

"How you feeling?" Jericho asks me over V-cog as Seb, Enni, Igor, and I finish getting suited up.

"How do you think?"

"Like you might need to pee from excitement one more time before departure?"

"That's what bioreclamation is for." I give the space suit a loving pat just above my hips. "No pit stops needed."

Magellan calls out over the team channel, "Docking in ten seconds." He counts down the last three, and then a dull thud sounds from the other side of the airlock.

"*Bliss Mobile*, this is *Sagan Explorer*," Mishra says. "We have you. Confirm airlock seal."

"Positive pressure confirmed, *Sagan*."

"Roger. Science Team you are clear to proceed."

"Copy that," I say to Mishra. "*Bliss*, we're headed your way now."

"Roger. Ready to receive."

It takes us two minutes to move through the airlock and get aboard the *Bliss Mobile*. The AOPC 13's shape reminds me of an eagle. Pointed nose and sleek shoulders push out from tapered wings and four engine cones in the stern. The ship is matte gray and black, like most everything else Marine-spec, and trimmed in the deep scarlet and gold of their insignia. Inside, the vessel is very military, which is to say it's utilitarian. Bare interior hull, hard seats, and lots of webbing for hand holds and storage.

We float to the aft cargo hold where five pairs of seats line the room's center, tip to tail, back to back. Hatch helps us stow our research equipment and then points us to our seats. The members of Rook's scaled-down squad are strapped along the starboard side of the row, while we take our places on the port side. Meanwhile, Magellan and Eddie are in the cockpit, getting ready to push back from the *Sagan*. The only person unaccounted for visually is Fergus.

"How you doing down there, Fergy?" I ask over V-cog.

"Thank you for inquiring, my lady. I am faring well. Though I might contest two points to that effect."

"Which are?"

"One is that I am not actually *down* anywhere since direction in space is relative. Unless, of course, we are using Orson Scott Card's magisterial work as our reference point, in which case—"

"The enemy's gate is always down," Geller interjects. "You taking up reading as a new hobby, bot?"

"When I'm not needed elsewhere, yes. The ship's entertainment resources boast a number of fascinating titles that I think are quite—"

"And your second point, Ferg?" I ask.

"That my current position, one of being folded up inside a dark space, hardly constitutes a desirable state, especially when I am absent from your countenance, my lady."

"We got a real Casanova on our hands here, Marines. Look out," Grabowski says.

From the cockpit, Eddie says, "Oi, everyone ready back there? 'Cause we ain't fucking waiting anymore."

Magellan confirms pushback with Mishra, and then we're off. I watch the *Bliss Mobile*'s exterior cams through V-cog as we depart the *Sagan*. The massive Horizon-class science exploration vessel makes our shuttle seem like a fly. But having a small form factor is the only way to get from orbit to the surface and back again without expending a huge amount of fuel or having access to a space elevator. The *Bliss*'s wings and control surfaces are worthless in the vacuum of space. But once we get in-atmo, glide ratio and fuel efficiency will make all the difference in the world.

"How's our destination looking?" I ask Magellan over the ship's V-cog lobby. It's a suite built to resemble the cockpit but with seating enough for the entire crew, if the ship's captain wanted everyone there. In our case, Magellan and Eddie only have Rook, Jericho, and me to bother them. Everyone else is monitoring the external cams and sensor data on their own.

"Drone B01 reports clear skies and wind out of the southwest at six knots. Temperature 22.3 degrees, and barometric pressure holding at 30.24. Local time is 0952."

"Thanks."

"No problem, Queen."

Seb is seated across from me. I wave and get his attention. "How about the landing zone?"

He pings the team channel with an augmented reality topo map. I open it and overlay the image in my natural vision. It shows the planet flat, like two pancakes conjoined in the middle, separating east and west hemispheres while a thin line runs along the equator to mark north and south.

"The largest continent is here, in the western hemisphere," he says. "I've designated it A for lack of a better term. Based on its size and that it houses eleven sub climates, it stands to have the largest levels of biodiversity. Likewise, Enni and I have chosen this easterly point along the equator as it will give us access to the ocean, an inland river, and both tropical and humid subtropical climates. This mountain range due west, if we have time, also gets us humid continental and highland samples."

"Sounds good. Just remember that we've allotted ten hours for this outing."

"A drop in the bucket for the decades of discovery that lie ahead of us, but it will do."

"You'll be first to return after a meal and a good night's sleep in the *Sagan*, Seb."

"And double decontamination with quarantine," Igor reminds everyone. "Is very important we are remembering, yes?"

"Copy that, Doc," Jericho says as everyone else nods.

"We can't just stay overnight in basecamp?" Grabowski asks, referring to the recon tents Rook has brought. "Burning a lot of fuel for all this out and back work."

"Not until we know what we're dealing with," Enni replies. "There are simply too many unknown variables. Trust me, the last thing you want is to find out Soteria has some critter that likes nanocarbon visor glass for a midnight snack while you're sound asleep."

"Unless it's a good kisser," Rodgers replies and starts wiggling his tongue at Grabowski, to which Grabowski punches him in the helmet. "Hey!"

"Cool it," Rook says as Rodgers hits back. He picks up the conversation as we start to encounter the very first tremors caused by the atmosphere. "Plus ten hours puts our cutoff at 1955 hours. A reminder to everyone that our days here are twelve minutes shorter than on Earth because of angular velocity and circumference. I've updated your mission clocks to suit."

"But we'll be gone by the time that matters," Enni says.

"Agreed, *if* everything goes according to plan," Rook replies. "Always be prepared."

"Plus," I say, "the sooner we get used to Soteria's time, the better. Something tells me we're gonna be here for a while."

"Don't get my hopes up, Evelyn," Seb says.

The next five minutes are bumpy as we dive into Soteria's gravity and slow through the upper atmosphere. But after that, it feels like any other descent to Earth with occasional turbulence and the sound of air rushing over the fuselage. It stirs me knowing that we're the first humans to fly here, the first to hear this wind, to see this view. Honestly, the number of firsts is so dizzying that I have to force myself to stop counting them so I can just enjoy the journey.

The *Bliss Mobile*'s forward cam shows Continent A's east coast stretching north and south, reminding me of Old Brazil's border. The ocean's blue turns aquamarine as it meets the undulating shore near our landing zone. Far to the west lies the mountain range Seb indicated earlier. Its treeless snow-topped peaks rise over four thousand meters into light cloud cover. And as far as I can see between the coast and the foothills is a blanket of green that rolls up and down. The foliage is interrupted in certain places by rock outcroppings or severe changes in topography. One such variation is a giant gorge that cuts inland, presumably a watershed from the mountain range that channels rain toward the ocean. According to Seb's topo, this is the inland river he mentioned earlier.

"Listen up," Rook says, directing his attention to our science team. "So you know what to expect, after our bird circles the LZ, the squad will deploy and set security. Once we've cleared the area, we'll call you in. If the LZ is compromised, fall-back and alternate pickup positions will light on the beach-head to the north, as noted on the topo map. Please remain seated until our maneuvers are complete and Magellan and gives the all-clear to unbuckle. Copy?"

We all nod, and I thank him for the briefing.

As planned, Magellan circles our landing zone three times, each bringing us a little lower to the landing zone marked on our map. It's a grass-topped promontory maybe a hundred meters off the ocean with gently sloping sides that sweep to wide beaches lined with palm trees. Except, they're not palms, at least not like ones I've ever seen. The fronds are less leafy and more willowy, trailing white and pink strands that look like they belong on an evening gown. I also catch my first glimpse of animals. A small flock of red birds stirred by our engines rise from the trees. Their long tails look almost identical to the white and pink palm strands.

"Avian camouflage," Seb whispers in amazement. "Dios mío. Enni, are you getting this?"

"I am. Making the entry now."

"The wingspan must be… I'm guessing one and a half meters?"

"Noting."

"Hookbill, rhinotheca."

"A what now?" Jericho asks.

"Uh, a… parrot-like beak, but the characteristics—"

Rook cuts off Seb as he and his squad stand. Corporal Hatch is by the aft door waving them forward. Each Marine has their helmet on, rifle held tight across the chest, and face looking toward the closed ramp.

"Thirty seconds," Hatch calls out, relaying a message from Magellan.

Seb looks worried. "Please don't shoot anything, Master Sergeant."

"No promises, Priest."

A notification in V-cog asks if I'd like to view Drone B01's live feed of our final descent. I accept, and get a new view added to my menu options. In it, the *Bliss Mobile* hovers some twenty meters over the grassy patch, superimposed with a military LZ icon. The ship looks like a raptor ready to alight on a perch. All at once, daylight bursts into our hold as the ramp door opens along the ceiling. The air buffets me, and I'm suddenly caught up in the euphoria of being exposed to Soteria's atmosphere. I look at my gloves, forearms, and thighs, wondering if I might spot particles or moisture. Nothing, so far. So I watch Rook and his squad ready to jump clear.

With ten seconds and ten meters left, Rook orders his people forward and then gives the go ahead. Ibrahim is out first, followed by Rodgers, Grabowski, Geller, and then Rook. Part of me wishes I was Ibrahim. First boots on the ground. But I understand the need for caution. As soon as the Marines are clear, Magellan applies throttle, and we climb. The engine wash flattens the grass and rustles more birds from the tropical fronds, only these birds don't flap two wings…

They flap four.

"Enni," Seb yells. "Are you capturing this?"

"I am! Dorsal and ventral wings. *Perkele*, I… I can't believe it."

"Rook?" I ask, cutting off my two scientists. "Anything?"

Rook

I GIVE Hatch a parting nod and then leap from the aft ramp to join the others in a security perimeter. Boots down, weapon up, eyes scanning, I give Magellan orders to depart. The *Bliss Mobile*'s engines buffet our position as the shuttle peels away.

I'm facing east where the grass-topped promontory falls away to a view of the ocean. There's nothing to see but the tops of alien trees, fleeing birds, and sunlight reflecting off the water.

"Pixies out and up," I say on the squad channel.

Each Marine deploys their Personal Exo-Sensory Environment Experience drones and pairs the feed to the unit V-cog channel. Unlike civilian models, our four-thruster units have EMP and shock shielding, extended battery life, plus several sensor bands not allowed on the open market. Our pixies also have micro-mag rail delivery weapons, giving us each five rounds to send downrange. The two millimeter tungsten slugs can pierce a human skull clean through from up to 5,000 meters away. No mess, and one hell of a headache.

With all connections solid, I order, "Heads on swivels. Let's push out."

Our security perimeter expands, aided by the small drones. The shore runs north and south from the promontory and is covered by standard debris coughed up from an ocean. Lumps of vegetation intermingle with foam, while marine birds feast on the remnants of small black carcasses along the sand. I zoom in to get a better look at Soteria's version of winged rats. They're blue, and seem to have feathers so fine they're almost... skin. Hell, maybe it is skin. Like a small pterodactyl or something. Whatever they are, they're having a grand ole time pecking and tearing their oyster-looking snacks to shreds.

With the promontory clear, I order the squad west toward the woods. Our pixies advance ahead of us while we use tree trunks and boulders as cover. Attentions are split between scanning the area down our rifle sights and watching from six meters up as the pixies spread out.

Thermal identifies dozens of small animals in the woods, none of which appear to be larger than a monkey. All seem to have frozen or are fleeing in our presence. This bothers me. I'm no biologist, but if creatures are afraid of something the size of humans, then chances are that things our size or bigger might not be friendly.

Evelyn cuts into my channel. "Rook? Anything?"

"Lots of curious critters. Standby."

Given the environment's lushness, I'm not surprised by the presence of so much wildlife. I also don't need to see full grown dinosaurs to be leery of what's out there. We might not have plopped down in the middle of a Jurassic period, like Dr. Fernández Parra said, but I've seen a dog tear a man apart. No need for velociraptors to ruin a perfectly good day.

My pixie tags Natalie Mason's RD-24, marked as B01, which has ducked under the treetop canopy to monitor our progress. The one-meter wide drone shows signs of wear and tear from atmospheric entry on two planets now, but it's still chugging away. Built tough. I give it a friendly wave, knowing that Mason and the other scientists watching might appreciate it.

Our pixies head deeper into the forest, skimming the floors and scanning debris. We examine six legged tree climbers with enormous eyes, twirling fliers that look like mini ballerinas, and skittish ground animals that dart away before any of us can get a good look. We'll need file reviews on all of this, that's for sure. I can only

imagine the heart attacks Sebastián and Enni are having
with all this.

"Any immediate causes for concern, Rook?" Evelyn
asks again.

"We haven't been attacked yet, if that's what you
mean."

"Well that's good."

"Yup. But it's only been"—I glance at the mission
clock—"three minutes. Give us a few more. We're going
to expand our search area now. I'll come back to you in
five."

She sounds reluctant, but complies. "Stay safe."

"That's the plan."

Our patrol pushes another hundred meters into the
forest with our pixies another hundred beyond that.
Aside from minor variations in elevation and the occasional boulder cluster, all of which seem clear of any
beasties that I consider dangerous, there's no terrain
element that provides a significant tactical advantage nor
creatures demonstrating aggressive behavior. Again, the
native predators might see things differently and have no
doubt evolved to make use of things I'm probably not
seeing. But in my book, high ground is high ground, and
claws are claws, no matter which part of the galaxy you
hail from.

I'm about to start giving orders to return to the LZ
when I see something of interest in my drone's thermal
layer. I assume manual control and dive toward the

forest floor. There, half hidden by a wide-leafed bush, is a pile of... "Shit."

"Send it," Geller says, asking for directions.

"No. I mean, actual shit. One hell of a pile too." I mark it, knowing the scientists will be keen to sift it for all the things scientists like to find in animal excrement. I still hate that class trip where my biology teacher made me sort through an owl pellet. Bizarre. "Unless a bunch of animals like to pool their excrement, this came from an ass a lot bigger than ours."

"Copy that," Geller says.

"I want motion sensors 200 meters out with overlapping coverage of 10 meters set on an arc to close off the LZ," I instruct Geller.

"Loiter the pixies. And then set a tighter stun line at fifty meters. Low voltage. Just enough to make any passersby second guess their desire to check us out. They can be curious from a distance."

"Roger."

"I also want the MS265 set up at the LZ, on the highest point and facing west. The brains won't like it, but if we have a major land threat, like whoever dropped that load, it'll come from the west."

Geller starts giving orders while I point back to the LZ and hail Magellan. "*Bliss Mobile*, this is Rook. You're clear for landing."

"Roger that, Rook. We'll see you in sixty."

Jericho

OBSERVING Evelyn as she steps off the shuttle is a bit like watching a child enter their favorite amusement park. She's giddy, realizing the culmination of her life's work. Hell, even for me, it's a head-trip—finding a pristine, unsettled planet in a star system nearly a thousand light years from Earth. She spins around twice, hands on the side of her helmet. I worry she's gonna try to pull it off, but then I realize it's a gesture of wonder. Next thing I know, she takes a knee and touches the grass, brushing her gloved fingers across it. A lone purple flower gets a tender touch, and then she's on her feet again, heading to a section of exposed rock that serves as an observation platform above the south beach.

With everyone else helping move gear out of the powered-down shuttle, I take a second to join her at the overlook. A seemingly endless strand of tropical beach parts the ocean to the east and the forest to the west.

"Like what you see?"

"Do you even need to ask?"

"Nope." I fold my arms. "Just making sure you're happy."

"I'm… the happiest I've ever been. Beyond happy. This is… well, it's…"

"Your life's work."

She takes a deep breath and then echoes me. "My life's work, yeah. But it's more than that."

"How so?"

"Well… for so long, everyone accused us, NUESSA and SESI, of being elites, right? The 'select few' who go to escape the tragedies unfolding on Earth."

"The beautiful ones," I add, using the Tantum's term for spacers.

"Exactly. But we weren't. If anything, we were the ones leaving our families and our homes to try and make life better for everyone else. Almost four years I spent on *Astraea* Station, four years of never setting foot back in the Southlands. And don't let anyone fool you: I would have given anything for a few weeks away on a New Zealand beach." She inhales as if she can smell the ocean air around us. "But we were never doing it for us. It was always for them. Always to give the generations to come a fighting chance at survival. And now?" Evelyn's eyes look to the horizon.

"And now we just need to find a way back to tell them the good news," I say when she doesn't speak up.

"Right. For now, we have a lot of work to do, and a whole planet to explore."

"You know, most people get depressed when they reach the pinnacle of their careers."

"The pinnacle?" She spins on me and scoffs. "This is a whole new beginning! I'm looking at a new mountain to climb, you dork."

"Just making sure."

A gloved fist hits me in the upper arm. "Wanker."

I pretend to rub pain away and then refocus on white strand curving away to the south. "You sad about not meeting any Naqualla yet? 'Where's the galactic welcoming committee?' Stuff like that?"

She waves a dismissive hand. "That's for the movies."

"So you're not sad at all?"

"Maybe a little, yeah," she finally says. "Just wanted to thank them, ya know? For taking a chance on us. For going out of their way to... help us find this."

I laugh.

"What's so funny?"

"It still amazes me that you don't believe in a higher power, but you've spent your whole life trusting that aliens would help save us."

"Because I can explain the existence of additional sentient beings. I can't explain God."

"Maybe. But both require faith, something you seem to have a lot of."

"It's called evidence, and I have plenty about aliens."

"I have plenty about God. Either way, someone we can't see saved us."

She smiles at me. "Maybe Seb isn't the only priest on the mission. I think you missed your calling."

"And miss this? No way." I gesture to the shuttle. "Come on. We've got some unpacking to do. Time to explore."

Just then, the hull emits a knocking sound, then a muffled, "Hello?" comes from inside the belly. "Is anyone out there?"

"Oh my gosh." Evelyn starts running toward the *Bliss Mobile*. "We forgot Fergy!"

"We're coming," I yell and then catch a twinkle in Evelyn's eyes. "What?"

"Think he misses my *countenance*?"

I laugh. "No doubt, your ladyship."

21

EVELYN

IT'S TAKEN the better part of thirty minutes for Seb and Enni to get all their equipment set up. Jericho, Eddie, Fergus, and I have been on tent duty, erecting a four-by-six meter awning to cover the makeshift field lab. Meanwhile, Rook and his unit have split their time between ensuring the area is well-monitored and erecting tents of their own, ones meant for sleeping. We're not scheduled to stay here overnight, but Rook insisted we need the option "just in case." By the first hour's end, our shuttle looks like it's given birth to a cluster of tents and workstations.

"Welcome to Camp Evelynton," Rook says with his arms spread apart.

"Excuse me?"

"Home of POET Lab One and the First Soterian

Marine Squad… for now. I imagine we'll have a division eventually."

"We can't name it after me."

"Who said I named it after you?"

"Cute."

"He might be on to something," Jericho says. "After all, this is your fault. So it seems to me that naming something after the planet's discoverer is appropriate."

"I didn't discover any—"

"So it's settled then," Rook says to Jericho, and they shake on it.

"No! It's not settled. We have to—"

"Camp Evelynton," Jericho replies. "Has a nice ring to it."

"It does *not* have a nice ring to it," I protest.

Igor disagrees. "I make song, yes? Official country patriot one."

"Oi, you mean a fucking national anthem," Eddie says.

"Yes. Is anthem. Perhaps song goes"—Igor clears his throat and starts singing—"*There is much greatness in fairest camp of Evelyn*—"

"Please stop," I say.

"No, no," Jericho replies. "I think he's onto something."

"—*where is hidden treasure of beauty in secret gardens.*"

"Oh, stars."

"*What bountiful riches await us from bosom of lands?*"

"He's not even fucking rhyming," Eddie says.

"Doesn't need to rhyme," Grabowski replies and then points to the west. "What about rolling hills? We need twin peaks, Doc!"

"*—twin peaks stand firm in wind for viewings.*"

I cover my visor. "Can someone mute him, please?"

"Okay," Rook says after a moment. "Let's, uh, continue the songwriting later."

"Or never," I interject.

Fortunately, Seb rescues all of us from Igor's singing and motions to a workstation under the central tent. "The air is clean. First analysis complete."

"How clean?" I ask and step around to his monitor.

"Enni and I need to run a few more tests, and I'd like Igor's eyes on the particle scan just to be sure. But, according to our first passes, I'd say we're more likely to contract something life threatening in London than we are here."

"So, helmets can come off then?" Rodgers asks.

"Not for you, Marine," Geller says. "Covers stay."

Seb seconds this. "We do need to run some more testing. Like I said, Igor's assistance with the particulates will be helpful. But I'm optimistic."

"So what you're saying is that the air is, so far, compatible for us?" Jericho asks.

"Yes." Seb gets a big smile. "That's exactly what I'm saying. Give us another hour, and we'll know better."

This news seems to buoy everyone's spirits even

higher. I imagine we're all keen to get out of our gear. But not at the cost of our lives, so discretion is still the order of the day.

"What's next?" I ask Seb.

"We need water samples, both from the ocean and from the river. After that, soil samples."

"We can recon the river for you, Priest," Rook says.

"And I'll grab the ocean sample," I say.

Rook eyes me. "Not without an armed escort, you won't."

"Shall I take up arms in her defense?" Fergus asks.

"I don't need anyone protecting me." I thrust out a hand. "Side arm."

Rook gives me a grin that's half annoyed and half amused. Finally, he demags his pistol, frees the biolock, and presses the weapon into my hand. "Try not to kill anything. It's a brand new world."

SINCE THE RIVER is farther from basecamp—still not gonna call it Evelynton—than the beach, Rook has ordered Fergus to accompany him, Geller, and Grabowski to serve as a runner once the freshwater samples are collected. Rodgers and Ibrahim have been tasked with camp security and the machine gun, and Corporal Hatch has control of the *Bliss Mobile*'s point defense turrets.

In the meantime, Jericho, Magellan, Eddie, and I have just picked our way down the promontory's south-facing slope. As I take my first steps onto the strand and feel my boots give way, countless memories of walking across beaches culminate in the strong desire to kick off my footwear. I want the sand between my toes, the surf licking my ankles, the salty air whipping through my hair. As it is, our space suits' atmospheric regulators are working overtime to cool us from the sun's high-noon heat. But I understand the need for caution. Just wish we could hurry things up.

"So, anywhere is fine?" Magellan asks, holding the sample kit.

"No, Seb said he wants it from that flat rocky area with the tide pools up ahead. It'll be safer for us too."

"Roger."

The four of us step off the beach and spread out on the ocean-worn rocks, looking for places to collect the samples. I find a tide pool about half a meter deep and walk in until water is swirling around my knees. The gentle push and pull takes me back to surfing in New Zealand after classes. Only in my wildest dreams did I imagine this… being here, on an alien planet, wading into a foreign ocean. And that's just it: those were dreams. No one expects them to come true, at least if they're being honest with themselves. Fantasies are for kids. Then even most of those get taken away when we grow up and get wise to the ways of the world. But somehow, fate has smiled on this moment. Smiled on me. And here I am.

"Twenty-five centimeters down," I say to the team, reiterating Seb's instructions. "Hold it for thirty seconds." They acknowledge, and then I activate my sample kit and plunge it underwater. The moment I do, something flashes around my hand. I instinctively pull back, glancing at the device to make sure it's okay. Which it seems to be. I inspect my glove—all clear—and then lean closer to the water. I don't see anything notable beyond a fine layer of undulating white sand some thirty centimeters below the surface. I look up to see if anyone else is encountering this, but they're all hunched over or kneeling in tide pools without looking up. So I try again.

The moment my hand goes under, the flash comes back. Bright neon yellow. Only this time, I see it's not one large event, but dozens of smaller ones. And they're blinking. Like… "Underwater fireflies."

"Come again?" Jericho asks over comms.

"I've encountered some sort of marine lightning bug. Are you guys seeing this?"

"Negative."

"Nothing here," Magellan adds.

"Same," says Eddie. "Must like you better than us."

I kneel in the knee-high water to stabilize myself and then move my hand a little.

"Careful, Evelyn," Jericho says.

I ignore him and strain to see the animal's shape. It's

not until my visor is almost in the water that I spot a school of transparent and gelatinous creatures, each about three-centimeters long. "Seb? Enni? Check my POV."

A few seconds later, Enni says, "Pleuronectoidei… but phylum Cnidaria?"

Seb nods in a V-cog sub window. "Fascinating. And bioluminescent."

"English, please?" I ask.

Seb shakes his head. "Ah, sorry. The, uh, *mesoglea* there—that's the main jelly-like substance of its body—along with the trailing tentacles of its medusa-phase definitely put it in line with what we'd call jellyfish. But the overall shape is more like a flatfish, making it a member of the ray-finned demersal fish."

"You mean flounder?"

"Precisely."

I gently swirl my hand a little more and find the flickering speeds up as the tiny creatures adjust and investigate. "They sure are curious little guys. Bioluminescent flounder jellyfish."

"Also known as Evelynfish," Jericho says.

"Cosmic stars! Would you all knock it off already? I'm… naming them Serenity fish, after my favorite fictional spacecraft. We are *not* naming these creatures after me."

"She's got a point," Rook says, clearly monitoring our conversation on his own expedition. Glad he's coming around to my side of things. "If they don't punch, bite, sting, or talk back, then we really can't name them after her."

"Why don't you come back here to test that theory yourself, Rook."

"Too busy discovering my own namesake."

I can't tell if he's being serious or not, so I bring up his POV. Rook's about twenty meters from the edge of a shallow canyon lined with tall trees. Despite their height, the trees's branches emerge from the main trunks about a meter off the ground and then shoot straight up where they bloom in fluffy pink tops. Like cupcakes. In fact, the vertical branches appear like ridges in a wrapper. "Cupcake trees. I never knew that's how you saw yourself, Rook. Proves everyone's got a soft side."

"Not the trees, you… *Eck*. I mean the *raptor*." He zooms into one of the uprights below a pink tuft where a hawkish bird with a single claw grasps the branch. Narrow yellow eyes with black pupils scan the woods. When someone in the fire team steps on a twig, the animal snaps its head toward them and unfurls its wings. The plumage reveals a giant version of the bird's own eyes, but colored as if hit by black light.

"Holy shit," Grabowski says and raises his weapon. "Take it out?"

"No, no," Enni yells. "That's a defense mechanism! It's scared of you."

"Like a butterfly with giant eyes on its wings," I say.

"That's right. Based on the size of that display, I suspect it's more harmless than harmful, and will choose to retreat if you antagonize it."

"Awww," I say in the most pandering tone I can manage and still not laugh. "Looks like Rook found out his big scary raptor is really a fluffy butterfly birdy."

"It's got a sharp beak, hasn't it?"

"So does a parakeet," Grabowski adds. "Uh… sorry, Master Sergeant."

"Moving on," Rook replies, and then shoos the new bird away with a few flails of his arm.

Rook is the center of attention once again about fifteen minutes later as he, Geller, Grabowski, and Fergus make it to the canyon floor. I've led our team back to base-camp and delivered the water samples to Sebastián when Rook pings us.

"I think we might have a real predator this time," he says softly.

Jericho waves his arms and gets everyone on V-cog to monitor. The Marines and Fergus are positioned behind large sandstone-colored boulders leading up to the river's edge. As Rook leans around one side, his HUD targets an animal some twenty-seven meters upriver. The dark creature is hunched over on four legs, probing the water with a long snout lined with teeth—from the looks of them, sharp ones. Short oily skin, like that of a marine mammal, covers hard sinewy muscle that rolls under each snappy movement.

"Jesus," Grabowski whispers. "Looks like a sea otter and an alligator had a little too much to drink and a little too much Melvin Studebaker on audio, know what I mean?"

"While breeding Enhydra lutris and Alligatoridae is biologically impossible," Enni says, "it is plausible that something with their various traits has evolved on this planet to create whatever magnificent creature we're seeing here."

"Magnificent? Thing's uglier than Rodgers in a thong."

"Hey," shouts the targeted Marine from beside me in the real. "I'll have you know I dropped three kilos recently, and your mom said I looked hotter than ever."

"Cool it," Rook says. "Let's just wait it out."

We all watch with fascination as the canine-sized animal wades through the water, scouring for food, I presume. Eventually, it snags a dark brown fish that flails on either side of the animal's snout. The predator returns to shore where it proceeds to disembowel the catch with stubby clawed forepaws while snapping up bits of flesh until the meal is done.

"Should have waited to claim your namesake, Rook," I say at last. "I think Grabowski gets this one."

"Hell, yeah! Wait… I'm not ugly."

"Really?" Rodgers says. "'Cause it explains a lot."

"Shut up, man. I'll take the freakin' cupcake bird back there. Jeez."

THE DISCOVERIES CONTINUE to pour in as the sun heads toward the western horizon. Yup, the stellar orbital vector is a bonus. While I'm all for the outlandish creatures Soteria has to offer, it's important that any new homeworld for humanity is as close as possible to the original. If little things like the antiquated practice of changing times by one hour around the spring and fall equinoxes can have detrimental effects on a given population, just imagine having the sun rise in the west and set in the east.

So far, we haven't encountered any super predators, which is fine by me. The Marines are disappointed that they haven't been able to square off with anything yet, but I keep reminding them that's a good thing. The more peaceful this paradise is the better. Plus, as Rook points out, there are hard limits to ammunition without setting up our printing operations and mining raw materials. So while it's all but certain we'll meet some baddies eventually, it bodes well for the mission's long term viability that they haven't found us yet.

The time is closing in on 1900 hours when Seb says, "We have our final sample quality results in."

The entire team stops what they're doing and moves under the lab's main tent where Seb, Enni, and Igor look like futuristic mad scientists crouched over workstations in spacesuits. The rest of POET shows up in the V-cog command theater, alerted to the news. When everyone's finally assembled, I say, "And? Whadda we got?"

Sebastián chuckles, shares looks with Enni and Igor, and then says, "After careful analysis, I… *we* have a planet, at least in this region, and, granted, there's *so* many regions that we'll need to explore, and then we'll have to—"

"Sebastián? The results?"

"Ah, right. Forgive me. Losing myself. Soteria is… as perfect as we could hope for."

"What? Really?" I take three steps toward him. "You're kidding."

"No. No, I'm not. The air, the water, the soil, pH and mineral composition… it's all… it's biocompatible."

I grab Seb's helmet and then hug him. He laughs and hugs me back as the rest of the team give gloved high fives. The sounds of celebration are more lively in V-cog and serve to heighten the drama.

"It's a miracle," I say at last, knowing how that word will be taken. But I don't care. Because it really is a miracle, at least in terms of getting the odds right.

Seb smiles. He's even crying. "Truly a *milagro*, Evelyn. Dios has smiled upon us."

"And the Naqualla." I point a finger at his visor. "Don't get too carried away on me, Priest."

He laughs and then admits, "And the Naqualla." But then Seb holds up his arms in an effort to calm everyone down. "This doesn't mean... Listen, please."

"Quiet down," Rook yells. That does the trick.

Seb continues. "This doesn't mean we can't be harmed out here. You can't just go around eating plants or meat or what have you. Half of it could still be toxic to us. We'll need a whole set of pathology tests to find out what's compatible or not with our physiology. That could take... well, that could take the rest of our lives and then some!"

"But for now?" I ask hopefully.

"For now I recommend we leave everything here overnight, let our extended tests keep running while we get back to the ships for some sleep, and then return tomorrow. Barring any unforeseen results with negative implications, I vote we remove our suits and start settling in a little more. Maybe even bring some of the others down to help establish a makeshift settlement using NUE protocols."

Hearing Sebastián use that term—NUE—snaps me out of my revelry. He goes on, outlining a science plan for the next two days, whereas I find myself disengaging.

"Everything okay?" Jericho says on a private channel.

"Oh. Yeah. Fine."

"Bullshit."

"Huh. Alright. Not fine. Just… Hearing Seb say NUE—"

"Soured everything for you, didn't it?"

"You too?"

"Yup. Kinda makes you feel like your parents are coming in to ruin playtime."

"Something like that."

Rook's voice comes over the general comm. "Alright, you heard the man. Let's prep for exfil. Grab essential gear. Everything else gets locked down and stays put."

"If I may?" Fergus says.

"What is it?" I ask.

"I would like to volunteer my services and remain here overnight. Even the shabbiest garden needs a faithful scarecrow, don't you suppose?"

"It's not a terrible idea," Rook says. "Your systems are all still operating okay?"

"According to my own diagnostics, yes. However, I pray thee take up the matter with my Creator as he will inevitably have superior discernment."

"Kit?" Jericho asks. "You copy that?"

"Hey, yeah! I do… *did*. Err, *am* copying everything just fine. And everything on Fergus looks nominal, and power levels are hunky dory. Nothing seems off at all. So, unless there's some sort of, ya know, metal-eating microbe that's quietly chewing its way through his hardware hoping to engorge itself on his main power bus where it lays nano parasitic eggs in his neural quantum matrix, he should be totally fine."

"Hear that, pal?" Rook gives Fergus a gentle pat on the shoulder. "Totally fine."

"Uh, but, my lord, he suspects that—"

"Bot stays. Kit, can you reroute all security drone feeds and early detection sensors to Fergus?"

"Uh, sure can, Master Major. Only take a second."

"Good. Fergus, you'll have firing capability on the MS265, but only when cleared by the Marine on watch who will be monitoring from the *Belle*. Copy?"

Fergus does a double take on the machine gun and then points at it. "You actually want me firing that weapon?"

"Not unless you absolutely have to, but you're as good an option as we're gonna get right now."

Fergus snaps into a salute. "You may rely on me, my lord. I shan't disappoint you. And if the very hordes of Hades storm our gates, I will champion the clarion call of my , attesting to their—"

"Got it."

Jericho addresses the camp. "Let's close up shop for the night and clear out. Skids up in ten."

Just like that, our first day on Soteria is over. We haven't even left yet, and I can't wait to come back.

22

JERICHO

Until I see everyone's faces lit by the *Bliss Mobile*'s cargo bay lights, I was pretty sure I was the only one who didn't sleep more than an hour last night. But based on all the bags under the crew's eyes, I can see I'm in good company.

Evelyn straps herself in next to me and says, "You look like shit."

"Takes one to know one. You sleep?"

"Not a wink. You?"

"Maybe one. But definitely not more."

She smiles and finishes securing herself, but then her grin eventually fades.

"What's got you? Besides no beauty sleep."

"I went to see Olivia again. In V-cog this time. Quarantine and all."

One eyebrow climbs my forehead. "You're quite the glutton for punishment."

"So I've been told."

"And?"

She shrugs. "Filled her in on our findings. She was…"

"Ambivalent?"

"I wish. I could see the… the damn delight in her eyes. Like she was genuinely… you know."

"I'm telling you, Evelyn. She might have a history with the Tantum, but her future is with—"

"Don't."

"I was just gonna say—"

"Whatever it is, I don't wanna know right now. Just… let's focus on the mission, okay? We've got a full day in front of us."

"Roger that." I tighten my straps one more time and then sit back as Magellan pushes away from the *Sagan*.

Unlike our last departure that saw the *Bliss* collecting crew members from all three ships, the expedition team bedded down on the *Sagan* together. It made quarantining easier, and the old Horizon-class has plenty of space, which was a nice change from the *Kogarashi*'s smaller confines.

The flight to Camp Evelynton—there's no changing that name now—clocks in at thirty-eight minutes. It's twice that climbing out at high velocity, and will be four times that for an average return trip. Longer with heavy payloads. But the *Bliss Mobile* is efficient and, for the most part, a smooth flier. I've always been a fan of the Tiger-class shuttle design. Sleek, mean, and yet still elegant. She's a classy dame with an edge.

Magellan lets Rook's squad out as before. They've already checked all drone footage and sensor data; this is just an in-person ground inspection. Once they give the all-clear, Magellan sets us down and shuts off the engines.

"Fergus," I say as the bot comes toward us. I grab him by the shoulders. "Good to see you, pal. You fare okay?"

"I am pleased to report that no nano parasitic eggs were laid in my quantum neural matrix. I'm sure that comes as a relief to all of those gathered here."

"That's weird."

"What?"

"Well, Kit created a diagnostic checklist for us to reference in the event we thought you were co-opted by foreign contagions."

"He didn't tell me of this."

"Had to be a blind test, right?"

"Ah… I suppose so, yes."

"Weird part is, he said that if your systems had been compromised you would say, and I quote, 'No nano parasitic eggs were laid in my quantum neural matrix'."

Fergus looks back and forth between Evelyn and me several times, each head swivel moving faster than the last. "But, my lord, I can assure you that my systems have not been comprised."

"Also something he said you'd say. You sure you're feeling okay, buddy?"

"Well... I... That's not..."

It's Evelyn who bursts out laughing first. "Oh stars, Fergus! He's messing with you. I can't..."

"Messing with me?" Fergus tilts his head. "Are you jerking my chain, my lord?"

"Consider it a rite of passage, pal."

"For what?"

"Becoming more human. What can you tell us about last night?"

Fergus seems to take a second to compose himself and then straightens to full height. "Well, there is much to say. Shall I provide you with a minute-by-minute review of every insect and animal that chose me as a defecation receptacle?"

"Uh... why don't you save that for doctors Fernández Parra and Mäkinen. Cool?"

"Very good, my lord."

"Anything missing or damaged?" Evelyn asks Seb, Enni, and Rook simultaneously.

"So far so good," Seb replies. "Just a lot of dew. Couple insects that died in the night too. Enni? Log these?"

"On it."

"What kind of visitors did we have?" I ask Rook as he reviews military drone footage.

"Seems the area has quite the night scene." He gets Seb's attention. "You have a couple hours of content to sort, Priest. The nocturnal activity is… wild, we'll just say that. Mostly ground animals. A few primate-looking creatures. And a pair of those sea otter gators we saw down at the river."

"I can attest to said wildness," Fergus says. "As previously noted, I suffered the bodily emissions of many species, several of which were engaged in numerous levels of coitus."

"La la la," Rodgers says with his hands on the sides of his helmet.

"Send it over, please," Seb asks. "Both of you."

"Already done," Rook replies.

"Same, sire," adds Fergus.

I look at Evelyn and catch the morning sun reflecting off her visor. "So… we doing this?"

"Excuse me?"

I tap the side of my helmet. "You breathing first or what? I think it's only fitting. Assuming all the levels still check out with Seb."

We look over at the scientist. He's busy typing away on a holo interface.

I have to get his attention. "Sebastián? How we looking?"

"Uh… everything… looks good. Amazing, actually. No changes, all experiments are running in the green, tests are negative. Uh, for toxins, I mean. Negative is a good thing."

"Roger. So it's still safe, in your mind?"

"I mean, is any person's mind really safe? Come on." He laughs at his own joke, but no one else joins him. He lets out a long sigh. "Uhhhhhhh, it's safe. The air, I mean. Not my brain."

I turn back to Evelyn. "Ladies first."

"No. Queen first," Rook says with a smile.

Huh. He's certainly getting more… *familiar* with her. "Queen first," I echo.

The next thing I know, everyone's gathered around Evelyn like she's the first kid for Show and Tell. She gives the group a half-nervous half-excited look and grabs the sides of her helmet with both hands. The V-cog actuated seal releases with a hiss. Then she gives the hardware a three-centimeter pivot to the right where the tines pop free of their receivers. Evelyn pushes the helmet straight over her head and smiles, inhaling her first breath. It comes out with a laugh sounding like something a child might make. "Ha ha ha! It's amazing!"

"I ain't waiting," Grabowski says. He unlocks his armored headpiece and pulls it away in a well-practiced motion. It's not two seconds clear of his head when he lets out a loud, "*Ehhhhh-choo!* Son of a bitch."

"Pollen count's high," Enni adds with a laugh.

"Smells like… chamomile and vanilla," Rook says with his own helmet clear. "It's… quite lovely."

I don't know what I'm waiting for. Helmets are coming off left and right. I guess I was just caught up with the look on Evelyn's face. With how happy she is. It's not every day you get to see someone take their first breath on a planet.

"You coming in?" she asks me. "Water's fine."

"Oh. Yeah." I release the seal, twist to the right, and push up. The air is warm and humid; it's not even 0830 hours. But like Rook said, there's a rich botanical scent to the air, mixed with the ocean's saltiness. Instantly, my mouth waters, craving non-printed food. The whole experience is somehow more enjoyable than I thought it would be. Breathing air this… *full*, this *alive*… It's kinda intoxicating.

"Is it just me, or does Earth air not even come close to this?" Geller asks.

The question meets with head nods and verbal agreements all around.

"Technically, Earth air isn't close to this," Seb replies. "At least not anymore. The increased oxygen levels and lack of toxicity here should make everyone feel pretty good. Higher brain function, concentration, cognitive ability, energy levels… they'll all be up."

With everyone enjoying the freedom of breathing the open air, it's time to get a little more comfortable. The civilians among us shed our space suits and enjoy the freedom of movement offered by our various crew uniforms. Evelyn kneels to touch the grass while others stretch freely in the planet's virgin air, much to the chagrin of Rook's unit.

The Marines have opted for what they call rock plate—shorthand for a ground-based armor configuration. Their suits are far less bulky and lack the zero-g thruster packs and backup life support modules. Instead, they've got lean setups that look much easier to move in, similar to the config I've seen Space Marines use when posted on-station. Rook's team has opened their visors and vented chest plates to help with the heat. Long term, I know they're gonna be uncomfortable, but that's all part of the routine for them. However, Rook has assured me that he established a roster that allows each Marine to go off duty on a rotating basis, giving them time to get out of their armor, eat, sleep, and inevitably flirt with the science officers.

With everyone feeling more comfortable, I turn to Seb. "Alright, what's our business for the day?"

"As I mentioned last night, I want us to expand our sample radius to one kilometer while the *Bliss* brings down the remaining scientists to accommodate the increased workload. We'll need to train many of them on procedures, anyone who wishes to help actually, but that won't take long."

"That many boots on the ground will make daily

ferrying costly," Rook says. "Do you feel it's safe enough to conduct overnight stays?"

"Isn't security more of your thing, Master Sergeant?"

"It is. But I'm talking biologically."

"Until we have cause to suspect something destructive, we have all the reasons to stay and pursue rapid information gathering. The more we can learn and the faster we can do it, the better."

"Roger. Geller will initiate camp expansion ASAP. Meanwhile, I'm going to have Popov use our second shuttle to ferry our confined Navy crewmen here in the hopes of winning hearts and minds to our cause. Their logistic and administrative experience will be key if we can secure their willing participation. Might take some convincing, slow and steady. But I'm hopeful."

I jump in. "And if we do get that window of opportunity to head back and bring word to the NUE, their testimony will be critical."

Rook stares at me flatly for a second before saying, "Agreed."

"Alright then," Seb says. "Enni, Igor, if you can prep to train new recruits, I'll start work on mapping grid search sectors."

"I'll oversee science personnel ferrying with Magellan and Eddie," I say. "Can we retain Corporal Hatch as our loadmaster?"

"Roger," Rook says.

"Forging paths?" Evelyn says.

"Through the darkness," the rest of us in earshot reply.

TWO HOURS PASS before the *Bliss Mobile* returns with its first load of gear and personnel. In addition to eight more of the *Sagan*'s scientists, I've brought Kit and Eddie along for their first trip to Soteria. Kit's first-hand monitoring of Fergus will be important. Plus, he's earned it. He needs to enjoy the spoils of our discovery as much as anyone. As for Eddie, he'll be key in equipment oversight and maintenance, as will Nairobi when she comes in the next wave. Right now, she's on watch aboard the *Kogarashi*. Each starship has its own duty roster, leaving one soul aboard at all times.

"Holy biscuits," Kit yells from inside his helmet when he steps onto the matted grass.

"You can take it off, pal," I say and point to his helmet.

"Oh, right." He pops the seal, twists, and pushes up before taking a deep breath. "It's… beautiful."

"Oi. You fucking crying?" Eddie asks.

"No." Kit sniffs and rubs the back of his wrist against his eye. A second later, he sneezes so loud I can't believe the sound came from him. "*Sniff.* Sorry."

"Interesting," Seb says, head popping above a row of

equipment. "Mr. Smith, can I examine you for a moment?"

"Already? I just got here."

"And you're having a near instantaneous reaction to something in the air, much like Mr. Grabowski."

"Does that… mean I'm special?"

"Oi, you're special alright," Eddie says.

"Easy," I say quietly. Then to Kit: "See Seb, and then I want you monitoring Fergus."

"You… you… *Ahhhhh-yeah-chooo!* —got it, Cap. *Sniff.* Sorry."

As Kit strides away, Eddie says, "I think we found a new predator deterrent."

"It would make me think twice. Listen, I want you keeping an eye on all the hardware. Especially for anything out of the ordinary."

"Oxidation, deterioration?"

"Exactly. We need to ensure that everything stays functional. If something in the environment is gonna break things down, I wanna know before it becomes a problem."

"Copy that, Knight."

The eight new scientists clomp down the ramp like draft horses and then start shedding their exploration suits in the gear tent. Protocol requires that we make transfers fully outfitted for hard vac emergencies, but I suspect that policy will lighten as time goes on. Then again, we haven't encountered any inclement weather or atmospheric anomalies that would put the fear of God in us. Time will tell.

The *Belle*'s second shuttle arrives from the west and sets down just behind the *Bliss*. V-cog has it labeled the *Rubenking Special*. Sounds like a good sandwich. And probably a punchline to a Navy joke. Who knows.

I wave Evelyn over to join Rook at the bottom of the bird's ramp as he greets our newcomers. If the Master Sergeant wants to win hearts and minds, it's important the three of us be present and united. The sailors come down the ramp uncuffed. Not even Dregs and Krutz, two of Popov's fire team members serving as security, have their weapons drawn. But heaven knows they can draw and fire before these Navy men could blink.

"Lieutenant Jaffa," Rook says as he offers to shake the man's hand. "Welcome to Soteria."

The commander doesn't shake right away, but I don't think it has to do with the bad blood between them, at least not entirely. Jaffa can't seem to help but look around in wonder and then points to his visor. "It's safe?"

"We're not dead yet," Rook replies with a half grin. "All the brains say the atmo checks out." Then Rook encourages all six sailors to remove their helmets. They do and breathe in. Surprised looks cross their faces, and even some smiles of amazement.

"Listen," Rooks says. "Why don't we try this again, seeing as how that last introduction didn't go so well."

Jaffa locks eyes with Rook. "You hijacked my ship, Master Sergeant. You… you'll be…"

"Oh, I don't need to be reminded, sir. I'm well aware of the ramifications of my actions… once I return to our star system."

I can't help but notice the special emphasis he places on those last words.

Jaffa looks like he doesn't know if he should be livid or stunned. It's almost comical. But I know there's a lot on the line here. Evelyn seems to sense that too and steps forward, extending her hand.

"Lieutenant, my name is—"

"Dr. Evelyn Park."

"Yes. And, contrary to whatever feelings you have toward Master Sergeant Farooq, I am the one responsible for getting you involved in all this."

"You're in one deep pile of shit, Dr. Park."

"And you're standing on a fully habitable exoplanet, Lieutenant Jaffa."

His stern gaze seems to melt some as his eyes divert toward the treeline, then the mountains… the ocean. "It's real?"

"You tell me." Evelyn turns slightly and admires the surroundings with him, giving a moment for the rest of Jaffa's crewmen to take in the view. "This… this is what we were hoping for. *More* than what we were hoping for. An answer for humanity, and now we have it. At least, we know where it is."

"And where is that, exactly?"

"Almost a thousand light years from Earth."

Jaffa's lips remain parted. He blinks. Then shakes his head. "That's impossible. We—"

"Don't have that kind of tech? You're right. But the Naqualla do. And that's who have made it possible for us to be here, sir."

"Aliens."

"Indeed. The real question is, will we be able to get the rest of our people here too. And when I say our people, I mean—"

"All of humanity."

"Precisely. But before that, we not only need to find a way home, we need—"

"To establish a level one settlement here."

She nods. "We could use your help, Lieutenant. All of you. I won't pretend to know about your policies and procedures. Rook and his squad are no doubt going to get court martialed—"

"They'll be executed."

"—but I do know that you've pledged your service to protect people's lives and ensure interplanetary peace. The way I see it, your job just got a whole lot bigger. We all knew there were risks for that stunt we pulled. But we also knew that if Sallsworth had his way, none of us would be here right now. Seeing this. This amazing place."

Evelyn takes a moment for the surroundings to speak for themselves. "If you choose to assist us, that means we have your full support, 100 percent, no questions asked. You buy into what we're trying to accomplish, and you take orders from Rook, Jericho, and myself like we are your commanding officers. This mission requires that we work together and have each other's backs. I'm not exaggerating when I say that the fate of our species depends on it."

"And if not?"

She gives him a curt smile. "If you decide that's too much for you and wish to remain in holding on the *Belle*, we'll make sure you are treated humanely for the duration of your confinement." Something glints in Evelyn's eye… a look I've seen before. "However, if you choose not to help us, know this: I will not vouch for you or your team when I'm asked about what we did to save the human race. When we find a way to save our people, and the world asks, you will not be a part of that story. Your name will never be remembered. I'll make sure of it."

So much for slow and steady.

The moment grows tense, and Jaffa doesn't seem to be budging. But neither is Evelyn.

"May I take a moment to confer with my crew?" he asks.

"Of course. Be my guest."

The lieutenant gathers his people into a huddle while

Evelyn steps back and joins Rook and me in our own huddle.

"You've been reluctant to talk about heading back to Earth," I say quietly to Rook. "It's been about—"

"I forfeited my life long ago, Knight. This is about my squad."

"They'd really do that? The Corps, I mean? Execute all of you?"

Rook gives me a nod so slight I almost miss it. "Depends on how they end up viewing what we did in the context of what we bring back. But chances are—"

"Dr. Park?" Jaffa interrupts.

"Yes?"

"We'll stay and help you. Our only request is that we be allowed to return to… uh, our home solar system at the first opportunity."

"Done." She extends her hand. "A pleasure to have you with us, Lieutenant. Now, let's get you squared away."

As Evelyn leads the Navy crew toward the main tent, I shrug at Rook. "I think she missed her calling as a politician."

"Or a general," he adds and then moves to catch up.

INTRODUCTIONS ARE MADE ALL AROUND. Our newcomers are Jaffa's XO, Ensign Lowery, Petty Officers Second

Class Claire Richards and Dre Hammond, Petty Officers Third Class Dumont Hill and Bryan Stack. All in all, I'd say they look happy to be off the *Belle* and, more than that, inspired by what they've found on Soteria. I get Jaffa being upset and cautious. I'd be too if someone took over my ship. But these are exceptional circumstances, and so far clear heads are prevailing.

I'm walking with Rook to watch the shuttles lift off for their second run when he stops in his tracks. Something in V-cog, I'm guessing.

"What is it?" I ask.

He turns around and looks toward the forest. "Contact, due west."

"With what?" The words are barely out of my mouth when a throaty whistle echoes from the treeline that makes the hair on the back of my neck stand up.

"Something big. Come on."

23

ROOK

AFTER GIVING KNIGHT A WEAPON, a helmet, and a light plate carrier, we head into the forest and connect with Geller and the rest of Teams One and Two. They're spread along a fifty-meter line, each taking cover behind a tree or rock. We approach Geller, careful to stay down when he motions for us to slow.

"Looks like we found the source of the giant shit," Geller says.

I peer around his cover to see a big animal seventeen meters away. Closest thing I can think of is a gray elephant, but instead of ears that come off its head, it's got an entire body of flappy skin that drapes down to brush the ground like a giant skirt.

"You getting this, Priest?" I say over V-cog after I ping Sebastián.

"Yes, yes! Keep it coming. This is excellent! Can one of your people zoom in on the face?"

Korvich pings Horowitz who's closest to the head. "Zoom in."

"Roger," he says.

I pick up the feed to see a giant blocky head with two elephant-looking eyes on the side. But instead of a long trunk and two tusks, there's a single horn about two and a half meters long coming from the center of its face above a small mouth.

"Holy hell," Horowitz says. "It's a freaking land narwhal!"

"Closer, please," Seb asks. "If you can, focus on what it's doing with that tusk. Ground level."

"Roger," says Horowitz. Again, the camera gets tighter, and the angle shifts toward where the animal seems to be probing some rotting wood.

"There," Seb exclaims. "Do you see the hole at the end of the horn?"

I can't tell if he's talking to me or the other scientists around him, but I decide to chime in anyway. "Is it a straw?"

"My thoughts exactly, Master Sergeant. It appears as if the creature has some sort of… channel running through the horn, which might explain—"

A throaty whistle fills the woods like before, but far louder, given our proximity. The sound takes me back to being a kid and inhaling hard enough on a drinking straw to make a tone. My mother hated it, especially when my brothers and I did it all at once, just to annoy her.

"Fascinating! Are you able to—"

A second sound rattles the air, but this one is more familiar. A predatorial growl. And if sound betrays size, then whatever made the noise is large.

The *narephant*, for lack of a better name, hears the sound too. It reacts by tightening the skin around its body, forming what I can only guess is some sort of protective shell. Likewise, most of its face is covered, leaving only the tusk pointing straight out.

"Looks like it morphed into a rock or something," Grabowski says.

"Always beats scissors," Rodgers replies. "Which is weird, right? Because scissors stand a better chance against rock than a piece of paper. Never understood how a—"

The growl comes again, but much closer.

"Anyone have eyes?" I ask.

"Negative," fire team leaders Geller and Korvich say.

"What about thermal?"

"Workin' it," Geller replies. Two seconds later, he adds, "Contact. Range, forty-one meters, bearing 76 degrees. Speed… three meters per second."

I switch to thermal and notice a pink glow moving

amid the trees, ground level. The blotch undulates in rhythmic fashion. "We've got a stalker. Anyone have visual?"

"Roger," Ibrahim says. She's on the far left flank of Geller's line and furthest south. I pick up her POV and see a shadow pass through patchy sunlight filtering through the canopy. It's brown. And speckled. I can't be sure, but I think I saw fur too.

"Can you get any tighter?" I ask.

Ibrahim is trying, I know, but the shadow is elusive. So she overlays thermal and uses it as a guide. The result is still not great, but there's at least some form. It's got the bulk of a bear, but moves with the elegance of something more lean. Like a panther.

The narephant lets out another whistle, but this time it's shrill. Piercing even.

"God dammit," I yell and switch on my helmet's noise canceling feature. The tech helps lower the pain. Knight uses his hands to cover his ear flaps until I show him how to make the sound suppression active. The noise has slowed the predator too.

"Tango holding. Eighteen meters from target," Ibrahim says. The thermal blotch is crouched low, and I still can't see all of it in the light. "You want us to open up?"

Before I can say anything, Seb yells, "Please don't! We must not interfere."

"Let it play out," I tell Ibrahim.

"Copy that."

As soon as the narephant is done bellowing, the predator resumes its vector, careful to stay low. Another ten seconds pass, and the narephant seems to get wind of its adversary's approach. It pivots like a dancer, raising its fleshy dress off the ground a few centimeters before dropping back down again. Now the three-meter horn is pointed toward the approaching enemy. Another shrill blast comes from the narephant, and the predator shrinks to the ground.

Part of me, the more cautious side, wants to order everyone to fall back. We can get good footage from the drones. But the other side of me, the one that never backs away from a challenge, wants to stay here and watch. I feel confident our weapons can put down either beast should things get out of hand, and we have a squad's worth of feeds going back to Seb. Plus, our team needs the experience if we want to learn how to defend against whatever this thing is.

"Ten meters," Ibrahim says.

For the first time, I get a good look at the incoming beast as it prepares to strike. Half bear, half jungle cat, and three times as big as either creature on Earth.

"Holy shit," Geller says. "It's gotta be the size of a grid car."

"Grid truck," Korvich counters. "Damn, son."

"Hold," I remind the unit as their weapons come up. "Keep those itchy fingers where they belong."

The *banther* steps into the sunlight and then leaps onto the narephant's side. Giant claws sink into the folds of flesh, drawing blood. The prey emits another deafening blast, one that forces the banther to let go and roll away, shaking its head from the noise. The half cat, half bear shakes its head and then roars several times. It looks annoyed, and its vocalizing is getting louder.

Aware of the fallback, the narephant adjusts itself and then charges the semi-retreating predator. The massive beast is quick—way faster than I would have given it credit for. But not fast enough. Its horn meets the air where the banther was a second before and then pierces a tree trunk. Amazingly, the horn goes straight through. But now the animal seems stuck. The banther seizes the opportunity and jumps on the victim's back again, this time on the hindquarters. Another loud blast comes from the narephant, but the banther doesn't fall away. It just digs its claws in deeper, gouging furrows that fill instantly with red blood.

I'm feeling bad for the narephant when a new sound ripples through the air, one I was not expecting. It's the world's biggest emission of gas through the alimentary canal, complete with flecks of dung flying all over the place. Despite the poor narephant's pain, the banther is getting blasted in the stomach by a fart that still hasn't stopped. Marines laugh as it dawns on them what's going on. And the flabby ass explosion continues until the banther has no choice but to jump away.

Eventually, the narephant pulls its horn free, pivots to face the distracted banther, now covered in fecal matter, and then charges. Using the same surprising nimbleness it displayed moments before, the prey becomes the predator as the tusk punctures the banther's left side. A violent scream cuts the air as the bear-cat tries to un-skewer itself. The banther's thrashing causes the pair to spin in a circle, stirring up dead fronds and debris along the forest floor. It's nearly wriggled free from the tusk, only to have the narephant fling it the rest of the way off. The banther crashes into a tree and looks stunned. Just then, the scent of ass hits me hard. I'm not alone, based on the expletives pouring over comms. It is, quite literally, one of the most heinous smells I've ever encountered, and that's saying something. I'm starting to feel bad for the banther. But I also understand why it just got stuck: there's something in the odor messing with my focus. And my balance. I reach out to steady myself on the rock.

"Priest," I say. "We're getting dizzy over here. Methane exposure?"

"Possibly. I suggest you get clear, Rook."

"Roger that." I'm about to give the order to fall back when the narephant does something truly shocking. It leaps, like a freaking ballerina, and lands atop the banther in a bound. The resulting *thud* sends a tremor up my legs, and the crack of bones makes me shudder.

Then the folds of skin descend and envelope the banther underfoot, hiding it from view. As if it were never there.

"What the hell?" Rodgers asks no one in particular.

The narephant stands there bleeding from his hide, all while stomping down on the animal caught under its fleshy dress. More muffled pops and cracks sound as the large animal pummels its aggressor. A muddy mix of blood and excrement appears along the ground. And when at last the narephant seems content, it moves off its victim to reveal a circle of pulp that looks like it came out the ass end of a meat grinder.

"Don't *ever* underestimate your opponent, class," Geller says.

"Can we go home now, teacher?" Grabowski asks. "I haven't smelled something this foul since Rodgers decided to—"

Another growl comes from the woods. Strike that: *three* growls.

Damn.

"Sounds like they travel in packs," I say over comms. I'm about to give the order to fall back when the sound of beating drums distracts me. It takes me a second to realize the banthers are charging. "Ibrahim. You have eyes?"

"Roger," she says, and pings the battle channel with her thermal. Three blotches are running through the forest at… "Damn! They're booking at eleven MPS!"

I wrestle with giving the order to fall back. We could

move out of harm's way while the predators are distracted, yes. But if these creatures are as sensitive to smell as I think they are, given how negatively they responded to the narephant's shit show, then our scent might lead them right back to Evelynton. If we're going to assault them, we're doing it on our terms, and as far from camp as possible.

"Hey, Priest," I say over comms. "Remember how you mentioned wanting to know if local game was compatible with our biology?"

"Not in so many words."

"Well, looks like you might get some sample tissue. Popov, prep for close air support on our position. Possible five line gun run. Stand by for coordinates."

"Roger that. Skids up."

A beat later, someone yells, "Contact!" and I pivot to see two banthers leap on the narephant's flanks while the third keeps the animal occupied from the front. The larger animal whistles again and then lets another fart rip. But the banthers aren't driven off. If the first predator was the scout, this is the kill team.

The victim tries side-stepping, swiveling, and even hopping in futile attempts to shake the predators free. They stay on, clawing at flesh until blood rains down the animal's sides in sheets. For the first time, the narephant falters, stumbling to the right. The lead banther dashes around the horn and bites it from the side. A loud *crack* sounds, and the weapon breaks free a few centimeters from the face. Blood pumps from the wound, and the big animal stumbles again.

Horn tossed to the side, the third banther lunges for the prey's neck and then clamps its toothy maw around the throat. The three predators ride their meal around as it stumbles through the woods, hitting trees and bumping into boulders before finally collapsing to the forest floor. And just like that, it's over. The victors squat on their hindquarters, heads on swivels to make sure there's no competition. Fat tongues lick lips, preparing for the feast. Satisfied that their kill is uncontested, they turn on the carcass and start ripping flesh from the body.

"*Rubenking Special*, this is Rook," I say to Popov. "Disengage and return to camp. We have…" Something flits over the kill area. "Goddammit, Priest! Your drone is too close. Pull back."

Before Seb can answer, one of the banthers cocks its head sideways and tracks the drone for a second. That's all it needs to gauge range and height before leaping into the air. A giant paw bats the drone sideways. While not destroyed, the unit is out of control, trailing smoke, and careening toward me. A small explosion pops from the drone's side, drawing the enemy's attention, then the unit crashes to the ground and tumbles end over end before plopping to a stop a meter from my feet.

Well isn't that just grand.

I pull behind the boulder and motion for Geller and Knight to hold.

"Rook," Korvich says, and I know what's coming next. "Hostile closing on your position."

"Yeah, figured that was coming. Prepare to engage. Popov? Looks like we might need you after all."

"On my way."

24

ROOK

IBRAHIM'S HELMET cam provides the best view of the animal closing on my position. The banther isn't fully crouched, like it's stalking prey, but it's far from relaxed. The posture exudes hostile curiosity as it nears the downed drone. I sense the creature's presence as it nears. Blasts of hot breath push leaves aside and emit a foul odor. The best case is the animal sniffs the drone, dismisses it, and then returns to the more interesting kill. Worst case? Well...

"*Aaaaah-chooo*," yells Grabowski ten meters to my right, visor up.

The panther's head swivels and locks on Grabowski's position. A low growl confirms that it has him sighted.

"Permission to engage?" he asks.

"Hold." I motion for Knight and Geller to follow me

out of Grabowski's field of fire. "Team Two, prepare to flank right on the main group. Team One, hold your ground. We go on Grabowski."

I get behind the next boulder and then give Grabowski the all-clear, but the animal must sense something because it roars and charges his position. Grabowski yells and opens fire, putting two three-round bursts into the animal's head and open mouth. The percussive *zip-zip-zip-whir* ends with blood splatter arching through the air.

I fire a three-round burst on the tango's midsection while Geller pegs it in the ass. Grabowski pulls behind his tree and narrowly avoids a snapping jaw. But the animal hits the trunk with its shoulder hard enough to send Grabowski to his back. He fires straight up, drilling the creature's chest. I can't even tell if our rounds are doing anything until the animal stumbles forward and then lands on Grabowski's legs. He's swearing up a storm and empties his magazine into the tango's skull. Bits of white bone and chunks of flesh fly away until the weapon goes silent. The creature is dead, but the other two are on the move.

Team Two has moved to create the right side of a V formation and splits their fire between the pair of banthers while Team One forms the other leg. I'm guessing nothing on this planet has seen MAW fire before, let alone people, so the targets don't retreat as other animals might back on Earth. The bullets shred their flesh but fail to dissuade them from pursuing us. One banther darts behind a crop of rocks only to circle around and then lunge at Engleman. He's ready, however, and opens up with his Bellaire MS265. The canister-fed weapon spits 7.62 ammo in a stream that pelts the encroaching enemy in the chest. Blood showers the forest floor, but the animal keeps coming. Horowitz doubles up with Engleman, focusing on the eyes and forehead. Their aim is true, and the skull blows open in pieces. Unable to function, the banther dives into the ground and flips ass over head before coming to a stop against a tree.

The last banther charges Team One, heading right for Grabowski, Rodgers, and Ibrahim. But they spread apart and converge fire on the tango's head, splitting it in two. The animal drops a shoulder and gouges a furrow through the dirt. Like the aftermath of the narephant, the air goes still, interrupted by the *Rube*'s engines as it does an overhead pass.

"First you need me, then you don't. But then you do, only to not need me," Popov says. "You're worse than my high school girlfriend."

"Something you need to talk about?" Rodgers asks. "Grabowski has a lot of experience there."

Grabowski would come back, but he's stuck beneath the bulk of his banther. "Little help here?"

"Rodgers, Ibrahim, help him out," Geller says.

To Popov, I say, "Make sure we're clear to the west, and drop some extra sensor beacons while you're at it."

"Roger that."

I ping Seb. "Got some steaks for you, Priest. Hungry?"

"I certainly wish it would have been through a different means, but I'm glad you're okay."

"Send Fergus with a container and a list of needed parts. We'll start butchering. And, a word of warning?"

"Yeah?"

"These things smell like death warmed over. Might wanna clear camp and give everyone a stretch break. God knows we need showers over here."

"I appreciate the word of caution. We'll send Fergus now. Stand by."

I make my way over to Grabowski who's on his feet again, brushing gore off his trousers. "You good, Corporal?"

"Yeah. Hell, yeah. Besides needing a bath and a bottle of something strong."

"We'll set you up with both soon enough. Head back to camp. Ibrahim, go with."

They nod and head out while Jericho and I turn back toward the main engagement area. The narephant's body doesn't look as big as it did when it was alive. But the stench is just as bad... if not worse. Banther bodies lay where they fell, and Engleman and

Horowitz already have their KA-BARs out, ready to start fileting.

"How do you think they're gonna taste?" Engleman asks. Everyone within earshot answers at the same time: "Like chicken."

A rhythmic *thud thud thud* signals Fergus's arrival. He sets down an insulated storage container and flips open the lid. "Your transfer bin, as requested, my lord."

"Thanks, Ferg. What does the Priest want?"

"Several samples of bone and muscle tissue, as well as brain matter, eyes, teeth, and stool. The full list is in your V-cog now. Where do you desire my assistance?"

"Grab a knife and take the narephant there."

"The what, my lord?"

"The big ugly one. It smells too bad for us to approach without being fully suited. And try not to puncture any glands or gas sacks. We don't need more noxious fumes in the area."

"Ah, very good. It is my supreme privilege to be of service to you in this way."

"Normally, I'd say you're being a bit overdramatic, but in this case, we're all really glad you're here, buddy." Before the bot can come back with some outrageous reply, I turn to Jericho. "Why don't you head back to camp. We got this from here."

"You sure?"

"I mean, do you want to stay and help butcher animals for the next hour?"

"I'll head back."

He smiles. "Warm up the grill in case the Priest says it's a go."

"I'll get the beer."

Jericho

As IT TURNS OUT, we do fire up the grill. Granted, it's some Bunsen-burning research apparatus care of the science team, but it cooks the meat to a consistent well-done. Sebastián is first to volunteer eating the narephant flesh after the sample passed his biocompatibility tests. No one's arguing either. Dog muscle and cow muscle might be near enough each other on chemical and molecular levels to pass a lab test, but you don't see me opting for the former when going out for a meal. Still, if we are to inhabit this planet as a species, I fully recognize that alternate versions of filet mignon will be required. Who knows? Maybe the next generation thinks cow meat is repulsive and narephant is mouthwatering. It's all relative.

"Well?" Evelyn asks Seb as he works the morsel around in his mouth.

"High fat content. And then a little gamey in places. But… with enough salt and pepper, I think it's tasty in its own way. Anyone want to try?"

Several onlookers wince at the prospect.

"Why not?" I say and step forward. "You're sure it's safe though? From contamination or something?"

"I am. But if I'm wrong…"

"Yeah?"

He holds up a knife with a sliver of meat toward my face. "We'll suffer from the flying fecal matter defense together."

I pluck the sample with my fingers and study it. "Not the most reassuring statement, but misery does love company."

The first few seconds of chewing is a mental game more than anything else. I fight the image of the giant animal showering its enemies with fecal matter and choose instead to see a Black Angus heifer grazing in a green pasture. Then my taste receptors kick in, and I'm struck with a savory blend of something between venison and the one time I had whale meat.

"And?" Kit asks me.

"It's… unique. Not one thing or another. Just… narephant meat."

"You see?" Seb says. "And it stands to reason. This is, by all counts, a creature unlike anything we've seen before, so why would it taste like anything we know?" He reaches for the banther sample that's been cooking on another rack. "Who's next?"

Every Marine in earshot raises their hand.

THE DISCOVERIES COME in waves for the next month. Some days, the science expedition teams bring back dozens of species samples, ranging from insects and plant clippings to stool material and video footage. Other days are quiet. But our knowledge of Soteria feels exciting and daunting all at the same time. Despite the flood of data, everyone knows we're just scratching the surface.

There's never a lack of work to do either. Whether it's being a lab assistant, weapons cleaner, construction worker, or ship mechanic, everyone has a variety of jobs to pick from, and we all cross-train where possible. Since there's no telling how long we'll be stranded here, no one can afford to be the only specialist in a given field in case the worst happens. Redundancy and endurance are not accidental; for POET, surviving is intentional.

True to his word, Lieutenant Jaffa and his crew are

fully committed to expanding Evelynton. His administrative energy is inspiring, to say the least. I swear the man never sleeps. He's also a competent and patient teacher, replicating his pragmatic approach to resource management in anyone willing to look over his shoulder. Combined with Eddie's competency in 3D design and manufacturing, the two of them have built walls around our camp that can be pushed out as more space is required. They've also engineered a small energy production plant, water desalination and sewage treatment systems, and the beginnings of a food storage facility for all the edible goods the science division is discovering.

More permanent housing is popping up too. While the 3D printers haven't stopped creating two-story habs from the local substrate, Fergus has taken to repurposing the boulders and lumber the Marines are harvesting to provide our new quarters with some "homey aesthetics," he says... not that he's ever set foot in a real Earth-based house before. But with his knowledge base being what it is, thanks to Kit, I'm not surprised that he has a notion for comfortable and even fashionable living environments. The first time I walked into one of his sample apartments and saw that the kitchen had been printed around a giant boulder, which also served as a hewn-out oven, I was impressed. The raw-cut overhead beams were also a nice touch to the otherwise bland schematic provided by NUESSA.

As for the Marines and all those raw materials that Fergus has been using, Rook's unit has been clearing the forest to the west of Camp Evelynton for security reasons. Apparently, military strategy dictates that all forward operating bases have clear lines of sight and lots of open space between them and any encroaching enemies. Not only is the immediate vicinity laid bare, but new weapons are printed and installed on the wall-tops, much to Evelyn's chagrin. But not even she can argue against Rook's hypothetical scenario where a pack of banthers charge camp from multiple angles in the middle of the night.

The warriors have also taken to hunting and foraging. Their experience clearing the woods has made them the leading forestry experts. Where Seb and Enni's expertise can tell us all about molecular composition and evolutionary adaptation, Rook's squad is fast becoming experts on how the flora and fauna behave and how best to live in harmony with them—not something I would have pegged Marines to ever be concerned with. Turns out, Grabowski and Rodgers are regular botanical connoisseurs. Who knew?

Kit and Fergus have also become quite the pioneers. They often head out for days at a time, camping in the forest and expanding our map of ground-explored territory. They act like a medieval Lewis and Clark, sharing tales of their adventures around campfires when they come back from a few-day's trip. I haven't been too concerned about Kit's safety since he has Fergus with him. But I have questioned some of their decision making, especially when they both returned one time with tattoos—Kit's face laser-etched onto Fergus's bicep, and Fergus's face burnt into Kit's thigh. God, it's ugly, and probably hurt like hell for Kit. But he's been super proud of it. They haven't told the story yet, but I'll be damned if I miss that campfire late-night.

Another practice that most everyone has taken a liking to is weapons training and hand-to-hand combat lessons with the Marines. At first, most of the scientists were scared of the rifles and pistols. Only a few had ever fired one before. But once Eddie started making science lessons out of the process, not only did the civilians take to the guns, many of them have become good marksmen. Likewise, they seem to be enjoying the sparring and grappling exercises, if nothing more than for the cardiovascular benefits.

There's also been a lot of talk about contacting Earth and even the Naqualla. But since we haven't been able to activate their rings, reaching Earth is futile. Likewise, since we don't know where the aliens hail from, picking a direction at random and sending out a signal over who knows how many lightyears is equally pointless. Still, Evelyn set up a repeating transmission from the *Sagan* broadcasting in all directions in the hopes that one day, maybe years from now, our benefactors will get notice of our arrival. Whether or not those expectations are even realistic is anyone's guess, but she and the rest of the science team felt it was our responsibility to make the effort. Likewise, similar transmissions have been sent toward Earth. Granted, we all understand they won't be heard for a thousand years, which is crazy to think about. There could be a generation in the future who receives a foreign transmission from a colony of humans believed to be a myth. Talk about a head trip.

Now that our fifth week here is drawing to a close, I find it amusing that I haven't been back to the *Kogarashi* in a while.

"What's so funny?" Evelyn asks me as she takes a seat to my left along the eastern wall that faces the ocean.

"It's been three weeks since I was on the *Koga*."

"Same for me with the *Sagan*."

"You miss it?"

"Not one bit. Which is ironic."

"How's that?"

She shrugs. "I'm a SESI lead scientist. My whole adult life has been spent in space. And I think it's safe to assume that everyone thinks NUESSA employees love being aloft. But the irony, at least for me, is that everything I've ever done to make sure that this"—she gestures around us—"was the inevitable end. I never wanted to stay in space."

"You wanted paradise."

She gives me a smile complete with a twinkle in her eye. "Yeah."

"Well, Dr. Park, you got your wish."

"Just have to find a way to give everyone else theirs too. Say, what's yours?"

"What?"

"Your wish? This whole time has been all about, ya know, *Parallax One* and Kep-C and *Astraea* and *Telemine* Stations. But you never signed up to find extrasolar sentient life. I mean, not at first anyway."

"You certainly changed my mind there, Dr. Park." I hold up the Sentia Aux tat on my palm and give her a smile, but it fades as I think about how little our politicasts mean in a virgin world like Soteria. Then again, how long will it be before we're fighting over resources? Before we're creating a disproportionate class system that claims to be egalitarian but inevitably favors a powerful few at the expense of a weakened many?

I draw in a deep breath of the ocean air and savor the smell. "I guess, at the end of the day, I just want people to have a shot, ya know? And I have to believe that the things I've designed, built, and tested… things like the *Kogarashi*, that they'll make some of that possible for people. To overcome the odds stacked against them. To reach the places they want to go. That desire hasn't changed. It's why expanding Evelynton has been fun for me… why the time has flown these last few weeks. I get to help people create a better life for themselves so they can keep dreaming. It's like you and me."

"I beg your pardon?"

"You've had big dreams, Evelyn. Communicating with aliens and saving the human race. I'm just the guy who helped make sure you got to the appointment."

All at once, Evelyn puts her head on my shoulder. I don't quite know what to do about it. So I just sit, trying not to move. Like hoping you don't scare a bird away that's alighted on your hat's brim. You freeze, taking the moment for what it is. A gift.

"Thanks," she says in a barely audible whisper. "For believing in me."

"You're welcome. And thank you for—"

"Hey, Fox?" comes a new voice over V-cog. A camera feed of Nairobi's face opens in an augmented reality window. She's doing her twenty-four hour shift on the *Kogarashi.*

"I'm a little busy right now," I say in the real, and then turn to Evelyn when she lifts her head. "It's Nairobi."

"Oh, okay," she replies.

"Fox," Nairobi says again. "We have a situation up here."

"What kind?"

"The 'something just came through Ring W' kind."

"What did you say?"

"What's wrong?" Evelyn asks.

I wave her off so I can focus on Nairobi. "Like debris or something?"

"Negative. Like a ship, and it's burning toward Soteria. Fast."

"Jericho? What's going on?" Evelyn asks again.

"Did you say a ship?" I ask Nairobi but slip and say it out loud too.

"Sure did, boss."

"What ship?" Evelyn says.

I stare her in the eyes. "Looks like we've got company."

25

LEMUEL

TRUE TO HIS WORD, Director Lemuel Brown reached out to his half-sister, Vivian Matthews, and asked after his nephew, Tré. The young man had a troubled youth on account of his father's recklessness, which made Marine Corps enlistment a logical option in channeling Tré's anxieties and boundless energy. But trouble followed him through the Corps as well, and he was eventually discharged—honorably, thanks to political connections on Lemuel's side. That was the last Lemuel had seen his nephew. But not the last he'd heard about him. From there, Tré used everything he'd learned about combat and counterintelligence from the Marines to forge his own way in the world, one where he could charge astronomical fees to anyone willing to employ his services as a

spy and, as far as Lemuel could discern, an assassin. He
knew all this because of Vivian, though they'd fallen out
of touch in recent years. She, ever the doting mother,
had become his handler. His rep. Partly because it
allowed her to keep tabs on her only child. Partly
because she was good at negotiating. But the biggest
part, Lemuel knew, was because of the money that kept
her own vices thriving.

"Hi, Vivian," Lemuel said, standing alone in his half-
sister's public lobby. "Can you talk?" He waited, hands
clasped behind his back, in the stark white construct that
was devoid of any items or walls. A perfectly blank slate
that betrayed nothing about its owner. Lemuel didn't
bother repeating himself. He knew she'd heard him, and
that if she wanted to talk, she'd show up. He'd give her
twenty seconds. After that, he'd bow out.

"Lem," she said, appearing in a black tracksuit with
white pinstripes. Her hair was gathered behind her head,
and she propped a hand on the side of one hip. Between
chomps of gum, she said, "What's shaking, big bro?
Haven't heard from you in a while."

"I'll, uh… cut to the chase, given the circumstances."

"That you don't call no more? Don't write?"

"Would you read it?"

"Maybe." She thinks for a second, chewing loudly.
"Eh, probably not. Whadda ya need?"

"I need Tré to look into something for me."

"For you? Or someone you know?"

"Does it matter?"

"Sure. Always matters, big bro. Always matters."

Lemuel knew better than to keep secrets from her. She would find out in the end; better to eliminate points of leverage from the outset. "Caleb Nowen."

"Sugar Buns?"

He cringed. It was the childhood name Viv had given Caleb when she was sixteen and he was a freshman in college with Lemuel. "Says there might be someone blackmailing general council members in the Chamber of Politicast Representatives."

"Huh. Honey, that's been going on long before you and I were around, and it will keep going on long after we're dead."

"Yeah, but this sounds serious." He related the details that Caleb had brought to him, about Lemmens in his pool, Phillips and his car wreck, and Latif being a no-show for his budget meeting. Celeb had provided two more cases after they hung up. Lem handed her a dossier with what he knew. "He believes they're connected somehow. I do too."

"Sure, they're connected. Doesn't take a rocket scientist to see that. Present company excluded, 'course."

Lem gave her a half smile. He wasn't feeling very chummy at the moment, even for his baby half-sister. "Think you can have Tré look into it? See what he can find?"

"Sure, sure. You paying?"

"No. I told Caleb this was on him."

"Smart." Vivian winked at Lem and then blew and popped a bubble. "Knew I'd want my money's worth with him, did ya?"

"Something like that."

Vivian weighed the dossier in her hand like doing so might magically reveal the work ahead. "I'll get you something by tomorrow. Might be a lot, might be a little. But Tré will do his thing."

"Thanks, Viv. I appreciate it."

"Don't thank me. Thank Sugar Buns. I'm doing this for all that. Mmmm, lord."

How Vivian managed to stay alive after running in the circles she did was anyone's guess. They broke the mold with her.

THE CALL CAME JUST after dinner the next night. But it wasn't Vivian who pinged him in V-cog. It was Tré himself. They met in Lemuel's den construct, standing on the back patio as the sun sank behind the pines.

"Uncle Lemuel," Tré said with a cool Janusian air and slicked back hair. He and his mother were as opposite as they came. Guy could've had his pick of roles in any political thriller or spy movie he wanted. But something told Lemuel that Tré liked real knives and bullets over the prop ones. "Nice to see you again."

"Same. It's been a while."

Tré nodded but didn't comment on that. "Vivian… *mom* forwarded your intel. Seems Uncle C. was right to be concerned."

"Oh?"

Tré produced a small holo window for each of thirteen people that, judging by the accompanying crime scene pics of their bodies, were recently deceased. "To the average on-looker, these are legitimate accidents. Varied in means and methods. Random, even. Sure, it's interesting that they're all major politicast members or direct relatives, but that's not enough to be conclusive. You need evidence to put that together."

"And you have some?"

"Every killer has their strengths and weaknesses. Crime families have their go-to axes. But these? These are varied, and clean. Which means we're either dealing with a savant who can be in several places at once, and one who no one has ever heard of, or…"

"Or more than one criminal organization is working together."

Tré eyed Lemuel. "You sure you don't wanna slide into the family business? I can set you up."

"This is as much as I can handle, son. What did you find out?"

Tré closed the smaller windows and opened a new one. The photograph was of a gaunt man in his early twenties wearing blue eyeshadow and, Lemuel noted, enough facial piercings to outfit his wife's earring collection for a month. "Meet Eldon 'Skitz' Pearlman, leader of Radio Ultra."

"The crime syndicate?"

"Indeed. Quite the chatty man. And he happened to be at the same club I was in this morning, as fate would have it."

"Which was where?" Lemuel stopped himself. "Never mind. I'm better off not knowing."

"While Mr. Pearlman isn't threatened by anything I could do to him with a computer… blackmail, forgery, racketeering… he is highly motivated by promptings of the more physical kind."

Lemuel raised his hands. "Again, not interested."

"I understand, Uncle. Just trying to let you know that the information he had was not given up lightly."

"You killed him?"

"And tip off whoever he's working for? Bad tradecraft. I incentivized him to be honest with me. And, yes, he's still alive."

"Did he say anything? Does he know who's behind the murders?"

Tré nodded. "He is. At least a few of them."

Lemuel noticed his jaw hanging open after a few seconds. "And… and we can get proof of this to the authorities?"

"Probably not, no."

"But we have to. These are… are assassinations of high level government—"

"You won't be able to get evidence of Mr. Pearlman's activities, I can assure you that. Radio Ultra has been untouchable precisely because they are consummate professionals in covering their tracks. Even if the confession I secured were admissible in a court of law, which it isn't, Pearlman and his stim rats would have a field day with corrupting the data as soon as it hit the archives, secure as they may be."

Lemuel didn't like that, but he also couldn't argue against it. This was a field he wasn't fit to play on. He already felt out of his league as it was. "Did he say why? The representatives who were targeted?"

"He did. But before I tell you, you need to decide if you really want it. I've been in this game long enough to know that some secrets paint big targets on your back. They make it hard to sleep at night. Get too restless, and it's amazing who will notice. Who will put poison in your drink or a bullet in your head. And this is one of those kinds of secrets, Uncle. Maybe the biggest of its kind. The sort that puts you, Aunt Ray, and everyone you know at risk if you can't keep your lips shut." Tré's eyes softened; Lemuel hadn't seen that since he'd let Tré know about the strings he pulled for his honorable discharge years ago. "I'm not even sure I want to tell you."

Lemuel heard the darkness in his nephew's words… heard the warning. He didn't doubt for one second the truth of everything Tré had said. He only doubted whether or not he'd be able to do something about it. "Will it keep people from dying? If I know? If I can do something about it?"

"A few, maybe. But many more could be put in harm's way too."

"Then that's a risk I'm willing to take. Been doing that my whole career, it seems."

"Uncle Lem, there's—"

"No going back from this. I know." Lemuel walked over to a wicker lawn chair and invited Tré to sit in an adjacent one. "Let's hear it."

LEMUEL HOSTED his second call with Caleb in as many days, knowing his college friend would think the SESI director's V-cog channel was more secure than a politi-cast representative's. But after what Tré had told Lemuel, he was beginning to think neither option was a secure one.

"You have something already?" Caleb said as he took a seat in the leather office chair.

Lemuel nodded but didn't speak right away.

"And?" Caleb was finally forced to say.

"Cale, how long have you and I been friends?"

"Jesus." The Sentia Aux representative for Auckland ran his hands over his head and fell back into his chair. "It's that bad?"

Lemuel interlaced his fingers and ran his tongue along the inside of his cheek. "You and I have been through a lot together. Seen some crazy shit."

"Crazy."

"But this…" He didn't even know how to qualify it. So he'd just start. "I can't confirm anything I'm about to tell, at least in a way that would appease the law. Everything's second and third hand. Hearsay. Gossip. And any first-hand information I have was… extracted." He didn't feel like expounding. "There's no evidence besides eyewitness accounts from people the world would sooner forget than trust. Which leads to a second issue."

"I'm listening."

"Even if it's all true, I don't know what can be done. The players at the table… they'll find out if something doesn't go according to plan. And they have the means to follow the leads wherever they go, smoke out the culprits, and then end them. For good."

"So these deaths… they're not accidents."

"They're assassinations, Cale."

"Shit. Shit, shit, shit. See? I told you, Lem. I *told* you."

"But it's more than that."

"Blackmail? Extortion?"

"Of the highest degree. I got a hold of Tré, and he

was able to connect Lemmens, Phillips, and Latif's deaths to over a dozen other incidents, some involving representative's family members, and all conducted by members of three different radical groups."

"You know them?"

Lemuel called up holo windows for each senior leader and their respective organizations. "Androsia Behr of Leonidas X. Eldon 'Skitz' Pearlman with Radio Ultra. And Tonka of the Bemba Militia. They've all been tied, at least in the underworld, to the majority of the incidents."

Caleb studied the files for a few seconds. "These are midlevel terrorist groups. And none of them would be caught dead with the others."

"Which is why they make ideal scapegoats for someone else's bidding."

"Let me guess, the Tantum."

Lemuel summoned another window and placed it above the trio. "It appears that in Neon's absence, her daughter Gemma Birdwhistle has taken her place."

"She has a daughter?"

Lemuel gave him a painful smile. The whole world knew of her son, Jack, following *Astraea*'s demise. But the daughter would be news to many. "Something tells me she's even worse than her half-brother."

"Half?"

"Different fathers. Where Jack was brought back into Neon's life in his early twenties following an issue with her estranged ex-husband, Gemma was raised at her side. Got early degrees in advanced bioengineering and virtual cognizance integration from the University at Helsinki and SJIT under the name Gemma Ridell, a registered member of the Viatoribus."

"So… she's an incog?"

"Has been most of her life, it appears."

"Christ."

"It gets worse. According to Tré, she broke V-cog."

Caleb blinked at him a few times. "Excuse me? *Broke* V-cog? As in…?"

"Developed a way past the quantum neural security firewall that every tech firm swore was impenetrable."

"But their testimony is the entire reason that—"

"That every human on the planet adopted virtual cognizance. I know. And she hacked the firewall. Tré says they call it Gaia's Blood, Neon's name for it."

"In honor of the maternal spirit of the Earth… that she's trying to save."

"Or serve. Depends on how fanatical you believe she was."

"So you're saying Gemma's behind all these assassinations? What does she hope to gain? After what they've done, there's no way the Tantum Terrae would be let within a hundred kilometers of a chamber seat."

"That's because she's not at the top of the food chain." Lemuel opened a fifth and final holo window above Gemma's. It was a picture of one of the most recognizable men in the star system.

"Sallsworth? Are you fucking kidding me? *He's* calling the shots?"

"According to Tré."

"Jesus Christ." Caleb's avatar stood, which probably mirrored his behavior in the real too, if Lemuel had to guess. Avatars often mimicked the user's physical body when certain inputs lagged. "Did Tré say if he knew what Sallsworth was up to?"

"He did. Part of it you already know about."

"His bid to be the first President of the Nations of United Earth," Caleb replied and waited for Lemuel to nod before elaborating. "He's going to call for a vote with him as the only candidate... trying to leverage the *Parallax One* situation to justify a special vote. Argue for an existential threat, consolidate power, and weed out dissenters. That's the historical play anyway, isn't it?" Caleb put his hands on his seat back and leaned forward, head down. "God, I'm gonna be sick." After another moment, he looked up. "This tech that cracks V-cog, Gaia's Blood, did Tré say what it does? Are we talking about mind reading, security breaches, what?"

"That's the second part. We're talking about the ability to kill the mind."

"I'm sorry, what?" Caleb didn't move. Not for three interminably long seconds. "Kill the mind? As in—"

"Murder."

"No. No way. I don't believe it. That's impossible. That means that every person with V-cog—"

"Is at risk, yes."

"Are you fucking kidding me right now? We're talking about billions of people who are potential targets, Lem! How... how are you so goddamn calm right now?"

"Because I already had my freakout earlier today."

"And you're sure about this?"

"That part was from Tré himself. He was the one who stole the tech from Neon and Gemma, and then delivered it to Sallsworth. And it's what Nigel used to kill Neon with."

Caleb looked like he was about to come unglued. "Sallsworth? Sallsworth killed...? But she died on the night of—"

"Of his system-wide address locking down *Parallax One*. Tré claims he assassinated her moments before he went live."

"The man's a sociopath! How do... How do you do that and then come off so... so slick? God in heaven."

Lemuel let Caleb have a minute to process everything. It wasn't enough time, he knew. Lemuel had needed an hour to settle down himself, and that was with some help from a few fingers of Jameson. Caleb was doing this dry, which wouldn't last too long, Lemuel supposed.

"So it's out there," Caleb said at last. "Gaia's Blood.

Gemma's got it, and now Sallsworth has it. And they're buddy-buddy?"

"Tré couldn't answer that part. He knows they're working together, even though it isn't clear why. The logical assumption is that he's going to reward her with a seat at the table."

"Something that will never happen," Caleb said as a reminder. "Not in a million years. Especially if the NUE knows who she is."

"And maybe that's it: keep her identity as Neon's daughter and the TT's new head from ever getting out."

"But we know."

"And we'd probably last ten seconds after leaking, Cale."

His dark face somehow managed to look pale. "Gaia's Blood. She can get to us."

Lemuel nodded solemnly.

"Holy hell…"

The lack of talking and the heaviness in the room gave way to the subtle sounds of wind blowing through the opened glass doors. Birds sang somewhere in the distance, and a woodpecker hammered for bugs inside a tree.

"So what do we do?" Caleb asked.

"We fight like hell to ensure that the crews of the *Kogarashi*, *Sagan Explorer*, and *Bellerophon* have a chance to get home."

"And you have any idea on how to do that?"

"I do," Lemuel said with his fingers steepled. "But you're really not going to like it."

"Career suicide?"

"That's the least of our worries, honestly."

"How do you figure?"

"Because if we don't do what I have in mind, we'll be committing genocide by abdication."

26

EVELYN

I NEARLY MISS the rungs as I climb off the wall and head down the ladder to camp. For whatever reason, the *Kogarashi* picked up the anomaly even before the *Sagan*. Then again, the science officer on duty was Bart Clement, and he's not exactly the most self-aware. Guy was probably napping. But once he was roused, the *Sagan* confirmed what Nairobi was tracking: an unidentified spacecraft vectoring away from Ring W and headed toward Soteria.

"Give me visual," Rook says from inside the new command building. It's a five room tech building with a command theater in the middle. The central room offers two rows of workstations and a floor to ceiling holo display along the far wall. Rook likes it dim and requests that Jericho and I close the door to keep out the daylight.

A camera feed from Lance Corporal Dregs is in the main display's upper right hand corner. She's the *Belle*'s Marine on watch and moving frantically through the ship's data systems to send the Master Sergeant what he wants. With a few final moves, she says, "Annnnd should be yours now."

Rook confirms acquisition and orders the live feed on the holo. When the images come, Rook says, "Holy God. We've got a bogie. Burn ID?"

"Drive sig fails to meet any known parameters," says Petty Officer Claire Richards.

"Nor does the hull design," Ensign Markus Lowery adds. "I think it goes without saying that this vessel isn't one of ours."

"And by ours, you don't mean NUE," Jericho says. "You mean…"

"Human," I add.

Lowery nods. "Affirmative."

The ship's most noticeable trait is its silver fuselage that glints in the sunlight as it starts to enter Soteria's atmosphere. It's triangular in design but has too many additional parts to be purely geometric. Wings, a tail, some sort of canopy, and curved lines on side pods and an underbelly section. It also has markings, none of which are in any language I'm familiar with, though they do seem to be script-like… maybe it's not even writing, but art. No way to be sure.

The command room's door slides open again, and

Lieutenant Jaffa enters dressed in work clothes and wiping his brow with a cloth. Lowery makes an attempt to brief him, but Jaffa waves him off. "I've been following in V-cog."

"What do you make of it?" Rook asks.

Jaffa leans toward the metadata streaming down the main holo's left side. "I'd say that's a transport shuttle of some kind. Small. Five, maybe six crew."

"Weapons?"

"Doesn't look armed. Plus, it's not exactly trying to hide." As if to emphasize his point, the star's light reflects off the hull and sends a lens flare to the *Belle*'s camera.

"But it is moving fast," Richards says, her voice taking on an amazed tone. "It's covered the distance from the ring to the planet's Kármán line in under three minutes and hasn't showed any signs of—"

I know she's about to say 'slowing' when the shuttle snaps 180 degrees and fires its main engines in what I can only assume is a full burn. The *Belle*'s camera adjusts for the sudden increase in light. Likewise, the shuttle's friction in the upper atmo throws off fire like a meteor.

Jericho thumbs toward the screen. "That's either one hell of a pilot, or they've got a death wish. Lot cheaper ways to end it all."

"Clement," I say. "Are you picking up any other activity from the ring?"

"Negative. It, uh… looks quiet. There's a fading

power signature, like maybe it opened for a second and then shut again or something. Maybe just enough to let this one through. But that's it."

"I want eyes on Ring W," Rook says. "Notify us the second anything changes."

"Roger."

Rook looks to Jaffa. "Mind handling ship management?"

Suddenly concerned, I ask, "You're not planning on opening fire, are you?"

"No, ma'am," Jaffa replies. "I'm just going to make sure all three ships are in their optimum positions should things deteriorate."

"And for us?" Jericho asks Rook. "Orders?"

"I want all personnel inside the wall and taking cover in the most shielded buildings. Our Marine element will set security. We'll hope for the best but plan for the worst. Where's the bogie's position?"

Richards comes back with a flurry of data. "Currently over the eastern ocean, lat 1.05, long 40.69, bearing 270 degrees, range—"

"That's directly toward us," I say.

"All the more reason to be concerned," Rook replies. "Range?"

"Range, 11,824 kilometers and closing. Altitude, 90 kilometers and falling. ETA on our position at current vectors, not accounting for the decel burn we're seeing, is twenty-five minutes."

"Thing's moving like a bat out of hell," Lowrey says.

"And yet still not burning up in atmo," Rook replies. "Which means it's tough."

"And means we have twenty-five minutes to figure out what we're going to do when and if it gets here, right Evelyn?" Jericho asks.

All eyes turn to me.

"We'll be ready," I say.

As it turns out, the ship hasn't arrived yet, and it's been almost two hours. Scratch that, it's been two hours and four minutes. Which has given me, Seb, Enni, and Natalie plenty of time to review SESI first contact protocols—too much time, in my view. Something's off with this whole thing. According to our ship-to-surface V-cog grid, which is still tracking the *bogie*, as Rook is keen to call it, the ship won't be here for another twenty minutes. It's slowed down with no explanation why.

"All dressed up and nowhere to go," I say, studying the live feeds, and then blow some hair out of my face. My team and I are back inside the command building after sending out some broad range signal patterns to see if the vessel will respond. We've even had time to change into cooler clothes, grab a snack, and hit the lavatory. But so far, it doesn't seem like the ship wants to talk. "Anything new?"

"Nothing," Lieutenant Jaffa says and then looks at Rook. "Thoughts?"

"It's clearly capable of faster speeds. This"—he glances at the latest telemetry—"this whole 515 klicks per hour business is a show."

"How do you mean?" I ask, genuinely curious, because I have my own suspicions.

"Well, it's inbound in a straight line, no deviation. It's also crawling, relative to what we know it can do. Both of those are poor strategic measures when approaching a potentially hostile force. So it either doesn't see us, which I highly doubt given the precision of its trajectory, or—"

"It isn't hostile," I say.

He seems reluctant to agree; none of us have forgotten Fred's account of the alleged Naqualla conflict with the Ganese. But he eventually nods. "Sure, the pilot could be a nut job hellbent on torturing its prey by conducting excruciatingly long approaches that end in total annihilation, but even I know that's a stretch. In the real world, if you want a target taken out, you don't hesitate."

"You think it's curious," I state.

"And it doesn't want to raise our hackles. Yup."

"Sounds like the lead Marine in the room has changed his tune from earlier," Jericho says.

"Well, when you consider the behavior, it's at least plausible that maybe they're not trying to assault us. And

I still haven't bought into Fred's interpretation of events over Kep-C."

I decide to offer my analysis, which support's Rook's optimistic view. "Come in low and slow, set yourself on a predictable flight path, and hope those on the ground see that as a friendly gesture. Do I have that right?"

Rooks grins. "The recruiter is next door. You should fill out an application."

"Not to question either of you here," Jericho says, "but isn't this wishful thinking?"

"Sure," Rook says. "But not when you consider the alternatives."

"Like?"

"It could have arrived with a fleet at night. It could have maintained that original speed and come in from the west across the continent where we wouldn't have line of sight until the last second. And if it's just a scout, it missed the class on concealment and evasion." Rook sends a live scope feed from the *Bliss Mobile*'s nose cannon. "As it is right now, we've got eyes on target and effective range dialed in. Assuming it can see us too and has made some sort of judgment call about our defenses, the fact that it hasn't veered off course means it might be interested in talking. So, in my world, this isn't a military operation until she says it is." He looks at me.

"And we can't know that until we get some sort of reply," I say. "So far, nothing we've broadcast has elicited any sort of change in behavior. And it's not emitting comms energy on any known bands."

"But even that could be seen as hostile, right?" Jericho says. When I give him a sour look, he holds up his hands in mock defense. "I'm just playing devil's advocate here since the two of you suddenly seem to be all fine with this."

"Ignoring communications can be seen as a hostile act, yes," I reply. "But it can also mean that they don't know what we're saying or…"

"Or what?"

"That they'd rather talk in person."

This raises everyone's eyebrows a little.

"Just for the record," Rook says, eyeing Jericho. "I'm still ready to pull the trigger, and I'm moving assets now. I'm just… slightly more afraid of what she can do to me than our new alien friends."

"Smart man," Jericho says and gives me a wink. "So what's the plan?"

THE FINAL TWENTY minutes are an interesting mix of discovery and apprehension.

We're getting much better images of the alien vessel, which have prompted Kit and Fergus to map a 3D model using the combined orbital and surface-based sensor data. It's rough, of course; nothing will be as good as traditional laser scans, but the duo has done well with what they have. The ship is a strange combination of design features that feel familiar, such as the bird-like wings and brow-shaped canopy, but also foreign, like the hull's angular geometry. And we still have no reference for the markings on the body. The language, if that's what it is, is as mysterious as the intentions of the ship and its pilot—if it even has a pilot.

The Marines have used the time to set up along the wall. Between the shuttles' weapons, newly installed point defense guns, and personal arms, Camp Evelynton is bristling with barrels pointed east. All drones, both scientific and military, have been set to loiter at various altitudes, providing multiple angles and scans. While Rook agrees with me that the incoming ship isn't behaving in a hostile manner, he has admitted that all of that can change at a moment's notice.

I don't even recognize my hand is patting the desk until Jericho puts his hands on it. "One step at a time, Evelyn."

"Right."

"Crossing ten nautical kilometers," Richards announces from the row in front of me. "Bogie decelerating. ETA three minutes."

"You copy that, Rook?" Jaffa asks.

"Roger," he replies from the wall.

I give Jericho's hand a squeeze and then stand up. "I'm gonna go outside with Rook."

"You sure that's wise?"

"And miss seeing this with my own eyes?"

"Well, when you put it like that..."

He follows me out of the command building and into the noon sunlight, then walks beside me across the quad. We take a metal stairwell to the rampart and join Rook who's looking through a handheld scope.

"It's slowed to a crawl," Rook says and then offers the device to me. "Have a look."

The warm ocean breeze whips at my hair, forcing me to move it aside as I take the optical device and press it to my face. The viewfinder is laden with sensor data and unfamiliar military nomenclature, but two obvious readings stand out as the optics focus on the silver bird: speed and elevation. "One meter per second, eleven meters off the water," I say.

"Low and slow."

"So we add hovering to the list of ship's features," Jericho says.

"Indeed," Rook replies. "ETA revised to five minutes. Either it's toying with us, or it really wants to be a sitting duck."

"It means us no harm," I say, trying not to draw conclusions prematurely.

"You think it's them?" Rook asks me. "The Naqualla?"

"Until they self-identify, it doesn't matter what I think."

The next four minutes feel interminably long. I glance up and down the line of Marines to see each of them training their weapons on the unknown ship. The featherless blue marine birds screech overhead as they take turns diving for food in the shallows, oblivious to the events playing out beneath them.

"It's dropping," Jericho says and then passes the scope back to Rook. None of us need the magnification anymore. The vessel is half a kilometer away and looks like it's about to crash when it sets down on the water with ease. Rather than sink, the vessel surges forward, still aimed at our promontory's eastern point. "Annnd now it's a boat."

"Multipurpose," I say. "You might need one of those."

"Order is already in."

Somehow, seeing this unknown craft go from space-ship to airplane to hovercraft to boat has deescalated whatever initial sense of apprehension I had. Granted, I'm sure I'm the one who wants this to be the Naqualla more than anyone else. Well, maybe save Kit. But that doesn't mean I want us to be cavalier.

The ship rides a final wave and then slides onto shore like a beached trimaran. Surf surges around the hull, leaves some foam on the high water line, and then recedes. Some fourteen meters below us, the ship just sits there. No metal creaking after extreme heat exposure, no idling engine. Just the sounds of the ocean.

"Now what?" Grabowski says a few meters to my right.

"Hold position," Geller replies.

When sixty seconds pass, Rook looks at me. "I'm with Grabowski here. Now what?"

"Maybe it's uncrewed?" Jericho says. "A drone?"

"Or maybe they need to pee and get ready to meet us," Kit says as he and Fergus walk up the stairs behind us. "Primping and all, ya know. It's a thing."

Rook looks Kit up and down once and offers a barely audible, "You don't say." Then his eyes return to the ship.

Before anyone can say anything else, I decide to make an offer. "I'm going down—"

"Like hell you are," Jericho says.

"You didn't let me finish. I'm going down *if* you all think it's a good idea."

Jericho shares a look with Rook and gives me an approving smirk. "If we think? Well isn't this refreshing."

"But no weapons," I add.

"Evelyn," Rook says. "I would suggest—"

I spin on him. "You can't hit it from here? Really?" I try to keep it playful, but I'm also quite serious.

He frowns but doesn't say anything more.

"Listen, so far, whatever that ship's intentions are, it clearly hasn't shown any signs of being hostile. The only thing I can even think of is that it hasn't communicated its intentions to us, at least in ways that we might understand. So I vote that we show a little more trust here and at least allow one of us to head down there as a sign of the same. After all, *we're* the ones with all the guns out right now."

"How about a compromise?" he asks.

"No, I'm not taking a sidearm."

"I was talking about him." Rook thumbs at Fergus. "He has fast response times, can shield you in the event of an attack, and can return you here with ease. And if that ship is any indication of our visitor's technological capabilities, then I wager they understand a thing or two about robots. Fergus here is a helper, not a weapon."

"Look at you being anthropomorphically sensitive," I say with a wide smile. It's a good idea, and stars know I'd appreciate the company. "Whadda ya say, Fergy?"

"I say that I am ever at your disposal, my lady. Do with me as you desire."

"Woah, woah, easy there," Kit says while tugging on Fergus's arm. "You can't talk like that, Ferg. Double entendre and stuff."

"Forgive me, my liege. I was merely trying—"

"You can explain yourself later," I interrupt. "We've got somewhere be. Let's go."

MY LEGS FEEL numb as I follow the footpath down to the beach. The closer I get to the alien vessel, the more my body feels like it's walking on autopilot. The ship's just sitting there, unmoved by the surf swell that surges around its hull and then slides away. I keep expecting some hatch to open, but nothing does. So Fergus and I march on until the dirt trail flattens out and gives way to sand.

"Would you like me to proceed ahead, my lady?" Fergus asks.

"No. Just... let's give it sec."

"And by *it* you mean..."

"Whoever's in there. *If* anyone's in there. You picking up any life signs?"

"Regrettably, no. The ship may be too heavily shielded, or perhaps their biological composition is so foreign that my sensors are not calibrated to detect their physiology."

"Or that thing was flown here remotely, and they want me to jump in and head off to La La Land."

Fergus cocks his head at me. "I'm unfamiliar with this location."

"I'm being facetious."

"Ah. Very good. Then I will plan on joining you in La La Land and wear my best tunic."

"There ya go."

After almost thirty seconds, Rook's voice comes over V-cog. "Anything?"

"Negative. It's just... sitting here."

"You wanna send in Fergus?"

"Not really."

"Might be the wisest course of—"

"Stop." The sound of running water—not like the ocean, but like a trickling stream—catches my ear. "I hear something." My eyes track the sound to a hole opening in the ship's port side. A hole that's becoming a doorway. "You seeing this? It's like the hull is evaporating."

"Copy that."

Once the hole reaches something close to three meters high and two meters wide, the sound stops, as does the disappearing hull material. There, above the main wing on the ship's port, is a door. I can almost make out a glow inside, but the sun's strength all but casts it in shadow. I shield my eyes and take a few steps sideways.

A cold hand touches my shoulder and startles me. "Perhaps I should circumnavigate the perimeter in your stead, my lady."

I hold a fist to my chest, bite my lip, and shut my eyes for a second. "Fergus? Please don't scare me like that."

"My apologies."

"Yes, if you can get a better angle, that's fine. But don't approach it."

"Understood." He moves away to my right, maintaining a consistent radius from the ship as his metal feet plod through the sand. Servos and their repeated whine sound above the waves rolling in the background. Meanwhile, I tap into his V-cog feed and watch his camera adjust for the shadows within the hull. The exposure washes out the surroundings, but the ship's inside becomes more clear. There's... some sort of corridor. A smooth back wall with what looks like scroll work etched into the surface. It almost seems Celtic. Leaves and spirals. I prompt Fergus to zoom. The detail gets clearer. Yellow light pulses behind the designs. The shapes even seem to be... to be moving. Then, all at once, everything goes black. "Fergus, your camera—"

"My lady."

Fearing something's happened to him, I snap back into the real and see a figure in the ship's doorway.

27

EVELYN

THE FIGURE, or *person*, is easily two and a half meters tall and half as wide. It looks… hairy. Short fur. With a surprisingly cute face. Something like a marsupial. Short ears, and stubby snout—Seb would know the proper terms. Large, bright, intelligent eyes lock with mine, and a chill goes down my spine. Not from fear…

From wonder.

There's no respiratory mask, no equipment on its back. Instead, the creature seems to be breathing just fine on its own. It's clothed in some sort of stiff gray vest with a high collar, made from a dark synthetic looking material. Blue writing adorns the chest and then flows out to the edges where it trims the garment in neat lines. A tunic of less rigid material covers the abdomen, hips, and upper thighs, while black boots stop just above the ankles.

The two of us stay locked on each other for a few seconds, neither moving. This is... is too wonderful for words. I can't even believe... 'cause there's a... and it's... stars, it's amazing. Without thinking, I do the most natural, stupid, and human thing I can. My hand comes up and I say, "Hi."

Evelyn, you're insufferable! Of all the—

Its ears turn, and then it bows its head.

Did... we just have our first semi nonverbal communication? My knees are weak. Heart's beating a million times a second. And now I'm exaggerating. *Get a grip, Eves!*

The creature spots Fergus, gives him a once over, and then looks to the ridge where the Marines line the wall. For a second, I'm worried this might be it. The moment where someone fires a shot heard 'round the world. But the visitor doesn't seem to mind the weapons pointed at it. Assuming it knows those are weapons. It has to, right? Cosmic dust, this is happening. This is really happening!

As the creature steps from the fuselage and onto the wing, I make note of its thick thighs, biceps, and a powerful prehensile tail. It's like looking at some highly evolved... kangaroo. Wearing clothes. And flying a spaceship! Stars, I—

"Wuaaa-kuk-kuk-kuk-kuk," the creature says.

I was not expecting something so adorable to sound like a grizzly bear coughing up a chainsaw. It makes the hair on the back of my neck stand up. The visitor walks along the wing to where it meets the sand and then hops down. I hardly hear the landing despite the creature's apparent mass, no doubt a product of its tail that seems to help it maintain perfect balance.

As the visitor faces me, I spot bare areas of gray flesh along the insides of its arms, neck, and inner legs. The inner ears are the same color too. I also catch a faint sparkle above the brow. There's some sort of silver circlet around its forehead. Then I notice the same kind of jewelry wrapping its wrists and a few of its nimble fingers. Yes, it even has opposable thumbs, as I'm sure Seb and Enni will be keen to point out. No claws here.

Stars, I still can't believe this is happening. But it is. *Keep it together, Eves.* 'Cause the last thing I want to be remembered as is the woman who passed out when meeting humanity's first extrasolar sentient being.

Before the alien takes a single step toward me, it does something incredibly... human, or maybe it's just incredibly biological. It opens its palms, hands held up to its sides. I understand it as an act of deference. The creature also lowers its chin slightly, not so low to be considered subservience, but not so high that it feels like dominance. Just... neutral. Nonthreatening. The lexicon of body language—assuming it's universal somehow. Stars, I'm making so many damn assumptions.

As the lifeform begins to walk, Fergus comes back to my side. The alien studies him and tilts its head, but returns its attention to me. A small part of me wants to back away. I'm exposed. Weaponless. But the larger part of me wants to stay right where I am, feet planted. No, it wants to move forward to meet the newcomer.

So that's what I do.

The moment I take a step, the alien slows. It's ears twitch, but that's all before it resumes pace to meet me. I decide to hold my hands out in the same manner, hoping the reciprocated gesture might build trust.

"My lady, would you like me to join you?" Fergus asks.

"No. Stay where you are."

"Very well."

I half expect Rook or Jericho to scold me over V-cog, but they don't, which I appreciate. The alien looks back and forth between Fergus and me, presumably curious about our quick discussion, but doesn't slow. We're about eight meters away, and I'm getting a deeper sense of this being's presence. It's even bigger than I imagined and seems to have a... I don't know... an aura around it. Probably just my imagination projecting the intensity of this moment. Feels like I'm meeting a superstar or respected dignitary or something. Like that illusion of fame that makes someone out to be more than they really are.

As if on cue, we both slow and then stop about two meters apart. Me, a human female dressed in a SESI t-shirt and NUESSA workout shorts; the visitor, a non-gender-revealed kangaroo-looking alien decked out in a hardened vest, tunic, and boots. I'm not sure who should speak first. Technically, I guess we're the hosts, but this being came from Ring W and probably discovered Soteria a millennia ago.

"Wuaaa-kuk-kuk," it says. The sound startles me. It's so much louder up close.

"I… don't know what that means, but"—I place a hand on my chest—"Evelyn. I'm Evelyn." Like that's going to mean anything. *Cosmos*. I feel like such an idiot. But where are you supposed to start?

The creature's ears pivot, eyes blinking. Then, after it narrows its eyes, something glints in the background. Just over its shoulder, I spot something fly out of the ship.

"My lady," Fergus says with a note of caution in his voice.

"It's okay, Ferg," I reply as a small silver ball floats toward us. "Let it play out." The sphere is the size of a baseball and has some of the same script-style markings as the ship does. The lines emit a soft green glow, and I have no idea how the object is flying. It's not making a sound, at least any that I can hear above the surf.

As the sphere comes to a stop beside the alien's head, the creatures lets out another "Wuaaa-kuk-kuk" that sounds indistinguishable from the previous two utterances, other than it's shorter in duration. I'm sure to my undeveloped ear, there's much more variation in there somewhere, I just can't discern it. The being raises a hand toward the sphere, drawing my attention to it, and then the ball floats toward… toward Fergus. It stops a meter from his head, and then a green horizontal laser line runs up and down his body.

"I do believe she is checking me out, my lady," he says while the sphere circles him slowly. "Do you wish me to stop it?"

"No, please. Let's see what it does."

"Very well. I shall endure said probing, as per your request."

The orb wraps up whatever process it's conducting, presumably a scan, and then returns to hover at the visitor's shoulder. The creature stands there for several moments, just blinking at me. No effort to speak, to explain what's been done to Fergus. Nothing.

"Fergus?" I say softly. "Did you… detect anything? Feel anything?"

"No, my lady. It was painless, and there was no transmission of any kind."

"Interesting."

"Wuaaa-kuk," the creature says, but more softly this time. The words are barely out of its mouth when the orb zips over to Fergus and then stops above his left shoulder just as it had done to the creature upon exiting the ship.

"Oh my," Fergus says, somewhat startled. "By Odin's beard, it's transmitting!"

I spin on him. "What? What's it's saying?" I look

back at the creature who appears completely content, eyes peaceful, ears relaxed.

"It's… well, it isn't anything that I am able to understand, my lady. But it is successfully resonating a primary receptor on a quantum level inside my neural matrix."

"Does it hurt?"

"No. The transmission does not seem to be destructive. Rather it's"—he freezes and looks up at the creature —"Korbix."

"What?"

"I'm not sure how I know exactly, but the sphere has identified the individual before us as Korbix. It is the closest English approximation, as I understand it."

My eyes must double in size as I look at the alien. "Korbix?"

It lowers its head.

"Your name is Korbix? Or your species is Korbix?"

"I believe that's its name," Fergus says. "But it's really more of a…"

"Of a what?"

"Of a *feeling*, my lady. Which is strange for me. Sorcery, I am quite sure, not empirical as I am accustomed."

"Are you able to speak back to it?"

"I'm unsure. Would you like me to try?"

"Yes. Yes, I very much would! Can you try saying my name in reply?"

Fergus points to me but looks at who I'm going to

call Korbix until I have a better reason and says, "Evelyn."

Again, Korbix lowers its head ever so slightly.

"Did we just introduce ourselves?"

"I believe so, my lady. Bravo."

"Starry night." I run a hand down my face and then cast a glance up the hill behind me. Everyone's still there. Over V-cog, I say, "You getting this?"

"Crystal clear," Jericho replies, sounding as awestruck as I feel.

"Fergus, if this is some sort of… I don't know, a communications bot interface thing, maybe you can try establishing a lexicon with it."

"A sound idea, my lady. How do you recommend I proceed?"

Before I can get another word out, the sphere shines a laser on the sand, this time as a focused pinpoint of light. Fergus and I both look down. The beam is on a seashell, one devoid of its former inhabitant—whatever Soterian invertebrate it may have been.

"I believe it…"

"What?"

"It seems to wish to know how I feel about this," Fergus says.

"The shell? How you… feel?"

"Yes."

"Do you have any feelings about it?"

"I'm not sure. But I will at least communicate the

word we use for it." There's a pause, and then he adds, "Tell me, how do you feel about it, my lady?"

What an unusual way to start a lexicon, if that's what Korbix and this orb are trying to do. Then again, it… makes sense. Language isn't just about rote identification. It's about meaning, inflection, tone, sentiment… and memory. Natalie would have more to say in this, but she's not the one on the beach right now. So it's up to me.

"I feel… fondness for it. It reminds me of my childhood. The good parts. It's… magical."

Suddenly, the laser light points east, right into the ocean.

"And how do you feel about the ocean?" Fergus asks.

"I… love it. The sounds, the power, the mystery."

Next the light lands on a boulder to our right. "And this?"

"I don't really have feelings about a rock. But… I guess, strong, maybe? Enduring?"

Right then, I notice Korbix looking back and forth between me and every object that the sphere sets its beam on. A palm tree. Some sort of sand crab. One of the parrot-like birds we first observed. Even a stick being tossed about in the surf.

Then the beam alights on my t-shirt and shorts. It moves further up the promontory and touches the wall, and then one of the Marines. Grabowski.

"What the hell, man? It's targeting me! Son of bitch, it's—"

"Stand down," Rook orders.

As soon as I tell Fergus how I feel about Grabowski, which is a mix of security and comic relief, the beam flicks over to a point defense gun.

"My lady?"

After a second, I say, "Danger."

The sphere spins and places the beam on the starship. Again, I tell Fergus my sense of it, and then the light lands on Korbix.

"Now it wishes to know how you feel about the newcomer," Fergus says.

How do you feel about this creature, Evelyn? About meeting your very first extrasolar sentient life form? About this appointment that you've dreamed of all your life? That you read about in stories and watched in movies? That you lobbied and labored for? Contended with bureaucrats over and fought tooth and nail for funding to make happen? Gave your entire career to? Lost friends, and made enemies over? How about risked your life for and put others in jeopardy to get? And now, after all that, here you are, face to face with the impossible. With the dream made reality.

"I feel... overwhelmed. And grateful, very grateful."

The beam hits me in the eye. It's not painful, but causes me to wince.

"And this?" Fergus asks.

I reach a hand to my cheek and feel something wet. I'm crying. "Tears. But... good ones. I'm happy."

"Wuaaa-kuk-kuk," Korbix says.

"Oh my," Fergus replies.

"What? What is it?"

"The being known as Korbix"—Fergus turns to me—"she feels the same way too."

"She?" I wipe the rest of the tears away so I can get a better look. "You discussed gender?"

"We have discussed many things, and conveying the female gender was appropriate when I communicated your name."

"You're a… you're female?" I ask her.

Korbix lowers her head a centimeter. That must be an affirmative, like us.

"Hold up, Ferg. You can understand her?"

"I understand the sphere, it seems, in as much as I'm able to *read between the lines*, as it were. We are far from an articulate level of communication. It's at the broad strokes level, you might say. Where before, with the Ganese, I was given access to a concise and limited optical data file that I was then able to decipher with Fred's assistance, this interaction is far more…"

When he doesn't reply right away, I have to prompt him. "Is far more what?"

"Meaningful. But therefore slower, as conducted in real time. I am not connected to the origin of information."

"What do you mean?"

"Fred was a digital construct. Equal parts artificial

intelligence and data archive. This situation, however, is far more... organic."

"How?"

"The sphere seems to be connected to her, to Korbix. I am unsure how, exactly. But this is not a straightforward *data dump*, as you are fond of saying. Rather, it is a learning process in which meaningful acquisition takes time."

"So, maybe it's their version of V-cog or something. The orb's a pixie maybe?"

"Perhaps. There is a vast amount of missing data before anything of certainty may be decided upon. I wonder, would you permit me to roam a bit with Rose?"

"Rose?"

"Yes. While the sphere has not self-identified, I have taken the liberty of naming it. I have selected Rose as a sufficient forename. Unless you think otherwise?"

This makes me chuckle a little. First Fred, now Rose. I can only imagine what's next. "No, it's fine. Rose is great."

"Very well. Additionally, might I summarize and therefore infer what humanity as a whole might feel about the objects in question should you not provide an alternative? I suspect it will speed things up, as it were."

I'm not exactly thrilled with the prospect of letting an excipion give an alien its interpretation of what humanity as a whole thinks about anything. Apparently, someone else shares my apprehensions.

"I could do it," Kit blurts over comms.

I look over my shoulder and spot the kid on the wall with his hand up.

While Jericho pulls Kit's hand down and they start up their own conversation about the matter, I ask Fergus, "Why don't we just follow you around and keep this going?"

"Because Korbix seems to want you to explore her ship."

I glance at the vessel, at Korbix, and then back up the hill.

Right on cue, both Jericho and Rook talk over each other with a combination of "Absolutely not" and "Stand down, Evelyn."

While I appreciate their mutual concern, I ask Fergus, "Why does she want me to explore it?"

"I lack the vocabulary and have yet to combine motivations with proper descriptors, but the sense I'm getting is one of... *hospitality*."

Seb cuts in for the first time since this encounter began. Honestly, I'm surprised he was able to restrain himself this long. "Treatment of the other, of the stranger. It's, uh, perhaps one of humanity's oldest forms of expressing trust, to invite in the stranger."

"He could also fly away with her," Rook says.

"You mean she," Jericho replies.

"Right."

"But this is where you place yourself at the host's

mercy," Seb continues. "Yes, she could carry you off. But you could also learn information that might compromise her safety, even damage her vessel and prevent a return to where she came from. I would caution any view that does not place equal cause for concern upon Korbix as it does for Evelyn."

Rook's avatar works his jaw in my augmented overlay. "Does it bother anyone else that we haven't gotten intel on the biggest question yet?"

"The Naqualla," I say.

"Right. I vote that before this goes any further, you get an answer to that one, and then we see whether or not we keep going with show and tell."

"I agree," Jericho says.

The idea has merit, but it also concerns me, because I'm not sure how the word Naqualla will translate from Fergus to Rose to Korbix, and invariably, we're going to get on the subject of the Ganese. The last thing I want to do this early is create unnecessary tension. Then again, if Korbix knows we've stopped by Kep-C on our way here, then she knows we'll have seen what's left of the Ganese. Might as well rip the Band-Aid off fast and get it over with.

"Fergus, before I agree, I would like to ask her a question. Is she… are her people… the Naqualla?"

28

NIGEL

THE MEETING with his new constituency, as he called them, were going reasonably well. Nigel no longer considered himself a man elected by the majority of the populace, but a pioneer supported by those who represented the people. Three out of four Solum Terram representatives were not only favorable of forming a new presidential office, they were emphatic that Nigel was the "only logical fit," "a man for the times," and "the Winston Churchill and George Washington for a new generation," all bylines he'd make sure ran in the marketing campaigns to follow.

Of those Solum Terram representatives who balked at the proposal, more than half came around once he'd had a chance to explain himself... some needing more direct language than others. It was only a handful that he needed to send Gemma to convince, and even fewer who needed to be given "special attention," as he'd termed it.

The other politicasts, namely the Preservationists and the Viatoribus, weren't seeing things as clearly, as was evidenced by the numbers coming in from Gemma's *persuaders*—he didn't like using the term assassins. The good thing about using the radical groups was that if authorities did start poking around, it would be easy to out whatever faction or leader he disliked. Not only would anyone fail to lose sleep over Leonidas X getting the axe, but nothing could ever be linked back to Nigel. It was a beautiful arrangement, one that Gemma came up with herself, further evidence of her resourcefulness.

While certain things, like Gaia's Blood, put Nigel and Gemma on an even playing field, Nigel considered himself her superior in everything from age and experience to politicking and strategy. But if she came to heel as he hoped she might, the young woman could become quite the leader herself one day. All she needed was time, direction, and training.

But that had to wait.

Nigel's most pressing matter was courting a Sentia Aux vote. He knew this would be the hardest to acquire. His positions on the Infinita program and every other space settlement initiative were well known and well despised by every spacer in the system. But he couldn't get the 80 percent majority vote needed to pass his bill if he couldn't secure at least some of the alien-lovers—God help them. Which was why his next appointment, in the real, with Representative Caleb Nowen was so important. The man was well connected to both NUESSA and SESI, and was adored by the space community. He'd gone to school with several key leaders, including SESI Director Lemuel Brown. If Nigel could somehow earn *or* coerce this man's support—all options were on the table—then it might go a long way in building momentum toward that 80 percent threshold he needed.

And if Nowen didn't indulge? Well, that's why Gemma was on standby. Where dissenting ST reps could be handled by the likes of Radio Ultra and the others, dissenting spacers would need to be handled delicately. There was no room for even a hint of foul play since the ST and the SA were sworn enemies.

Nigel decided to meet Caleb Nowen on his home turf and flew overnight to New Zealand. The two rendezvoused at Caleb's favorite country club, Tara Iti, which lay north of Auckland between Pakiri and Mangawhai. The stunning ocean vistas rivaled those of any course Nigel had played, and the drinks weren't bad either.

"Cheers," Nigel said to Caleb as they took seats on a sun-drenched patio surrounded by suit-clad security.

"And what are we drinking to again, Secretary General?"

"Paths forged in the darkness *together*," Nigel said, making a play on the politicast's cherished mantra.

Celeb toasted, but it was a half-hearted effort. Then they sipped their drinks of choice and sat back as an attendant brought over a rolling umbrella to shade them.

"My secretary didn't say what this meeting was about," Caleb said.

"That's because *my* secretary didn't give her one."

"I see. Would now an opportune time to let me in?"

"It is. So long as I have your word."

"On?"

"That what we discuss here concerns matters of system-wide security and can never be repeated except with my permission and the permission of those within the knowledge base."

"As are all security matters of the NUE. Why the melodrama? Begging your pardon."

Nigel set his drink down. "Because this one has implications that will make most everything else we've done together pale by comparison."

"Well now I'm really on the hook. Don't leave me hanging."

Over the next fifteen minutes, Nigel outlined his bill, including carefully crafted arguments for the new presidency office and his intentions for all NUESSA and SESI space settlement initiatives. He knew Caleb would be keen on those, and decided to lead with them rather than make the man dig. It might be seen as an act of validation, though the tactic hadn't worked according to plan the last three times he'd tried. Then again, he barely got to his space initiative policies with those meetings; the reps had rebuffed him right away for the claim of presidency.

But not Caleb. Nigel was surprised, and pleasantly so, he had to admit, that the Southlands Representative had let him finish at all. When Nigel had nothing more to say, he sat back, opened his hands, and said, "So?"

"So what?"

"What do you think?"

Caleb gave Nigel a half smile and adjusted his sunglasses. "I think you're a goddamn fool, is what I think."

"Aren't we all," Nigel said, realizing he'd overestimated Caleb.

"*Annnd* you're off your rocker if you think for one second that a single Sentia or even Viatoribus rep, for that matter, is gonna support your ass with those kinds of sanctions on settlement expansion."

Curious. Caleb was skirting the presidency issue altogether. This was new. "Do you… have alternative suggestions?"

"Of course. But why waste my breath if you're not interested in hearing them."

"Let's say that I am." Nigel leaned forward. "But before that, you're not put off by the idea of—"

"The world's first President of Earth? Jesus. It was

inevitable. I'm actually kinda surprised someone hadn't proposed it a generation ago. Now, do I like the idea of a presidential appointment, much less the creation of the position in the first place? Hell no. But I'm a realist, despite whatever you might think about my Sentia Aux predispositions. It means that I realize I might not be offered the same opportunity the next time around."

"Next time?"

"That someone as insane as you tries this. 'Cause you'll fail. But let's say you don't."

"Yes, let's say."

"Then I'd rather be first at the table than last. And given that none of my counterparts have gotten a personal fly-in from you, at least to my knowledge, I'm guessing I still might have that distinction."

"Of being the first spacer to endorse me?" Nigel considered whether or not to show one of his cards. But so far Nowen had surprised him. "Yes. As a matter of fact, you would be."

"Which also means I have some leverage."

"Such as?"

"Your pledge never to destroy *Parallax One.*"

And there it was. Nigel had anticipated this, of course. Every contingency his advisors could come up with had been fielded behind closed doors. Nigel was just surprised that Caleb had been so prepared. Was it cause for concern? That was too soon to tell.

"You want to recover the crews of the *Kogarashi*, *Sagan Explorer*, and *Bellerophon*," Nigel said.

"Among other things."

"And find out exactly what they discovered on the other side."

"Aren't you the least bit curious, Sallsworth? Come on."

Nigel dodged the question. "Let's say I'm willing. What do I get in return?"

"Isn't that obvious?"

"Indulge me."

Caleb gave him a sly grin and pulled his sunglasses to the tip of his nose, looking over them. "Every last Sentia and Viatoribus vote I can swing."

"Is that a fact?"

"No, Secretary General. It's a promise."

29

EVELYN

"Is she… are her people… the Naqualla?"

Fergus hesitates and then turns to Rose and Korbix. "I will pose the question as best I can, my lady."

"Thank you."

Several seconds pass while I rub my left palm with a thumb. My hands are sweaty, and it's not just from the midday heat.

All at once, Korbix lets out a sharp blast of air from her nostrils. Her brow furrows and ears lay back. I even catch one side of her lip twitch. It's the first time I've felt genuine fear since this began. Before I know it, I've taken a step back.

"Evelyn," Rook says in a tone that sends a warning to my adrenal glands. My heart rate's up.

Korbix sees me back away. Suddenly, her countenance changes from something like anger to wide-eyed disbelief.

"It's not directed at you," Fergus announces with his hands raised like a herald in a court. "The body language that connotes anger, it is not against you or yours."

"She's angry about the question?"

Fergus shakes his head. "She is… distraught over the Firsts."

"The Firsts?"

"Also, she feels it is too much for words."

"Can she at least answer if they're the Naqualla? Granted, that's probably not even what they call themselves… we just have the Ganese version. But ask along those lines."

A few moments pass before Fergus says, "She can indeed confirm that her species is the Naqualla. The word is an appropriate interpretation of the variation given to the Ganese, and she seems comfortable that the word is both appropriate and suitable for our purposes in English. Though the correct form, if you must know, pronounced in her native tongue is Nee-kwee-kuk-kuk-ooo-wah."

I can't believe it. My eyes lock with Korbix's. The emotions swirling behind those glassy irises are turbulent. I suspect pain, obviously anger, maybe even… is it regret?

Korbix inhales, allows her belly and chest to expand,

and then lets the breath out much like a human would do who's trying to control their emotions. The level of kinship I feel with this wonderful being is…

Getting ahead of myself, is what it is.

Korbix gestures to her ship.

"The offer stands," Fergus says. "Until then, Korbix has released Rose into my care. Moreover, his eminence has been released to join me in educating Rose."

"Kit?"

"Indeed."

At this, Korbix turns around in the sand and heads back for her ship.

"Where's she going?"

Fergus looks at Korbix, then to me, then back to Korbix, and then back to me. "She's… returning to her vessel, my lady. Are your ocular receptors malfunctioning?"

"No, I mean… She's just going to sit in there and wait for me?"

"I believe that is part of it, yes."

"And the other part?"

"I believe the appropriate word is *grieve.*"

"Well I'm not gonna just stand here and do nothing," I say to Jericho and Rook in our shared V-cog suite. We've been conferring for the last minute, and with every second that's gone by, I get more frustrated. "There's an alien, a real life alien, sitting in that ship waiting for me. And, by Fergus's account, it feels pretty strongly about whatever went down at Kep-C. So I say we keep the relationship moving forward until we have reason not to."

"But why one representative?" Jericho asks. "And why now?"

"Your guess is as good as mine. But we don't get any answers by standing around."

"I still don't like you going inside, Evelyn," Rook says. "It could be—"

"A trap?" My hands are on my hips in the real. I even turn and face the hill. "Don't you think that Korbix could have taken me long before now if she wanted? And I'm no engineer or military specialist here, but given how fast her ship flies, something tells me she could have done us in a while ago if she wanted, right? But more than that, we already have notions that the Naqualla are out to aid us, not harm us. So unless either of you have any legitimate reason for me to keep standing out here aside from some overly masculine urge to protect me, then I'm going."

Jericho and Rook exchange glances and then shake their heads. But Jericho seems to think of something and raises a finger. "How will you communicate without Fergus?"

"Women find a way, Jericho. We always do."

I step out of the suite and ping Kit. Augmented reality tags him and Fergus as being on the north side of Evelynton, moving up the hill. "How's it going?"

"Very going, Miss Evelyn. Uh… I mean very good. It's going very good. Rose is asking lots of great questions. Or maybe it's Korbix we're talking with? I still don't have that down fully. But anyway, yeah, we're like adding lots of nouns and stories to its database. And it's fun too, ya know? Like teaching a little kid stuff who keeps asking 'Why? Why? Why?' Only way less irritating. I had this little cousin once, Matilda. She could talk your ear off, let me tell you. This one time—"

"Kit, I'm about to head into Korbix's ship, so can you save that for later?"

"Oh! Golly, yeah. Sorry about that. Just, uh, be careful, okay? Even though I really don't think you have anything to worry about."

"I will. Thanks."

As I've been walking to the ship, I keep expecting the doorway to re-materialize and shut me out or something. Which doesn't seem logical because Korbix is the one who invited me in. Still, I know how quickly we humans can change our minds about things when we get angry. A pang hits me in my chest as I picture Olivia. Part of me wishes she was here… and at the same I'm glad she's not. Damn. Being caught between two opposing emotions really sucks sometimes.

The tide is coming in, and my trainers get soaked by

the next wave that rushes the shore. I suddenly feel bad about the water and sand I'm going to track into Korbix's shuttle, but I try to rest in the fact that she's just done the same. Then I laugh out loud, amused by the absurdity of my concern—soiling the inside of an alien spacecraft, as if it could be remedied by simply asking, "Should I leave my trainers on the mat before coming in?" And then Korbix replying, "Don't be silly. The maid will be here tomorrow, and what's a little mess, especially between friends?" Then I laugh again at how completely unqualified I feel to be doing this seeing as how I'm having an internal monologue about etiquette.

Or... maybe that's precisely what makes me qualified.

My first step onto the ship's wing is electrifying. Not literally. But I'm stepping onto an alien vessel. I keep going, walking the same path I saw her take and marveling at the craftsmanship. The surface is silver, yes, but it's also iridescent this close up. And very smooth. I don't mean to take liberties with the invitation to join Korbix, but I have to kneel and touch the surface with my fingertips. To my surprise, the metal—if that's what it is—is cool. Considering how long it's been sitting under the sun, that seems unusual.

Fearing I might be caught fondling the wing, I stand and keep moving toward the door. I'm almost three meters up in the air here with a little further to go. A meter away from the entry, I smell something that reminds me of lavender. Which makes me smile. I guess because I wasn't really thinking about how an alien ship might smell. The assumption has always been... well, bad, I guess. Weird how we draw conclusions like that. There's also a woodsy scent, like being inside a forest. Not musty or moldy. Just... fresh. Alive.

I decide to tap my trainers against the side of the door to knock out some of the debris. I'm about to take them off and look for slippers when I think better of it. None of this is Naquallan custom, I bet, but my aunt and uncle would never forgive me if I did otherwise. At the same time, I offer a quick, "Hello?" and look in. The corridor is big for a human but seems about right for someone of Korbix's stature. The scroll work that I saw earlier is gone. Instead, a flat white wall greets me and beckons me out of the direct sunlight and into the shadow toward the cockpit, maybe even a small bridge. I enter the ship and give a soft, "I'm coming up," even though I recognize she probably can't understand a word I'm saying.

The air is cooler here, and the smell of forest lavender is stronger. It's lovely, really, and I suddenly wonder why we don't take as much care of our own spaceships. Every vessel I've ever voyaged on smells like BO and industrial cleaning agents.

There's a narrow opening at the end of the corridor. It's certainly large enough for me, but I imagine Korbix needed to take her time. I see two pairs of captain's chairs in the bridge beyond, including the edge of Korbix's arm coming from the front right seat. Sunlight from the canopy silhouettes her body hair, but the room still feels shielded from the outside, giving me a sense of security as I step inside. Though I admit that seeing her in what I can only presume is the pilot's seat does leave me feeling a little uneasy; she could definitely take advantage of me and fly away, as per the guys' concern. Nonetheless, I forge ahead, walking carefully through the center aisle, and then gesture to the left hand seat. "May I?"

"Rrrr-kuk," she replies.

I no more understand her than she does me, but I think we get the gist, so I sit, immediately feeling awkward in the larger chair. I'm practically swimming in it and trying not to get my rear end stuck in the cutout for my non-existent tail. It takes me a few seconds to get comfortable and not look like a total fool. Korbix has one eye raised at me, and when I finally look up, she glances away as if she hadn't been watching. That makes me smile. Perhaps we're more alike than we know.

I look around the spartan bridge. There's no obvious controls or gauges. Just lots of white surfaces that look like they might contain or project controls if activated. The console shapes themselves are elegant, weaving around the room like ribbons. Whoever designed this space was definitely concerned with aesthetics. Like the fragrance in the air, it's beautiful. And then it hits me that I'm sitting on an alien spaceship. Stars... there's a lot of firsts happening right now. I try not to let them distract me and focus on being present.

That word, Firsts, comes back to me.

I decide to try a little pantomime-to-speech communication, knowing I'm about to sound like every tourist whoever tries speaking to a foreigner. Cosmos forgive me. I point to her and say, "Are you, Korbix"—I wave my hand over my chest, which she tracks curiously— "Okay?"

"Whaaak-ruk."

"Yeah. This isn't gonna work."

Not only are my words subjective, even if she knew the meaning, there's really no commonality in our vocal ranges. I feel like I'm talking to a wild beast. Not because Korbix isn't intelligent. If anything, I suspect she has a much higher IQ than me. It's more because there's simply no way I can even attempt to make the sounds she's emitting, much less understand the nuances involved. And based on the sense of frustration I'm picking up from her, I suspect she might feel the same. Maybe I was wrong to come in here before Fergus had some sort of conversational link established. Still...

I need to do something.

Something brave. Or stupid. Or just because I really want to make actual first contact. I reach over the side of the chair, across the aisle, and rest my hand on Korbix's arm. She looks down sharply but doesn't move. She

seems frozen in consideration of my action. And perhaps
it was a bit premature. For all I know, this is a sacred sin.
Or maybe I'm deathly allergic to her fur. Stars, the more
I think about it, the more I realize this was a very
very bad—

Korbix lays her hand on mine and then meets my
eyes with hers.

A chill goes up my arm.

We don't say anything. And yet, I have a sense that,
right here, we're saying all needs to be communicated.
So I keep my hand on her arm until she finally lifts hers
away. She leans back in her chair and then seems to
content herself with waiting. I'm not sure for what.
Maybe for Fergus and Kit to come back. Maybe for
Rose to turn something on and start translating. Maybe
for the population of Evelynton to march down the hill-
side with a welcome band and a key to the town.
Annnnd now I'm daydreaming, because what else are
you gonna do when you're on a freaking alien ship and
can't talk?

I glance up at Korbix and see she has some of the
same sullen face she did before when I asked her about
being the Naqualla. Whatever has caused this, and I
suspect it has something to do with the Ganese, she's not
getting over it. So... I sit. And I sit. And I breathe in the
luscious lavender scent and enjoy the beautiful wondrous
space I'm sitting in. Finally, after several minutes, Korbix
seems to have found herself and motions toward the

ship's aft. She gestures again and raises an eyebrow like a question.

"Go back?" I say, not even sure why I'm speaking aloud; she certainly isn't. I nod and motion for her to lead the way. This seems acceptable to her. Korbix climbs out of her chair, and I think we're headed outside when she heads past the entry door and then into a spacious room with more captain's chairs. Only this furniture isn't like that in the bridge. The seats are more luxurious and look like they can change shape around the body. Picking up serious high class aviation vibes here. I count six chairs altogether, along with more white ribbon-like forms weaving up walls and across the ceiling. Narrow vertical slit windows line either side of the curvaceous room, and soft circular lighting adorns the ceiling and floor's edges.

It feels a little odd that Korbix would be showing off her shuttle like this. Unless it's her custom. Or maybe she's a gearhead showing off her tricked out grid car—how should I know? Or... maybe she's showcasing the ship's capacity because she wants to take me and several other passengers somewhere.

Korbix moves to a door at the room's far end, which seems like it's positioned amidships. She touches the wall with her hand and the door vanishes. As in, it just evaporates right before my eyes. I recall the exterior door behaving much the same way.

"Do that again," I say with a smile.

Korbix gives me a quizzical look and holds her hand up to the empty space that the door occupied seconds before.

"Yeah. That. Can you… ya know…" I flutter my fingers and try to imitate the door re-materializing.

The corners of Korbix's mouth pull up in what I assume is a smile, and then she activates the door. The material, whatever it is, re-materializes like water pooling inward. Only, it's not water. The final product is far too hard. But it flowed. Some sort of nanotech maybe?

Korbix appears to be as delighted with my interest. I wonder if it's not unlike a child discovering something new and wonderful that an adult finds utterly dull. Like a 3D printer or their first time in V-cog.

Again, Korbix dissolves the door, and we pass into the next room, this one less comfortable and more sterile, though still fashioned with the ribbon-like consoles flowing along the walls and overhead. I keep imagining control surfaces appearing across them when activated. Or maybe… maybe they don't turn on at all, and I'm just projecting my own imagination on things.

This room is laid out with definitive sections… chambers even, each with tiny holes in the ceiling and reciprocal holes in the floor. My guess? It's a water closet. Toilets, showers, grooming, all to accommodate the passengers and whatever cleanliness customs the Naqualla hold dear. As if to aid my conclusions, Korbix gets my attention and moves two hands over her head, back to front. It reminds me of a rabbit grooming itself. Then she looks at me like she's hoping something will be confirmed. So I mimic the gesture, but move my hands front to back over my hair as if washing soap away. This seems to please her, and she gives a short grunt.

A third and final room boasts what I can only guess is some sort of multipurpose print facility. Like the other spaces, it's elegant, refined, and minimalistic. Cupboard-like compartments line a waist-height countertop that runs along one wall, reminding me of a kitchen. The opposing wall has two chairs with mechanical arms that come up and over the sides reminiscent of a medical suite. Meanwhile, the aft wall is consumed by what appears to be a large 3D printer. It boasts a recessed nook large enough for me to squat in, a grated floor, and articulated robotic arms with silver-tipped nozzles. Whether or not any of this is as I suppose remains to be seen. But time will tell, I hope, because I want to learn everything I can about Korbix and her people. Does that make me a xenoanthropologist then?

"It's beautiful," I say, offering a wide smile in the hopes that it translates somehow.

Korbix replies with a purr that I haven't heard yet. I take it as a good sign. Though I am curious why she hasn't powered the ship to show me everything in action. Then again, that might be cause for alarm, especially from the likes of Rook and the Marines. Which means

Korbix is either remarkably self-aware… orrrr she just doesn't feel like turning everything on.

Somehow, I get the sense that showing me the ship has buoyed her spirits. There's a lightness in her step as we make our way back to the bridge. We take our seats as before and then sit there quietly. Whether or not the feeling is reciprocated, I'm enjoying Korbix's company. Just being with her is amazing, and I catch myself smiling at her like a kid looking up at Santa Claus. Korbix notices and then seems to smile too.

"Miss Evelyn?" Kit says, not in V-cog, but from outside the ship. "You in there still?"

I glance at Korbix, climb out of my seat, and then stick my head out of the ship's portside door. "Everything okay?"

"Oh, sure, sure. Fergus says he and Rose are about wrapped up with phase one."

"Phase one?"

"What he believes is enough vocabulary for him to create a translation construct within V-cog to serve you and Korbix. Well, you Korbix and then anyone else who wants to know what's being said."

"Understood. Thanks, Kit." I glance at Fergus who's further back and strolling along the beach with Rose like they're old friends.

Kit follows my gaze and says, "They're just exchanging notes and stuff. He's ready though."

I ping Jericho and Rook. "Looks like Ferg has

enough for us to initiate a dialogue. I'm going to propose that we move to Evelynton and see if she's—"

"I don't think that's a good idea," Rook says. "Not until we know more, anyway."

"Agreed," Jericho says. "What don't you see what you can learn from there, and then we'll proceed accordingly."

I don't particularly like the lack of mutual hospitality this presents. Korbix has shown me the inside of her property; etiquette says we should do the same. But I get the apprehension. "I'll start things off. But if it goes well, then we'll need to at least propose a tour." Before either of them can combat that, I add, "You wanna gather everyone in the virtual command theater?"

"Will do," Jericho replies. "Let us know when you're ready to start."

Back in the real, I sense Korbix move next me. I give her space, and she peers out at Kit and then waves him in.

"Is she, ya know, inviting me inside?" he asks in astonishment.

"I believe so, yes."

He puts a hand on his chest and looks around. "You want me to come onboard?"

Korbix inclines her head as if she understands.

"And why not?" I say to him. "You're a valuable part of the team and crucial to Fergus's development, right?"

"Uh… I mean, I guess so, yeah."

"Korbix apparently thinks so too. You don't want to keep her waiting, do you?"

"Holy biscuits, no ma'am! Not at all." Kit scrambles up the wing, takes his shoes, and bows deeply in front of Korbix. She lets out some sort of warbled grunt that I think might be a laugh and then motions him toward the bridge.

While Kit follows her, I wait just inside the doorway watching Fergus and Rose as they near the ship. For some reason, I can't help picturing them as some old couple who have spent so many years talking together that they no longer need to use words. There's a deeper connection at work, one that transcends spoken language. I also can't help but wonder if Fergus, with his newly granted freedoms, feels he's found a kindred spirit, albeit alien in origin.

When they finally reach the ship, Fergus does his best to walk lightly up the wing while Rose zips past me and darts into the bridge. "Everything good?" I ask Fergus once he's near enough.

"Yes, quite so, my lady. I trust you will be pleased with our progress. For the moment, Rose and I will be actively translating your verbal communications in real time. As our accuracy increases, we will shift resources to your virtual cognizance networks."

"So... she has some sort of V-cog system too?"

"In a sense, yes. Though it is far less intrusive than the human system."

"Intrusive? Meaning... it's not implanted?" I remember the circlet around her head. "It's external."

"Yes, my lady."

"Fascinating. Let's get going then." I point him to the bridge, and he sits behind Korbix while Kit is already seated behind my chair. Eh, *seated* is a relative term. He's eyeing everything in sight like a squirrel who's discovered sugar cubes. But that changes when the chairs start rotating inward so that we're eventually facing one another in a circle.

"Well isn't this nice," Kit says.

Over V-cog, I say to Jericho, "Looks like we're all set here."

"Roger." A moment later, the command theater appears in my mind's eye, filled with every member of POET. All but Olivia. Though she's hardly a member. Jericho sends a security request for optic and auditory nerve pairing; it means the entire crew is going to see and hear everything that I do. Unnerving. But the situation calls for it. So I hit accept and then sit back.

Silence fills the bridge and the V-cog theater alike. Once again, I'm not sure who's supposed to speak first. The sense of anticipation is heightened now that Fergus is assured we can communicate reasonably well. My palms are even sweatier than before.

Here goes nothing...

30

EVELYN

"GREETINGS. My name is Dr. Evelyn Park," I say, barely able to contain my excitement.

"And I'm Korbix," says an elegant female voice in my head mere fractions of a second behind the alien's percussive speech. It will take some getting used to. "I'm happy to meet you, Dr. Evelyn Park." Hearing her say my name makes me shudder. Fergus, or maybe Rose, has her sounding like a princess who's aware of her royal position but distrusts hierarchy.

"And I'm happy to meet you too. I've been waiting… all my life for this."

"We have been waiting a long time as well."

The smile on my face is impossible to erase. Likewise, I seem to have a permanent flutter in my stomach. "I have so many questions for you."

"May I start with one of my own?"

"Anything."

"What do you call your species?"

I laugh at the simplicity of the request. Of course she'd want to know that. "We call ourselves humans."

"Humans." Hearing her attempt the word in her language sends another chill down my spine.

"We come from a planet called Earth, though I suppose you are familiar with it, at least from a distance."

Korbix bows her head ever so slightly. "We have seen."

Of course she has. Stars. "Uh, before we continue, I feel it's important to let you know that our team is watching this encounter right now through our"—I glance at Fergus—"It's okay to say V-cog system? You'll interpret?"

"I will, my lady."

Back to Korbix I say, "They're watching through V-cog."

It takes a little more time for her to finally reply as I assume Ferg and Rose are explaining virtual cognizance to her. "I am familiar with this type of connection."

"Is… that what you're using now? To hear Rose in your mind?"

"No. But our people once used something similar to your solution," Korbix explains. Then her posture straightens and she takes on a slightly formal tone. "Greetings to those humans participating in this conversation. I am pleased to make your acquaintance."

Jericho says to me, "Tell her it's mutual."

"They are pleased to make your acquaintance as well," I reply to Korbix. "I hope I can introduce you in person shortly."

"I look forward to that. My name is Korbix Kōs Limmia, Chief Naquallan Ambassador of the Resettlement Council, and First Representative to Humans here on…?"

When she doesn't finish, I ask, "Yes?"

"What have you chosen to name your new planet?"

"Our new…?" *Holy cosmic stars*. That's not a question you get asked every day. "Uh… Soteria. We've named it Soteria, an ancient name for salvation and deliverance in one of our older cultures."

"Soteria. A fine name."

"Thank you. So, you've come to meet us then? To see who answered your call? It was you, after all, the Naqualla, who built the transmission ring here as well as the one above the previous planet we visited? You sent the signals?"

"We did."

My heart races. "And your reason?"

"To provide your kind and those you wish to preserve with a second chance."

"To settle a new world."

Korbix inclines her head. "Soteria."

Kit's knees are bopping up and down. Korbix notices the behavior and asks, "Does this make you anxious?"

I answer in his stead. "We thought this might be the reason for your contact. Well, some of us anyway."

"Not all suspected as you did?"

I worry my reply might put her off, but it's the truth. "No."

Korbix lays a hand on her belly. I'm not sure if this is a gesture to denote unease, sickness, or maybe she's just hungry. At last she says, "And yet the majority of you decided to take the chance, build the ring, and activate it."

"Enough to make it possible, yes." I don't want to delve into the quagmire of NUE politics just yet. There's way too many other things I want to talk about. "The Naqualla, where do you come from?"

"Our homeworld is called Tria, located over 1,000 lightyears from here."

My mouth opens but I can't speak right away. Eventually, I say, "Another thousand lightyears… from here? That's nearly—"

"Two thousand from your home."

"You must be a very old starfaring species."

"More than some, less than others."

What in nebula's name is *that* supposed to mean? "Others?"

"Yes. Though I recommend we save such talk for a later day."

"Of course." *One mystery at a time, Evelyn.* "May we discuss the Ganese?"

Korbix's nostrils flare fractionally, but she nods nonetheless. "What do you wish to know?"

"As much as you are willing to share. Am I correct in assuming that it's a painful topic?"

Korbix sighs and then looks at Rose. "My assistant will provide Fergus with the imagination as I speak."

I glance at Fergus. "Imagination?"

"Forgive me, my lady. The word is better translated as visual content. They have video, apparently historic, though I'm detecting annotations that would seem to make some of this redacted, as it were."

"So it's confidential?"

"That is one interpretation, yes. Here it comes now." Rather than port the data into V-cog, Fergus sends it through his chest-mounted holo projector, creating a 3D display in the middle of our seating area. A lush planet appears, colored in blues, greens, and whites. Something like a Dyson sphere surrounds it, only instead of harvesting a star's energy, like the twentieth century theoretical physicist and mathematician Freeman Dyson proposed, this cage-like apparatus seems to serve a civil and space engineering need. Vertical and horizontal bands of monolithic proportion crisscross thousands of kilometers above the surface. Each band seems to boast its own atmosphere and is teeming with life across cities, countryside, and mountains. Space stations and ships of all kinds float between the circular bands and the planet, giving the impression of a highly advanced and thriving species.

"Behold, Tria," Korbix says. "Home of the Naqualla."

"It's spectacular," I say, regretting the less commonly used word. But Fergus is on it because Korbix wastes no time in replying.

"Thank you. This is, however, not our first home. We, like you, sought another, one provided by benefactors who believed we would benefit from a second chance."

"Your people suffered a crisis?" I can barely contain my astonishment.

And neither can Kit. "Holy biscuits," he whispers and then cups his mouth with his hand. "Sorry."

"A meteor that wiped out life on our origin planet," Korbix continues.

"How did you have time? To mobilize an evacuation, I mean?"

"We knew for many years what was to come, and so did those watching us from afar."

I squint at her. "You were contacted like we were?"

"In a certain sense, yes. Though the means were very different, as their technology was and still is above our own. But it not only empowered us to avoid catastrophe, it gave us the possibility to do to others what had been done for us."

"Rescue other planets, other species in peril…"

She nods and then waves her hand. Millions of stars sweep in the background as if Korbix whisked the camera through space at light speed. A few seconds later, the view slows and comes to rest on another habitable world, far less kind than Tria, and even more arid than Earth.

"Is this the Ganesian homeworld?" I ask.

Korbix nods. "Six hundred of your years ago, yes. And it was found by using the gifts the Lithnōgé had bequeathed to us."

I shoot Fergus a sharp look and whisper, "*Bequeathed?*"

"A fitting word, my lady."

"Mmmm." Back to Korbix, I ask, "Wouldn't Tria's distance from Kepler-16… excuse me, from *the Ganesian homeworld* have placed it almost 1,700 light years away?"

"Conventionally, yes. But we did not find the Ganese from Tria. We discovered them from here, on Soteria."

"You… came here first?"

"Yes. You have no doubt noticed the lack of transmission components on the second ring in orbit."

"We noticed. Assuming there wasn't a species here to intercept a signal, we haven't had any ideas as to how it got here."

"Except space towing," Kit interjects. "Which would

have taken a super duper long time if it came from a planet like Tria over a 1,000 light years away, ya know?"

Korbix nods. "I will save the story of its arrival for another time. Needless to say, from Soteria, we sought for the next closest Goldilocks and the Three Bears who might find this porridge just right."

"Fergus?"

He snaps his head toward me but says nothing.

"Goldilocks and the Three Bears?" I ask.

"Ah! I beg your forgiveness, my lady. That was an oversight. Much to process here."

"Did I say something wrong?" Korbix asks.

"No, you're fine. We're still working on the translation protocols."

"I see."

"So, you detect the Ganese and see their predicament, then you send a signal their way and, what, wait?"

"For five hundred fifty years."

"The time it took for the transmission to arrive."

She nods. "They discovered the schematics within a year and had the ring constructed in half that time."

"How did you see all this? The light across those distances is—"

"We didn't. The quantum connection between the light transmission and our origin ring let us know they'd received the gift and built it."

"The gift." This makes me smile. That's what it felt

like we were receiving too. At least it did for me. Her statement also confirms my suspicion that there was some proprietary link between an origin ring, its signal, and the constructed ring. "What about the war?"

Korbix takes a breath, and then a hexagonal ring appears in the display, one I've seen before. Ring X. "The Ganese built their ring but never activated it, allowing it to remain dormant for nearly 100 years."

"That corroborates what Fred said," Kit adds.

Korbix turns to Kit. "Who is Fred?"

"Uh… he's, uh…" Kit gives me a panicked look.

If we're going to continue to build trust with Korbix, I might as well be up front. "Fred is our name for an artificial intelligence we encountered on a derelict space station above the Ganesian homeworld."

Korbix's ears twitch like she's heard something in the distance. "There are survivors?"

"If you count an AI." I remember the Gan swarm. "And some sort of cyborg cousin species that survived in space."

Wrinkles grip Korbix's eyes, ones that cause me to assume that this is news to her. After a few seconds, she seems to find herself and continue. "After so long a time, we decided to investigate. It was our first attempt to help a species, and we had grown… impatient."

"Pardon me, the Ganese were your first?"

She nods. "And our greatest failure."

I exchange looks with Kit in the real as well as with Jericho and Rook in V-cog. I have a feeling that whatever intel Fred gave us about the Naqualla being the antagonists in the Ganesian conflict are about to be challenged.

In the holo display, Ring X activates and produces a vessel much like the one I'm sitting in now. It looks more dated somehow, but the design elements feel the same. "When our ambassador first arrived—"

"You?"

She shakes her head as the edges of her lips curl on the side of her snout. "We live long, but not that much."

"Of course." Not my finest moment. But how should I know what a Naquallan lifespan is? "Please, continue."

"Our ambassador arrived to find a fractured society with multiple heads of leadership. Some wished to hear what our representative had to say while others did not. Many of them felt that us activating the ring was an act of violence... an act of war."

"Did they attack you? Your ambassador, I mean?"

"No. Not at first. Ambassador Tosheen Gil Tamtik brought a full report before the Resettlement Council— that's the body formed to govern how we might aid other systems. But it seemed that the Ganese were not the only species who had differing opinions about how to respond to our offer. Where Tosheen and the majority of the council were in favor of working things through with the Ganese, the Talv were not."

"I'm sorry, the Talv?"

She sighs. "A sect of our people who do not believe it is our responsibility to seek out the suffering and lend assistance. They voted against measures to work with the Ganese, but their attempts to thwart council efforts failed. So we undertook the necessary steps to begin relocating any Ganese who wished to move to Soteria."

"But they never arrived," I say, guessing.

Korbix's snout twitches like she has an itch at the end of her nose. When she speaks again, the words feel like they're said with a seething tone. I imagine her lips circling up over her teeth were she saying them in the real. "Despite being among the minority, the Talv still had great power. They arrived before Ambassador Tosheen's delegation and opened fire on the Ganese orbital defenses."

Black ships, like those made from the scraps we saw in orbit over Kep-C, surge from the ring. Their menacing elongated hulls pierce Ganese space stations like arrowheads splitting targets, all while using some sort of force field to maintain their structural integrity. Enemy vessels swirl around the newcomers, but each thin pyramid-like ship fires energy beams that incinerate the defenders. Before long, the dark ships turn on the planet itself. Orbital rounds streak to the surface and produce billowing clouds that ripple from the impact points in all directions. While I assume the conflict took far longer, Korbix's visual retelling is over in a minute.

"By the time Tosheen arrived, it was done. Nothing survived... until learning of this *Fred* just now."

"And the Talv?"

"They returned home. The council dismissed them and accused them of genocide, demanding that Tria's highest court take action against them. But many saw them as heroes, doing what the council was too weak to do. Those who praised the Talv argued that our people's resources were best spent on protecting our own kind and not aiding others."

"Holy biscuits," Kit says and then turns to me. "That sounds like, ya know, a little like us."

Korbix eyes Kit. "Such infighting is not foreign to you either?"

"I'm afraid not," I reply. "But to wipe out an entire planet? Surely this wasn't just dismissed?"

"In the end, the Talv were acquitted since the act was seen as mercy."

"Mercy? How does that make sense?" Kit asks.

"Because the Ganese were already doomed," I reply to him and to Korbix.

"That was part of the argument, yes," she replies. "The other was that to lend aid would have placed Naquallan lives at risk given the forecasted Ganesian hostility. Whether or not they would have retaliated violently will never be known. Ultimately, the council came up with an idea that they hoped would redeem the Tragedy of the Fallen Firsts."

Fergus interjects, "That has a nice ring to it in English, does it not?"

"If you remove the genocide context, sure," I reply.

Fergus raises a finger as if to say something but holds short.

Back to Korbix, I ask the question I already assume the answer to. "And the idea for redemption?"

"To find another compatible species in need, and then build an origin ring."

"That's when you discovered us."

"It was, yes."

"But we were hundreds of years removed from the technological discoveries that would bring about our climate's most dramatic changes. How could you anticipate that?"

"Your species, we knew, was well on its way to planetary dominion. Thus history and experience told us that only one of three remaining outcomes was inevitable."

"And they were? If you don't mind me asking."

"One, that your species died before it was space-faring due to civil war, disease, or an extra-local catastrophe."

"Meteor, solar flare…"

"Among others, yes. The second possibility was that you continued on your course but could not develop fast enough to account for the damage you'd already set in motion."

"Which has been our current path."

"Yes. It seems the proclivity of most sentient species to outpace their own mortality. The third option was the least probable."

"That we became spacefarers and solved our own problems before it was too late."

"Correct," Korbix replies, seeming satisfied with my answer.

"So it really didn't matter what we chose. It was worth sending a signal."

"That is also correct."

Even though the construction of Ring Y predates Korbix by who knows how long, she represents the species who took a chance on Earth. "Korbix, I... I don't know how we could ever say thank you enough. For taking a chance on us."

"You're welcome. But I dare say you also owe your species equal thanks for allowing you the freedom of building what you discovered."

"I'll make a note to remind them... *if* I ever see them again."

"Are you not planning to?"

"We haven't figured out how to get back.... how to turn on the rings from this side."

"A problem easily solved whenever you're ready."

This gets wide eyes from just about everyone in the command theater, including me. "You have a way for us to return?"

"What kind of rescue would this be without the ability to make return trips?"

I exchange gleeful looks with the other leaders while saying to Korbix, "That's... incredible! We're delighted to hear that. Thank you."

"My pleasure." She pauses, seeming to consider something else. "Are you looking to return now?"

"To be honest, we probably need to send some word back, yes. Though, if given the option, I would rather stay here. This is kind of a big deal for us."

"And for us," Korbix replies. "You are, after all, the first species that we have successfully served."

For whatever reason, that fact hasn't quite dawned on me until just now. "But I thought you said you had a governing body who decides what worlds you aid?"

"We do. After the Ganese tragedy, the council decided only one more attempt was to be made before any more worlds were ever considered."

"Earth."

Korbix inclines her head but says nothing more.

"What has this council been doing in the meantime?"

"What most committees do when no actionable direction is apparent. We bicker and argue until the best minds leave the conversation and the group dwindles away to a staunch few."

"Oi," Eddie says from the V-cog theater. "We sure these wankers aren't taking notes from our playbook?"

"Fergus, don't translate that please," I say.

"As you wish, my lady."

Back to Korbix, I ask, "And what will your people think now?"

"Hopefully, that the efforts of our ancestors weren't wasted. You are proof that their hopes were well founded. That another species can rise above their calamities, respond, and resettle, just as we did. And that the considerable resources committed to such ends are indeed worthy of investment."

"You sound as though the debate is still ongoing."

"No small thanks to you."

"I... don't understand."

"Yours is the Forgotten Gate. The one buried in time. While the Resettlement Council still exists, its presence within our larger government became a footnote... marginal at best. But with news of the Forgotten Gate's activation and your subsequent arrival, you can imagine the spoon it's caused."

I glance at Fergus. "The *stir* it's caused?"

"Yes, my lady."

Korbix continues. "I am told that our current debates rival those of our ancestors. Long dormant opinions about resources and energy as well as sentiments toward aliens have resurfaced."

"Aliens?" Kit asks.

"I think she means us," I reply.

"Oh. Right, right. Sure. 'Cause we're the aliens to them. *Phew!* That is so cool."

"There is also mounting fear of what you will do if we don't stop you."

This makes me sit up straight. "What we'll do? To Soteria?"

"To us," Korbix says more flatly. "Those of the Talv's persuasion fear that you will attack us and take Tria for your own."

"Attack you?" Kit says, looking aghast. "With what? Your ships are like a bajillion times more technologically advanced than ours."

"While I cannot validate your mathematical proposition, I believe I understand your sentiment. And yes, you are severely under-armed for the task. But other concerns include contamination, disease, and questions that your species will raise about ethics and metaphysics."

"Huh?" Kit asks.

"Spirituality," I whisper.

"Oh. Gotcha." But he wrinkles his forehead. "Yeah, still don't get it."

"Don't worry about it." Back to Korbix, I say, "I can assure you that we have no desire to overtake your planet or do your people harm." But even as those words come out of my mouth, I think about all the harm humans have done to themselves and countless species in our own biome, whether intentionally or not.

"While I believe you, Dr. Evelyn Park, I suspect that your civilizations are much like ours: fractured by contending ideas. For every person who means no harm, there is another who will do violence, and all in the name of what they believe is right."

After a moment of frustrated sadness, I say, "You are more right than I care to admit."

She seems to share my sentiment and extends the silence for several seconds. "In any event, while my first priority as ambassador is to ensure your safety and the successful settlement of your new world, Soteria, I do have a proposal for you."

"And that is?"

"That those who you feel best represent your species would return with me to testify before the Resettlement Council."

"Testify?"

"As to the merits and efficacy of our program, the one that brought you here. Doing so would not only go a long way in validating the original beliefs of our ancestors, but it would go a long way in ensuring that other species in similar peril would be given a chance at survival. Not to mention the benefits your species would experience in partnering with us, and us with you. At present, I am able to take up to nine passengers—more if and when your willingness requires it. The decision is yours, of course, and the offer stands indefinitely, so long as you wish to keep channels open between our worlds."

"Of course we do," I say. "And I want that on record."

Korbix nods, as do most of the crew from what I can see. They surely understand as much as I do that eventually one numb-skulled politicast leader or another will say something to jeopardize this relationship. Even though I feel so small in the grand scheme of things, I want humans in the future to see that we were willing.

"If I may? How long will you need this team of witnesses for their testimony?" I ask.

"A year. Perhaps more."

"A year?" Jericho says, sounding a tad bit exasperated. "Why so long?"

"Great matters take time on Tria. And this is surely one of the greatest. Plus, we will have much to learn from your ambassadors, just as we trust you will have much to learn from us. I cannot speak to who is best to return to my homeworld, but I must insist that the most compelling, most intelligent, and most persuasive members of your species form the initial delegation if we are to have any chance at healing the wounds that have scarred our collective memory for so long. Moreover, they will be essential in forecasting what I hope will be an expanding vision for bringing salvation to other species in need." After a few moments, Korbix adds, "I will leave you now. But before I do, I will show you how to re-open your gate to return to Earth. I also hope that some of you will consider coming with me. Your presence would have great impact on the council and expedite our efforts in assisting your resettlement."

This shocks me bolt upright. "Already? But you just arrived."

"Indeed. And yet there is much to be discussed with the council... much to be done."

She can't go. Not yet! "You're sure I can't persuade you to stay a bit longer? See our settlement?"

"Perhaps that is a bit premature, Dr. Evelyn Park. While it is clear that *you* are more than eager, I imagine for others on your crew this meeting has come as a bit of a shock. In my experience, trust is built over time, and consistently so."

I can practically hear Rook smiling over audio. "But we have so much more to discuss," I reply. "Maybe... maybe I can come with you?"

"Woah, woah. Hold up," Jericho interjects. "Evelyn, can we, uh... talk about this first?"

"What's there to talk about?"

"Uh, the safety and wellbeing of our entire expedition."

Stars, he's right. And I'm getting ahead of myself. Still, the opportunity to go back with Korbix is... well, it's too important not to discuss and make a decision on. "Korbix? Can you give us a few minutes?"

"Of course. Please strongly consider my proposal as it would benefit both our peoples."

"Great. Just"—I hold up both hands in the hopes

that somehow it will keep her from vanishing—"stay right here, okay?" I must sound like an overreacting parent. Or a control freak. Probably both. But she gives me a reassuring smile and bows her head slightly. Thank the cosmos for that. "Jericho, Rook. Picnic table."

"Picnic table," they reply in unison.

31

JERICHO

THE MARINES HAD PRINTED a picnic table and set it under a canopy on the beach just south of Evelynton. It's made for a great spot for a break during daily rotations and a popular hangout after hours. I hear there are plans to print some more to populate what's lovingly been dubbed Margaritaville. But for Rook, Evelyn, and myself, it's become a makeshift conference table, one that will hopefully help Evelyn come to her senses…

And probably Rook and me too. While I think it's premature for Evelyn to go anywhere, I also recognize that time is of the essence, and that if anyone is destined to venture off to a strange new alien world, it's her. Sitting here with them, listening to the sounds of the ocean and the birds overhead, I get the feeling that whatever we decide will have wide-reaching implications. For all of us.

"The way I see it," she begins passionately. "There's no better option than for me to—"

I grab her hand. "Before we get going, can I just say that... Wow. Right? We did it. We just made first contact. There's a freaking alien in a starship on the beach over there." I give this a few seconds to settle in as we smile at each other. "Bravo."

They nod and repeat the word.

"Now, before you say what you need to, Evelyn, as far as the three of us are concerned, there aren't any easy choices here. One way or another, whether today or tomorrow, we're breaking up the band. It sucks. But if we go into it giving ourselves permission to know that it sucks, then I think we'll be better suited to face what we *need* to do instead of what we *want* to do."

Evelyn pulls her hand away. "And I need to go."

"I know."

"Don't argue with me about, Jericho! There's a whole... *What did you say?*"

"I know," I say again and take a deep breath. "Our first contact with an alien species, and we're being invited to sit at their table. How can we afford not to say yes? And there's no one better than you."

"Agreed," Rooks replies. "You were born for it."

Evelyn looks between us a few times and then settles on me. "But back there, you—"

"I know what I said. And while I don't want you to go and think there are plenty of reasons why you should wait, I also know that there's no one better to represent humanity in this situation than you, Evelyn."

"Roger that," Rooks says. "The moment we fly back into our system, the questions will come fast and furious, and from all sides. We'll need a mountain of answers and explanations, and we don't get those without having people in key places. The best way to win any conflict is to get as far out in front of it as possible."

It's clear from the look on Evelyn's face that she was not expecting this from either of us. Hell, I wasn't expecting it from Rook myself. "What about the year-long commitment?" she asks.

"We'll manage," I say. "Maybe we'll get more done without you. Christ knows you can be a real pain in the ass."

"You wanna run that by me again?"

I look at Rook. "See what I mean?"

"Woah, leave me out of this. Nooo comment."

The wind kicks up for a moment and then subsides.

"Who would you take?" I ask.

She thinks for a moment. "It has to be their choice, of course, but… I'd ask Sebastián for starters. Not only will he be more interested to know about the Naqualla and every other species we are bound to meet, but he'll be best to give a biological and evolutionary account of human development… to argue why it was imperative that we find a new home. Natalie is probably the sharpest mind on the *Sagan*, which… don't tell anyone else you heard that from me. She could help me wade through any logical and political issues that come up. Having Igor along could be critical if the Naqualla don't know how to meet human health needs. He can treat but also teach about our biology."

"Can I make a recommendation?" I ask.

"Of course."

"Take Eddie."

Evelyn grimaces. "Really?"

"He's rough around the edges, we all know that. But when it comes to systems analysis and breaking down problems, whether it's hardware, software, or even people, he's a bulldog. Plus, there's no one more committed than him. He'll fight tooth and nail for you in any argument and win. I'd want him in my corner. He can also fast track any learning we'll need to do as a species if and when it comes time to integrate."

"Well, when you put it like that…" She laughs a little. "Let's just hope he doesn't learn Naquallan expletives. One language for Eddie is enough for the universe."

We chuckle with her and then grow silent again, the sound of the ocean reclaiming the space.

"What about security?" Rook asks eventually.

"Any recommendations?" she replies.

He seems to grow thoughtful. "Lance Corporal

Hatch would be my first choice. A good rifleman, self-aware, diligent. And as a corpsman, she can complement Igor but won't leave your side."

"Any others?" I ask.

He shakes his head. "Hatch should be enough, assuming Korbix is planning to assign a Naquallan security detail to Evelyn. We'll need all hands here to maintain security and help expand the camp in preparation for new arrivals. That said, I would actually recommend Fergus go along."

"Fergus?" Evelyn asks. "Really?"

"How else are you planning to communicate with them?"

"That had crossed my mind, but you seem to think he'd be good for protection?"

"I do. With both of your permissions, I'm going to have Kit and Lieutenant Jaffa give Fergus access to the *Belle*'s Marine Corps Manuals and training doctrine tutorials. I know it breaks every rule in the book, but like Kit said, we're not in Kansas anymore, and where you're headed, Evelyn, having a superhuman at your disposal could prove advantageous."

Evelyn squints at Rook and then finally nods. "If you're okay with it, so am I."

"This means Kit's going too," I add.

They both look at me.

"You're… willing to part with him?" Evelyn asks me. "Just like that? I thought you—"

"He'd be heartbroken not to follow Fergus."

"But you—"

"I'll be fine."

"You're gonna miss him."

I laugh. "Actually? Yeah. I will. He's a pain in my ass too."

"You seem to collect those," Rook adds.

"And don't I know it." I rub my left butt cheek. "Anyway, the kid's smart. Kind. And having some youth around will do you all some good."

"That leaves one seat," Rooks says.

I stare right at him. "Which belongs to you, pal."

His eyes go wide, as do Evelyn's. "Negative," he says. "I'm needed—"

"Wherever she sets foot," I reply, pointing to Evelyn.

He looks from me to her. "But what about the camp?"

Evelyn smiles. "I thought Lieutenant Jaffa was best suited for administration and logistics? At least that's what a little birdie told me once."

I'm glad Evelyn's keen on the idea. "Listen, Rook," I say. "Hatch is a good recommendation. No doubt. But our friend here is about to go somewhere completely foreign. For my money, there's no one I trust more than you to ensure her protection and care. A hundred coins says she feels the same. And ten times that amount says you don't want to let her go without you."

Rook just blinks at me. It's not often anyone catches a Space Marine off guard.

"If Jaffa stays, who will give a report to NUE Space Command about what we've seen here?"

"I can handle that just fine," I reply. "Plus, we all know, at least I think we do, what awaits you back on Earth."

Rook's eyes waver. The military will not be easy on his dereliction of duty. There will be hell to pay, even if he did it for all the right reasons. He knows that. And so does every member of his team. I've seen the look in their eyes whenever the subject comes up.

"She needs you," I say to him. "Plus, you need this. And I need you to do this too. For all of us."

"I agree," Evelyn adds, giving Rook a warm smile and then offering him an open hand. "So, you coming or what?"

Watching Rook finally accept the invite is strange. I know it's the right call. But I'm not okay with it… personally speaking. I wish it was me going with her. Because, if I'm being honest, I wonder if I'll ever see Evelyn again.

"What about you then?" Rooks asks. "Earth?"

I nod, shaking myself from the start of a pity party. "Yeah. Someone's gotta tell the story, right?"

"You need to prepare yourself," Evelyn says. "The number of interviews alone is going to be killer."

"I've done my share."

"I'm talking about Willow Shade interviews."

The thought of the outrageous verb superstar makes my stomach turn. "Hey, on second thought? I'm gonna tag along with you guys."

We all chuckle for a second, and it feels good and sad all at the same time. Because it might be the last time. We'll have our discoveries, but not together. We'll have laughs, but not at the same table. And we'll probably shed tears, but not over the same drinks.

Damn.

"You okay?" Evelyn says, taking my hand.

I blink a few times. "Sure."

"Really?"

I shake my head once. "I'm gonna miss this."

"Same," Rook says, looking back up the hill toward the camp, then turning toward the mountains beyond. "But until someone else steps up, we have jobs to do."

"Agreed." I let go of Evelyn's hand and hold mine out flat, palm down. "Forging paths?"

They place theirs on top of mine and we all say, "Through the darkness."

EVELYN CHECKS in with Korbix and asks for a few more minutes before returning to camp. We find the other leaders as we left them in the command building. The mood feels somber despite the amazing revelations of the day. But everyone knew going into this that we would be pushing the limits of the known universe… at least what we knew of it. And now we have even more boundaries to push.

"Alright," I say. "Listen up. Evelyn, Rook, and I have a plan to propose. It's not the final word; that will have to come from those of you who we're recommending for service. But this is what we think best, so please recognize that when considering alternatives. No one wants to order anyone to do anything outside their will—"

"Except the Corps," Grabowski says.

"And your mom," adds Rodgers.

Rook shuts them both down hard, and finishes with a sharp, "Focus."

They nod and lower their heads. Then Rook gestures for me to keep going. It wasn't agreed on that I would be the spokesman for this part. It's just… happening. Like everything else in the whirlwind of our last year.

"Korbix's presence has come with its own understandable sets of discoveries, questions, and opportunities. While it could be argued that we let some time pass to investigate her claims, the news that we can head back to Earth right now combined with the opportunity to send some of our own with her means we can't afford to wait. Therefore, it seems to us that we have three immediate priorities before us. The first is that we maintain Camp Evelynton's security. Likewise, since Soteria is a gift, we need to treat it as such in preparation for the lives of those who will enjoy it in the future. Rook?"

He nods. "To that end, Lieutenant Jaffa, it's our recommendation that you oversee both orbital and ground-based assets in conjunction with Corporal Geller. Your leadership will be critical to maintain operational integrity and ensure camp security for the long term."

"Accepted," Jaffa says without hesitation.

"Roger that," Geller adds. "What about you, Master Sergeant?"

"Stand by." Rook nods for me to keep going.

"I will be leading a return run to Earth aboard the *Kogarashi* with anyone not otherwise committed since she's the fastest vessel we have. Our mission will be to update the NUE about what we've discovered and begin coordinating the largest resettlement operation in the history of humanity."

"What about Korbix and the whole testifying thing?" Kit asks.

I turn to Evelyn.

She smiles and addresses the room. "Based on our consensus, the reasons to say yes to Korbix's offer of departing for her homeworld with a delegation outweigh the precautions of waiting. I want the delegation to include Sebastián, Igor, Natalie, Eddie, and Lance Corporal Hatch for security. We also want Kit and Fergus to come along."

Kit looks like he's about to pass out.

Grabowski takes him by the arm. "Keep those legs under you, boot."

"M-m-me? Are you sure, everyone? Because, holy moly, I thought I'd be the last person you'd, ya know, ever want to represent humanity to a high falutin' intergalactic space council where the fates of a billion trillion souls hang in the balance."

"Don't make us change our minds, pal," I say while using my hand to pump some imaginary brakes.

"Right, right. Sure. I'm cool." He shrugs away from Grabowski. "I'm cool, man."

"Whatever you say," replies the corporal.

Kit looks at Fergus. "You up for it, Ferg?"

"I am ever at your disposal, my liege. Mine is to serve with ne'er a question."

"I know. But… I think this time it's important that you, ya know, decide for yourself and stuff."

Fergus tilts his head as if in thoughtful consideration. "You are saying I have freedom to choose my fate?"

"I mean, maybe not your *whole* fate. That's kinda up to destiny. But at least this part, yeah. So? Whadda ya say?"

"I say, I'm in like Flynn. Though I'm still not clear on who he is and what he's into. If it's obscene, I may not be into everything Flynn is into."

"Thanks, Ferg," I say, hoping to stop him from taking this to places none of us want it to go, at least not without a few beers in us.

"What about the last seat?" Geller asks. "I believe Korbix said she has room for nine."

"That seat belongs to Rook," I say. Everyone seems a bit surprised by this, so I move to explain. "Soteria will be in good hands with the Lieutenant and Corporal Geller. Likewise, the *Koga* doesn't need security where we're headed. But Evelyn and her team? Rook belongs at the tip of the spear with them. I also imagine he'll be instrumental in establishing inter-species security protocols."

"Not to mention the fact that I don't want any of my Marines heading back to Earth, at least not for the foreseeable future, until we know how things shake out back home," Rooks adds. This gets head nods from his entire unit. Even the Navy sailors seem to agree. "As for my role, I'm honored to be asked to help the delegation, and I won't turn it down."

"We're behind you, Master Sergeant," Geller says. This gets punctuated by several "Oorah!"s around the room, and even one from Private First Class Ibrahim who's joining via V-cog while aboard the *Bellerophon*.

Once the room settles back down, I glance at Evelyn and then Rook. "So we're good?"

"Yes," Evelyn replies.

"Assuming no one has objections they'd like to air," I say, looking around, but no one makes a motion. "Then there we have it."

"You gonna let Korbix know?" I ask. "Or are we just gonna stand around here telling bad jokes for awhile?"

Evelyn laughs and turns to Fergus. "Mind patching us through to Rose?"

"Please stand by, my lady." A moment later, a live picture of Korbix appears in our crew's V-cog theater.

"We agree to help you, Korbix," Evelyn says. "Given all that your people have done for us, it seems the very least we can do for you."

I'm no expert in Naqualla body language, but so much of their behavior shares a lot with humanity. The way her eyes brighten and her back straightens sends a message of relief and hope. "Thank you," Korbix says, and then places a hand-paw on her chest. "We are most grateful." But Rose seems to interrupt the moment with fast chatter in the Naquallan tongue. Korbix's eyes grow wide. I'm not sure if that's a look of satisfaction or surprise.

"Is everything okay?" I ask.

"No," she replies, ears laid back. "It seems they didn't wait for the council to decide and have taken matters into their own hands."

"What? Who?"

"The Talv. They have entered this system."

32

ROOK

ACCORDING TO KORBIX, we have under four hours before the Talv are within range of detecting us. That's not a lot of time, but it's also more than I might have expected from such a superior fighting force. I've ordered Evelyn, Kit, and Fergus to escort Korbix up to our settlement. No sense planning an operation like this through Fergus and Rose remotely; it would just waste time. If an enemy like the one that appeared over Kep-C is here now, we're in trouble… the no contest kind. Furthermore, if that hostile force were to navigate to Earth, humanity wouldn't fare any better than the Ganese. Sure, we'd put up a fight, at least I'd like to think so. But I'd be lying if I said we had a chance, not against the weaponry Korbix showed us. It would be a massacre.

Korbix took a moment to temporarily disable her

vessel before leaving it and ordered Rose to turn off something called auto-follow. Sounds like a loiter mode that protects the pilot in the event of a capture scenario. I take the act as another effort to build trust with us, which I appreciate. I still don't know exactly who the good and bad guys are in all this, but Korbix is making the most apparent effort to protect the same humans I'm charged with keeping safe. That works for me.

"Evelyn's at the east gate," Private First Class Krutz announces over the squad channel.

"Let them in," Geller replies. "Master Sergeant?"

I look up from my display screen in the command building and follow Geller into the sunlight. It takes a second for my eyes to adjust, but when they do, I get my first up close look at the Naquallan alien. She's head and shoulders above Krutz and the other Marines escorting her across the square. Korbix also has an air of dignity about her, one that's at odds with my impressions of a kangaroo. God, that's gonna be a hard comparison to break.

Jericho steps beside me, and we meet Evelyn and Korbix just outside the command building.

"My name's Jericho Fox." He inclines his head to Korbix like she'd done to Evelyn. "It's a pleasure to meet you."

"The pleasure is mine, Jericho Fox," Korbix replies, her audio and probably some brain data getting translated into V-cog audio through Rose and Fergus.

"And I'm Master Sergeant Farooq, Camp Commander," I add, trusting the translation matrix to work out the military jargon into equivalent terms. "But you can call me Rook. Welcome to Camp Evelynton."

Korbix bows again. "A pleasure," in her alien-sounding tongue.

"Let's get started."

We duck out of the sunlight and walk through the command building to the conference room. Everyone clears away from the newly printed table. I gesture to an empty seat and invite Korbix to sit but then realize there's no way she'd fit in the chair. Her tail alone makes it impossible.

"Thank you, but I'll stand," she says.

"Then we all will." The rest of the leadership team arrives, including my fire team leaders and Lieutenant Jaffa, all of Jericho's crew, and five of Evelyn's key leaders from the *Sagan*. I gesture to Korbix and ask the question I know is on everyone's mind. "What can you tell us about the Talv threat?"

She summons the floating orb known as Rose to the table's center. It descends to within a few centimeters of the top and then emits a bright holo display. Soteria, about the size of a basketball, floats in a starfield with the two rings tagged on opposite sides. Likewise, our three ships circle in low orbit.

"My ship's sensors indicate that a *ker-kuk'kerrr*-class starship has entered your new star system through our ring." A slender arrowhead-shaped ship like those we saw in the footage from Kep-C arrives through Ring W.

Lieutenant Jaffa asks Korbix, "Is this vessel armed?"

"Heavily."

"But it's small? Like yours?"

"No. At least six times the size of mine. Crew capacity averages forty-five members." At her words, the display zooms in to give us some more detail.

Jaffa meets my gaze. "That's a frigate," he says, betraying neither concern nor boredom—ever the Navy man.

"In addition to crew and weapons, this ship also has four landing bays, at least two of which will contain landing craft." Korbix looks at Jaffa. "Those *are* like mine."

"And your estimated time of their arrival remains?" he asks.

"Three to four hours, yes. They will take their time to scan the system first and then enter high planetary orbit."

"And what do you expect they'll do upon arrival?"

She seems to think a moment and then says, "They will approach your vessels in orbit, possibly boarding them. Then they will deploy the scout ships to make planetfall here, centering on your settlement. From there, I expect they will make a determination based upon their findings."

I ask, "Which could include…?"

"They could choose to leave you alone and then disable the ring behind them."

"But that cuts us off from you," Evelyn says.

I'm quick to jump in. "Yeah, but it leaves us alive. And Earth."

"It is also unlikely," Korbix says. "The Talv have little interest in protecting any assets beyond their own. I merely offer it as an extreme possibility. The opposite is that they destroy your ships and conduct an orbital strike against your settlement."

"Not ideal," I say.

"Not anything," Korbix replies looking confused. "You'd be dead."

Apparently, sarcasm isn't part of Fergus and Rose's communication style yet. "If those are the extremes, is there a middle option?" I ask.

"Yes. If I remain among you, they will be forced to deal with me first."

"And then you'll what?" Kit asks, taking on a more dramatic tone… like he's recording his V-cog sensory stream again, goddamnit. He's also chewing some marinated meat off a bone. "Fire up your proton torpedoes and blast 'em out of the sky in a blaze of glory that, ya know, tells the whole galaxy, 'Hey! Don't mess with Korbix or the Earthlings, or else!'"

"My ship lacks such capacity. Plus, how would it alert the entire galaxy?"

"Um, well… I was kinda speaking figuratively, ya

know? Like, your actions would just send a message or something. Kinda put everyone in their place and make them think twice about messing with—"

I interrupt. "Korbix, can you be more specific about how the Talv will act toward you?"

She examines Kit a moment longer and then turns to me. "For one, the presence of my vessel will force them to be more cautious, perhaps even diplomatic, at least for a time. They know I will be documenting their behavior. That said, it does not mean the absence of violence."

"Because they could eliminate you as easily as they could us," I venture.

"Not as easily, but yes, they could kill me. First, however, they would need to ensure that none of the data I capture has any capability of returning to Tria."

"And does it?"

"I have many means at my disposal. None are secret to the Talv, but that does not mean my devices lack power to achieve their purposes."

"Insurance?"

She cocks her head at me, probably processing the word from Rose. "Yes. In a manner of speaking."

"You sure we couldn't just shoot back?" Kit asks, still recording, and still licking his fingers between words. "After all, we are *smick* the Parallax One Exploration Team, which *smmmack* includes one Master Sergeant

Ishaq al *smmmock* Farooq, feared and fabled leader of the Space —"

"Kit," I say, unable to take his lip-smacking anymore. "Enough with the eating already."

"Sorry. My blood sugar was low. I can't help it if I'm skinny. If I don't eat enough, then I get in a bad mood, and you do *not* want to be around me then. *Phew*. Have you seen the movie *Two Fists of Danger?* Well, it's like that, but waaaay—"

"Kit," Jericho says.

"—worse?" He sets the animal bone down and gives everyone a sheepish smile.

"In answer to your questions," Korbix says. "You have no chance of outrunning them, based on the scans I made of your ships. Nor are your weapons able to match theirs."

"Oh," Kit replies, looking quite dejected. "Even if we're, ya know, at our best?"

"The *best* you can do is hide and wait things out."

"Oi, I hate fucking hiding," Eddie says.

"But it might be our only option," I reply. "We have caves to the west. Would that provide sufficient protection from their scans?"

"It should, yes."

"Jesus, Mary, and Joseph," Eddie says. "It's like *2001 Space Odyssey* monkeys getting visited by a Monolith. Only this one shoots. Christ, if that's not a mind fuck, I don't know what is."

"Eddie, please," Evelyn replies.

"A what?" Korbix asks Fergus.

Before anyone can stop him, the bot says, "A deity, followed by two others saintly names, followed by a reference to a late twentieth-century cinematic masterpiece, followed immediately by a derogatory expression in which an unfortunate recipient's head is the target of an unwelcomed sexual advance used to connotate a revelation exceeding expectations."

"An odd but surprisingly poignant expression."

"Oi. See? She fucking gets it," Eddie replies and then stuffs his hands under his armpits. "Wankers."

"Korbix," I say. "Do you expect any secondary forces? Any other ships coming?"

"Not right away. This is most likely a scout vessel. But that does not mean you aren't in grave danger. For now, I recommend we come up with a plan to hide your presence and hope that I can deter them."

"Alright, people. We're on the clock and we've got the best minds on the planet."

"We're the only minds on the planet," Kit says, but suddenly stops and picks up the bone he was working on. "Best minds, huh?"

I nod, skeptically. "Why? You got an idea, kid?"

"I think so, yeah." Then he smacks his lips one more time, and I swear to God I'm gonna glue them shut.

WE'VE GOT A PLAN. Not a very good one. But a plan nonetheless, all thanks to Kit. It hinges on my least favorite tactic, both at the poker table and on the battle-field. Bluffing. But if you're forced to play, and you've got nothing in your hand, then you'd better bluff like your life depends on it. And in our case, it does. We can't get back to orbit without being noticed, and we can't win in a direct conflict, so Korbix is going to lie. She's going to tell the Talv that we're not here, and us? We're finding concealment.

All three crews of Evelynton's forty-nine-member population have been divvied up into four groups, each with an equal distribution of skills and experience in the event that the teams are separated, captured, or killed. The only exceptions are Private First Class Zara Ibrahim, currently aboard the *Belle*, and Dr. Jimmy Bolton who's standing guard on the *Sagan* and watching the prisoner, Olivia Tomlinson. They've taken the neces-sary precautions to make the starships appear as dormant as possible. Even with life support shut down, there's plenty of air and heat to keep them safe for a few days.

I've assigned groups to my three fire team leaders, plus a fourth to myself. Likewise, I've designated each unit a different location to conceal themselves in the surrounding area. While Korbix won't guarantee the positions will keep us off the Talv's sensors—because what guarantees are there in combat?—she has confirmed that the caves to the west of Evelynton will provide the best chance of staying off the enemy's radar.

Team One, headed by Sergeant Geller, is heading southwest with Jericho, Afumba, and a distribution of our navy and science officers. They'll take position in a shaft buried between boulders at the eight o'clock position relative to Evelynton. Team Two is heading a few degrees north of Team One and being led by Corporal Korvich. Evelyn's in this unit, flanked by Lieutenant Jaffa and Fergus. I've charged them with protecting her life at all costs. They'll be in a bowl-like room hidden twenty meters behind a waterfall. I trust the deep bedrock combined with the flowing water will provide the most protection. Corporal Popov is leading Team Three, heading to a cave in the side of a ravine at the ten o'clock position. And I've tasked myself with Team Four, taking cover in a hole halfway up a bare rock incline with a good view southeast to Evelynton. We'll be the most exposed, but I need the high ground for command oversight if things go sideways.

All teams are maintaining local V-cog connection provided by the *Bliss Mobile* and the *Rubenking Special*, our two shuttles still parked in Evelynton. But soon, we'll be terminating that connection since Korbix says it can be traced. Instead, she'll be ordering Rose to provide a one-way untraceable signal to Fergus who will distribute it to the rest of us at a low enough wattage that it shouldn't be a problem, or so Korbix claims. Part of me wants a total comms blackout, but if there's an issue in camp between Korbix and the Talv, I need to know, so I opt to keep the signal plan in place.

"Those look like Korbix's shuttle," Kit says beside me as we watch two enemy ships streak across the eastern sky.

"Sure do. Just a lot meaner," I reply. They're the pair of smaller scout vessels Korbix mentioned. "I'm guessing those side pods are weapons. Possible turret bulge under the nose."

"You think, maybe, they might, ya know, hurt her?"

"She doesn't seem to think so, but there's one thing you can count on when dealing with a bully."

"You're bound to get shoved in a locker?"

I look over at him and smile. "They don't act reasonably."

"Oh. Yeah, that too."

Back to the horizon, the pair of Talv ships close on Evelynton, and Korbix orders us to kill our network signal. We do, and then switch over to the one-way feed coming from Fergus. He's outside the waterfall at Team Two's position to provide the transmission, posing a minimal detection profile, according to Korbix. But should the enemy close, he has orders to drop the relay service and get to cover.

The two Talv vessels flare for landing on the beach to the south, sending up huge plumes of sand. A few seconds later, the ships drop below the treeline and out of sight. In my head, I pick up Rose's camera view. She's hovering a meter above and behind Korbix as the ambassador emerges from her vessel and walks along the strand to the newcomers. Two squads of what I'll call Talv combatants move down their ship's wings and move toward Korbix. All twenty of them are dressed in black versions of the same vest and tunic style clothing as Korbix, but with more angular insignias as well as dark plate armor on their chests and shoulders. They also wear helmets and carry strange alien-looking rifles. The only person without a cover or weapon is the foremost *roo*. He or she is a little shorter than Korbix and maybe a 100 kilos lighter. And, yup, that's the nickname I'm giving the bastards who want to kick us out of paradise.

As the two sides converge, the audio channel fills with the sounds of awkward Naquallan speech, making me wince. Fortunately, Fergus dials the volume down and features translated audio from Korbix and the Talv leader, who Fergus has given a squeaky sounding male voice. Whether following some parameters from Rose or due to his own dislike of the newcomer, Fergus has certainly made the guy sound irritating as hell.

"Ambassador Korbix Kōs Limmia," says the male roo. "Why am I not surprised to see you here?"

"I could say the same about you, Pohge. Then again, shouldn't you be licking Ilso's toes about now? Seems you've missed your daily appointment."

The one called Pohge thrusts his snout in her face,

forcing her to avoid an impact. "Watch the height of your head, *kerr-kuk*."

Fergus whispers softly, "It's untranslatable, I'm afraid."

"You've come alone from the looks of it," says Pohge.

"Does that surprise you?"

"Considering that the worms have, at long last, come to grovel at your handout, yes."

"And yet you've wasted no time in coming to see these *worms* yourself. Tell me, how long did the council take to grant you permission?"

"You would know if you had waited yourself." Pohge snorts at the air. "Where is your grand entrance, Ambassador? Have you not come to impress them?"

"I came to greet them officially, yes, and with the charge of doing so quickly should any parties with less than honorable intentions arrive first. Unfortunately, it seems that my efforts were wasted."

"What do you mean?"

"I believe they're all dead," Korbix said flatly. "I found remains in several locations west of their settlement."

Pohge shoots a glance up the hill. "And you've scanned the area?"

"Just as you have, I assumed."

"Indeed."

"Anyway, there is little to report, sadly."

"We'll see about that." Pohge flicks a hand. His squads surge forward and start up the promontory, tails bobbing as they go. The Talv leader tilts his head at Korbix. "Shall we?"

The cohort of Talv combatants enters through the southern gate, weapons shouldered, heads on swivels. This is obviously my first glimpse of any military type behavior, and it's clear that, at least according to human standards, these aliens are trained for combat. They're smooth. Precise. Moving intentionally from building to building, checking corners, covering one another's progress. That coordination alone is something to be concerned with. Couple it with powerful weapons, and we have ourselves a proper enemy fighting force.

Private Horowitz shares a look with me. "Not good," he says.

"All the more reason this plan needs to work," I reply.

"Roger that."

The enemy scours Camp Evelynton, opening doors, searching buildings, and examining our belongings. The shuttles get a once over, as do our mounted wall defenses. But, surprisingly, nothing gets trashed. When the camp is finally deemed clear, Pohge rounds on Korbix. "Show me the remains."

"I will upload the data now."

"No. I want to see them with my own eyes."

Korbix hesitates, which seems to perk Pohge's interest.

"It's too far," she says.

"I have all day, Ambassador."

Finally, Korbix relents. Now let's hope she can sell it.

IT TAKES the Talv combatants fifteen minutes on foot to reach the first staged encounter southwest of Camp Evelynton. It's not ideal having them move in our general direction, but it's only logical that any fights with land-based apex predators would happen in the forest west of camp. Our four teams are still safe several klicks away in the foothills region.

Korbix leads Pohge to a grizzly scene where body parts, armor, and clothing are strewn across a ten-meter-wide area. Dirt and leaves are displaced in signs of a violent struggle, while several trees look like they've been rammed by a hover truck carrying a blood bank. On the far side is the decaying corpse of a banther complete with a shredded limb trapped in its jowls.

"What happened?" Pohge says, looking over the scene as his lackeys check the remains.

"I logged several level six species when I arrived. You can see part of one here, as it looks like the aliens managed to slay it. But it appears that more arrived and fought over prey."

"You staged this," Pohge says, not sounding entirely convinced, although that could just be Fergus's misinterpretation.

"Yes, Pohge. I staged this." My heart skips a beat, hands squeezing my weapon. "I came out here, opened fire on a bunch of aliens, arranged them with an apex predator's mutilated corpse, and then led you here for fun. That sounds perfectly reasonable, and I'm sure the council will agree with you."

Huh. Apparently they *do* have sarcasm in Naquallan culture. Noted.

Pohge works his jaw and turns about as if a temper is raging inside him. "You said there are others. Show me."

"Let's just go back to—"

"*Show me*," he spits.

Korbix swallows. "Very well. This way."

Over the next hour, Korbix tours Pohge through three additional death scenes, each more decomposed than the last. The hope was to make the fatal incidents look successively older by increasing the state of decay and reducing the amount of content—both things that would happen naturally over the course of days and weeks as lesser predators discovered the meat and the weather covered over the signs of struggle. It also stood to reason that the *aliens* who survived each encounter would gather their dead along with any items of value, making us have to part with less of our actual hardware. Still, we needed to leave some sign of foreign presence, so more clothing and bits of broken armor were used.

As for the "human" corpses, they were harvested from a local population that reminded me of overweight deer. Seb called them *xenocervidae* or something. In addition to the deer body parts, our makeshift special FX department used massive amounts of blood care of a recent narephant kill. Seb, Igor, and Enni had quite a bit of fun dressing things up despite the time crunch.

After seeing the fourth location, Korbix doesn't even ask Pohge if he wants to see more. She just starts walking west to the next—and last—of our staged areas. "Enough," he shouts. "I've seen enough."

Korbix turns to face, almost looking disappointed.

"Easy," I say under my breath. *Don't oversell it.*

"As I said before," Korbix continues. "I will share the data with you since I know all your many superiors will be curious as to their underling's findings."

Pohge snarls at her. The guy's patience seems to be wearing thin. "And risk giving my partners infected data that would expose us? I'll capture my own footage, thank you."

"As you wish." She starts walking away. "I'm heading back to camp."

"Camp?" Pohge looks up. "What do you mean?"

"The settlement."

"Yes… but you said camp."

Kit is right next to me and backhands my bicep. "It's

a different word!"

"What?" I ask.

"Camp! It's more… *colical*."

"Colloquial?"

"Yes!"

Shit. He's right. It's something *we* would say, and probably something Rose and Korbix picked up during our discussions, making Camp Evelynton sound familiar and not just some disconnected alien settlement. Apparently, there's a Naquallan equivalent that she's lapsed into without thinking.

Korbix tries to cover her tracks, but I don't think the Talv leader is buying it. He looks her up and down like he's searching for clues. Then he glares at Rose. Pohge's direct stare into the camera make's my trigger finger tingle. His head tilts, and he withdraws something from his vest. It's a device of some kind, a tablet maybe. He checks it, then looks back at Rose. Right then, the signal terminates. Whether because Korbix shut it down or Pohge interrupted it, I'm not sure. But what I do feel certain of is that the Talv leader just detected Rose's transmission, or at least suspects one. Which means he knows Korbix is lying.

"Uh, Master General?" Kit says. "I don't think, ya know, that's a good sign."

"No. It's not." I address our team members who are standing in the cave's mouth. "We've got tangos inbound."

33

EVELYN

"Fergus?" I yell above the sound of the falls. "What happened to the signal?"

"The transmission was terminated," he replies as I join him beyond the waterfall's veil.

"By Rose?"

"Uncertain. If it was her, and I suspect as much, then I must assume it was done to protect us. However, the larger concern is the implication behind Rose transmitting at all."

"Pohge will assume that someone else is watching," I say. "This isn't good."

"I agree, my lady. Our orders from Master Sergeant Farooq in this contingency are to—"

"I know what he said, but we can't just stay here."

"But we must. Secrecy is paramount, and remaining hidden ensures the greatest…"

After a moment, I ask, "Fergus? What's wrong?"

His head tilts. "I must leave."

"Leave? Why?"

"I have reason to believe that I have been detected by a foreign sensor scan." He turns away from me and starts walking along the wet rocks toward the trailhead that leads up and away from our hiding place.

"Fergus, wait! You—"

"My continued presence here may jeopardize your safety, my lady. Please, return to the cave and await contact from Master Sergeant Farooq."

I run after him. "Where will you go?"

"As far away from you as possible."

The thought of Fergus getting destroyed hits me harder than I would have expected. He's just an excipion, after all. Nothing more. And yet, he *is* more, at least to us. But then I consider something else: what if he's captured? What if the Talv have a way of interfacing with him like Rose has and are able to extract information?

"Fergus, stop! If you're captured, I'm worried that you may inadvertently give the enemy information about humanity that could compromise us all. Put Earth at risk."

"I will never be captured alive, my lady." He turns sideways and arches his back like he's showing off fancy new clothes. Only instead of drawing my attention to imaginary attire, he points to the small of his back. "I still got it."

"The fragmentation grenade."

"Indeed. Maglocked and secure. If I go, the enemy is going with me."

"Fergus, I…"

"Do not fret about me, my lady. Care more for those beneath the shadow of your wing. It is my honor and rare privilege to serve someone such as the great Dr. Evelyn Park."

"Thank you, Fergus."

"Now, please. Go back inside, and with haste."

I meet him and place a hand on his chest. "Be careful."

"I shall endeavor not to disappoint you." With that, Fergus resumes walking to the trailhead and then eventually disappears around the corner.

I take a breath, forcing my frustrations to dissipate, but it doesn't work. So I return to the waterfall, skirt behind the veil, and rejoin the others.

"What's the situation?" Corporal Korvich asks, clearly unhappy that I went outside. Muted beams of sunlight hit his face, illuminating the concern in his eyes.

"Fergus suspects Rose was discovered by Pohge."

"Which means he'll assume Korbix isn't alone."

"Fergus also believes the Talv may have detected his

presence. He's drawing them away from our position. We need to do something."

"We follow orders and stay put, Dr. Park."

"But what about Korbix? If the Talv suspect that she's been lying then—"

"Then she'll have to deal with the consequences herself. She knew the risks."

"And just like that you want to abandon her?"

Lieutenant Jaffa stands to join Korvich. "What we want is to make sure someone among us survives to return to Earth and finish what you started."

"Yeah? And using what ship, Lieutenant? Because I can guarantee that those invaders aren't going to leave any of ours in orbit if they think for one second that we *aliens* are still alive down here. Would you?"

Jaffa chews the inside of his lip and glances at Korvich. "No."

"Then I say we try to mount at least some sort of response. You Marines are all trained for this sort of thing, right? Time to put it to good use."

"Dr. Park, begging your pardon," Lance Corporal Hatch says, lowering her voice. "But if the Talv force is as advanced as Korbix says they are, then no, we're not trained for this sort of engagement."

I lock eyes with her, wanting to take her rifle myself and head out. Problem is, I believe her. This is me being impulsive. Being frustrated. And mad. Me feeling power-less, which I hate.

"Dr. Park?" Hatch says.

"What?"

Ever so gently, she places a gloved hand on my arm. "Please. Come sit down."

I feel my chest rise and fall, my beating heart slow.

Bhavna joins Hatch and takes my other arm. "Evelyn? Come on."

I nod and decide to listen against my better judgment. Or is it against my worse judgment? Maybe, if I'd listened more, we wouldn't have gotten so deep so fast. Maybe we could have won the politicasts to our side, taken our time with the NUE, and entered *Parallax One* together, united. Maybe we could have had a stronger presence to receive Korbix, stop Pohge, and keep us from...

"Evelyn?" It's Bhavna again. "Why don't you come and—"

The light dims as if a cloud has crossed the sun. I turn and spot a shadow moving behind the waterfall's wavering veil. "They're here."

Jericho

"Two bogies, closing on Team Two's position," Geller says and then hands me the scope.

"Son a bitch. Evelyn."

I don't need the optics to see the ships, but I hold them up anyway and zoom in on the vessels descending toward the forested waterfall north of us. Geller and I have risked climbing on top of the boulder pile surrounding our cave but are still hidden under an overhang. The aircraft look even more menacing up close. Weapons are clearly visible now, having emerged from pods that kept them shielded during atmospheric entry. They're ready to shoot something, and I feel powerless.

"What can we do?" I ask Geller.

"Nothing, I'm afraid. Unless you have a death wish."

"We can't just sit here."

"I understand your frustration, Knight. But I have to believe that Korbix knows the enemy's force strength. We're infantry forces pitted against superior airpower. Even by Earth standards, it's a bad match up. In a ground contest, maybe we stand a chance, assuming their armor isn't impervious to magnetically accelerated tungsten rounds. But anything we attempt against those ships right now would only put more lives in danger. That's why we split up in the first place."

A loud *zrack-BOOM!* echoes through the woods as birds take flight. A second noise comes with a blast of light followed by an explosion of fiery rocks. The debris shoots a hundred meters up, trailing smoke through a rising dust cloud.

"Jesus," I say. "They're firing!"

A hand hits the top of my head. "Stay down," Geller yells.

Another shot from the enemy ships flings more rock into the air, this time accompanied by a fiery plume. I can't think of what ignited other than the munition itself. But now one ship has descended beneath the treeline while the second has gained altitude to, presumably, provide cover.

"Geller, we have to—"

"We need to get off these rocks, double time."

I cast one more look at the enemy ship as fire rises from the woods and then reluctantly follow Geller back down. I don't know if Evelyn and the rest of Team Two are alive, but my heart is beating fast. I can barely keep my balance as we navigate through the gaps in the rocks and make it to our hideout. The thought that Evelyn has come all this way only to be hunted and slain by the sentient species she placed so much hope in is... well, a shitshow is what it is. Goddammit.

"That sounded like weapons fire," Grabowski says as we re-enter the cave.

"Shook the ground like a mofo too," Rodgers adds.

Geller confirms their suspicions. "The bogies have opened fire on Team Two's position. One bogie has set down hot, the other in support."

"Shit," says Grabowski.

"Are you okay?" Afumba asks me, ever the guardian angel.

"Fine." I pull the assault rifle from my back and stare at it.

"I know that look."

"As do I," Geller says. "And I advise against everything you're thinking right now, Knight."

"We can't just sit here waiting," I protest.

"Welcome to combat," Rodgers replies and then looks at Geller. "Orders?"

"Hold for one mike, then I want the two of you"— he points at Grabowski and Rodgers—"topside for a SITREP on the bogies. I don't expect them to sit still for very long."

Afumba places a hand on my shoulder. "We will find a way."

I don't really know what he means by that, as it's pretty non-specific, but his calm demeanor and simple reassurance are appreciated. I'm also grateful that he didn't say something stupid like, "Everything's going to be okay."

We wait out Geller's one minute, which feels like one hour, and then Grabowski and Rodgers snake out of our hole and start climbing. We don't hear any more weapons fire during their absence. When they return a minute later, they're both out of breath from the effort.

"Both bogies are headed north," Grabowski says. "Looks like they're flying recon toward Team Three. But the bird that touched down is up high, flying support."

"Trading places." Geller squints and looks past the corporals toward the exit. "They're taking prisoners."

"I thought they wanted us dead," Rodgers says.

"They still might," Afumba replies. "But a true commodity has more value intact than broken."

I'm relieved at the prospect that Evelyn may have survived that explosion. But at the same time, the idea that she and the others could be captured is making it hard for me to think. I don't even want to imagine what the Talv might do to her. So I don't. I shut the thoughts out like I'm ignoring a warning alarm in a cockpit telling me I'm about to stall. *Focus, Knight. Use the assets at your disposal.* "Alright, Geller. Remind us of the contingencies."

"Orders are to hold position for thirty mikes until the last bogie is away. Rendezvous at Evelynton, scout for signs of sabotage, and then regroup when it's safe. Plan from there based on what assets and intel are available."

I grit my teeth at the orders. I know they're wise on paper. Rook had reasons and experience to back their creation. But it doesn't mean we can't improvise. "Geller, I can't wait thirty minutes."

"Neither can I, Knight. But orders are orders." I'm

about to buck him when he adds, "However, if you were to move early, we'd be forced to follow you. No plan survives contact with the enemy or a headstrong NUESSA captain."

"You mean POET captain."

"Those are even worse."

Rook

"THEY'RE HEADED TO THE RAVINE," I say and then pass the scope to Horowitz.

"I thought Korbix said the caves would hide our heat signatures?"

"She did. But she could be wrong. Or maybe someone popped their head up. Or…" I hold short of the third explanation.

"Or they tortured Korbix for intel."

Looks like I didn't need to. "Roger."

"Which means we're not safe here," he concludes.

As if to accentuate his point, the bogie on point fires

another energy round toward Team Three's ravine. The hideout is beyond the line of sight from here, but I can still see the dust plume rise skyward. "Shit."

"Orders?" Horowitz asks.

"Hold position"—the worst order for any card-carrying Marine to hear, but an order that saves lives nonetheless. One that lets you live long enough to fight another day. Hopefully. "Get everyone as far back as possible. If they are tracking thermal, we need to minimize our footprint. We scout again in five mikes."

"Copy that." Horowitz heads back through the cave while I take one last look at the enemy ships. There are prisoners onboard, my gut says so. Which means that I'm going to spend everything I have left to secure them—to secure her—or die trying.

34

NIGEL

THE VOTE WAS HELD in a closed-door session of the Chamber of Politicast Representatives at the Nations of United Earth headquarters in Oslo with 348 of 375 representatives present, more than enough for quorum. The tally took less than one hour, with the Speaker of the Chamber, acting as Secretary General since the vote concerned Nigel, declaring 83 percent of the voting members in favor of the historic measure. Upon his swearing in the following Tuesday, the 8th of June, 2252, Sir Nigel Sallsworth became the first President of Earth, Commander In Chief of NUE Military Forces, and Regent of Space Settlement Territories, including Mars Nation, the Belt Lands, and the Moons of Jupiter. Never before had so much responsibility been given to one individual. But, it was reasoned, never before had humanity encountered such a need.

And it was not without new accountability. The joint chambers of Politicast Representatives and Presidents, along with the Security Council and Space Council, were assigned new powers that established new checks and balances for the office of Earth's President. The framework made it clear that he was not a lone agent, wielding unanimous powers excessively, but a servant of the Republic, bound to democracy and the will of the people.

Nigel, of course, was fine with the language. It sounded good to the people, eased the concerns of the chamber members, and provided the attorneys years of tantalizing paid-by-the-hour busywork as they hemmed and hawed over every jot and tittle of the agreement.

The decor of his current office had been updated with flags and signage to suit his new position while his new office was being constructed. And even that bureau would not be his final home; he'd already commissioned a team to design a new building worthy of a system-wide president. He would abandon Oslo, choosing instead to look over the Gulf of Finland from a perch in Helsinki. With any luck, he would move into the modern architectural masterpiece by 2254 and, he hoped, linger in those hallowed halls for many years to come.

In the meantime, he had more pressing matters to attend to, namely keeping good on his promises to Caleb

Nowen and the other spacers while also ensuring that the pesky business of *Parallax One* would never trouble him again. He figured that Caleb and his ilk had gotten so excited over their victory, one in which Nigel vowed never to destroy the ring, that they failed to imagine all the other things he could do to prevent anyone or anything from ever passing through it again.

"First Fleet Admiral Bronheim has reported that all vessels have arrived at *Parallax One* as ordered, Mr. President," said one of his new staffers whose name he hadn't yet made time to memorize. The kid sat at the briefing room table amidst twenty other young faces, all eager to attend to their new president. All impressionable. This was as much to keep old political wrenches out of his office and build a new team from the ground up as it was to appeal to the next generation of voters. By the time Sallsworth was up for reelection, he wanted the new voter base to recognize their own among his advisors, not the dreary curmudgeons of a bygone era. Earth's Presidential Office had to endure and resist all future efforts to rescind it.

"Very good. Any issues?"

"No, Mr. President. *Telemine* Station is secure. Admiral Bronheim said he looks forward to your inspection of the facility."

"What about the new command center?"

A hand went up from a young woman with long dark hair but she didn't say anything.

"You don't need to raise your hand, people. If you have information, just speak it out. We'll get used to this together."

"Yes, sir. Sorry, sir," the young woman said. "*Valkyrie Command* development team has been assembled and are starting the design phase. They expect to have initial proposals ready by month's end."

"Keeping us on schedule?"

"Yes, sir. Ahead, actually."

"Excellent."

Valkyrie Command was Nigel's concession to the chamber members on the Security Council in exchange for their votes. Since he'd committed to never destroying *Parallax One*—publicly, at least—that meant that more money needed to be spent on vigilance. In order to patrol the region around the ring and keep space navy guns pointed at it and *Telemine* Station at all times, a new forward operating base was needed, one to serve as permanent oversight of *Parallax One. Valkyrie Command* would not only provide operational and logistical support, but it would house the largest RAGE array in history—that is, rail assault gatling equipment. In fact, *Valkyrie*'s entire design was based on building around the central rail platform, effectively wrapping a two-kilometer long RAGE cylinder with a ring-city capable of supporting one-g permanent human residence. When finished, it would be the largest weapons installation ever built by humans.

Of course, it was all a sham. Nigel had no intention of allocating the funds needed for building yet another piece of megalithic hardware in space, just as he never intended to keep his word about not destroying *Parallax One*. *Appease and smile*, he told himself more and more these days. *But always delay.*

"What else? Anyone?"

"Post-election polls are on the rise, sir," said a blonde haired twenty-something man near the back. "The people, they…"

"Spit it out, son."

"They love you, Mr. President."

This got several smiles and a few chuckles.

"Does that surprise you?" Nigel countered. "I have exceptional taste in staffing." A few more polite laughs and nods of approval came his way. "What's your name, son?"

"Carol. Alexander Carol, Mr. President."

"Well, Alex. Remember this: everyone loves the first guy. But they love to hate the last. I got lucky."

"It pays to be first," Alex shouted back.

"Hear hear. Which includes all of you. Congratulations on being selected." Nigel started clapping, which set them to doing the same. When the self-congratulating finally died down, Nigel closed out the morning briefing. "Keep up the good work everyone. We'll see you here tomorrow morning, same time, 8:00 AM. Stay hungry."

Walter Brunell, Nigel's chief of staff, held the doors

for the young aides as they filed out. Only a few recognized him; the rest were too high on euphoria to notice the older man. He smiled and nodded as they passed, closing the door behind himself once they were gone. Then to Nigel he said, "A few look promising."

"And the rest will be gone within the month, I wager."

"I'll make sure they land somewhere that they can't do any harm."

"Any word from the Canary?" Nigel asked, choosing to use his codename for Gemma Birdwhistle. Even though his plan had gone off without a hitch, it didn't mean he could get lazy. *New levels, new devils.*

"As a matter of fact, yes, Mr. President. She's requested—"

"A position?"

"A *tour.*"

"Of?"

"*Telemine* Station, sir. In your company."

"Odd."

Ever since the Vote to Change History, as the pundits began calling it, Gemma had gone radio silent. Which was rather odd. Nigel had gotten his end of the deal; it was only a matter of time before young Birdwhistle came calling for Nigel to make good on appointing her to one chair or another. Most people would have demanded it before the victory cheering had stopped. But Gemma was not most people. And, Nigel suspected, she was not only interested in gaining a position of power but in having his head.

"A fitting place to kill me, wouldn't you say?"

Walter nodded once but said nothing.

"Arrange it. Inform heads of security, but keep it quiet."

"With utmost discretion, sir."

The notion of putting an end to the Tantum Terrae once and for all thrilled Nigel. But rather than let emotions distract him, he channeled his energy into plotting his final act against Birdwhistle. He'd bested her mother; how much easier the daughter. Then he would be clear of all encumbrances, free to lead the system forward and do what was needed. Do as he pleased.

35

JERICHO

"CAMP'S CLEAR," Geller says to me and Rook as he and the rest of the Marines file out of Camp Evelynton's western gate.

"Which means we need to assume the Talv have taken them and Korbix hostage. That's best case scenario," Rook says.

"Best case?" Kit asks. "That's hardly what I would call a—?"

"Think about it," I say to him.

Kit does, and then answers, "Oh. Gotcha."

As it stands, our current roster is twelve members in Team One, which includes Geller, Grabowski, and Rodgers. Ensign Markus Lowery and Petty Officer Third Class Dumont Hill round out the military contingent. Myself, Afumba, and five science officers make up the civilian portion. Team Four is eleven strong, including Rook, Private Horowitz, and Petty Officer Second Class Claire Richards. From there, it's Kit, Magellan, Eddie, Natalie Mason, Enni Mäkinen, plus three more scientists. Current readings from the *Belle*, *Sagan*, and *Koga* show them operational and in orbit. Ibrahim and Bolton have maintained the communications blackout, and I have to assume that Olivia Tomlinson is still in custody.

I call everyone to gather around just inside the western gate and then say, "Alright. Listen up, everyone. It seems pretty safe to assume that the enemy has captured Teams Two and Three, hopefully alive, and are holding them prisoner on their frigate, using their smaller shuttles as transports."

"Didn't realize they had so much room," Grabowski says.

"If they utilize the aft compartments for cargo instead of luxury accommodations like Korbix's ship. Plenty of power to haul the weight too."

"Roger."

"Fortunately, it doesn't appear as though the Talv have damaged anything in camp nor our ships in orbit. I wish we could update Ibrahim and Bolton on the *Belle* and *Sagan*, but transmission is too dangerous. I'm hoping they maintain the blackout for as long as possible in order to avoid detection. As such, we're taking risks ourselves by coming out of hiding, but both Rook and I believe it's time to go on the offensive."

"'Bout fucking time," Eddie replies.

Grabowski asks, "You have a plan?"

"We do. At least the start of one anyway. First…" The sound of fast approaching footsteps distracts me. I glance back through the western gate and see someone running toward us. "Fergus?"

"Oh, Knight," he cries as he slows to a stop in front of me. "Thank Odin's beard, I found you. The Talv have absconded with Dr. Park and the rest of Team Two!"

"We know, buddy. You okay?"

"Okay? I am responsible for delivering my charges directly into the enemy's hands! I might as well detonate myself here and now lest I cause any further—"

"Belay that," Rook says. "We need you, now more than ever."

He tilts his head at Rook. "To what, betray *you* now and cause irreparable harm to—?"

"Do you think you can reactivate the auto-follow feature that Korbix disabled when she left her ship?"

"You… desire that I turn it back on?" Fergus looks between Rook and me a few times.

"We do," I reply. "But only in part. I still want to be able to fly the ship manually. You think that's possible?"

"Perhaps. That is, if I don't make a mess of things again and cause us to fly right into the local star on account of my boneheaded lack of direction."

"Easy there," Rook says in a calming tone. "Did you do something to alert the enemy?"

"In a manner of speaking, though it was hardly intentional, I can assure you."

"Go on."

"Well, once I realized I'd been detected, I sought to put as much distance between me and the waterfall as possible. However, in my haste, I inadvertently ran in the direction of Team Three. I honestly don't know what came over me. Perhaps a latent need to see if they were in satisfactory condition, who knows? Whatever the reason, it led the Talv straight to their position. The enemy even managed to incapacitate me for a moment... I believe it was some sort of stun ray that temporarily disabled my audio and visual relays... a drive-by *muting*, if you will. The fault is mine, and I will never forgive myself."

"You made a mistake," I reply. "Welcome to being human. What counts now is getting back in the game."

"Did you just say... welcome to... being human?"

"Sure, yeah. Can you——"

"You think of me as human?"

"Maybe a little. What we need now is——"

"I'm touched, my lord." He places a hand over his would-be heart. "I never knew that you felt his way."

"All that's gonna change fast if you don't listen, Ferg."

"Ah! Of course, my lord. Apologies. I shall begin work on the task in question posthaste."

"Good. Eddie? I'm gonna need you and Kit to work on setting up a local V-cog channel for us to use that won't ping the Talv's sensors. Think you can come up with something?"

"We'll see what we can do."

"Good. Rook?"

He nods and says, "Marines, I want you in full kit, void-combat ready in ten mikes. Everyone else, you've all been cross-trained on our basic weapons systems. Now's the time to put what you've learned to good use. Grab weapons from the armory. Meet back here in fifteen mikes."

"Pardon me, Master Sergeant," Enni says. "But where are you expecting to engage the enemy? Here, defending Evelynton?"

"Negative, Mäkinen." Rook points straight up. "We're taking the fight to them."

IT TAKES JUST over ten minutes for everyone to return from their respective tasks. Fergus has successfully reactivated the auto-return feature, and I've double-checked our proposed weight loads against the tolerances of Korbix's shuttle. Meanwhile, Rook and his Marines have the Navy personnel and our scientists and engineers armored up and ready to fly. We're piled into the command building where I get everyone's attention and then start things off.

"The plan is to load into Korbix's vessel as soon as this meeting is done," I say.

"We're calling it *Banshee*," Rook adds.

"And our destination? The Talv frigate, aka *Behemoth*."

"What about using the *Bliss* and the *Rubenking*?" Natalie Mason asks. "More room, and they gives us more firepower—"

"Negative," Rook says. "Not only would our ships alert the enemy of our approach, but those ships are our only transport off the planet. They must remain intact."

I continue. "The *Banshee* doesn't risk discovery because it has a built-in return and loiter mode paired with the pilot. In this case, Korbix, who is currently aboard the *Behemoth*."

"And it's still connected with her?" Petty Officer Second Class Claire Richards asks.

"Not to our knowledge. But that doesn't matter," I reply.

"Begging your pardon?"

"We're going to assume that this feature is well-known to all Naqualla pilots, including the Talv. As such, while they may be surprised to see the ship, their guard will be down. If any humans did survive, we wouldn't approach them using alien tech, especially when we have—"

"The *Bliss Mobile* and the *Rubenking Special*," Lowery finishes, putting it all together. "The fact that we *don't* use them reinforces the ruse."

"Precisely," I reply. "Kit and I will be flying it manually, and Fergus has worked to ensure our life signs are minimal, if any. Which means that to the Talv, the *Banshee* is simply following its pilot like a puppy after a kid walking home from school."

Rook adds, "They should see the ship as another spoil of war and bring us into port."

"And if they don't?" Rodgers asks.

"Marines head out solo. Void breach, secure packages, and exfil to the *Banshee*. The only deviation between making orbit and approaching the *Behemoth* is that we'll be letting Fergus out midway."

All eyes turn toward the bot. "Me? You're... kicking me out of the club? I knew it was bound to happen eventually. And it serves me right too after all the things—"

"Fergus! We're sending you to the *Bellerophon*."

"To keelhaul me? Confine me to the brig? Run me through with the Iron Maiden?"

"What?" I ask, squinting. "No. You're going to retrieve one of the warheads in the TST-21 torpedoes, pull the manual detonation device, and bring both to *Behemoth* for us to plant onboard."

"Oh. I see. Going down with the ship. Confining me to quarters. Falling on the sword so that I will no longer be a—"

"Fergus, we really need you to relax," I say. Then, in a more measured tone, I ask, "Can you do what we've outlined?"

"Of course, sire. With ease, especially once I am space bound again. I readily admit that half of my missteps are due in part to—"

"Just be ready."

"I shall. O, how I shall!"

"We'll also need you to alert Ibrahim about phase two," Rook says.

"Which is?" Fergus adds.

"Putting the *Belle* on overwatch to help us get clear of the *Behemoth*."

"Won't that compromise Private First Class Ibrahim's life?" Fergus asks.

"It might. But it might also save everyone else's. I hope it doesn't come to any of that, but we need the option. And I need you to provide the target package when you see her. Copy?"

Fergus's shoulders slump. "I will do as you request."

"Good. Once we're inside we'll be relying on Eddie and Kit to come through with a comms solution. Anything?"

Eddie shakes his head. "Not yet, but we're working on it, mate."

"Roger. Mason, we'll be relying on whatever intel you can gather from the *Banshee* to interface with *Behemoth* and try to locate our hostages. Floorplan, schematics… hell, I'll take wall placards. At the same time, you"—Rook points at Fergus—"will set the payload."

"Where, my lord?"

"Wherever it will do maximum damage, bot. Use your noggin."

"Consider it used, my lord."

"Once we have the hostages secure, we'll break comms silence and alert the *Belle* to standby. Then we haul ass to the *Banshee*, pull back to a minimum safe distance, and then flick the switch."

"The switch, my lord?"

"He means the detonator, Fergus," Kit says. "Fire in the hole and stuff."

"Ah, very good. I shall ensure that the Master Sergeant has the remote detonator so he can stuff all holes with fire."

"Oi, and that's it?" Eddie asks, looking at me.

"That's it," I reply. "It's a Hail Mary, we know. But it's the best we could come up with on short notice."

Eddie gives an approving frown and then nods his head a few times. "Fucking love it."

I smile at Rook. "There you go."

Rooks smiles back and says, "The key is that the Talv aren't expecting us. Which means we have the element of surprise. They've never dealt with humans before, and they just picked a fight with the wrong species."

This gets a round of "Oorah"s from the Marines and even a few civilians who've picked it up. Others nod, a few clap, and I see Fergus and Kit give each other a high five.

"Anything else you wanna add?" I say to Rook.

The Master Sergeant thinks about it for a second and then says, "I know for many of you, this will be your first combat experience. You're going to be scared. That's normal. You might freeze up. That's also to be expected. But you're heading into the fight alongside professional trigger pullers. So let the Marines take the brunt of the assault. Listen to their orders and do as you're told. They'll do their very best to make sure you get back here in one piece. Understood?"

Agreement spreads around the room.

"All in?"

"All in to win," the Marines call back. It startles several civilians, but they shake it off.

"Stay together, think on your feet, and listen to your leaders," Rook says at last. "Let's get our people back."

"You heard him," I add. "Skids up in three. Let's fly."

M**Y** **ANXIETY** **LEVEL** rises in proportion to our climb toward space. Whether or not anyone realizes it, we've taken a huge gamble on this op. Specifically, by putting all our eggs in one basket… all our people in one ship. If something goes wrong and the Talv suspects us, they have one target to shoot down. But, as Rook told me, if we can get behind enemy lines and deliver our payload, the enemy will have a chigger under its skin that it can't get out without bloodshed.

The alternative plans that Rook and I had weren't any better. Dividing us between the *Banshee* and the two Tiger-class shuttles was a non-starter. Leaving anyone behind in Camp Evelynton would have made them an easy target for an orbital strike. And remotely tasking the *Bellerophon* to fire on the Talv frigate or the *Sagan* to ram it would have been a waste of resources, not to mention a suicide mission for those aboard.

No, this was the right call. Or at least the best of all the bad options.

"How's she's handle, Cap?" Kit asks me as we leave Soteria's bumpy air and climb into the exosphere.

"Like butter. I'd let you have a go but—"

"Oh, no. That's okay. Monitoring flight systems is plenty-o-work for me. *Plenty-o-work.* Plus, I got me a case of the jitters." He holds up one hand flat so I can see it trembling. "The shakes don't make for smooth flying and all."

"No, they don't."

"But I appreciate you asking, Cap. Thanks. Maybe next time."

Just then, Magellan chuckles in the seat behind Kit's where he's monitoring our orbital trajectory.

"What's so funny?" I ask.

"Not funny. Fortuitous." Magellan taps something and then points at the main hollow display, center console. "Turns out the *Behemoth*'s orbit puts it just behind the planet's edge when we need to let Fergus out. Can't get better cover than that."

"Fortune favors—"

"The bold," Magellan answers.

I give him a pleased nod. "Someone's read Virgil."

"By my calculations, if Fergus can retrieve the munition quickly enough and get out of the *Belle*, he might have time to fly back in our shadow. Granted, I would think he's small enough to get written off as debris. But every advantage helps, right?"

"Sure does."

With the *Banshee*'s thrusters off, I unbuckle, pass the controls to Magellan, and push myself out of the bridge. I pass the cramped crew compartment and head toward the aft sections. Fergus is ready to exit from a rear service airlock. Rook and Rodgers stand beside the bot at the door, or at least the outline of what will be a door when the nanotech on this ship is ordered to create a hole. I need me some of this tech.

"You ready?" I ask Fergus.

"I am indeed, my lord."

"And you understand what you need to do?"

"I do."

"Good."

Rook adds, "Do me a favor when you see Ibrahim? Tell her we're sorry to keep her in the dark."

"I shall."

Rook gives him a grunt and then pat his shoulder. "Happy flying, Ferg." I echo the sentiment.

"And to you, my lords," Fergus nods to Rook and me as he enters the airlock.

Rodgers counts down the last ten seconds as the ship's hull dissolves like a sandcastle being washed away by a wave. I blink several times… as if that's gonna help my brain figure out what I just saw. It doesn't. When Rodgers yells, "Go," Fergus pushes out of the airlock and fires his thrusters. The acceleration is impressive, and even gets a "Dayum" of appreciation out of Rodgers. "Wish I could handle those g's."

"As it is, you can barely handle two, Corporal," Rook says.

The door re-materializes, and Rook and I make our way back through the ship. Rook takes the seat behind the captain's, and I swap out with Magellan. "Shame we can't put her through the paces though," he says. "I bet she screams."

"You never know," I reply. "The night is young."

"Don't get my hopes up, Knight."

Once I'm back in the captain's seat, Magellan points out the *Behemoth* on the scope. It's an outline, hidden by Soteria's western edge, but within the next fifteen minutes, it will emerge as a Talv frigate.

"Hurry up and wait," Rook says from behind me. "Anyone know any good jokes?"

"I do," Kit says.

"Anyone but Kit?" Rook replies. Magellan and I shake our heads.

"Guess that means I'm up," Kit says, and adjusts his flight suit's waistband.

"Come to think of it, I think someone needs me aft."

"You don't wanna hear the one about the scrambled egg?"

"Nope."

"That's a shame. It was a good yolk."

BY THE TIME *Behemoth* has come around Soteria's horizon, any lighthearted banter in the bridge is gone. In its place, I'm gripping my chair arms white-knuckled. It all comes down to whether or not the Talv take us in or decide to blow us to kingdom come. The only ship-worthy weapon we have is strapped to Fergus who is now closing a few thousands kilometers behind us... assuming he found the warhead and detonator. We won't know for sure until we're face to face again. But those components aren't hard for a Stellar Dynamics SME-31 space maintenance excipion to find and retrieve. So we should be good to go.

"I can hardly make it out visually," Magellan says. He's referring to the *Behemoth* dead ahead. As per the renderings we've seen, the Talv frigate is shaped like a severely pointed arrowhead, and looks black as space. No lights, no reflective surfaces, just pure stealth. Were it not for the Naquallan version of a transponder system on Korbix's vessel and its faint silhouette against the starscape, there's no doubt we could have flown right by it unaware.

"Any sign of energy build up?" Rook asks.

"Negative," Magellan says. "I'm hardly an expert on alien ship status indicators, but I believe no changes of any sort are a good thing. Plus, we have green indicators everywhere, color-coding all thanks to Fergus."

"And we're still hidden?"

"At least according to the *Banshee*'s sensors, we are," Kit says. "No life sign signatures allowed out; this forward window is in some sort of one-way mode; and we're broadcasting an autopilot transponder code that, according to Fergus's notes, is nominal. Easy-peasy. We're essentially an un-crewed vessel on autopilot seeking a single roo female who likes long walks on the beach and meaningful conversation."

"I know just where we can find one," I reply. "So far

so good." Although, I actually don't know if Korbix is single or not.

The next five minutes pass in silence as we all await some sign of hostility from the *Behemoth*. But none comes, which means one of two things: the frigate thinks we're what the *Banshee*'s flight computer says we are, or it knows we're bursting at the seams with humans and flying right into their clutches. Either way, we're not dead yet, and that's a win in my book.

"Good news, ya wankers," Eddie says, popping his head inside the bridge. His voice startles me. "I got you some comms."

"You don't say," Rook replies.

"Now, it ain't pretty, and it won't reach far, but it should get the job done as long as the squads stay together."

"How'd you figure it out?" I ask, curious.

"After Fergus was detected, his sensors ran some passive sweeps. I compared those against the radiation parameters that the *Banshee* is set to block and got some interesting results. As it turns out, the Talv actively scan a wide range of frequencies and power levels, which makes sense. They're monitoring for enemy activity."

"But…" I say.

"But… all systems have their prejudices, and Naquallan builds are no exception. I was able to isolate a few freqs that, for whatever reasons, they don't seem to care about. As long as we don't broadcast V-cog too loudly, we should stay off their radar. I've set limiters in a suit-based local area network that will take care of it. Add in relay pucks every ten meters, and we should have low-power coverage throughout the ship."

"Nice work, Eddie," I reply. Rooks says the same and gives him a fist bump. Turning back to the Talv frigate, I add, "Now let's just hope the rest of the plan comes together as smoothly as that."

"Don't jinx it, Cap," Kit says and winks at me.

"Right."

The *Behemoth* is bigger than I thought it would be, a fact made more overwhelming as the frigate overtakes us and draws Korbix's ship toward a darkened bay in the aft section. The shuttle-sized gap opens like the dematerialized doors on the *Banshee*, but no lights shine from within the hold. The only reason we know the space is even there is because of our holo display. Either the *Banshee* is using some sort of passive scanner to map the area or it's got data on the frigate to overlay as a 3D schematic. The visual contrast between light and dark is so extreme that the only way we know we're truly inside the *Behemoth*'s hull is because Soteria disappears as the nanofloor re-materializes beneath us. After ten seconds, the planet fades away leaving us in total darkness.

"Time to get this party started," Rook says. "Let's move."

36

JERICHO

I GIVE Kit and Magellan a smile as we unbuckle. "Nice work, you two."

They nod in reply, and then we retrieve our weapons from the bridge's side compartments before heading out. Meanwhile, Rook floats back to the crew compartment and says, "You sardines ready to get out of here?"

"Thought you'd never ask," Geller replies.

"I dunno," says Grabowski. "Rodgers is nice and warm. No wonder his sister likes him."

The second Marine throws an elbow into Grabowski's ribs. "She's not the only sister who likes me."

Rook cuts them off before it devolves further. "Mr. Carr has set up a V-cog LAN for us that should allow for basic comms in a short range without risk of Talv detection. We'll need to strengthen that with relays every ten meters; team leads, that's on you. Alternate with anti-personnel cubes. Additionally, you'll find the frigate's schematic is in V-cog. Everyone, follow your team assignments and make sure to ping all items of interest. The less time we spend aboard the *Behemoth* the better. Any questions?" No one responds. "Let's move."

Kit gets the *Banshee*'s port side door open, and the Marines are the first out. They float away and form a spherical perimeter, feeding our V-cog grid with new data. It's still visually dark in the hold. The only room details come from their helmets' LIDAR. The scans show the *Banshee* clasped around the hull by wide bands affixed to the bay's ceiling. Below us, where we entered, is a solid floor.

The rest of the assault team floats out and joins their respective fire team leaders. I'm a part of Alpha Team along with Rook, Afumba, Kit, Natalie Mason, and a *Sagan* scientist named Cartwright. Bravo Team has Geller, Lowery, Richards, Eddie, and two science officers. Charlie is Grabowski, Petty Officer Hill, Magellan, and two scientists, while Delta has Rodgers, Horowitz, Dr. Igor Kalashnik, Enni Mäkinen, and two of her colleagues.

"I've got eyes on door one," Rodgers announces over our local area network. A waypoint indicator tags an outline in augmented reality on the wall heading toward the bow. It appears where the schematic says it should. That's good.

"Door two, starboard side," Geller says, noting the other exit that heads toward the ship's center spine.

While not having light to see by is a nuisance, I consider it a good sign the enemy hasn't lit us up like a Christmas tree yet. It means Korbix's ship is still of minimal concern to the Talv. But I suspect that won't last long.

The team leaders call their units away. Alpha moves opposite Bravo at door one, ready to push toward the bow, while Charlie and Delta arrive at door two to head starboard toward the ship's middle. Unlike the hull exit walls that are made of the dissolving nano material, these doors are the standard sliding kind that seem to part down the middle.

Before pressing a fist-sized button on a wall mount that's aug-labeled Open in V-cog, Rook orders Geller to place his first anti-personnel explosive. From what I've been told, the cube pulls apart in two equal sections, both of which get maglocked against opposite sides of the door frame. The matched gel explosives, each stuffed with ball-bearing projectiles, are triggered by an optical switch. Since every POET member's V-cog is pre-cleared as a passive transponder key, they can pass safely. Each Marine carries a second fob version for Korbix or anyone whose V-cog hardware has been compromised. But anyone without a key will trigger the device, which will send hypersonic metal into their bodies from both sides. Nasty buggers.

"Set," Geller says and then hits the open-door button.

The partitions retract to reveal a left-right corridor. Soft white ceiling and floor lights illuminate the hallway. Afumba and Ensign Lowery call clear on the hallway. Bravo heads to port while Alpha heads to starboard. Based on the corridor design, this ship is far more utilitarian than the *Banshee*. Gone are the smooth white surfaces and leather-like furniture. In their places are exposed electrical panels, gritty metal grates, and signs of wear ranging from boot scuff marks to equipment impacts.

"And here I thought the aliens would be neat freaks," Mason says.

"Feels military," Afumba replies.

"Agreed, and poorly maintained," I add. "At least by our standards."

"Maybe they're mercenaries," Kit says. "Ya know. Less spit and polish, more brute force and cash. In it for the babes."

Rook says, "Keep the chatter down, people. We need the line clear."

I give Kit a skeptical eyebrow raise and then get back to scanning the passageway. Rook maglocks the first of our V-cog relays against an inconspicuous metal wall panel. The signal strength indicator in my helmet's HUD jumps to 100 percent.

"It's solid," I tell him and then continue to float down the corridor. The passage begins to bend toward the bow, and we take extra care to stay concealed as the angle straightens out. Fortunately, there aren't any Talv ahead. Rook gives Afumba orders to plant his anti-personnel charge and then says over squad comms, "Hallway one clear."

"Copy. Hallway two terminates in a cargo area," Geller replies. "Nothing of immediate interest."

To Charlie and Delta Teams, Rook asks, "SITREP?"

"No hostiles," Grabowski replied. "Two rooms clear. Engineering, we think."

"And I'm pretty sure we found ourselves a head," Rodgers adds. "Shitters haven't been cleaned in a while. There's also a brig in section nine toward the stern."

"It's too small to hold our people," I call back, feeling more confident as I take in the size and scope of the corridors firsthand.

"Agreed," says Rook. "Keep scouting. Stay frosty."

After a few seconds, Kit says, "If we don't find them soon, you think we should power up V-cog all the way and try to establish a connection with Dr. Park?"

"Not worth the risk yet. Give it time," Rook replies. "Alpha and Bravo, moving to waypoint Hotel Zulu."

Hotel Zulu is the place my gut says our people are

being held. It's on deck two toward the bow, just one deck below the bridge. In the schematic, the room looks large enough for twenty-three humans and a Naqualla ambassador. But what really gives it away is the reinforced walls, single access door, and a side room that appears to have a shared window with the hold. Perhaps an observation suite.

We cross two intersections before coming to a third. Geller pulls back and holds up a fist, then he orders everyone against the walls. "Tango approaching, starboard passage." The Marine maglocks his SR-90 to his back, pulls out his combat knife, and waits with his body wedged against the near wall so the enemy won't see him…

Not until it's too late.

As soon as the Talv enters the four-way intersection, Geller springs out and drives the knife into the side of the enemy's neck. The alien lets out a wet *kerrr-kuk-KUK!* and backhands Geller, which throws the Marine off. He swears as he slams into the wall. Rook launches forward as the alien tries to pull the weapon from its neck, but the Talv whips its tail around and slams Rook into the opposite wall. Geller is back in the game, feet tucked beneath him, and then jumps toward the alien. His hand meets his knife and starts pushing it deeper while shoving it back and forth. The pair of bodies spins in zero g as purple blood spirals away in large globs. The alien shrieks again, threatening to give our presence away. I want to jump in and help, but there's too much going on. Plus, Rook has recovered and joins Geller by grabbing the enemy's head and yanking it back and forth. The motion accentuates the blade's damage, which seems to be having an effect on the alien. Its cries are getting weaker, as are its tail swings. Finally, Geller twists the blade and then cuts through the front of the throat. Severed tissue flings forward in ribbons, each flicking with droplets of blood. The Talv warrior goes from hitting Geller and Rook to grabbing its neck. Geller withdraws his blade and shoves the body away. It hits the ceiling and twitches, still trailing a lot of blood.

"I believe that gives you the first alien kill, Geller," Rook says. "As in ever."

"Oh, shit. I didn't even think about that."

"Why would you want to?" Mason says, grabbing her throat. "That's… that's…"

"That's a Marine saving our asses," Petty Officer Richards says as she helps Geller search the alien corpse for items of interest and then guide the body into a side space that looks like a utility room. "Had to be done."

Mason looks like she might be sick. "Right."

"You okay?" I ask her.

She nods but doesn't say anything in reply.

"Keep moving," Rook says. "We're on the clock."

All the more reason to keep moving.

"Oi, found this," Eddie says, holding up something that resembles a pistol.

"Keep it for now," Rook says. "But don't go trying it."

"What, you think I'm gonna point it at my face and shake it to see if it lights up? Jesus, I'm not a complete knob."

"Just making sure."

Eddie shares a look at me as I fly past. "Bloody Marine wankers."

By the time Alpha and Bravo have made it to the final intersection before facing Hotel Zulu to the left, Charlie and Delta teams report that the small cargo bay is clear. "Nothing to see but crates, Sarge," Grabowski says.

"Roger. Move to us. Keep laying anti-personnel cubes."

"Roger. Moving."

Ahead, Geller finishes scouting around the next corner to port using the HUD-linked cam on his HG-11 sidearm. He sends the live feed to the rest of us, and says, "One sentry, eight meters, weapon present. Looks bored."

"Take the shot on my go," Rooks as we all close on the intersection.

"Roger." Geller holsters his sidearm and then pulls his rifle into his shoulder. "Ready."

I suck in a deep breath, knowing that once Geller fires, our element of surprise is gone. I also wonder if we should wait for Charlie and Bravo teams to catch up, but we need to get to the hostages, and our Marines know what they're doing.

Rook says, "Go."

Geller pivots around the corner, aims, and fires three rounds into the unsuspecting Talv alien with a *zrrrr-cra-cra-crack!* Geller's battlesuit compensates for the weapon's discharge with vectored puffs of air that keep the Marine stationary in zero g. The first two bullets fail to puncture the enemy's armored chest, but the third strikes its face, leaving it shattered and trailing blood. The enemy convulses reflexively, but freezes two seconds later. It's hung up by its tail that's gotten lodged between two wall plates.

Cartwright, one of our scientists, vomits inside his helmet. I grab him to keep him from flailing and wait for his suit's vacuum to kick in.

"Eyes on me," I say. "Hey, Cartwright! Look at me. You're okay."

He nods and settles down a little, but his eyes are still darting around.

"Try not to look at it," I say.

"But it's... everywhere," he replies. The end of the hallway is a mess of gore and bone. But we don't have time to discuss it further. The vocal sounds of Talv come from somewhere behind us. Afumba surges ahead to free the corpse and looks for a side room to stash it. Meanwhile, Geller bypasses the body and reaches for the open button beside the next door. He waits for me, Rook,

Lowery, and Richards to join him; without a window to see what's beyond the barrier, we need to take extra precautions in case it's an ambush.

The voices behind us are getting closer.

Rook nods at Geller.

He hits the button, and the doors spread apart.

37

EVELYN

"Lieutenant? You need to stay awake," I say, pushing his shoulder gently.

"He's lost a lot of blood," Nairobi says. Despite our best attempts, the dressings are soaked through and allow red spheres to fling away in zero g.

"Lieutenant Jaffa? Come on. Stay with us." Try as I might, I can't get the commander's eyes to keep from rolling back, and he passes out again. I look across our holding cell to Korbix. "Are you sure there's nothing in here that can help him?"

"I'm sorry, no," she replies through our translation protocol.

To Nairobi, I say in a barely audible voice, "If we don't get Jaffa some help, we're gonna lose him too."

Both of us look to room's far corner where Private First Class Krutz and Science Officer Joe Aubertine's bodies are stacked. Krutz fired on the enemy when they entered the waterfall. Even killed one, I think. But Krutz got hit in the chest as payment. The Talv made us carry his body, which has served as a constant reminder of what the enemy can do. Likewise, Aubertine got whipped by a Talv tail when he took too long to load the corpse into the ship. I suspect the blow was meant to punish him, but it ended up breaking his back, not to mention whatever other internal damage it did. His heart stopped twenty minutes ago. Probably intracranial swelling, but without someone like Igor here with the right equipment, there's no way to know. Worse still is that if we don't find a way out of here and obtain medical care, more of us will share Krutz and Aubertine's fate.

Just about all of us have suffered injuries of some kind, whether from the initial attack or the mistreatment that followed. After stripping the Marines of their weapons and armor, the enemy used some sort of voltage wand to keep us moving like cattle. Several crew members fell under beatings that followed, bruising hands, knees, and wrists. Others hit their heads on the ground. Some twisted ankles. Outside the cave, we were taken to the awaiting ship, thrown into aft cargo compartments, and left unsecured for the ascent into orbit. Even with the superior Naquallan technology, we suffered turbulence that broke bones and even knocked two members unconscious: Sebastián and then Jericho's assistant Alice Ortega. They've since come to, but now I think they're suffering from concussions.

Pohge took particular delight in prodding Korbix with his voltage wand and kicking her in the ribs when she failed to get up. Her treatment discourages me, not just for her own sake, but for all of ours. It seems to me that if the Talv were interested in returning her or any of us to the Resettlement Council, they would have done more to keep us free of injury. Instead, scenes play out in my head of surviving just long enough to appease some shadowy overseer only to be disposed of as soon as the viewing is done.

Then there's the trivial but pressing issue of water and sanitation. I'm already noticing signs of dehydration, and people are complaining about needing to go to the bathroom. It won't take long for the smells and bacteria from urine and excrement to build in such a confined space, adding to everyone's discomfort and eventual health issues. We humans are far more frail than we'd like to believe.

The remaining Marines have tried to escape twice, once in an attempt to overpower two guards, another time faking a medical emergency. Between weapons, armor, and determination, the Talv made sure to dole out extra punishment. The beatings resulted in one broken forearm for Private Engleman and a serious concussion for Corporal Hatch, our only medic. Marine morale is low, which doesn't bode well. They're the ones conditioned to take hits like this and keep moving.

And here we are, so close…

So close to having it all. To giving humanity a second chance. We had it. And now, if we can't find a way out of here, we've lost it. Which means the doubters were right: the aliens *were* coming to kill us. Maybe not all the aliens. Korbix and those of her kind certainly had our best interests at heart. But sectarianism isn't just a human trait, unfortunately. The critics were right to be skeptical.

"What was that?" Nairobi asks me. When I give her a confused look, she adds, "Talking to yourself?"

I nod sheepishly. "Happens. Just… frustrated. Seems the naysayers were right about an alien invasion."

Nairobi squints at me. "No. Uh-uh. No way. You're Dr. Evelyn Park. You don't get to give up."

"I'm not giving up. I just…"

"Hey." She works to catch my eye. "Do you see them invading Earth right now?"

"Well, no, but Soteria—"

"Then the critics are still wrong. Earth is still safe. And so what if we found a few bad apples? Korbix isn't. And it seems like there are a lot more of her kind than Pohge's kind."

"I just thought… Did it *have* to devolve into shooting and bloodshed? I mean, really?"

Nairobi shrugs. "Biology fights to survive, right? In way, that makes them more like us than we may have wanted. But I think that's a good thing."

"That they're like humans?"

"That we're like each other," she corrects. "That if the Naquallan got it right, there's hope for us too. Plus, you've been through worse, right?"

I think about surviving *Astraea* Station's destruction. About avoiding not one but two assassination attempts. About almost being shot out of the sky by Navy destroyers and a swarm of alien cyborgs. I nod at Nairobi. "I've gotten out of some pretty big pinches."

"Good." Nairobi gives me a wide smile. "Now. How would Dr. Evelyn fucking Park get herself out of this one?"

Yeah, Eves. How would you get yourself out of this one? I scan the room one more time, looking for anything that I haven't taken into consideration already. But nothing stands out. Not until I spot a peculiar gap between two metal sections above the sealed door. And for a split second, I think I spot a wire inside.

"You got something?" Nairobi asks me.

"Maybe." I push off the floor and float to the arch. My fingers play with the gap to see if the metal is loose. Sure enough, one the panels isn't screwed down all the way. We don't have any tools, and I'm certainly not strong enough to pry it free, especially not with my bandaged wrist right now…

But Korbix is.

"Korbix?"

Her ears perk up.

"Can you try pulling this plate free?"

She glides across the room and lands between Nairobi and me, eyes fixed on the panel. Interest sparks there, and the next thing I know, she's ripped the cover free. Beneath is a mess of wires.

"Jackpot," I say and start trying to separate them, but Nairobi pushes me aside gently.

"Let a professional handle it?"

"Please, help yourself."

Nairobi starts sorting the wires and talking out loud as she does. "Funny thing about electrical current: it works the same way in every star system. Electrons are either flowing or not. Positive, negative, ground." She looks like she's stripping wires with the cover ripped open by Korbix and attempting to cross them. "Sheath colors vary, sure. But so long as you're not disarming a bomb or anything, it doesn't hurt to poke around, right?" Something shorts in the panel and all the lights go out. A second later, a small bank of secondary lights turn on. "Okay, so it's not door number one. Let's try you next…"

At the same time that Nairobi shorts out some fans behind a nearby vent, I hear something outside our door.

Part of me thinks to back away, but if she can get this thing open, we might be able to catch whoever's out there off guard. And we already know they have weapons that we might be able to secure. "Maybe cross wires a little faster?"

"*I'mmmmm tryyyyyying*," she says, with clear annoyance. Another *pop!* sounds from inside the small bay. Nothing happens.

"Try again," I say, feeling my heartbeat quicken. There's more noise outside. "Nairobi?"

"Working on it." There's more sparks, and then…

The doors slide apart. I reel around, fists up, ready to lunge at the enemy.

"Evelyn?" It's a human. *In a void suit!*

"Jericho?"

His visors flips up. "Evelyn!"

"Stars! Is it really you?" I push forward and throw my arms around him, tears blurring my vision. He returns the embrace, and I spot more void suits lined up behind him. "How did you all get up here?"

"Long story. How did you get the door open?"

"Nairobi."

"Eh, she spotted the exploit," Nairobi says.

Jericho moves me aside to make room for Rook. "Good to see you, Evelyn," he says and gives me a gentle squeeze on my shoulder. Then he waves at our people. "Howdy, everyone. Who needs a lift?" This gets several cries of relief, but most are too tired to shout.

"We've… we've lost Krutz and Aubertine," I say. "Lieutenant Jaffa is hurt pretty badly, as are Engleman and Hatch."

"I'm sorry to hear that," Rook says with a pained face. "We need to move." He waves more void suits into the room, which include Afumba, Kit, and Natalie. I can't see the rest of the faces because I'm still crying in relief. Damn emotions.

"You're hurt," Jericho says, looking at my bandaged wrist.

"I'll be fine. I'm just glad you're all here."

Rook gets Jericho's attention. "It's time for phase two."

"What's phase two?" I ask them both.

"Putting our gunship on overwatch," Rook replies.

Jericho adds, "Which means turning V-cog back on all the way."

"Won't they know you're here?"

Rook smiles and thumbs over his shoulder at a mess of purple gore splattered on the hallway walls. "They already do." A second later, my V-cog system notifies me that it's picked up a full-strength local area network. Then both aloud and over V-cog, Rook says, "*Bellerophon*, this is Rook. Ibrahim, how read?"

"Lima Charlie, Master Sergeant! Where the hell are you?"

"Aboard the hostile frigate. Marking in your TACHUD now. Prepare to power up all weapons systems and open fire upon our departure, but not a second before."

"Copy that."

"*Sagan*, this is Rook. How read?"

Nothing comes back.

"*Sagan Explorer*, do you copy?" After another three seconds, Rook looks at me. "Remind Dr. Bolton to keep his notifications on during nap time, would you?"

I'm about to reply when a voice from just outside the doorway yells, "Contact," and weapons start firing down the hall.

Jericho

ROOK MAKES A CALL OVER V-COG. "Grabowski, Rodgers! Hostile engagement outside Hotel Zulu. Request immediate support."

"Roger," Grabowski replies. "Support inbound. Sixty seconds."

Geller and Afumba are on either side of the utility room's opening, shooting down the corridor at the enemy. The Talv are firing back with some sort of energy round that chars the far wall. I join the other voices shouting for everyone to stay against the sidewalls when one of the women takes a hit to the upper torso. Her left shoulder and half her head vaporize in a single blast, leaving only flakes of glowing ash and swirls of steam. It's Bhavna Mishra, the *Sagan*'s comms officer.

Evelyn lurches toward the body in horror, but I catch her by the arm. "No! You can't!" Incoming rounds cut in front of Evelyn, reinforcing my words. She lets me pull her back but still shouts after Mishra.

"We're pinned down," Geller yells, pulling inside to change magazines.

"We need cover to advance," Afumba adds.

With everyone against the side walls, the crates strapped to the floor stand out. "Hey! Why don't we cut those free. Use them as floating shields?" Each one is about a meter and half square and can easily shield a person.

Rook nods once and gives orders to have the webbing sliced. Lowery and Richards pull out their knives while Geller and Afumba return fire to cover them. It takes less than ten seconds for the large crates to float free. I help Rook move the boxes toward the exit and start directing people to line up behind them. At the same time, spare weapons get demagnetized from our backs and distributed to anyone who can still shoot. Eddie parts with his newfound alien pistol and passes it to Korbix. The ambassador looks surprised and touches several buttons on the weapon before giving Eddie a satisfactory nod.

"You'll need this too." I pass her a transponder fob so she doesn't inadvertently set off the anti-personnel ordnance in the hallways. "In here," I add and pantomime stuffing the device inside her tunic.

The wounded and the fallen have been distributed to those able to tow them. Rook gives everyone a final once over and then says over V-cog, "Grabowski, Rodgers! Where's my support?"

"Still en route but got slowed up. Twenty seconds," Grabowski replies.

"We can't wait." Rook nods at Geller, Afumba, and me stacked behind the first crate. Eddie and Kit have Evelyn and Nairobi behind the second, and then the rest of the hostages are paired up with the remaining members of Alpha and Bravo Teams behind the last crates. "Move out," Rook shouts.

Geller and Afumba lead the charge, pushing the first crate through the doorway and down the hall using short bursts from their jets. They fire around either side and manage to keep themselves from bashing against the walls. Rook joins them, firing around a third edge while I shoot around the fourth. To the enemy, it must look like a cargo container with four weapons attached to the sides. But they certainly sense the weak spots because a new volley of energy fire skips across the hallway's walls. Geller pulls his arm back for a moment and yells. He's taken a hit to his forearm, but it looks like his armor took the brunt of it. "Son of a bitch, that stings!"

Behind Evelyn's crate, more follow. The weakest members stay in the middle, covered by Eddie. He's got Jaffa lashed to his back, while two of the scientists haul Krutz and Aubertine's bodies. A third carries Mishra's mangled corpse. Interestingly, Ambassador Korbix has chosen to bring up the rear; she'll be exposed from behind.

Ahead, we're almost to the four-way intersection. If we can push the enemy beyond the junction, we can make the right hand turn toward the aft. Unfortunately, I'm pretty sure that the last of the Marine anti-personnel ordnance was placed ten meters in that same direction. But if we can get the enemy to follow us, maybe we can use that to our advantage.

"Tangos inbound at our twelve o'clock, your nine o'clock," Grabowski says over V-cog. "We're coming up on your hallway now."

"Be advised," Rook replies. "Their energy weapons are a bitch to flesh and blood, but armor stands a chance."

"Copy that." Grabowski relays the information and

then orders Charlie and Delta teams to hug the walls. I pull Grabowski's helmet cam from the team roster and open it in a corner window in my field of view. His unit is using the bulkheads as cover. Then he says, "Let's light 'em up!"

Scorpion SR-90's hum as they fire on the Talv stalled in the intersection. The enemy takes a beating, damage made all the worse by the Bellaire MS265 that Horowitz had maglocked to a bulkhead. Ribbons of purple meat and blood peel away from the hostiles as the machine gun chews between armored plates and hits flesh. But it doesn't last long. The enemy has ordered their units to fall back…

Which leaves us the gap we need.

Rook sees it too. "Push," he orders.

We shove our crate forward and our line follows, but we're still taking heavy fire from the enemy across the intersection, and we have to make that right hand turn. Grabowski and Rodgers order their fire teams to advance to the intersection. Once there, they throw frags around their right corner and take cover. Double *BOOM!'s* sound, and a shockwave temporarily pushes us back. Those without helmets or hearing protection smash their eyes shut, some holding their head, a few yelling in pain. That damage can be remedied; a Naquallan blaster round to the chest can't.

"Advance," Rook yells, reminding our team to keep pushing.

Charlie and Delta fire around their right corner—our straight ahead—which gives us another window of opportunity to gain ground. Ten seconds later, we're at the intersection, and not a moment too soon. To our left, toward the bow, a new wave of Talv appears and opens fire. Before anyone can shove a crate that direction to provide cover, Petty Officer Richards and a scientist both take several direct hits. While the armor survives, the unarmored sections of their void suits do not. I catch a glimpse of deep burn marks and red flesh under an armpit, inside a groin, just below a helmet seal on the neck. Further back, hands reach out to grab the bodies but fail while other scientists scream. I just hope they don't panic.

"Leave them," Eddie yells and pushes people around the corner. "Stay focused!"

Thank God for that man.

Ahead, we meet Charlie and Delta teams and pass Grabowski, Rodgers, and the rest of their people as they continue to lay down covering fire and use the crates as shields. Ten seconds later, we're all through and headed toward the *Banshee*.

"Master Sergeant Farooq?" comes a familiar excipion's voice over V-cog.

"Send it," Rook replies.

"Tiz I, the Ardent Conqueror of Malquith. I'm aboard the *Behemoth* now, my lord, and preparing to place the warhead. That's the good news."

"There's bad news?"

"Yes. I'm unable to gain access to the engine room, and I think I've been followed by—"

His voice cuts off at the same time that reinforcements appear in the intersection in front of us.

Shit.

38

NIGEL

GEMMA BIRDWHISTLE WAS DRESSED in a canary yellow tracksuit with hot pink sneakers. Her hair was pulled back into a bun that protruded from the back of a black baseball cap with the Viatoribus logo embroidered on the front. An odd choice for one who so loathed the spacers, but then again they *were* touring the now legendary *Telemine* Station, home of *Parallax One*, so a literal tip of the hat to the politicast that had a majority stake in the station was fitting.

Between Nigel's Secret Service and Gemma's Tantum Terrae protection detail, over eighty armed agents monitored their progress through the converted legacy hab. Most stayed out of sight, giving the two plenty of space. Nigel met Gemma on the main observation deck that looked up through the station's cylindrical length. The far end, where the three *Parallax One* nodes were mounted, was exposed to the void. But rather than an unadulterated view of the stars, observers looking out the end saw massive warships suspended against the black, ready to strike should the portal ever reappear. The gate wasn't on, of course, which gave the impression of First Fleet aiming down the station and right into the observation deck. A fitting backdrop, Nigel mused, and so relished Gemma's choice of venue.

"Miss Birdwhistle, how nice to see you," Nigel said as he dipped his head at her but never averted his eyes.

"Mr. President. Congratulations on your new appointment."

"Thank you. Though, I must say, this is quite a long way to come just to congratulate me."

"Yes, but what a view, right?" He followed her gaze through the station to First Fleet. "All that power at your disposal… the most recognized man in the history of the world, they're calling you. If they only knew the lengths you undertook to secure it."

Nigel didn't mind her speaking so freely here. The station had been cleared of prying eyes, and transmission firewalls had been established to completely cut off the station's V-cog grid from the rest of the network. They were, after all, at Lagrange Point Two, 1.5 million kilometers behind Earth relative to the sun, so going dark wasn't difficult. Instead, everyone on station used a local V-cog network to interface. And if anyone was recording their neural sensors for later dissemination, well, he would ensure that information never left *Telemine*.

"I must say that I found your request for a tour rather unusual."

"How so?"

"Given your… contempt for all things space, I should have thought you'd want to meet atop some carbon sweepers or while wading the Siberian algae fields."

"Both excellent choices."

"But not yours."

She smiled and then seemed to look through him. "My brother died on a legacy hab."

"I remember."

"Don't we all. You know, it's safer and less expensive to live on the plains on Antarctica for a year than to spend one week in space. And yet, where do we spend our resources? Here. O'Neill-Oberth cylinders. Dome settlements. Outposts millions of kilometers away from the one place that isn't trying to constantly kill us."

"A shame, really."

"Yes, Mr. President. But what's more shameful is when leaders who claim to stand for one thing bend their knee to the opposite."

"Concessions had to be made."

"But at what cost?"

"I think the agreement we came to for the Viatoribus and Sentia Aux was rather aimable. We vowed to—"

"Keep all stations funded, including this one, in exchange for round the clock military protection. That's a far cry from defunding the space settlement program. If anything, it's directing more money away from Earth, not reducing."

"It was necessary to secure their support."

"For you."

"For the good of the system, Miss Birdwhistle."

"And the promise of *Valkyrie Command*? Pouring trillions into building yet *another* new—"

He waved her off. "I have no intentions of keeping that promise."

Gemma squinted at him. "Which leaves one to wonder just what promises you will keep, if any."

Now they had come to it: her position in his new government. "As it turns out, I am making good on the one promised to you. I would like to invite you to sit on a very special committee chaired by—"

"I'm not interested."

This was unexpected. The entire premise of their working together was providing her a seat at the top. Did her fundamentalist objections run so deep as to keep her from reaping the spoils of war?

"I really think you should consider it, Miss Birdwhistle. The influence you could have serving your own interest is—"

"My interests?" She scoffed at him. "Ha. That's what you think this is about? My mother was right to hate you."

"Your mother was more like me than she knew."

"She was nothing like you. And I understand why she wanted to kill you."

"And why's that?"

"Because you're not a true believer. You're an opportunist."

Nigel stiffened. "If by that you mean that I seize every chance to shatter the idealistic fantasies of powerful people hellbent on destroying Earth, then, yes, I am quite an opportunist. Everything I do is for the greater good."

"Everything?" She laughed and turned away. "Everything you do is to save your own skin, Sallsworth. You're a weak man who has conflated the mission of preserving our planet with your own personal ambitions."

"And that's a crime, Miss Birdwhistle?"

"Yes. When you aren't willing to sacrifice everything for the greater good, it is."

"And you would do better? You really think it's possible to reach such a lofty place without ego? I'd like to see you try."

She turned to glare at him. "Maybe I will. But I have an obstacle in my way."

Now it was Nigel's turn to scowl. "So we've come to

what you really want then. My head, is it? And how does that play out, Miss Birdwhistle? My security detail against yours? Or maybe a fight to the death inside V-cog to avenge your mum? And then what, you walk into my office, sit in my chair, and expect the whole system to bend to your wishes? We've already been through this." He let out an amused sigh. "I thought you were a naive girl before, but now I don't know what to think of you."

"Girl?" She chuckled and then picked at her teeth with a fingernail. "Is that what I am to you? Some small child who can be bullied into doing your—a parent's —bidding?"

"We had an agreement. I'm holding up my end of the bargain. Take the seat. Because you'll never have mine."

"Nigel, dear," she said, momentarily using Neon's term and tone. The sound sent a dark chill up his spine. But she reverted to our own voice. "I never wanted your seat, and you can keep your head. In fact, I'm counting on you keeping both."

"*Then what do you want?*"

"Not here. I don't trust your people, or even some of mine, for that matter."

Nigel held her eyes for a moment, figuring he knew what she meant. "If you think for one second I'm following you into V-cog—"

"A neutral room. No weapons. And your people can

inspect it with me inside, unprotected... even kill me if they like."

"You're crazy."

"And you're curious."

Nigel searched her face, seeing if he could detect the hint of deceit that hallmarked Neon's expressions but found none. She was right: he did want to know what she had up her sleeve. Like it or not, Gemma was a powerful player on the world's stage, and one he either needed for himself or eliminated. *Far better to keep your enemies close*, he reckoned, and so decided to take her up on the offer. "Very well." He called his head of security over and made the arrangements.

Chairs were placed in front of the observation window for both Nigel and Gemma to sit. Gemma entered V-cog first, loading in her supposed "neutral room," followed by Nigel's security detail. They searched the premises for weapons while Nigel's top slicers scanned for code anomalies. They were already well-versed in Gaia's Blood; they still didn't know how she overcame the firewall, but they at least understood how it operated, making Gemma just as susceptible to dying inside V-cog as anyone else.

After several minutes of watching Gemma sit motionless in her chair, eyes closed, Nigel felt Walter tap once on his shoulder. "Security says it's clean."

Nigel didn't reply right away. He was lost in thought. Finally, he motioned Walter to come close and then whispered in his ear, "If something should happen to me, take care of my family. And tell Esther and the children… I love them."

Walter didn't try to play down the request. He simply nodded once, keeping a firm upper lip, and then said, "Good luck, sir."

THE V-COG LOBBY was a log cabin interior. Natural finish. Vaulted ceilings. And furnishing reminiscent of the Adirondack period. Black bear and white tailed deer heads were mounted above the cobblestone fireplace while red plaid throw blankets lay neatly folded on the edges of two opposing leather couches. A rough-cut timber coffee table sat between them bearing a metal tray of coffee, cream, and sugar. If Gemma wanted to kill him with anything in the room, it would be her insatiable love for overpriced coffee.

"Shall we sit?" she said from beside him, motioning to the couches. He agreed and took the one to the right. "Coffee?"

"Tea."

"Forgot that, sorry."

She forgot nothing, Nigel noted as he watched her smile and pour a mug for herself. "So? What do you have to tell me?"

She sucked the spoon clean, set it down on the tray,

and then sipped her coffee. "Mother said you were always in such a hurry. *Tempus pecunia est*, eh?"

Time is money. "You said you didn't want me dead. But you also don't want a seat at the table."

"True."

"Then…?"

She held up her hand. Nigel didn't understand at first, but then he noticed what *wasn't* there. Her Tantum Terrae tattoo. "You didn't notice before, did you."

It could have just been a render choice in V-cog, but then Nigel thought back to their meeting on his yacht. After she'd left, one of his cleaners had taken extra care to remove a strange ink stain on the couch where she'd been sitting. As if to drive this memory home, Gemma leaned back and stretched her free arm across the top of the couch landing her hand in the same place.

"You removed your tattoo?" Nigel asked. "You're unaffiliated?"

"Perceptive."

"Why?"

"Because the future we're building has no place for sectarianism."

"Perhaps. Though it has its benefits."

"For you, surely."

"And you're exempt?" he asked, eyes narrowing.

"Yes. Because I don't plan to be in the public eye ever again. Not when I have you."

If Nigel was confused and curious before, he was

even more so now—confused, curious and concerned. "Explain."

"You said it yourself, didn't you? All that talk about systems, centuries of compounding dependence, layers of trust. 'Due process,' you called it. 'The acquisition of power through conventional means. Ruthlessly at times.' Have I got that right?"

"Where are you going with this?"

"Isn't it obvious? You secured for me what I could not for myself."

"But you're not President."

She laughed. "And I don't have to be as long as I'm smarter than you." Gemma withdrew something from her shirt: a gold locket on the end of a necklace. She snapped the chain off her neck with a sharp yank and opened the clamshell one handed. "You would be so proud," she said, speaking to what Nigel could only assume was a picture of Neon. Then Gemma set the locket on the coffee table and sipped from her mug again. When Nigel didn't move, she nodded to the locket, "Go on."

Nigel took the jewelry off the table and examined it. Sure enough, there was a printed photograph of the late Magnolia Birdwhistle in the locket's right half. He was about to reply when he noticed something in the *left* half... something that seemed like a button, small as it was. His eyes flicked up to hers, his chest tightening. His security had missed this. They'd been searching for weapons, ordnance, booby traps. They'd frisked her and scoured the entire construct. But they'd missed this, whatever it was, hidden on her person in plain sight. "What is this?"

"I built us a game."

"I think you've played quite enough of those. We're through here." He stood and exited V-cog…

Only, he didn't reappear in *Telemine* Station.

He tried to leave again…

Still nothing.

Panic rose in Nigel's chest like a fire. He tried hailing Walter. He tried calling for security. Tried accessing the verb. But all contact with the outside was cut off. He couldn't even open his eyes in the real or detect any sounds in the space station. Not even his body's sense of equilibrium was coming through. He was, for all purpose, completely isolated from the real world and bound inside this lobby.

"Something the matter, Nigel?" she asked between sips of her coffee.

"What have you done?"

"I told you, I—"

"*What have you done?* Let me out!" He crossed the room and batted the mug from her hand. "Let me out now!"

"Gladly. First, we—"

"There is no *first*!" He lunged, hands around her throat. "I will kill you, just like I killed your mother."

Strangely, however, Gemma did not fight back. Instead, she laid her arms on the couch and let him attack her. She stared unflinchingly into his eyes. It enraged him all the more, and he squeezed harder, wishing her to die so that he could be freed from this prison. It was certainly of her making, and would deconstruct with her death…

Won't it?

Unless her resignation signaled something more dangerous… more sinister.

Sensing he did not have all of the information, and that he'd allowed his fear to overtake him, Nigel eased the pressure from her neck and eventually pushed himself off the couch.

Gemma rubbed her flesh and cleared her throat. "Now that we have that out of your system, would you like to hear about my game?"

Nigel bared his teeth at her, but couldn't bring himself to speak.

"I'll take that as a yes." She gestured for him to sit down. When he didn't move, she added, "Nigel, this will take a moment. You'll be more comfortable, trust me."

Nigel stood, fuming, but eventually returned to the couch and tried to regain some of his composure. He sensed that, if he was to beat her at whatever this was, he would need his wits about him, and the rage he'd just demonstrated would get him nowhere. At last, he nodded for her to continue, and then sat back.

"Good. Now, you and I are both equally trapped in

this lobby. Yes, I made it, and the game began when I activated my locket. No, neither your slicers nor mine can get us out, I've made sure of that. And yes, there is a path to freedom for both of us. There is also something at the end that we each want. What good would a game be without prizes, right?" She eyed him, perhaps waiting for a response, but he didn't give her the satisfaction. "Right, well, *yours* is a button on a pedestal that releases you from this place. No questions asked. You're free to go."

"How can I be sure?" Nigel asked.

"You can't. You'll just have to trust me."

"I clearly don't."

"And you clearly don't have any other options now, do you."

"I could kill you."

"And lock yourself in here forever? Sure, I suppose that's an option, though hardly a good one."

"I don't believe you."

She scoffed at him. "If you're willing to take that chance, then by all means, kill away." She spread her arms in invitation. When he didn't make any moves, she lowered her arms. "Bear in mind that I'm bound to the same rules."

"You mean, if I die, you're trapped in here too?" She nodded. The thought of suicide crossed his mind, but that was a zero sum game, and one he would only entertain as a last resort. If ever. "And what's your goal?"

"My pedestal's button also frees us, but it gives me access to your V-cog. Any time. Any place. As long as it's in your head. And in here, I can see, hear, feel, and *do* anything I want."

Nigel squinted at her, trying to wrap his head around the implications. The breach of privacy was certainly the most obvious violation, but the others came quickly enough. Access to monitor every closed door meeting, every call, every appointment. She would experience it all with him, whenever she wanted. The technology needed for that defied what was available, just as it broke every law and safeguard protecting virtual cognizance technology. But this was Gemma Birdwhistle, so he had little doubt that she was capable of such terror whether he admitted it or not.

"And I can guess what you're thinking, Nigel. Why not pluck the V-cog nanos from your brain? I can think of two reasons. First, how does a person preside over the entire solar system without it? I mean, practically speaking? Interface with staffers, record notes, keep appointments, call foreign dignitaries, gossip with party members, flirt inconspicuously during soirees... the list is endless. We all think we can live without it, but the dirty little secret is, we can't. It's Pandora's Box, and society opened it long ago.

"The second reason is that when I reach my pedestal first, and I will, it will leave a little something behind. Undetectable and unrecoverable. An artifact of my own design left in your brain, such that with whatever new hardware you get—even a clean V-cog install—there will always be a connection point for me to exploit."

"To what end?" he asked, lips tight over his teeth, though he could well imagine the answer.

"To keep tabs... to learn... to leverage."

"Blackmail."

"Of the most intimate kind, Nigel. And, should you not wish to comply? Well, let's just say that if I can trap us in here"—she gestured around the room—"I can certainly keep you locked away up there"—she tapped her temple with one hand while pointing at his head with the other.

"You're insane."

"Such is what the lowly call the intellectually superior, I suppose."

"This... *this* is what you did to my opponents to secure votes, isn't it."

"I needed to test it out, and you provided the perfect opportunities, Nigel. Thank you. Now, you no doubt understand that I never wanted a seat at the table. I don't even want the Tantum Terrae. I have everything I need right here. The presidency, the nations, the star system at my fingertips. All thanks to you."

Nigel rested his hands on his lap and took a few deep breaths. He'd been played. And wasn't it just like the enemy to bowl a yorker when least expected? To deceive the batsman in flight? There was no choice left for him but to play whatever game she'd made. It infuriated him, because he hadn't seen it coming, as equally as it terrified him, because he knew beating her would be nearly impossible. And yet, he had to try.

"This… pedestal," he said, glancing around the room. "What does it look like?"

"You'll know it when you see it."

"Where?"

"Then you're ready to play?"

He nodded.

"Fabulous." She rubbed her hands together. "It's a race."

"To where?"

"Why, to the finish line, of course."

Nigel felt his lips curl into a smile. It was confidence. While she might be smart, she lacked his physical strength and stamina. Nigel was faster than her, thanks to his years of continued athletic engagement.

"But I should warn you," Gemma added. "This construct might play with your head some. My only promise is that you and I are both subject to the same rules at all times."

"Rules… governing what?"

"Why, physics, of course." Then she stood and gestured to the front door. Nigel joined her and then opened it. What he saw next took his breath away.

39

EVELYN

SOMEONE SHOVES me to the right where I stop myself against a metal bulkhead. The act saves my life as energy bolts zip through the place my head was a second before. I can't help replaying Bhavna's death in my mind's eye. She's... gone. Just like that.

And many more will die too if you don't focus, Eves.

"Gun," I shout to Rodgers who's taken cover behind the same bulkhead. "Give me something!"

He demags a pistol from his hip and passes it to me, biolock off.

I pull the gun close to my chest. Holding it gives me a sense of power. I can defend myself and others if it comes to it. Crate pushers pass me making a fortified front line against the new Talv attack. We've got enemies behind and in front of us, but the cargo boxes are serving as good barriers. Jericho may have saved us all with his quick thinking.

"Advance hard on this next push," Rook orders over V-cog. "Covering fire. Go!"

The sound of Marine weapons fills the air. I can't imagine anything surviving down the hall. The next thing I know, three Marines grab fistfuls of webbing and use their battlesuit thrusters to power the massive boxes down the hallway. Rook orders everyone to follow close behind, and we get halfway to a docking bay tagged in my V-cog overlay. Just then, an explosion throws me forward. My head slams into someone's backplate, and I see stars. But I'm still awake, buffeted by hot air and bits of debris. Ears are ringing too.

Someone's shouting at me. The person I flew into. But I can't hear. Then the voice speaks in V-cog. It's Grabowski. "You okay?"

I nod. "What happened?"

"Anti-personnel charges," he says and points to something in the wall beside me. It's a squat looking block with a faint NUE Space Marine Corps insignia. A matching one is affixed on the opposite side of the corridor. "They're ours. More coming, so be ready."

"Got it." I don't look forward to being thrown around again or suffering more ear pain, but if it means not dying, I'm all for it.

We cross the next intersection, and I spot three Talv corpses floating in zero g. While their chest plates look unscathed, their heads and bare arms have been shredded. Two more bodies farther down the left hand tunnel look like they've been blown apart, possibly from more anti-personnel devices, but I can't be sure.

"Contact, my twelve," someone ahead of me says. The calls come with another exchange of fire.

"Reinforcements on our six," someone else says. There's so much going on, I can't keep track of it all. People screaming. Marines yelling about changing mags. Several people switch places, fast, and all the while we keep moving down the hallway, stopping, starting, and stopping again.

"What's the hold up?" Rook yells, directing the question at Geller who's pushing the lead crate. The box is getting blasted by something, light splashing around the sides. I think it's starting to break apart.

"They've got a BFG," he yells. "Losing cover."

If that crate goes, so does Geller and three Marines. *And Jericho.* He's right behind them with Afumba.

"Can you take it?" Rooks asks.

"Negative. We're pinned down."

"Wait for their reload."

"We'll try."

I glance around my crate and see Jericho's cargo container glowing red. Bits and pieces of the front face are flinging past our heads as the Talv weapon sends an unrelenting barrage of energy against it. But still, the men keep it in place, somehow willing it to hold together.

Finally, the Talv assault stops. Geller and the others push out to return fire. But another explosion rips down the hallway and pushes us back. I grab a metal conduit to keep me from going too far. Debris pelts my side, and a few chunks hit me in the head and arms. As soon as the shockwave passes, I look ahead to see...

Fergus? And with his arms flexed over his shoulders! "I, Ardent Conqueror of Malquith, have come to save the day with a Holy Hand Grenade," he exclaims. "Come! This way. One, two, five!"

"Son of a bitch," Rook says as we all push off and shoot toward the excipion.

"Have I done well? Do you, in fact, feel saved?" he asks Rook as our line passes through the next intersection.

"Definitely," Rook replies, but then something seems to bother him. "Where's the warhead?"

"Positioned inside the hangar bay, my lord. As I said, I couldn't make it to engineering where I supposed the bomb would produce the greatest results. However, it should be sufficient to permanently disable the frigate."

"Works for me. And the detonator?"

Fergus hands Rook a cylindrical device.

"Nice work, Ferg. Help the weakest keep moving. And"—he pulls a rifle off his back—"make yourself useful."

"As you wish." Fergus accepts the firearm and then identifies two injured crew members who seem to be struggling to fly straight.

That's when I notice Enni. She's clutching the side of her shoulder where an arm used to be. The wound has been flash cauterized, but her face tells the story of immense pain and shock. I reach out and help her keep moving down the tunnel. "I got you, Enni."

She cries and lets me help push her along.

The terror is real.

A renewed gun fight breaks out behind us. It seems the majority of Pohge's forces were near the bow, which makes sense if that's where the bridge is. They pass several more of the Marine anti-personnel devices as we progress, but it doesn't seem to stop their assault.

For her part, Korbix is using her Talv weapon to fire around a crate to our rear. I can't see what effect it's having, but she seems to be adept at using it. But even with all our defenses, the Talv keep putting more pressure on us.

Just then, the rear-most crate breaks apart, and at least one person suffers a fatal hit.

"Grabowski, *nooo*," Rodgers yells toward the floating body. The dead Marine's chestplate has craters the size of baseballs in three places, each revealing burnt flesh-colored wounds. His limbs aren't moving either. Rodgers lets out a terrible roar and fires at the enemy while trying to pull Grabowski's body out of harm's way. But he too is struck several times. The first few hits don't seem to impede him much, but as more rounds hit the same places on his body, the armor gives way. The pair of them are flung against the bulkheads and take a dozen more hits. Tragically, their bodies serve as shields for those in the rear.

More team members are struck, but I can't see who. I'm being pushed and pulled too hard by hands helping me fly down the hall. One last cargo box serves as a rear shield, dashing incoming fire against the walls. Light flashes with a sporadic strobe-like effect that seems to match the rising fervor of the enemy's disdain over our escape.

We're close to the bay now. I think I see the hangar door ahead. Yes. Someone's standing at the entrance, pushing people in. There's no explosion of light bursts when they enter, so I take that to mean the space is clear of Talv. But behind us, the roar of weapons fire is getting louder.

"I'm out," someone says. It's Rook, I believe.

"Last mag," someone else yells.

That's not good. The Marines are running low on ammunition.

I get Rook's attention just before I enter the door and throw him my pistol. The weapon sails in a straight line before Rook grabs it by the handle. He spins in a continuous motion and then fires around the crate. A beat later, another anti-personnel device detonates. The explosion throws me back, but the doorkeeper grabs my arm and shoves me through. My wrist screams in pain. Heat flashes against my backside. A heartbeat later, I'm adrift in a large dark space. I'm flying away from the battle fires, combat sounds dissipating. For a split second, I wonder if I've been hit… if this is my soul disintegrating into nothing. Annihilationism. I've met my end. But then, in the darkness, a shaft of light appears…

It's a doorway… in the afterlife?

No… it's on the side of *Korbix*'s ship!

I can see the vessel's shape now, and the V-cog ident tag reads *Banshee*, which must be Rook's codename for it. They flew Korbix's ship here! I don't know how, but cosmic stars, am I grateful to see it. I spot another tagged item, something named Big Ass Bomb. It's Fergus's warhead, affixed on the ceiling just above the *Banshee*.

"Drop all remaining munitions in the hall, double-time," Rook yells behind me. I try to look over my shoulder to see what's happening, but without anything to push off from, the action is pointless. I pull up Rook's POV in V-cog and see the Marines throwing every last grenade they have into the hallway and then closing the door. Then everything goes black save for the ship's doorway ahead. I wait. And float.

A loud explosion sounds from behind me. The hangar walls rattle. I half expect the Talv ship's hull to breach. But it doesn't. I don't know how much time that's bought us, but hopefully it's enough. Meanwhile, I fly right past the *Banshee*'s open door and head to the hangar's far side. Just then, two hands grab me from behind, and a voice says, "I gotcha."

It's Rook. He adjusts my course and sends me toward the lit doorway. Two more people inside reach out, take me by the arms, and pull me in. My wrist explodes in pain again, but I don't care. I'm back on Korbix's ship and being pushed toward the bridge. She's secured herself in the captain's chair to the left, and Jericho is climbing into the right but freezes when he sees me. "You still good?"

I nod, then say, "I still can't believe this is happening."

"Believe. We're almost out of it. Buckle up."

I do, and watch as Korbix powers up her ship even despite the way she's wincing. Purple blood mats the hair along her neck and arms, and her breathing seems labored. But she's alive, which is more than I can say for so many in our crew. I glance toward the passenger compartment and see it swelling with people. The only person not fully inside the ship, however, is Rook. He's still standing in the doorway.

"What are you waiting for?" I ask. "Get in."

"Unfortunately, I'm gonna need to stay behind."

I give him a look like he's gone mad. "What are you talking about?"

Rook opens a hand and lets several pieces of debris lift from his palm.

A pit forms in my stomach. "The detonator."

He nods. "Someone's gotta stay behind to set it off manually."

"Don't be ridiculous," I say. "We can still get away without it." He counters with a blank face, which forces me to add, "Can't we?"

"Given the level of hostility we've encountered," Korbix says over V-cog. "The Talv will do everything in their power to make escape impossible."

"Can't we just shoot it as we fly away?" Popov asks from the aft compartment.

"With what weapons?" Jericho asks, referring to the lack of armament on Korbix's ship.

Before anyone else can jump in, Fergus pushes me aside and says, "Please, allow me."

Rook remains in the doorway. "You're needed here, bot."

"But I—"

"Can sit your ass down because you've become far too important to the ongoing success of this mission."

I push past Fergus and collide with Rook. "You can't do this. There's gotta be another way."

"Oi," Eddie says, pushing himself forward. "Like letting someone with less mission value take the fucking job."

"Then you'd better get in line," Nairobi says, trying to jostle for position.

"Well aren't you all just a sorry bunch of martyrs,"

Rook says. "Unfortunately for you, this is a military matter, one that falls under my purview. Now, if you'll excuse me—" Something hits Rook from behind and throws him into me. At the same time, I hear a weapon shooting... but not like any the Marines carry. I shield my head as we collide against the corridor wall. Rook turns to confront whatever new enemy lurks in the darkness but freezes as the nano door starts closing up. "What the hell?"

I catch a human floating just outside the ship, dressed in a SESI EVA suit. The door is filling in fast, but not before I glimpse a familiar face. "Sorry, Eves. Rook. This one's mine."

40

NIGEL

Sir Nigel Sallsworth looked through the log cabin's door at a body of water, but instead of the surface stretching out toward the horizon, it was perpendicular to him. Spellbound, he walked onto the cabin's covered porch to find that a sea stretched out in all directions as if he was looking down on it from twenty meters up. He glanced at Gemma.

"Go," she said and then ran off the porch and into mid-air. Her feet swung around and she fell away from him… not down, but *out*, flying toward the sea. Seconds ticked by as Gemma's body grew smaller and smaller. Finally, she landed with a splash. A moment later, her head popped above the surface and she looked up at him. "I'm winning," she yelled, her voice sounding far away. Then she conducted a surface dive and disappeared under the waves.

"Shit," Nigel said, then followed it with, "Right jolly bloody hell," before running forward and leaping off the porch. His body swung around like Gemma's and his feet pointed toward the water. It felt as though gravity itself had shifted. He twirled his arms about, trying to get his bearings and keep from tumbling out of control. The acceleration stole his breath, but he still managed a glance overhead to see the log cabin sitting on a rock ledge whose cliffside perch ran perpendicular to the sea. The mere sight of it messed with his head, but he didn't have time to dwell on it. The water was rushing toward him, fast, and he suspected it would be unforgiving. If he died in V-cog, he died in the real. So he straightened his legs, folded his arms across his chest, and took a deep breath. This was going to hurt.

A snap of pain shot up his spine as he hit the water. The sound thundered in his ears, and when he finally opened his eyes, bubbles blocked his vision. He kicked a few times to reach the surface, but stayed only long enough to take a fresh breath of air; if Gemma had gone down, so must he.

The water beneath was shallower than he imagined it might have been. Just ten or so meters separated him from the sea floor. He couldn't make out it completely, not without goggles, but it didn't seem like any seabed he'd experience before. Instead of sediment and algae

covered rocks, he only said red block and white stripes…
Bricks, his brain suddenly registered. He was swimming
down toward a wall of bricks. *And another door.* This one
was glass, like those leading into a store. He swam down,
pulling and kicking faster as his lungs started to burn.
Finally, he reached the door and pulled on the handle,
but it didn't budge. Through the glass, he could make
out the fuzzy shapes of a cityscape, like he was looking
up at buildings from the street. He pulled harder, but still
nothing. Then it dawned on him that this door might
push in. So he did, and the glass swung out, sucking him
through.

The moment Nigel crossed the threshold, gravity
shifted again, pivoting his body around his feet and
pulling his chest up until he was standing in the middle
of a street. The sudden movement disoriented him,
more than the last shift, but he didn't have time to dwell
on it. A horn blared behind. Nigel spun around to see
grid truck bearing down on him. Not being able to see
around either side, he took the safer option of dropping
to the ground and letting it go overhead. The horn
changed pitch as did truck raced past, leaving Nigel on
his back.

He sat up to find himself in the middle of three-lane
one-way city street. There was a gap to the next set of
vehicles, but they were coming fast, and he needed to get
off the road. But which way? Gemma clearly had the
home field advantage here, and that fueled another spat

of rage. He got up and tried darting toward the sidewalk, but just before stepping onto it, something prevented him. It was as if he'd struck an invisible wall. But a grid car was flying at him, so he dropped again, barely missing the front bumper. He stayed put for two more passing vehicles as the anger and frustration continued to well up in his chest. However, the anger also heightened his fight sense, and he spotted a sewer cover not six paces away—were he standing. Instead, he decided to crawl beneath the passing hover cars and see if he could lift the circular plate. Elbows striding across asphalt, knees pushing out, he reached the entrance in a matter of seconds and tried the metal cover. It lifted with surprising ease, and he slid it aside.

Expecting to see a dark sewer tunnel, Nigel was shocked to find that he was looking down at a white sand beach. Another car horn blared behind him, prompting him to dive through the hole headfirst. This time, gravity did not shift, and Nigel continued straight down, barely managing to somersault through the three-meter hole so that he landed on his back in the sand. The impact knocked the air out of him, but he was free of traffic. He propped himself up, breathing heavily, and found a luxury resort to his right, ocean to his left, and a woman running through the hotel's beach furniture ahead.

Gemma.

Nigel pushed himself up, electrified. The hunt was on, and he reasoned that he could catch her here, or at least close the gap some. He took off at a sprint, bounding over virtual people sunning themselves on towels and dashing around umbrellas. Gemma did the same, but seemed aided by her slighter build. Still, Nigel had more power, and if he could wrestle her to the ground, he could use his mass to incapacitate her. He wondered, however, if knocking her out would be detrimental to his chances of escaping the game she'd built. Better to tie her up or break a bone than risk messing with her consciousness. He'd use tools gathered from the environment.

A woman lay face down in a fully reclined beach chair, her bikini top draped across a drink table. He swiped the bathing suit and wrapped it around his forearm, thinking he could use it to bind Gemma's wrists and feet. Nigel mounted the deck of a beach-side tiki bar and shoved several digital guests out of the way. As he jumped the bar, Nigel grabbed a sommelier knife and then stuffed it in his pants pocket. The corkscrew and small blade might come in handy. Maybe he could bleed her out and escape just before she died.

Nigel jumped off the far end of the tiki bar and charged after Gemma again. The sand made running harder for both of them, but Nigel's powerful legs carried him further and faster than Gemma. He gained on her, though not without cost. In his eagerness, Nigel found himself gasping for air, winded from the leap into the sea, the swim, the adrenaline of almost being struck in the street, and now this—running in sand. His lungs burned, and he tasted the penny-flavor in the back of his throat. He wouldn't be able to keep this up forever, but he was getting closer, now just four meters away.

Gemma angled toward the incoming surf, looking as though she might plunge into the shallows. He needed to stop her before she entered the next level of whatever came next. A man stood from a short-legged beach chair as the surge pushed up the beach. Nigel grabbed the plastic chair and then, with all his might, side-armed it at Gemma and struck her in the back of the legs. She fell face first into the sandy water and letting out a sharp cry. Nigel was on her an instant later, pressing her head down and trying to get one arm behind her so he could begin binding her wrists with the bikini top. But no sooner did he have her in position than the surf began pulling him out to sea. Not like some gentle tug from the real ocean but a magnetic pull that took him off balance and yanked him into the receding swell. He lost his grip on her but still had the bikini top around his forearm.

Nigel was sliding away from the beach, accelerating as if he were heading down a slide at a waterpark. He shut his eyes against the salty sting and tried to keep himself upright but the rip current was too great. Soon, he was submerged, blind, and still accelerating. Then, just when he thought he would run out of air, his head popped above the surface. He was still accelerating, but now found himself sliding down a giant glass surface covered with water.

Nigel blinked again. He was on a skyscraper, sliding down an incline toward the edge. And there, across the gap, was a flat-topped building with two pedestals on it, situated in a sparse rooftop garden. *The finish line!* But there was no way he could leap that far. The distance was impossible. He needed to stop his descent. Nigel used his hands and feet to try to slow himself. It worked, at least partially, but the excess water that had come with him from the beach was making him lose his grip. So he pulled the sommelier knife from his pocket and jabbed the tool into the glass while also keeping pressure with his feet. A blood curdling *eeeeeeeeeeck!* sounded as the metal carved a line across the glass. Again, it didn't stop him completely, but enough to give himself some time to think…

And enough for Gemma to sail past him. "You lose, Nigel," she said and then, to his astonishment, she flew off the edge and disappeared over the side.

Nigel gaped. Had she just committed suicide? Was her plan all along to end herself and trap him in her construct forever? *It can't be.*

Just then, something caught his eye, movement from over the gap. He hadn't seen it before, but there was a garage-door-sized hole in the air parallel with the street below and just high enough above the advancing rooftop that as Gemma fell out of it, she had enough angular momentum to continue her course across the gap and land in the garden.

Nigel was nearing the edge, still using his feet and the knife to slow him, still carving a streak across the glass. With the water thinning out, he was getting more contact. At last, the soles of his shoes stopped him on a small lip, and he looked down a hundred stories or more to the street below. Sea water continued to rush past him, flying into mid-air. A crosswind caught it, disappearing the droplets into vapor. The same gusts tousled his hair and reminded him how very real this construct was. Then a wave of vertigo spun his head. Nigel leaned back against the glass in panic.

How did she get across? he wondered. But it was too late now. She was there, a meter or two from her pedestal, and he, still stuck on the edge of this building with what felt like eternity between them. She'd won. And he'd lost.

Gemma yelled something from across the street.

"What?" he called back.

"*You have to use your momentum,*" she said more deliberately.

Nigel chanced a look down again but didn't see how momentum saved him from not plummeting to his death. Until he spotted an anomaly in the scene some distance below. He didn't know if it was just his eyes playing tricks on him or if maybe there was a glitch in the render. *An intentional glitch,* he thought. *Like the garage-sized door in the air above. A portal.* Dropping into the one below might send him out the bottom one of the one above. And if he had enough forward momentum, he could carry that through and onto the other side of the street.

But, no, he would not be that stupid. She could easily get him to jump and then remove the lower window.

"I'm not trying to kill you, Nigel," she shouted over the wind again.

"Could have fooled me," he hollered back.

"I'm bound to the same rules you are, remember?" That didn't do much to ease the vertigo. "Jump! Just make sure you have enough speed." She pantomimed something... like she was crawling...

Back up the roof? She must be joking. But Nigel didn't see any other way around this, and Gemma already stated that she had no desire to kill him. Her whole plan was predicated on him surviving, on him remaining the President of Earth. "Son of a bitch." With the water gone, he reckoned he'd have better grip than before. He even kicked his shoes and socks off, knowing his skin would gain him even more friction, and stuffed the knife back in his pants pocket. Then he started crab walking up the side, slowly. Carefully. He figured he only had one shot at this. After almost a minute of climbing, he reached a height that he felt was sufficient and cast one more look at her. She still hadn't reached for her pedestal. Was she really so sadistic that she wanted to see him suffer? She could end this all simply by pressing her button and winning the challenge. He'd find ways around her intrusion. There was trickery he could employ, he felt sure of that. Not a perfect solution, but maybe enough to keep the devil at bay. And, perhaps one day, he'd find a way to kill her. *Bide your time, Nigel.*

He inhaled sharply and then picked his hands and feet up off the glass roof. Again, his body accelerated and his stomach lurched. The edge was coming faster than expected. Did he have enough speed? And what happened if he didn't? But it was too late now. The edge approached, and pushed away at the last second, avoiding the lip, and flinging himself out over the street.

Gravity took over next, yanking him down. His arms and legs flailed, his gut flipping inside. And the street below rendered out in perfect clarity, no doubt added by the adrenaline shooting through his veins, in V-cog and in the real. Everything seemed to slow down then, and in the blink of an eye, Nigel went from passing between the buildings toward the street to suddenly appearing higher than the adjacent building and flying toward its roof. And somehow, he felt that the top portal had slowed his descent down. *It worked!* He couldn't believe it… not that he had time. A split second later, he landed barefoot on the edge of the building, but barely. His center of gravity was off. Arms spinning to keep from falling backward.

"Gotcha," Gemma said, grabbing him by the shirt. Relief washed over him. Until she said, "Changed my mind," and let him go.

Nigel tried grabbing her arm but failed. Instead, he felt his stomach lurch again as he tumbled backward. A few meters down, he sensed himself pass through the portal again to appear higher than where Gemma was standing and falling slower. Instead of moving to the garden's edge, however, Nigel fell past the roofline and back into the lower portal. It happened successively three more times before he realized his fate.

"Make it stop," he yelled as he passed by her.

"Oh, I'm so sorry. I can't. Though, that's not really true," she said, stringing the sentences together to account for the delay. The period was short enough that they could have a conversation of sorts, strange as it was. "It's more like I don't want to."

Nigel suddenly felt more afraid of helplessness than ever hitting the street below. The insecurity, the incessant speed-up/slow-down nature of the motion, the *insanity* of the perpetual loop… it was tormenting. Because no matter how hard Nigel strained, he could not reach the ledge as it passed by. And no matter how much he wanted to throw his weight around, it was impossible to move his body closer.

"Is this how you did it?" he yelled as he passed her. "Tormented them?"

"Your opponents? Or course. Some more brutally than others. But always the same outcome. They relented or died."

He growled at her amidst his dizziness. "You got what you want! *Now end this.*"

"Maybe."

"What do you mean maybe? You bested me. Get us the hell out of here!"

"Oh, I'm getting out. The question is whether or not I want *you* out yet."

"But you said you need me as President."

"Need is such a subjective word, don't you think? Right now, a new opportunity has presented itself, one I hadn't anticipated." She tapped her chin, eyeing his next two passes. "How long might you stay here until you would do anything to get out?"

"You'd be stuck here too!"

She smiled. "I lied. My button gets me out, but I can keep you in as long as I like once I have access to your V-cog. It's *true* override permission at that point."

Nigel's code slicers had warned him that such a thing was hypothetically possible once they'd seen Gaia's Blood. The probability, they argued, was almost statistically impossible. He ground his teeth, cursing their lack of foresight… and *his* underestimation of his opponent.

"In fact," Gemma said after a few more trips through the loop, "I wonder if I might not keep you here indefinitely. I imagine the resources at your disposal, the banking codes, the dirt on all the slime you know, could come in handy."

"I won't yield."

She laughed at him, hard and loud, tearing through the sound of the wind. "You don't have to yield, Sallsworth. The moment I press that button, it all belongs to me, don't you see? *Full access.* The very thing they feared has come upon them. And the most beautiful part? Nobody knows."

"You're a monster."

"And you're not in a position to fight me."

Nigel raged inside. He had never felt so trapped in all his life… never felt so helpless. There had to be something he could do. That's when he saw the bikini top wrapped around his forearm. The sommelier knife was still in his pocket too. A thought crossed his mind. It was a long shot. And he'd only get one chance. She would have to be close too. Right on the edge. But if he could snag her and pull her into the loop with him, then he felt sure he could throw Gemma aside and use Newton's third law of motion to get himself to the building—*equal and opposite reactions.* All he needed to do was push away from her body once he captured her.

"You were there, weren't you," Nigel began on his next pass. "Watching when I shot your mother in the head." He could see Gemma's jaw stiffen, even in his haphazard state. At the same time, he took out the knife and shoved the handle through the buckle. "Can you imagine? To watch your own mother die and be so utterly helpless to do anything to save her?"

"We're done here. And I'm done with you, Sallsworth."

While she talked, he spread the corkscrew, knife, and lever arm out making a grappling hook. It would be flimsy, and he'd need to catch her around an arm or the neck to pull her off balance, but he had to try.

"And to think, it was your technology… *your* invention that made it all possible. I can't imagine how that must've felt."

"You're a bastard and not worthy of living, Sallsworth," she yelled, voice rising to a scream. He started unraveling the bikini top. "And it will give me great pleasure to know that you are here, looping, for the rest of your insignificant life." Nigel counted the passes, knowing he had to throw as soon as he slowed out of the top portal. "You won't be completely alone, though. I'll come visit you from time to time, and maybe I'll even release when it suits me." She stepped to the edge and raised a finger at him. "But know this. With access? It means I can send you back here *any time I wish.*"

"Not if I send you first." Nigel held onto the strap's end, threw the weighted end, and extended his arm as far as it would go to cross the two meter divide. The tool overshot her wrist, but as Nigel fell, the strap tightened and flicked the corkscrew around to catch on the elastic. It happened so fast that Nigel thought he missed. A heartbeat later, Gemma screamed above him. He looked up to see her pitch forward, his hand jerked by the sudden tension. The scream grew louder as she cleared the building, but Nigel had already dropped out of the upper portal and could see her below him. He flew past the building before she appeared overhead. Gemma was too far away for him to reach, so he tried pulling on the strap only to discover he'd lost it, nor was the other end wrapped around her arm.

That's when the horror struck him. He and Gemma were separated by more than three meters, never nearer.

"*What have you done?*" she wailed, frantically trying to reach for the building as it passed two meters from the ends of her straining fingertips.

Nigel swallowed. What *had* he done? In his attempt to free himself, he'd damned them both. And there was nothing that either of them could do about. Ever.

⁙

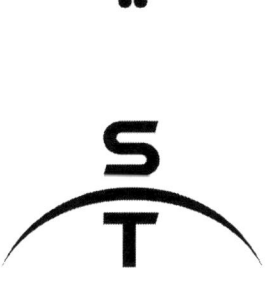

Walter

Walter Brunell stood over Nigel, seated in his chair, while Gemma's head of security lingered off her left shoulder. It had been over six hours since the pair had entered V-cog, and neither party showed any signs of cognizance besides rapid eye movement. While vitals looked stable, both Nigel and Gemma had experienced adrenal spikes five and a half hours before. Increased heart rate, above normal brain activity, and muscle twitching all followed. Then, shortly after the event, all the symptoms abated and their vitals returned to normal.

"What do you think happened?" Gemma's staffer asked in a conciliatory tone. Walter only knew him as Norkü, and he genuinely seemed concerned for Miss Birdwhistle. Though the question and the emotion behind it seemed odd to Walter, as if he knew what went on in their heads.

"It's your boss who shut us out," Walter said at last. "I'm not sure why you're asking me."

"Well, we can't access her neutral interface either, so…"

"So? Where does that leave us?"

"I suppose at an impasse. Unless their deliberations really are taking this long."

Walter shook his head. "I have worked for Mr. Sallsworth for over thirty years. Never once has he suffered a meeting longer than ninety minutes, even when a billion credits were at stake. Anything beyond that meant people hadn't done their homework, and he had no patience for the incompetent and ill prepared."

Norkü's countenance grew dark, but it was more akin to fear than anger. "So what are you saying then?"

"That something has happened to them both."

"What sort of something?"

"I don't know, Mr. Norkü. Why don't you tell me? Perhaps check with your research lab again?"

He bit a lip, then said, "We have. Every half hour now."

"And?"

"She's barricaded herself in."

"And him along with her then."

Norkü started nodding long before more words came out. "It appears so, yes."

Walter inhaled through his nose and blew out through his mouth. He had reservations about Nigel's collaboration with the Tantum Terrae leaders from the beginning—both Gemma and Neon. Granted, Gemma's more recent activities had ensured Nigel's election, but they had come with costs, and now Walter feared some were too great even for his employer's deep pockets to pay. "Oh, Nigel. What have you done?"

"Pardon me?" Norkü asked.

Walter raised his chin and swallowed. "We are leaving. I suggest you do the same."

Norkü hesitated. "You… won't prevent us?"

"Why? It seems we are both dealing with a tragedy

that we may never know the fullness of. Isn't that enough punishment for one day?"

Norkü nodded grimly.

"You have free passage back to Earth."

"Thank you, Mr. Brunell." He looked from Gemma's sleeping face back to Walter. "What will you do with him?"

"Make sure he's as comfortable as possible. And you?"

"The same."

Walter nodded once. "Good day, Mr. Norkü."

"Mr. Brunell."

Then Walter turned aside and began making preparations for long term palliative coma care. He also sent a memo to the heads of the Nations of United Earth explaining the President Sallsworth may be unable to fulfill the duties and responsibilities of his office. Last but not least, Walter began composing what he would say to Esther, Malcolm, and Fiona; while the star system had lost its first president nearly as fast as it had elected him, Walter Brunell was far more concerned for the family who had lost a husband and father long before his time. And he wept as soon as he was alone.

41

EVELYN

"Olivia? What the fuck are you doing here?" I say over V-cog, now that the *Banshee*'s door is sealed up. I move left to look out a port-side window, unable to contain the anger, frustration, and confusion in my voice. Olivia is in one of the *Sagan*'s EVA suits and holding a piton gun from our field exploration kits. She didn't hit me or Rook... So what was she shooting at? "Korbix, I need this door open!"

"I'm sorry, Dr. Evelyn Park," she calls back from the bridge. "But your fellow human has fired on my vessel activating an emergency lockdown protocol. It will take a few moments to clear."

"Don't bother," Olivia replies.

"How did you get here?" I ask.

From behind me, Fergus says, "I attempted to inform you that I thought I was being followed."

"Should've tried harder," Rook says.

Kit joins me at window. "Miss Olivia?" he says with the sound of wide-eyed wonder. "Well who in shiitake mushrooms land let you out of your room?"

"Pays to be a code slicer," she replies with a smile, revealing nothing. "Good to see you, Kit. What matters now is that you have someone to detonate your bomb. I suggest you get moving."

"Olivia, you…"

"Yes?"

My jaw tightens, lips pressing together before saying, "You're a criminal. One who'll be tried for crimes against—"

"Yeah. I know, Eves. And I deserve everything the courts say I have coming. In the meantime, however, I have a date with a warhead."

"Korbix, I need this door open!"

"Should be opening… now."

The nanostructure starts peeling away, but a moment later, Olivia fires the piton gun again, and the emergency protocol reseals the doorway. "Korbix!"

"I'm sorry, Dr. Evelyn Park. There's nothing I can do."

I whirl on Olivia through the window. "Stop shooting!"

"Sorry. If you'll excuse me, I've got some work to do."

"But you'll die!"

She chuckles. "Can't fool you SESI scientists, I tell ya what." A loud *boom* sounds from somewhere in the ship. Pohge's survivors are trying to get in. "You don't have much time. Now get going, would ya?"

"Olivia… Why?"

"Because maybe I want to prove you wrong. Even the worst of us are capable of greatness. You just need a little faith."

"Evelyn," Rook says. "We need to get seated."

I spin on him. "You're just going to… let her do this?"

"Yeah. And so are you. We need to go."

My last stern look at Olivia softens before Rook pushes me back toward the bridge. As soon as I'm buckled in, Korbix unclamps the ship from the Talv frigate and hacks open the *Behemoth*'s hull bay doors. Reflected light from Soteria floods the hold at the same time that the void snuffs out the fire coming from the blown apart hallway toward the bow. Debris and bodies fly out next, sucked into hard vacuum. Many of the dead are humans. Our fallen crewmembers. My throat grows tight, and I lament how many we're leaving behind. Olivia, knowing that the bay doors would have to open for us to escape, had grabbed onto an emergency hand-hold on the ceiling seconds before the bay doors opened.

She's now recovered and is headed towards the Big Ass Bomb. She's also swapped her piton gun for one of the Marine's discarded rifles.

Korbix moves us out of the bay but doesn't immediately fly away. Something's wrong.

Rooks must sense it too. "Their point defense weapons?" he asks her.

"They are dangerous once we leave the ship's shadow, yes." Her fingers move quickly across the illuminated console. "Which is why I am waiting."

"For?"

"To see if my attempts to subvert their weapons systems will work."

Jericho asks, "You're hacking them?"

"Trying to, yes."

"How long?"

"Fifteen of your seconds. Maybe more."

"And if you can't?"

She casts him a dark look. "Then we—"

"We open fire first," Rook interjects. He pings Private First Class Ibrahim on V-cog. "You still awake, Ibrahim?"

"Roger. Coffee's kicked in."

"Time to make it rain. Prioritize enemy weapon systems as they become known. On my go."

"Warming up the bus. On your go."

With a tone of warning, Rooks adds, "Ibrahim, be advised: this will make you—"

"A fatass with a bullseye tacked to it? What's new?"

Rook smiles, but it seems sad. "Stay frosty."

"Roger."

"How far clear do we need to be from that warhead?" Jericho asks no one in particular.

"At this speed, I'd say at least ten seconds," Rook replies. "Depends on several factors."

"Ten seconds should be enough, yes," Korbix confirms. "My shields can handle that, assuming your warhead is a *kerrr-kow*."

"Yeah, it's a *kerrr-kow*," he replies with a grin. I'm guessing the word is atomic or something close to it.

As Korbix sets up a countdown timer labeled Minimum Blast Radius, Rook hails Olivia. "Tomlinson, we need ten seconds to get clear."

A tagless indent audio channel comes back. "Copy that, Rook. Should I count with Mississippi or potato?"

"Dealer's choice."

"Potato it is."

When Rook gives Korbix the nod, she says, "Please prepare for uncomfortable acceleration. This will not be enjoyable for you in the least."

"'Long as it gets us out alive, Korby," Rooks replies and nods at Jericho.

The latter calls back to everyone in the stern. "Get ready for a punch, people! High-g maneuver coming up."

I lean back and brace myself just as Rook gives

Korbix and Ibrahim the same cue: "Let it rip."

Korbix advances a virtual fader on her console. The ship responds instantly, shoving me back in my seat. The acceleration is unlike anything I've ever felt before. Blackness creeps into the sides of my vision, but I grunt in an effort to will it away. Head pinned. Limbs pressed back. And I can't breathe.

"Hostile power signatures detected. Targeting now," Ibrahim says in V-cog from the *Bellerophon*, her voice rising. "Weapons away."

Ahead of us, power surge flashes appear out of nowhere. The *Belle* is too far to see with the naked eye, but weapon discharge flashes give away its position. Two seconds later, Korbix's console shows the Talv frigate behind us getting hit. Explosions tear holes in the black Talv ship, but the void snuffs out flames and fire, leaving ultra-fast debris trails in their wake. Despite the *Belle*'s preemptive attack, the frigate still manages to shoot us. Blue light washes out the camera feed, and I'm pushed back in my seat further. Warning indicators go off on the bridge. Korbix's hands work fast.

Ibrahim fires more from the *Belle*, this time hitting a turret that's shooting at us. A mini electrical storm erupts from the explosion, and more of the frigate's hull is carved away. I glance at the ten second countdown timer. We're only halfway to the minimum blast radius.

"Contact," someone yells in comms. It takes me half a second to realize it's Olivia's voice. She's got company in the hull. A video feed of her face pops into my head. "Eves?" She fires between shots. "You there?"

I send back my helmet cam and grunt out, "Yes."

"I just want you to know that I'm sorry, and you really did make me a believer. I told you I had your back." She returns fire and then glances at her gun as if it's run out of ammo. "Forging paths...?"

"Through the dar—"

The feed cuts, and Rook yells, "Incoming!"

A second later, we're consumed in light.

Jericho

I BARELY MANAGE to keep conscious. Chalk it up to experience and the best gene editing money can buy thanks to NUESSA's test pilot regs. The explosion has passed us, and according to camera feeds, the enemy frigate is nowhere to be seen. I'm no military man, but I'm pretty sure that constitutes a win.

Evelyn and Rook are still out, but Korbix is awake. She's already flipped the *Banshee* around and started a gentle deceleration burn. "Are you okay, Jericho Fox?" Korbix asks.

"Yeah." I attempt to rub my head but get stymied by my helmet. "We made it?"

"We have, yes."

"And the Talv frigate?"

"Annihilated."

"God in heaven, thank you." I pause, thinking of someone else I'm grateful for. "And you, Olivia. Thanks."

Still, the bomb she detonated doesn't explain the sudden acceleration we experienced. Since there wasn't any atmo for a shockwave to give us that kind of shove, something else factored into the equation. Something on the enemy frigate. "What happened?"

"Your warhead triggered a secondary reaction from the Talv drive core. The release of energy propelled us more than I expected. I hope all members of our ships are alright."

I call up the V-cog roster and skim vitals for everyone still on the network. "All accounted for. 'Least those who started out alive." A pang hits my chest as I consider just how many people we've lost. The crew summary tab shows that of our forty-nine original POET crew members, sixteen are registered deceased, and two offline: Dr. Bolton aboard the *Sagan* and Private First Class Ibrahim on the *Bellerophon*. Everyone appears to have injuries, some more than others. They'll need medical attention at camp right away.

"What about our vessels?" I ask.

"Your gunship appears to have been severely damaged with return fire, but the other two vessels are untouched."

"Could've been worse. What are the chances of another Talv ship coming after us?"

"Assuming I return to my system promptly? Low." She seems to hesitate. "Then there is the matter of you and your people. I recognize this is all ill-timed, but I need to know your final decisions."

I glance at Evelyn and Rook. They're still out. "Take us back to Camp Evelynton. We'll treat everyone and then go from there."

"Understood." Korbix enters the coordinates and then redirects the *Banshee*. As the ship comes about and takes up the new heading, I feel strange waves of both grief and relief wash over me. Relief that we survived; I can hardly believe we just did what we did. Grief over all those we've lost; it's the same sense of mourning I had after the *Perseverant*, after *Astraea* Station... that sense of knowing I had a hand in the deaths of good people. Because I'm partly to blame just by virtue of my involvement. I survived... they didn't.

I'm also tired. Adrenaline dumping out of my system, I think. Maybe extreme fatigue from all the g's we just pulled. Or pain meds pumping in from my suit. My eyelids are heavy. My thoughts drift toward Earth, to telling everyone that we have a new home to move to. New aliens to meet. It's overwhelming. And at the same time exhausting. Because I feel so damn tired. "Hey, Korbix?" I say just before letting myself close my eyes for a few seconds.

"Yes, Jericho Fox?"

"Thanks. For everything."

"You're welcome. Get some sleep."

"Copy that." I can't fight the tug anymore, so I close my eyes and let myself drift off to sleep as we head toward the Soterian sky.

EPILOGUE

Evelyn

SOMEONE'S CALLING MY NAME. It's repetitive. And irritating. So I bat at the voice in the dark.

"She's up! Holy biscuits, she's awake!"

"Kit?"

"Easy, Miss Evelyn. Easy…"

The darkness is replaced with soft light that gives way to shapes and then colors. "Where… where are we?" I'm on my back and definitely *not* in… in space, on Korbix's ship. Fleeing the Talv frigate and counting down the seconds until…

Until Olivia detonated her warhead.

"We're in camp," Kit replies warmly. "Yours, ya know? *Huh-uh huh-uh.*"

I massage my eyes against a migraine. "What's so funny?"

"I was just thinking that maybe we, ya know, could name the next one after me. Camp Kit. Eh, that's a stupid idea."

"I'd vote for it."

"You would?"

"Mm-hmm. Here, help me sit up?"

"Sure, sure." He takes my hand and pulls, but it sends a shooting pain up my arm. "Your wrist! Golly, I'm so sorry. Totally forgot."

I hold the wounded arm to my chest for a second until the pain subsides, then offer him my other hand.

"Slowly. Nice and easy, Miss Evelyn."

I'm in the medical building and sitting along the wall of patient beds. A few are still filled, but most are empty. "How many died?"

Kit's face grows sad.

"Kit?"

"Eighteen in total. Fifteen during the fight, plus Olivia. Then Rook found out Ibrahim died on the *Belle*, and then we lost Dr. Cartwright who was assigned to Jericho's team."

"So many…"

"Yeah." Kit rubs the back of his neck. "Leaves thirty-one remaining."

The figure hits hard. Somehow, I always envisioned that we'd all get through this. Stars, I also imagined that aliens *wouldn't* try shooting us. That didn't work so great, which makes me angry, confused, and... happy to be alive. Because things couldn't have been much worse. More could have died. What we did was desperate, dangerous. But it may have saved our entire species. So I'm grateful to be counted among the living, though it doesn't ease the pain over our dead.

"Miss Evelyn? You okay?"

"Headache. But fine. You?"

"Who, me? Golly, yes. I mean, I got a few bruises and a scar that I can flex for the ladies... but, you don't wanna see that."

"Sure I do."

"No, I... I mean you *really* don't wanna see it. It's that one thing I mentioned, 'member? On my bum?"

I laugh, recalling the incident with Fergus and him during one of their campouts. "And you expect to flex that for the ladies but can't even show me?"

Kit turns a deep shade of red. "Well... the right lady, maybe. Ya know. One day."

"Uh huh." I give him a pat on the shoulder. "We'll save the showing for later."

He looks up in shock. "Oh, golly, Miss Evelyn. I wasn't trying to imply that it was *you*! I'd never lead you on like that."

"So you don't want it to be me?"

He gulps. "Uh, no, no. Well, I mean, yes! But … ugh… I'd never want… but then you… Holy biscuits."

I lean in and kiss him on the cheek and then slide my legs off the bed.

"What was that for?" he asks, touching his face.

"For always being sweet to me. Men could learn a thing or two from you."

He swallows again. "Gee, thanks."

"Where's Jericho and Rook?"

"Command building with Korbix."

Once my feet are on the floor and I'm steady, I make a bend in my arm and offer it to Kit. "Mind escorting me?"

"It would be my pleasure, Miss Evelyn. And, one thing?"

"Sure."

"When I do meet, ya know, the *one*… mind putting in a good word for me?"

"It will be my pleasure, Kit."

"LOOK WHO DECIDED TO WAKE UP," Rook says with a smile, rising to meet me. Jericho and Fergus also come over and greet me as a wide range of emotions floods my chest. I hug each of them and wave at Korbix and Rose who remain on the far side of the table.

"You feeling alright?" Jericho asks.

"A little sore, but good overall. You?"

"Same. I think we're all there with you."

I turn to Rook. "I'm sorry to hear about Private Ibrahim."

"She died to buy us time. Saved our lives."

"For which I know we're all grateful."

"I certainly am," Fergus adds. "And, in a rather odd turn of events, I should think we have Olivia Tomlinson to thank."

"Speaking of which," I say. "Do we know how she got out?"

Jericho nods. "We recovered security footage from the *Saga* captured on a redundant system. When Dr. Bolton shut down the *Sagan* after the Talv arrived, he accidentally powered down the auxiliary power to the internal security system. On its own, that might not have been a problem, but Olivia knew how to reset the locks on her door and got out. Overpowering Dr. Bolton was easy. Then she paid the bridge a visit, caught up on what Bolton had logged, and decided to tail Fergus in an EVA suit. The rest, we know."

"But Bolton didn't know about our plan at that point," I say, still curious how Olivia figured everything out.

Jericho gives me a shrug. "I think she took a chance and came out on faith. She knew from Bolton's log that the Talv were bad news and that we were in trouble.

Between seeing Fergus and Korbix's ship, she didn't have to know what the specifics were…"

"She assumed we'd need help."

"Yup. The rest she probably figured out by watching Fergus plant the bomb."

The idea that Olivia saved our lives baffles me. She was a traitor. A Tantum Terrae incog responsible for taking untold thousands of lives. Nothing can bring those people back. Still, I can't ignore the feeling of gratitude I have for her. "What she did for us on the Talv ship… that counts for something."

"Agreed," Jericho says. "I think she genuinely cared for you."

"And I her." I hold my aching wrist, silently thanking her again, wherever she is. "We owe you both too," I add, eyeing Jericho and Rook. "Had you not attempted that rescue, I fear that we'd… well, we'd—"

"*You,*" Korbix interrupts, "would be dead, and I would be a pawn in a long political game, one likely ending in my execution. Needless to say, your praises will be sung in the hallowed halls of the Resettlement Council, and your testimony will go a long way, should you choose to represent our cause in an official capacity." Her eyes lock with mine. "I'm sorry to pressure you, but if we are to leave, it must be now."

"Right…" I look at Jericho and Rook. "Do we have an updated roster after…?" I find myself looking down. I still can't fathom how many we lost.

"Right here." Rook brings up a holo display in the table's center so we can all see. I scan the document, taking in the losses once again. I'm grateful we survived. But I'm saddened by all those who didn't. Rook clears his throat and says, "In Lieutenant Jaffa's absence, I recommend we leave Sergeant Geller in charge. He's my most trusted Marine. The rest of the surviving Navy personnel aren't in any condition to lead, at least not at present." He eyes Jericho and me as if looking for confirmation. We nod, and he adds, "So we appoint Geller and give him first pick of the remaining security forces to ensure that Camp Evelynton receives the attention it needs before the rest of the party wagon arrives."

"Party wagon?" Korbix asks.

"Figure of speech. Sorry. The first wave of human settlers."

"I'll take whichever civilians want to head back," Jericho says and then nods at Rook. "I'm guessing nothing's changed about the possibility of court martials for you."

"It'd be news to me," Rooks replies. "Thank you. I don't envy the heat you'll be taking for us."

"Well, I expect to be compensated in Naquallan libations when I get back, with interest." Jericho turns to Korbix. "You got strong drink?"

"Strong drink?" She looks at Fergus. He takes a moment to update her on the definition of alcoholic beverages. "Yes, I believe we should have many biologically compatible beverages meeting your requirements."

"There ya go." Jericho points a stiff finger at Rook. "With interest."

"Roger that."

Jericho eyes me. "Which leaves the expedition team to go with Korbix."

"Right." I scan the roster one more time. "All the original members are still alive. Should they wish to proceed after all they've been through, I remain committed to taking them."

Korbix bows her head. "Your efforts will not be unrewarded. Thank you, Dr. Evelyn Park."

"Please, just Evelyn."

"After what you all have done? It will never be *just* Evelyn."

That phrase, "it will never be" strikes me. So many things will never be what they were before. So many people I'll never see again. Even Earth. Something deep tells me I'll never go back. Strange how life can change so suddenly.

"Korbix," Jericho says. "We'll need you to provide us with the means of opening your rings."

"Of course. Though, it is just *ring*."

Jericho glances at Fergus. "I'm not tracking."

"I believe she means it as stated, my lord. Ring singular."

Back to Korbix, Jericho says, "I don't understand."

"You have only one ring to pass through should you wish to return to Earth."

"You mean, the one here in orbit connects back to *Parallax One*, bypassing Kep-C?"

She nods and gives him a slight smile. "Correct. Such is our design."

Jericho looks at Rook and me. "No more swarm."

"And fewer points of failure," Rook adds. "I like it."

"I will give you the activation device momentarily."

"Thank you."

"Time until skids up?" Rooks asks and then thinks better of the question. "Before you want to leave, Korbix?"

"As soon as possible. We certainly can't afford another episode of that. I will request the immediate deployment of security vessels that will ensure Soteria's safety."

"Thank you. Ten minutes okay?"

"Ten minutes will do."

WITH THE CAMP ALTERED, and those preparing to depart making their goodbyes, Jericho, Rook, and I head up to the ramparts on the east wall. The sky has started its shift toward evening, and the day's heat is falling away with the sun. Likewise, marine birds are gathering for their dinner along the shore while the forest behind us rings with the sounds of insects preparing for nightfall.

"I'm taking bets now," Jericho says as the three of us lean against the railing.

"On?" Rooks asks.

"How long it takes Geller to turn into George of the Jungle out here. Hundred coins says he builds himself a treehouse within six months."

"Over-under says three months."

"Done."

"Eh, I don't see him as a woodsman," I reply. "I'm pegging him as a beach bum myself. Cabana, south side, one month."

"Looks like we have a three way split," Jericho says, and then eyes me skeptically. "What are you smiling at?"

"Funny how fast you can get attached to a place."

"And the people." He eyes me with something akin to sadness for a moment and then his eyes turn toward the ocean. "Can't say I won't miss it here."

"All the more reason to get back ASAP," Rook says to Jericho.

"I'll do my best, Master Sergeant."

"Holding you to that. Listen, I've… got a few things I need to take care of before we're out. Give you guys a few minutes. I'll meet you at the *Banshee*."

"Sounds good," Jericho says.

He tips his head. "Evelyn."

"See ya in a sec," I reply.

Jericho and I watch Rook descend the steps and then disappear into the camp. After a few seconds, Jericho says, "This, uh… might be the last time we see each other."

"For a year or so, yeah. But it'll go by quickly."

"Yup." His fingers drum on the railing. "I guess sometimes you don't realize how much you needed to seize certain moments until it's too late."

"We seized plenty."

"Sure."

"You were expecting more?"

"I was expecting…" He smiles at me, then looks down. "I don't know what I was expecting. Probably because I wasn't expecting you, Evelyn."

"What's that supposed to mean?"

He thinks for a second. "I've had some really big successes, followed by big failures. Notoriety, then total obscurity. Feels like only yesterday that I met Kit, flying a dumpster through the desert outside Old Cheyenne. And I was sure that was it. The rest of my life. I wanted a second chance, but didn't think I deserved it. Didn't think they'd ever let me back in space again. But then you happened."

"Then *Sallsworth* happened," I correct. "He's the one you should be thanking."

"He was just responding to what you'd put in motion. Everyone has been. NUESSA, the Tantum, all of it. Because of you, Dr. Evelyn Park. You've always been in the middle of it… for all of us. You're the drive core. The spark. The thing that, as I look back over the last year, has been the single most consistent cause, for better or worse, of everything that's happened in my life. And now that we're parting ways, I… I guess I'm not sure what to say."

"You're welcome."

He smiles at me. "What?"

"Back when we were on the picnic table"—I thumb over my shoulder to the south beach—"you said thank you, and then we got interrupted. I never got to say you're welcome."

"Well, there ya go." His smile fades. "I just wish we had more time. Because maybe, if we did, I'd say something about how much I care for you. And then maybe you'd say the same, and we'd have a life together that was more than just *Parallax One*, Soteria, and the Naqualla."

"Well, maybe when you come back, we will."

"Maybe." He looks to the horizon and then over his shoulder, likes he's searching for someone. "Rook's not staying away from Earth because he's afraid of being court martialed. That man hasn't been afraid a day in his life." Jericho locks eyes with me. "He's staying away because he's set his compass to you."

My face gets instantly hot. I hold Jericho's stare as long as I can, but eventually look away. Because I know that, somehow, he's right. And I can't say I don't feel something toward Rook. I do. I just don't know what, or how much. Maybe because I've felt something for Jericho too. But there hasn't been… like he said, there hasn't been time.

"What's that?" Jericho says.

"What's what?"

He grins. "You were thinking out loud again."

"Stars." I push strands of hair behind my hair, hoping I didn't betray myself too much. "You're right. About Rook. I know you are. But I don't know what I feel about him."

Without warning, Jericho takes my hand and holds it. His eyes search my face. He seems sad, but somehow hopeful. Like he wishes this turned out differently… that *we* turned out differently. But maybe he believes something might come of it in the future. I just can't be sure because he's not saying anything. "You'll figure it out," he says at last. "And you'll have plenty of time to do it."

"And what about you?"

He eyes the horizon again, still holding my hand. "Not sure yet. But I expect I'll be pretty busy telling people about us. What we've done. About you, humanity's first ambassador to an alien government. Then I'll get busy making that dream of yours come true." I'm about to ask him what he means when he adds, "To get people to paradise. Someone's gotta drive the bus."

Dammit, I can't take this anymore. Before I can talk myself out of it, I grab his face and kiss him, throwing my arms around his head. His lips are warm, and his scent mixes with the ocean air, stirring something deep inside me. Jericho wraps his arms around my back and pulls me close, kissing back hard. Stars, why did we wait so long for this? But I know why… the mission, my work, it was always the priority. And suddenly, it all takes second place to this moment. Where it's just Jericho and me, and nothing else. Not exoplanets. Not ring portals. Politicasts. Or exploding space stations. Just two people colliding like stars in their own universe.

Finally, the kiss ends, and I pull away.

"What was that for?" he asks.

"You didn't like it?"

He grins and then pulls me back, putting his lips on mine. The sensation summons a second wave of desire… of never wanting this to end. Of building a life together, of making more discoveries. Exploring. And then of growing old. It all flashes in front of me like a glimpse of the future that might have been.

Jericho pulls away but keeps me in his arms. "Been wanting to do that for a while."

"Huh. Not me."

"What?"

Now it's my turn to grin, stifling a laugh. I rest my hands on his chest and stare into his eyes. But as I do, the hope welling inside me dissipates. Why? Because of reality. "Jericho. I don't think that we—"

"I know," he says before I can finish. "But we had this."

"Yeah." I look down and rest my forehead on his chest. "We had this."

"And you know what? It was definitely worth it." When I look up, he's smiling, eyes glistening. "Thank you. For daring to dream."

"Thank you too. For saying yes."

"Anytime, Dr. Park. Anytime."

Jericho

THE ENTIRE CREW is gathered outside the *Banshee* and the *Bliss Mobile* as the vessels idle on the camp tarmac. It feels strange to be leaving so soon after such traumatic events, but there's no time to waste. Korbix and the emissary team must return to Tria to send security forces and block any further Talv incursions, and I need to return to Earth with the momentous news of Soteria.

"And you're saying it will open upon approach?" I ask Korbix a second time, examining the briefcase sized device. According to her, it will activate any quantum portal regardless of who built it, so long as the ring was constructed using the Naquallan's carrier signal.

"Twenty-one point three of your kilometers away and the plane will appear, yes. Three additional openers are already in your cargo bay. Should you need more, you know where to find us. I have pre pre-programmed these to carry you from your Earth's ring directly to Soteria as previously noted."

"Amazing." I extend my hand to the ambassador. "Thank you, Korbix. For taking a chance on us." She looks quizzically at my hand, and then grasps it firmly.

"It was the right investment to make." Korbix turns to Evelyn. "Are you ready?"

"We are." She gestures for her team to board the *Banshee*.

Igor fist bumps the line of hands ending with mine. "Captain Fox, is great honor knowing you."

"Same, doctor. Take good care of them."

"Is privilege." He puts a hand on his heart, gives a small bow, and then heads up the wing toward the doorway.

Sebastián is next. He gives me a slight bow, hands clasped at his chest. "It has been a remarkable honor to serve with you, Captain Fox. I wish you the very best in your next mission."

"Same. I imagine you're gonna have your plate full for the next couple of years."

"Years? I expect to be for the rest of my life. It's a good season to be a xenobiologist."

"Sure is. You stay safe out there."

"I shall. Gracias, mi hermano."

Natalie Mason jumps in and gives me a big hug. "Take care of yourself, Fox."

"You too, Mason. Stay sharp."

"Always."

She's hardly let go when Eddie pulls her back. "Oi, quit taking up so much fucking time with him!" Next thing I know, Eddie's slapping my back pretty damn hard. Not sure if this is affection or torture. "Fucking hate good byes, Knight. So that ain't what this is."

"Copy." *Torture it is.*

He pulls back and then pushes something into my hand. At first, I wonder if it's another pair of dice, like the set he left in my office as an insult for taking chances with people's lives. But when I look down, I see it's a knight chess piece made from what I can only guess is locally sourced wood.

"Carved it me'self," he says.

"I can see that. Looks pretty rough."

"Which is exactly what your fucking face is. But you? You're a real knight now. It's not a fucking codename anymore. You protect 'em, Knight. Bring 'em all here. No one's better for the job than you."

I close my finger around the chess piece. "Thanks, Eddie. Take care of yourself."

Hatch gives me a salute next. "A pleasure, Captain Fox."

"Keep everyone safe, Lance Corporal," I say.

"I intend to. You do the same."

Then comes Kit and Fergus. And for some damn reason I'm getting choked up already.

"Hey, pal," I say.

He shuffles his feet on the tarmac. "Gonna miss you, Cap."

"Same. But about you."

I spot tears in his eyes. "You've done more for me than anyone except my mom. How am I supposed to, ya know, say thank you for that?"

"You just did. And, hey, you should know something…" I unzip the top of my flight suit to reveal a t-shirt with Kit's face and his SayMeKit hashtag underneath. "I'm a fan."

"Hey! Where in the world did you get that?"

"Had the team print me one. In fact, I had them printed for all of us." I direct Kit to look around, and right on cue, everyone spreads jackets and unzips suits to reveal a SayMeKit t-shirt.

He laughs while tears stream down his face, spinning around to see everyone. They smile and clap for him until he finally turns back to me. "I don't know what to say, Cap."

"You just need to listen." I put both hands on his shoulders. "You are the best damn flight engineer I've ever had, and the most faithful friend. Thank you, Leslie Christopher Smith, for being there for me when I needed you most. I'll never forget you."

"Holy biscuits, me neither." Kit rubs his nose with his forearm and then lunges into my arms. "I love you, Cap."

"Love you too, pal."

After a few seconds he pulls back, but not all the way. "Hey, could you, ya know, maybe do me a favor when you get back?"

"Anything." I freeze. "As long as it doesn't have to do with that reporter, Willow Shade."

"*Ha-huh ha-huh.* Gosh, no. Um, it has to do with Abigail."

"The ship?"

"No, silly. The girl. Ya know. The one who got away?" He winks at me while actually saying, "Wink-wink."

"Riiight." I remember the story about the crush he had in school on the "perfect woman" who got a scholarship to St. Johns but who Kit never quite got around to asking out. "I'll see if I can track her down for ya."

"And maybe, ya know, give her a copy of this before

you give it to Willow Shade? To make her feel special and all."

An incoming file prompt pings me in V-cog. It's labeled Season One, Episodes One Through Eight of Kit Smith's Incredible Discoveries of the Galaxy. "Kit, I said no Willow Shade business."

"You'll figure it out." He pats my shoulder. "And you"—he turns to Afumba—"watch this big lug's back for me, would ya? He gets into a lot of trouble."

"Every step," Afumba replies. "I give you my word."

Beside Kit is Fergus, who places a hand on his chest and bows deeply. "Captain Fox, I consider it my life's greatest honor to have served under your command. I pledge my sword and shield to your cause whenever you have need."

"Thanks, Fergus. What I need now is not to let Kit out of your sight. That's an order."

He bows again. "It will be my sworn duty to watch my Creator's every move."

"Well, maybe not *every* move," Kit says.

"Thanks, Fergus," I reply and point them up the *Banshee*'s wing.

Rook is next. I take his hand but then hug him with my free arm. "Take care of yourself out there."

"You too, Knight. Thanks for the adventure."

"Feeling's mutual." Over his shoulder, I lower my voice, "And take good care of her out there."

"Always," he replies just as softly.

Last but not least is Evelyn. She embraces me fast and squeezes tightly.

Words get stuck in my throat and come out garbled. "I don't know what to say."

"Which means words are no longer enough." She lets go and holds my face in her hands. "You're a good man, Jericho Fox. I'll be seeing you."

"You too," I say, hoping it will be true. "Be safe."

She scoffs at me. "Like that's ever gonna happen."

"Eh. People change."

Evelyn rises up and kisses me on the cheek. "Goodbye." We wave at each other as she walks up the wing, and then, just like, she's gone. I look for her silhouette in the cockpit window but can't make it out.

Fortunately, before I can get too sentimental, Afumba touches my arm. "We must be going as well."

"Right." I look over at Magellan, Nairobi, and Alice, my faithful PA. Her broken arm is set, and she's assured me that she's ready to fly. Normally, I'd say she needs a few days, but given the extreme circumstances and how much I'll need Alice's help in the coming months, I haven't refused her request to return with us. "You all ready?"

They nod, and Magellan leads the way to the *Bliss Mobile*. I say my final goodbyes to Geller, Enni, whose still recovering from losing her arm but has managed to make an appearance thanks to stim code, and some of the others, and then walk up the ramp and out of Soteria's evening heat. As soon as the cargo hold is shut and I'm secure on the bridge beside Magellan, he asks, "What do you suppose awaits us when we get back?"

"Probably more than we bargained for. But after everything we've lived through? I think we can handle it."

Magellan smiles as he powers up the main thrusters. "I like your optimism."

"Now that we've done the impossible, it's hard to have anything else."

Just then, through an exterior V-cog camera, I notice the *Banshee* rising off the tarmac beside us. In the cockpit, port side, I spot Evelyn's face. There are no windows in our Tiger-class shuttle, so she can't see me back. Which is probably for the best. But I can see her, and pray to God I always can, as long as my memory lasts. It will fade, of course; all memories do. But right now, I have a perfect view of the woman who discovered humanity's salvation, looking heavenward, her face alive and eyes filled with anticipation of the next discovery.

TRUE TO HER WORD, Korbix's remote gate activator—a device we've started calling the garage door opener—worked like a charm. One moment we were orbiting Soteria and flying into Ring W, then next we're at Lagrange Point Two pointed toward the speck that is

Earth. Our sensors and visual displays burst to life as they connect to the V-cog network. Ship idents, news alerts, and diagnostic updates stream down every piece of monitoring hardware both physical and virtual. A host of vessels far more numerous than what we left surrounds us. And then the hails begin.

Magellan activates the ship-wide silence feature which temporarily mutes all incoming requests. There are simply too many to count, let alone respond too. Meanwhile, I'm shocked at what I don't see—specifically, a fleet of Naval battleships, the kind I'd been anticipating this whole time. Instead, dozens of NUESSA and SESI space craft along with massive construction platforms circle *Telemine* Station, all pointed at *Parallax One* like doctors performing surgery. Just two navy ships are on the sensors, both several hundred kilometers to the outside of the action.

"Is it just me," Magellan says as he flips and slows us to a stop, "or has the Navy been given a back seat?"

"That's what it looks like." I can't say I'm not relieved either. I'd been squeezing my sphincter in preparation for what we'd find here. Hell, part of me wondered if the politicasts hadn't blown up *Parallax One* altogether. But with the sudden sense of safety, a thousand questions are filling my mind faster than I can keep track of them. "We need to find out what's going on," I say and then I scan the list of incoming communications, spotting one that supersedes all the rest... at least if I'm looking at this from Evelyn's perspective. It's categorized as a priority one alert from SESI headquarters and initiated from Dr. Lemuel Brown. Magellan sees it too and gives me a nod of approval.

I open the V-cog request and instantly find myself on the stage of a virtual command theater filled with over a hundred personnel behind workstations, each looking up from their respective terminals and eyeing me in disbelief. Above and behind me is a command wall filled with camera feeds, telemetry, and data streams. And standing a meter away from me is none other than the director of Search for Extrasolar Sentient Intelligence himself, Dr. Lemuel Brown. He's dressed in slacks, a white shirt, and a black vest with both NUESSA and SESI patches sewn on the lapels. The expression he bears is somewhere between astonishment and joy. "Fox?"

"Hi, Dr. Brown."

"Is it… really you?"

"Last I checked. Good to see you."

"Ha HA!" He claps his hands together and holds them to his mouth, eyes still wide. Then, as the room starts to erupt in applause, he steps forward and embraces me. Not something I was expecting from the famed director, but I can't say I don't appreciate the love. So I hug back. He shakes me hard as the room continues to cheer. Finally, brown pulls away but holds me by the shoulders. "I can't believe it. You made it."

"We did."

"And Evelyn?"

"No." His face is crestfallen, then I realize my mistake. "I mean, she's fine! She's just… not here with us now. She…" *She what, Fox?* How can I possibly explain everything? I quickly settle for, "She stayed behind for some important work."

Brown grabs his heart and lets out a nervous laugh. "You had me there."

"Sorry about that."

"And everyone else is okay too?"

"Uh… most of them. I have a lot to fill you in on, sir."

"I can imagine. You have data?"

"I have more than that. I've got a planet."

Brown's face seems to pale. "A planet?" he parrots flatly. "As in…?"

"As in Earth 2.0, sir. We named it Soteria. And we can't wait to show you. For now, though, this might help." I quickly route an image of the planet into the theater's resource list and send it to the main display overhead. Brown lets out a glee-filled yelp and stumbles backward. I catch him just as he starts clapping, which summons another round of applause from the room only far greater than the last. Within seconds, everyone's on their feet and cheering, the noise reaching pandemonium levels for scientists.

Brown spins to face me. "It's real?"

"One hundred percent. And there's more. We made first contact in the flesh."

Now Brown is laughing. He's almost hysterical. Like a child meeting Santa Claus. He even does a little dance. So I decide to push him over the edge and send a picture to the screen. It's an image grab from the *Bliss*'s nose cam of me, Evelyn, Kit, Rook, and Eddie just before leaving Soteria. And in the middle is Korbix, in all her human-kangaroo-like glory.

Brown is so taken aback, he sits down on the stage, mouth agape, and stares up at the image. A few tears run down his cheeks, and then he looks at me. "You did it. I… can't believe it. You actually did it!"

"No," I correct, looking around the room. "We all did it." This produces another round of applause. People are hugging and crying, giving high fives, and throwing fists in the air. A few headsets go flying, and one guy is actually running up and down the stairs with excitement. I decide to take a seat beside Brown and look up at the image.

"What do they call themselves?" he asks in a tone barely audible above the cheering behind us.

"Naqualla," I say, smiling. "At least that's our word for them. And they're very eager to meet us."

"The Naqualla," he replies in wonder. "How truly marvelous…"

I look around at the theater for a second and then ask him, "Dr. Brown, what happened to the Navy presence? All we see up here are NUESSA and SESI vessels."

He snaps out of his revelry some and casts me a rueful grin. "Called them off."

"What? How? I thought that——"

"Sir Nigel Sallsworth had moved against *Parallax One*? He was. And then he suffered a stroke and has been in a coma ever since."

I blink twice at him. "You wanna run that by me again?"

"He was on *Telemine* Station too. Giving a tour to Gemma Birdwhistle herself."

"Neon's daughter?"

"The same. One minute they're in secret talks, the next minute they're both unconscious."

"That didn't strike anyone as odd?"

Brown chuckles. "Struck the whole damn world as odd, Fox. But there was nothing anyone could say, let alone do. From what I understand, both of their V-cog systems were locked down tight. Not even the NUE's best cryptologist could get in."

Something about his tone piques my curiosity. "You think there was something fishy going on?"

He sighed. "Listen, I am a firm believer that we reap what we sow. I'm not sure we'll ever know the exact cause of Sallsworth's coma, or if he'll ever come out of it, but I do know that he seems to have bitten off more than he can chew this time. It's a lesson to anyone who has ears to hear."

"And Gemma?"

"Radio silent, I'm afraid. Though, I suspect that if her condition is anything like Sallsworth's, we won't be hearing from her any time soon."

"So much tragedy in that family."

"Agreed." Brown sat up a little. "In any event, the NUE General Council held an emergency joint session election for Sallsworth's replacement. It was a historic majority vote in both the Chamber of Politicast Representatives and the Chamber of Presidents, especially considering the new system leader hails from right here in SESI. "

"What about all the divisions? The animosity? How is that even possible?"

Brown smiles. "The people, Mr. Fox. It seems the *people* wanted to know more about our ring before we got around to blowing it up. According to public polls, they felt the best person for that job was Dr. Park and then yourself."

"I'm… flattered."

"Then you can imagine how I felt when my name was third on the list."

It takes me a second. "*You're* the new secretary general?"

"No. I'm the new President of Earth."

I blink a few times at him. "You... wanna run that by me again, sir?"

"Don't worry," he laughs. "My first act was to undo what Sallsworth had done. Secretary General is more than enough power for one person to wield. Plus, I wouldn't have the time to monkey around with my day job if I was president of anything. This"—he gestures around the theater—"is where I belong. And if they need me to oversee some meetings here and there? So be it. Hey, don't look so surprised."

I let out an astonished chuckle. "Congratulations, sir. Well deserved. Still, I wouldn't have guessed that—"

"Don't worry. I wouldn't have picked me either. But it allowed us to back the Navy off and keep *Parallax One* operational until you returned." He smiles a little. "Turns out the naval admiralty didn't really want to nuke it anyway. Plus, Sallsworth had fast tracked a concession for the military, a little something called *Valkyrie Command*. It's since been repurposed as a NUESSA jump point for future missions into *Parallax One*. Now that you're here, I'm trusting we can get even more use of *Valkyrie*."

I put my hands on the floor behind me and lean back, marveling at the turn of events. We had less to worry about than we suspected. Much less. And who knows, under Brown, Rook and his unit might not even get court martialed. They might get promotions.

"Evelyn looks happy," Brown says after a few moments, looking up at the picture on the display.

"She is. Very. And I suspect she's even happier now."

"Because she got to stay behind?"

"No." I smile at the picture, think of just how excited she must be right now, and how much I wish I was there to see her face as the discoveries unfold. "No, she's actually with the ambassador, heading back to the Naquallan homeworld."

"For what purpose?"

"To represent humanity," I reply. "To forge more paths in the darkness and see where they lead us."

⁂

Evelyn

"*GOLLY.* You look like a million... uh, wow. I mean, just... uh, *beautiful,* Dr. Park," Kit says as I enter the waiting room. "*Oof,* sorry. Am I allowed to say that? It's not offensive, is it?"

"No, Kit. It's not offensive. And thank you. I appreciate your kind words. Although, I must confess that I do feel a bit out of place." I smooth the dress down my abdomen. It's a gift from Korbix, and apparently made from material that's quite rare. The fabric is iridescent in nature, shifting through the colors prismatically as the viewer turns their head. The dress is sleeveless, following customs, and comes with a built in cape that flows behind me as I walk. The Naquallan designers and seamstresses spent two days getting me ready, not that I can blame them: trying to craft a form-fitting garment for an alien back on Earth would be an equally challenging task for sure. I also have a crystal lattice crown woven into my hair that has turned me into some sort of dignitary, though I hardly feel so important. I'm just me, Evelyn. A SESI scientist who's a long way from home.

No. Who's found her new home.

"You look handsome as well, Kit," I say, admiring his outfit. He turns around once for me, arms out. The suit —or maybe just outfit is a better term—is bright orange, which is apparently an important color to the Naqualla. It features a sleeveless vest buttoned down the center with golden closures and topped with a high collar. Baggy pants are tied off below the knees with yellow cords. Kit also wears large color-matching shoes that make his feet look twice as long as they really are. He looks a bit like a scuba diver when he walks, but he seems to be getting the hang of it. I secretly wonder if the smallness of our feet is somehow repulsive to our hosts; mine are hidden under my dress, and I noted more than a few disgusted looks from the designers yesterday. I suppose our general hairlessness is also less than desirable given their furry mammalian appearance. And where we do have hair—atop our heads—they've gone to great lengths to amplify it. Like my crown, Kit has his own crystal-like apparatus, one that resembles a lantern that takes advantage of his red hair, making it appear as if the vessel is glowing. Creative, but far from Earth's fashion sense.

"Well, I'm gonna go get seated now," Kit says. "Rook and the others are waiting. Just wanted to make sure you didn't need anything. You don't, do you?"

"No, Kit. I'm fine. Thanks for checking on me."

"No problem. Break a leg and stuff."

"I'll try my best."

Kit exits one door at the same time that Korbix enters another, the one leading to the main stage, at least according to the translation augmented through V-cog. "How do I look?" I ask. This is the first time Korbix has seen me in my new dress.

"Like a person of prominence ready to address a grand audience."

"I'm glad you approve."

She smiles, but then asks, "How do you feel?"

"Nervous. But also excited."

"Both fitting emotions. I share them. Your opening remarks?"

I tap the side of my head. "All set."

"Excellent. Remember, this is simply to say hello. Share only what you feel comfortable with. There will be plenty of time for you to share more in the months to come."

"Right. Got it."

According to the schedule, Korbix will be introduced first and share some thoughts on her year-long lecture, currently entitled Redemption of the Firsts: Humans and their Arrival on Soteria. Not that she's already prepared a year's worth of talks; it's simply an allowance of time that she has to document, organize, and lay out her findings. I liken it to how someone in a graduate-level program on Earth might present a doctoral thesis. Given the nature of her discovery, it's only fitting that actual humans be given center stage of which I am the first participant. The honor has both excited and unnerved me since learning about it.

"Thank you," Korbix says. "It's truly our privilege to host you, Dr. Evelyn Park."

I'll break her of using my whole name one day. But for now, I bear it with a smile. Plus, it's endearing. "And it's an honor to represent our species to you."

Our arrival three days ago was nothing short of miraculous. To see Tria from orbit in all her glory took

my breath away. The Naquallan version of Bishop
Rings, as envisioned by Forrest Bishop in the late twentieth century, are a technological feat unlike anything
I've ever witnessed. Only, instead of free-flying in space,
these wrap around the planet at various angles and sizes.
It was one thing to see them in Korbix's depiction; it's
quite another to observe them in the real… to fly
between them en route to the planet's surface and then
to look up and see them trailing across the sky. Whole
mega continents stretch end to end, appearing hazy as
they shoot off the horizon, growing crystal clear once
they span directly overhead, hundreds of kilometers
above. And all those people, both on the rings and
across the planet, are listening. Watching. Waiting to
meet the *kerrr-kuk-ooomans* that Ambassador Korbix is
talking about from her position in the middle of the
stage.

I step through the darkened doorway, careful to stay
in the shadows. It reminds me of being backstage in a
theater production during college. I never acted, mind
you. Just worked with the crew for one semester. Hated
being in the limelight. But that's all about to change.
The stage here is three times the size of any I've seen on
Earth. The audience, too, boasts thousands of attendees,
seats curving up and away like small pearls inlaid on a
clam shell. These, I'm told, are the members of the
Resettlement Council along with several dignitaries of
the government. Light glistens from round fixtures in the

ceiling, casting the entire space in an otherworldly glow —soft, yet somehow still radiant.

Korbix's voice is amplified through a public address system. She commands the stage with authority, at least that's how I interpret her body language and tone. I hope I can do the same. Part of me is trying to pay attention to what she's saying, trying to split the natural sound of her voice with the translation in my head. But another part of me is just taking all of this in. Thinking I might wake up from this dream any second now. I'm also wondering how Jericho has fared and who he's been able to tell about our discovery. I miss him. But we both have our jobs to do, our roles to play. I'm a scientist, yes. But tonight, I get to be an ambassador. I have a responsibility. To begin the slow and yet fabulously exciting process of introducing our alien species to this planet's population... our saviors. Our benefactors. And, if Korbix is any indication, our friends.

"Please welcome Dr. Evelyn Park," Korbix says, turning toward me. "First human on Tria."

I freeze at the mention of my name and the sound of the applause. Seeing her. All the people. And then my friends. In the front row, there's Kit. Rook. Seb, Igor, and Natalie wave. There's Eddie Carr, probably ready to cuss me out if I don't unglue my feet from the floor fast enough. Hatch, she's smiling. And Fergus, staring at me with his warm glowing eyes. A spotlight finds me in the shadows, nearly blinding me, and Korbix beckons me forward with an upturned paw. The applause rises in pitch. It's time. I take a steadying breath, step from backstage, and then stride toward Korbix. I'm not even halfway there when I turn to face the audience... thousands here... untold billions watching. And what will I say? My notes suddenly seem so small. So insignificant. Because of what they've done, a mission started hundreds of years ago. And here we are, right now, reaping the investment made by people we've never met.

"Hello," I say, suddenly aware that my voice is being translated a split second after I speak, causing the combined English and Naquallan speech to reverberate up the clam shell and disappear into the ether. "My name is Dr. Evelyn Park, and I stand here tonight representing... all of my people... to say thank you. While we can't wait to learn about you and your incredible civilizations, I am told you are equally as eager to learn about us." I glance down at my friends again, faces bright and smiling. "So it's only right that, from the very beginning, you know our hope, our deep desire, is to forge a friendship between our peoples, one that spans the entirety of our mutual existences. But more than that, ours in an endless debt... one that, with each breath we are given, will seek to repay you with gratitude for giving humanity one more chance. One more chance at living. At breathing. At being human. And finding out not just what it means to be the best version of ourselves, but what it means to be you. To be Naquallan.

"This mutual understanding... this... *learning* of one another's ways, of seeking each other's mutual peace, of fighting for one another's right to live, this is our desire as a species with you. Nothing less, and never asking for more. Though we are small by comparison, younger, and far less-learned, the best of us are passionate in our curiosity. Generous when asked. Sacrificial when pressed. On our darkest days, we suffer from our own ill-will; we are not perfect and have plenty of worries to share. But we hope... We do hope that each day will be brighter than the next. And you, the Naqualla of Tria, you have made this day brighter than any we ever could have imagined. We owe you our lives. And if you'll have our hand of friendship, we offer it freely. Willingly. And without expectation. If you'll have us, then tonight, let us begin."

I stretch out my hand as my voice rolls up the amphitheater, my heart stopping, my head wondering how they might reply. Hoping they'll say yes. And praying... yes, even praying that my species will do better today than it did yesterday. We owe our benefactors that much. And I believe we can do it. We must. Because the future is waiting on the other side of our choices.

THE END

SOTERIAN TATTOOS
KIT SMITH'S INCREDIBLE DISCOVERIES OF THE GALAXY

Curious how Kit and Fergus got their first tattoos? Find out in *Soterian Tattoos*, a short story from Kit's personal archives (also known as Season One, Episode Seven of *Kit Smith's Incredible Discoveries of the Galaxy*).

Available in print, digital, and audio exclusively at christopherhopper.com, with performances by Daniel Wisniewski and Rebecca Woods.

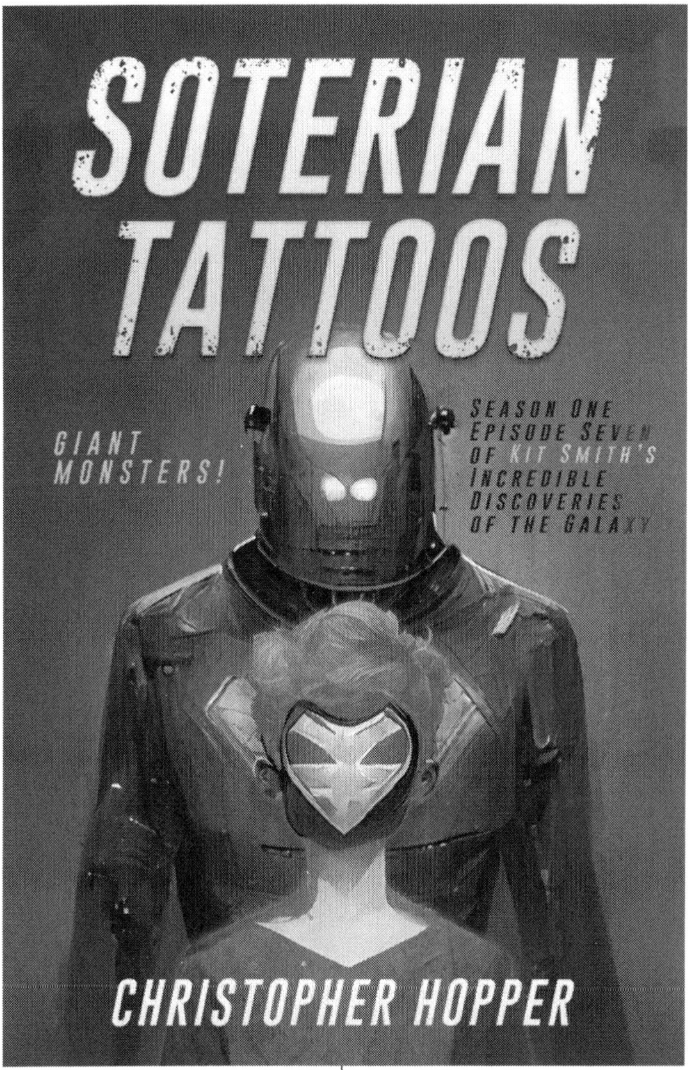

SOTERIAN TATTOOS

GIANT MONSTERS!

SEASON ONE
EPISODE SEVEN
OF KIT SMITH'S
INCREDIBLE
DISCOVERIES
OF THE GALAXY

CHRISTOPHER HOPPER

SECURE YOUR COPY NOW!

VIP

Become a VIP Club Member Today!

Membership is free, and you'll receive an official club poker chip, short story, and 10% off Christopher's store for life. Plus, you'll be signed up to get exclusive club perks in the mail and invited to join the private social media groups.

Visit christopherhopper.com to sign up now.

ACKNOWLEDGMENTS

This book would not be what it is without Matthew Titus, Christie Strahler, Gary Guilmette, Tracey Beattie, Neil Rubenking, Jon Bliss, and the amazing Dan Wong for his sharp attorney's eyes.

To my faithful alpha and beta readers for the thankless job of sweeping up the sawdust after the lights go out: Shane Marolf, David Seaman, Mauricio Longo, John Holley Jr., Kevin Zoll, Steve Janulin, John Walker, Mike McDonnell, Sean Ross, Eric Earley, Elijah Cole, George Hain, John Vermillion, Beverly Raymond, John Holley Jr, Brian Sinks, Joanne Sinks, Kathy Simonet, and Julia Camacho Monzon.

A heartfelt thanks goes to all the amazing spacers in my VIP club. Your encouragement and enthusiasm keep me positive and employed. I'm so grateful to have you as my most loyal fans.

Rebecca Woods and Daniel Wisniewski, thank you for bringing my characters to life for the audio version of this story. Once again, you have created a new piece of art from the rough medium of my words. Thank you for sharing your time and talents with us all.

I'm thankful for my fellow writing companions who know and share the highs and lows of publishing: Jeremy Davis, Jonathan Yanez, R.J Smith, Jason Anspach, Jeff Chaney, Ken Lozito, Wayne Thomas Batson, Nicholas Smith, Gerry Riddle, and Scott Moon. Your friendship is a blessing.

Thanks to my daughter, Evangeline, for running my store and taking care of our customers, and to my son, Luik, for populating the Infinita Codex with all my world building content. You guys rock. Your dad couldn't do this without you.

And to my wife, Jenny. Thank you for making the leap to fly into space with me. The journey has been amazing, and there are still more adventures to come. I love you.